THE SWITCH

THE
SWITCH

Lily Samson

PAMELA DORMAN BOOKS / VIKING

VIKING
An imprint of Penguin Random House LLC
penguinrandomhouse.com

Simultaneously published in hardcover in Great Britain by Century,
an imprint of Penguin Random House Ltd., London, in 2024.

A Pamela Dorman Book/Viking

LIBRARY OF CONGRESS CATALOGING-IN-PUBLICATION DATA
Names: Samson, Lily, author.
Title: The switch / Lily Samson.
Description: [New York] : Pamela Dorman Books/Viking, 2024.
Identifiers: LCCN 2023038902 (print) | LCCN 2023038903 (ebook) |
ISBN 9780593656013 (hardcover) | ISBN 9780593656020 (ebook)
Subjects: LCGFT: Thrillers (Fiction) | Domestic fiction. | Novels.
Classification: LCC PR6119.A49 S95 2024 (print) | LCC PR6119.A49 (ebook) |
DDC 823/.92—dc23/eng/20231113
LC record available at https://lccn.loc.gov/2023038902
LC ebook record available at https://lccn.loc.gov/20230389

Printed in the United States of America
1st Printing

Set in Adobe Caslon Pro
Designed by Cassandra Garruzzo Mueller

For L. K. and Andrew Gallix

And for Lyra, 2003–2023

PART ONE

1.

NOW: ELENA

Tonight it all begins.

As I sit on the sofa, watching a Netflix crime series with Adam, I can't quite believe I'm going to go through with the plan. My nails, once well-maintained, are now ragged and blunt. I feel certain that, at the last minute, I will chicken out and curl up in bed and escape into sleep.

"For God's sake, the weapon's right there, in her kitchen, with blood on it," Adam playfully mocks the detective onscreen, who keeps missing vital clues in the shakily scripted drama.

I resist the urge to yawn. I didn't sleep well last night. I tell Adam I need the toilet.

Upstairs, I flush without using it and tiptoe into our bedroom. Adam looked surprised when I gave it a thorough clean yesterday, even using the Hoover extension to spruce every corner, and ironing all the bed linen before putting it on. I've always been the messy one.

The new Habitat duvet cover is white with little green sprigs on it. I smooth away a crease with my hand.

On Adam's side is a bedside table where his iPhone is charging, a box of tissues and a few Arthur Conan Doyles. There's a small table lamp and I unscrew the bulb gently, centimeter by centimeter.

I click the switch. Nothing. If Adam gets anxious, if he reaches for the lamp in the dark, it won't help him.

From the window, I gaze out over the rooftops, lights going on in the houses as people settle down for the evening, the last rays of the sun faint in the pale pink sky. My eyes fall to the clock. *Seven thirty-six.*

Four and a half hours to go.

My heart trembles.

2.

THEN: ELENA

It began with Sophia MacInnes. I first encountered her in my local café three months ago on a March morning. Adam and I had just moved to Wimbledon Village and it felt like we'd won the lottery.

Our previous accommodation had been a flat in Walthamstow, which had been okay, if a little cramped, until some noisy neighbors moved into the flat above, driving us mad with parties and banging and music at all hours. It came out of the blue, the offer: Adam's aunt, aware that our lease was soon to run out, was going to the US for eight months and would we like to housesit? We'd be allowed to bring our cat. After moving in, we spent the first weekend wandering about, drunk with joy at the charm of our new area: the green beauty of the Common and the swans on Rushmere Pond, the old-fashioned feel of the Village with its quaint shops, the lovely local pubs. And the quiet! Peaceful nights; no need for ear-plugs; the joy of waking up and hearing birdsong from the garden and feeling human again.

Even for Adam, who'd had a much more privileged upbringing than me, this world was aspirational: the average house price ran into millions. We were conscious that we were temporarily existing in a bubble of luxury, which made our excitement bittersweet. Already two months had passed, way too quickly.

Adam had a new job in an investment bank in the City while I had given up office life for freelancing. It was too easy to spend the day in my pajamas with my laptop on my knees, surrounded by half-drunk cups of Earl Grey, so I had taken to working in a local café.

The day it happened, I was sitting there with a tea, toying pleasurably with a Word doc covered in red corrections, when I became aware of a commotion near the door.

There was a woman. Distressed. Early thirties. Blonde-haired. Glamorous. She hurried to the customer restroom, hurried back to the café entrance. "I just left it in there," she said, visibly distressed. "And—he—he took my bag!"

"I'll call the police," said Antonia the waitress.

I told myself not to get involved. I had a deadline for the end of the day. But the woman looked so vulnerable that my heart went out to her. I waved at her, calling: "If you need to cancel your cards or anything, you can borrow my mobile."

She sat down next to me, relaying her horror story: she'd accidentally left behind her handbag and when she went back for it, she saw a teenager had grabbed it and was dashing past her toward the exit. She had just moved to the area and was shocked.

"It's normally so quiet in here," I reassured her. "It's nearly always yummy mummies, to be honest. I think you've just been unlucky—sorry."

We chatted some more, Antonia brought her a free coffee, she called her husband to get him to check their insurance policy for her card numbers and got them canceled. Soon a policewoman arrived. At this point I left, walking home with a guilty zing of excitement. Meeting Sophia had been a thrill, broken the routine of my day. It made me reflect, later, that though we loved our new place, we were lonely. The trek back to Walthamstow was more of an effort than we'd imagined and often Adam was too tired after long days at work; we'd only seen our old friends a few times since the move. Adam didn't mind as he preferred staying in, but I've always enjoyed socializing.

Back home, it was my turn to cook dinner. Adam sipped a Siren beer and watched me chop veg as I enthused about my afternoon. "I found her on Instagram." I showed him my phone.

"Sophia MacInnes." Adam's eyes lit up. "She's hot!"

I gave him a sharp nudge and he grabbed me and kissed me, declaring that nobody was as gorgeous as his wench.

"Oh, wow!" My heart leaped as I noticed a little red person icon in my notifications. "She's just followed me back! And sent me a message, saying thank you for my 'extraordinary kindness' . . . She's actually an artist." I scrolled through images of her paintings. They were in the style of Vanessa Bell: vibrant colors and abstract shapes. "She's done designs for Liberty's . . . she's had exhibitions . . ."

"How many followers does she have?" Adam asked, a teasing edge to his voice.

"Over six thousand."

"And how many do you have?"

"Fuck off!" I gave him a cross kiss. "I only joined a few weeks ago. I'm *building* a base . . ."

"You should invite her over for dinner," he reflected. "Her and her chap. It would be nice to meet some new people."

3.

THEN: ELENA

The next time I bumped into Sophia at the Vicomte Café, I invited her and her husband, Finn, over to dinner for the following evening. I tried looking up Finn on her Instagram, and was surprised to find no trace of him. Just Sophia, looking impeccable with her hair scooped back with sunglasses, cool as a Hitchcock blonde. She'd mentioned her husband was older than her. I wondered if she was embarrassed by him, if he was a lecherous old goat she'd rather hide away. In my head he became a caricature: a ninety-year-old needing her help with his walking frame.

Adam and I were rusty at entertaining guests. We cooked together, chopping and singing along to the radio and joking about. At one point I splashed water at him and he tickled me and thwacked a tea towel against my bottom. This was what I loved about Adam, the way we could be childish together and let off steam and stress, knowing that the moment the doorbell rang we'd have to present ourselves as grown-ups.

I wondered nervously how we might seem to our dinner guests. People would sometimes do a doubletake at me and Adam, musing that we looked mismatched. He was wearing jeans and a black T-shirt with a rock music logo on it; he looked as though he could be the lead singer in a band. At the weekend he would grow blond stubble, to be shorn off for work first thing on Monday morning when it was back to a suit and commute. In contrast, I'd dressed up, putting on heels, an Oasis dress patterned with red flowers, and a bright slash of lipstick.

My cat Lyra sat at the end of the hallway, picking up on the tension in the air, flicking her tail with nonchalant curiosity.

The doorbell rang. Lyra fled. Adam and I froze: *they were ten minutes early.*

On my way to the door, I checked my reflection in the mirror. My freshly washed brown hair was still a little damp. Was the lipstick too much? The bold gesture helped to hide my shyness; I loved meeting people but found first encounters hard.

I opened the door.

I had been right to dress up. Sophia was wearing black velvet, and she looked stunning.

"Elena!" She gave me an exuberant hug and a kiss.

Her perfume was gorgeous: like walking through a cottage garden in the summer, breathing in shades of rose and jasmine. I noticed a small gold crucifix glittering at her neck.

"And this is—" she began.

"Hi, I'm Finn." He shook my hand. He wasn't what I had expected at all. His hair was as dark as patent leather, flecked with gray, his eyes like black olives framed with thick lashes, his tan light. He was older than Sophia by five years at most, I'd guess. Hadn't she said he was in business? He looked like a film star.

We went into the dining-room, where Sophia cooed over the table arrangement, the vase of freesias. There was something so gushing about her compliments that I felt on edge. Adam's aunt had a tendency toward clutter and sentimentality; old dressers and china, dull landscape paintings on the walls. Yet I didn't want to confess to Sophia that we just had a housesit. I wanted her to believe in us as a couple who could afford to live in Wimbledon Village.

"It's lovely here." Sophia went to the French windows. "So much light coming in."

We were proud of our garden, even if we couldn't take credit for it. Several camellias were still in brilliant scarlet flower, and a pretty cherry tree was covered in buds of blossom.

I wondered what Finn made of us. His expression was hard to read.

Adam, who had been busy in the kitchen, came in then, shaking hands, grinning, offering them rosé in his loud Scottish accent. I felt a flash of pride: everyone liked Adam. He had such a warm, sunny face, blue eyes framed by laughter-creased crinkles, freckles that reminded you of how cute a boy he must have been. He was confident, which rubbed off on me and helped me feel more bubbly.

We sat down to eat asparagus as a starter, drizzled with olive oil and topped with Parmesan.

Finn was on my left. The glow of his charisma kept tugging at my attention; even when I wasn't looking at him, I was aware of him, electrified.

"Elena says you moved here recently too," Adam said.

"In February," said Sophia. "We moved to Murray Road—just round the corner. We were in Cornwall before."

"I love Cornwall," Adam enthused. "I remember holidays there when I was a kid. Whereabouts were you?"

"In Crugmeer. Don't worry, nobody's ever heard of it!" Sophia laughed. "It's right on the west coast—quite cut off. It's been a big change, coming to live in London—but I love it. Most of the time . . ."

"Sophia tells me that you saved her life," Finn teased me.

"Oh, I just lent her my mobile."

"Elena was my guardian angel." Sophia spoke fast, with an almost theatrical delivery. "I was completely stranded!" she exclaimed, as though the café was in a foreign country rather than just down the road. "Thank goodness you were there that day, I don't know what I would have done otherwise."

"I just did what felt right, what anyone would do." I blushed, smiling at Adam. "I'm in there most days, actually—I call it my office."

"The freelancer lifestyle. Some of us get to sit in cafés every day drinking coffee," Adam teased me.

"Oh, but that doesn't mean her job isn't as important as yours," Sophia berated him with feminist disapproval. "Freelancing is hard work!"

"Yes, *Adam*." I mock-glared at him.

Adam looked chastised; I wanted to give Sophia a hug.

"So what do you do?" she interrogated him.

"I'm at Commerce Bank, in IT, programming."

"Sounds like hard work."

There was something a little dismissive about her tone; Adam bristled. He was proud of his breadwinner status, but he hated being defined by his job, which he did for money rather than love.

"It *is* hard work, long hours, and I sometimes have to do weekends."

Sophia patted his arm and he looked appeased.

"Oh, me too," she said. "People think being an artist is fun, and I know I'm lucky, but it can be grueling. I'm popping over to Venice soon. I've got an exhibition at the Contini Gallery . . ."

I felt a stab of envy, covering it up with praise. Venice was a city I'd always longed to visit. As Sophia described her exhibition, my gaze wandered to Finn's fingers, curled around the stem of the wine glass. He caught me looking and I was scared my attraction to him was evident, amusing to him.

I retreated into the kitchen to get the main course; Adam joined me.

"They seem nice," he whispered cheerfully. "Bit bourgeois."

I gave him an exasperated nudge and he grinned.

We served up the plaice, roast potatoes, beans, and took them in. Adam lit some candles, turned down the lights. An itch in my heart: for all the patter of polite compliments, I dreaded that they were bored.

A conversation about boxsets started up, Adam and I clashing over *The Sopranos* versus *Mad Men*, but Sophia and Finn fell quiet.

"We don't watch much TV," she confessed, lifting an eyebrow.

"No? That's refreshing," said Adam. "I waste hours staying up late getting hooked on some piece of rubbish."

"I like black and white films," said Sophia. "And the old-school stars: Sophia Loren, Cary Grant, Audrey Hepburn—what a goddess! My mother was actually friends with Audrey . . ."

Adam's eyes lit up; movies were his great obsession. Not a day went past without him enthusing about an obscure seventies classic or an old Hitchcock he'd just rewatched. Soon they were chatting away, forming their own bubble. For a moment Finn and I sat in silence, then he addressed me.

"You must have a precise mind if you're a proof-reader."

I blinked: mostly people assumed it was a very boring profession.

"It's quite wild," I said in a deadpan voice. "I mean, no two days are ever the same—it's semi-colons one day, colons the next. And I have to pay high insurance premiums to deal with the risk . . ."

Finn smiled.

"But I enjoy it, and it's been going so well I'm about to put my rates up." I was touched when he looked impressed.

A breeze slanted the candle-flames, rippling shadows across his face.

"How long have you been a proof-reader?" He made it sound fascinating, as though I was a spy.

"Three years. Before that I worked for a PR firm in the City. I ended up hating it," I replied. "I think I had a bit of a midlife crisis."

He raised a thick eyebrow.

"You're far too young for a midlife crisis." His gaze flitted to my lips, back up to my eyes.

"I'm thirty-seven."

"No! You look thirty." His surprise seemed genuine. *He's such a charmer,* I thought. I was conscious of how fragile the moment was. I wished we were at a party, in a corner, and could talk like this for hours.

"Adam and I joke that the average midlife crisis starts around the age of eighteen and finishes around the age of sixty-five."

When he laughed, Adam and Sophia looked over, each a little terri-
torial.

"Attends avant de te lancer! Rien n'a encore été décidé." Sophia addressed
him quietly in French and he replied in the same language. I felt the door
that had opened between us slam shut. My French was GCSE level, decidedly rusty.

Adam and I exchanged looks: how sophisticated.

"I know how to order a pizza in French. And a beer. That's about it,"
Adam reflected, and Sophia smiled in amusement.

At the end of the evening, when we were all a little tipsy, I gave Sophia a grand tour of the house. I was taken aback when she reacted badly
to Lyra, saying she was terrified of cats, and I had to shut my beloved pet
away. But she gushed compliments about all the rooms, gave me advice
on how I might jazz everything up—add a rug here, put up some curtains there. She admired the blackout blind in our bedroom, which I
recommended as the perfect antidote to insomnia. We all wandered into
the garden, gazing up at a moon that was nearly full. Finn was standing
by my side. I felt his skin close to mine, the kiss of our hairs just touching—
and a shiver passed over my body. I had never been attracted to any man
with this intensity before, and it scared me.

4.

THEN: ELENA

Murray Road, read the sign.

I twigged. Realized that this was the very road that Sophia and Finn lived on.

It was a Monday morning. I had woken early and, before going to the café, decided to take a quick walk on Wimbledon Common, when I saw the street sign.

On impulse, I turned on to it, even though the thought of Sophia felt like a sting.

We had planned to meet for a drink the previous week, but she'd canceled on me at the last minute. And an invitation back to theirs for dinner hadn't materialized. Adam wasn't fussed; he'd found them a bit overglossy and flashy. He had replied to my moans by saying I was being too sensitive, too impatient, everyone was busy. But Sophia seemed to have enough time to post on Instagram three times a day and while I had liked every one of her posts, she'd only liked one of mine. It was dogging me: I felt a sense of unworthiness that hadn't bothered me in some years, now that I had a proper, grown-up life with a fulfilling job and partner. Sophia and I clearly belonged in different worlds.

Adam and I were living on a nice road, but this one was in another league. Each detached house was a variation on grandeur and beauty.

One might be contemporary, the sort a James Bond villain might live in; another Edwardian, a glorious muddle of brick and chimneys, a porch gorgeously drenched in wisteria.

Number 195 . . . 193 . . . 191 . . . Hadn't Sophia said they lived at number 187? Or was it 186?

What on earth must it be like, I thought, *to have the required millions to buy a place like one of these?* While here I was, checking the Oasis website daily, hoping a dress I had my eye on would be reduced to less than £50.

Suddenly I saw them on the opposite side of the road. Finn was opening the door of a car parked by the curb; Sophia was on her mobile.

I was about to duck down when she called, "Elena!"

She looked so pleased to see me that the pain of her past rejections melted a little. "Sorry—got to go now—I'll call you this evening," she said rapidly into her phone, ringing off. "Oh, gosh, I am *so* sorry I had to cancel our drinks the other night—I was *so* looking forward to it, but a commission for a portrait came up and I had to see Lady Valerie. We *must* reschedule ASAP! And I've been thinking I might well join you in the café, it looks like such a lovely place to work even if thieves roam large!"

"You and Adam should come for dinner," Finn added. "We'd love to have you over."

"That'd be great!" I smiled, my eyes hovering somewhere around the lapel of his jacket.

A neighbor went past, calling out *hello* and *isn't it a lovely day,* and as they turned to answer, I grabbed a quick look at their house. The porch was decorated with the elegant green stems of a climbing rose. The neat lawn was framed with beds of beautiful violas, and I wondered how come theirs weren't mutilated by slugs or snails the way ours were. I felt a hunger to enter, to see their rooms, taste their food, use their bathroom, sneak glances into their bedroom.

"Are you heading for the station?" Sophia asked.

I nearly said that I had taken a detour for fun, but I feared the coincidence would seem too stalkerish. So I replied: "Um, yes, I have a meeting in London."

"Oh, Finn too. He can drop you off."

"Thanks," I mumbled.

Finn's car was a dark green Jaguar. As I slid into the front seat, I breathed in the smell of leather and aftershave and something smoky, like cigars.

Yesterday, sitting in the café, I had been slow getting into my work, too busy googling Finn. He was CEO of MacInnes Consultancy and there was a photo of him on his company website. I had enlarged it. Lingered on the details. The thickness of his eyelashes, like moths' wings; the way his smile quirked slightly to the left, giving him a lazy old-style glamour, like Cary Grant. The look in his eyes that was stern and yet had a hint of mischief.

I watched them in my wing mirror as they said goodbye. He kissed her forehead softly; she pulled back and seized his face between her hands, her eyes boring into his. A strange, intense gesture: one of possession? Or was she angry with him in some way?

"Hey." Finn slid into the seat beside me. Sophia tapped on the window, waving exuberantly, blowing me a kiss. With a start I noticed a little streak of dark hair at her temple. I'd thought she was a natural blonde . . .

As Finn turned the engine on, opera filled the car: a sensual, warbling voice, singing in Russian. I bit my lip—didn't he want to talk to me? Maybe he wasn't a morning person. We stopped at some lights, snagged in traffic. My eyes flitted to his hands. I'd noticed how sexy they were when he first came to dinner: both delicate and brutish, dark hairs on the back, feathering up to his wrist; the edge of a Chopard watch peeking out from under his sleeve. He turned to face me. His smile said, *Isn't the music beautiful?* And suddenly there was an intimacy in our shared appreciation. As though we were a couple so comfortable with each other we had no need of small talk. The singing soared, became so raw that it was almost embarrassing to share this intensity.

Finn slid into a parking spot. When he turned off the engine the silence was a shock.

"Going for a meeting, you said?" he asked.

"It's a big company in London—it might be a huge proof-reading job," I improvised.

"We might need a proof-reader for our new website. If so, I'll know who to turn to." He flashed *that* smile at me again and I nearly died inside.

We got out and he zapped his lock; we walked to Wimbledon station.

"What was that opera?" I asked as we approached the ticket barriers.

"It was Shostakovich—*Lady Macbeth of Mtsensk*." He Oystered in and I realized I was going to have to follow, flashing my card against the yellow circle.

"We'll have to all go together—there's a new season starting at Covent Garden soon." His gaze didn't quite meet my eyes, and it struck me then that despite his smooth manner, he was a little shy.

My heart leaped. "I'd love to—we'd love to."

"Well—I'd better head off now," he said. "I'm catching the District line . . ."

"I'm off to Waterloo," I improvised.

As he headed to the Underground, I danced down the steps to Platform 5, waited a few minutes, the Waterloo train rolling in and then out. My heart was still skipping. Our conversation kept replaying in my mind. I headed back up the stairs and slipped out of the station, about to head up the hill—but if I went back to my regular café, Sophia might bump into me. Instead I opted for Patisserie Valerie on the Broadway. I sat down, gave myself a stern reprimand, but it was no good: my crush had just got a whole lot worse.

5.

NOW: ELENA

Three hours to go.

    I enter the living-room. The TV screen is frozen, paused on the detective's bemused frown. From the sofa, Adam gazes up at me and something vulnerable in his expression touches me, evokes a flood of guilt.

Can I really go through with this plan? What the hell am I doing?

"Do you want another Siren?" I ask in a small voice.

That was the plan: to get him tipsy. Not drunk, but a bit blurry about the edges, so he wouldn't notice details.

"Nah, I'd prefer a tea."

"You sure? There's one left in the fridge . . ."

"I'm fine."

Tea, then. He's only had two beers tonight. Not really enough.

I'm just leaving when he suddenly asks: "What's up?"

"What d'you mean?" I reply breezily.

"You're being weird. You've been weird all evening."

I give him a look, as though he's the only weirdo around here. "I've had a stressful week, with that deadline." He carries on looking at me and I shrug, hurrying into the kitchen.

Weird: it's a word he's flung at me a lot recently. But what if this isn't about our recent relationship troubles? What if he's toying with me? What if he's seen my notebook, the list, suspected something? Or is that just my guilt talking?

I pop teabags into mugs. Yorkshire Gold for him, with a dash of milk; Darjeeling for me with plenty. He always mocks my "weak" tea versus his "manly" one. A joke we've made a million times over the years.

Suddenly the phone rings. I jump violently, the kettle veering, nearly spilling boiling water on my hand. *Calm down*, I tell myself, *get a grip*.

Nobody ever rings us on the house phone except his aunt—and his mother.

I hear Adam go into the hallway, pick up the receiver. "Hi, Mum."

I put away the milk, quickly wipe up a splash. I'm washing everything the moment it's used, not wanting Sophia to see our kitchen in a state. On our calendar, the picture for this month displays a stately home, with a garden in full bloom. Dates with Biro scrawls next to them: *15th— Mum check-up, 22nd—work drinks*. How will those days feel? The future already feels as though it's been shaped by today. Today—*May 5th*—the day that bisects everything, that is going to create a Before and an After.

6.

THEN: ELENA

It was a Tuesday afternoon, and Sophia had invited me on a shopping trip.

"I was looking at your website the other day," she said. "I saw that you studied at Cambridge."

I smiled, a little evasive. I sensed that she thought we were from similar backgrounds, due to my accent and job and partner. People tended to assume that I grew up in a world of ponies and privilege, but nothing could be further from the truth. And I wasn't going to let on, for now. I didn't want to risk it.

"I studied Art at Goldsmiths," Sophia added, picking up a thong. "My godmother knows Tracey Emin, so I was lucky enough to have her as my mentor when I was starting out . . ."

Of course you did, I thought, smiling affectionately. The moment we had entered the lingerie shop, everyone had turned to look at us. It wasn't just Sophia's beauty and the flair with which she dressed, but a quality in her that expected attention, demanded it.

I enjoyed being on the periphery of her spotlight. Even if she was theatrical, it was so charming, so endearing, the way she chatted with everyone, warmly and freely, making people smile. Over the past few weeks we'd met half a dozen times for work sessions in the Vicomte

Café, drinks or dinners out; I was flattered, even a little awed, that she seemed to have decided we should be friends.

"You're so clever," Sophia went on. "That's what I said to Finn, the night after your dinner party: 'Elena has brains.' Are you going to buy that?"

She nodded at the camisole I was fingering.

"Adam doesn't really go for this sort of thing," I mused. He was a man who liked cotton knickers, simplicity. Besides, the prices were exorbitant.

"Finn would love me in this," Sophia said, holding up a lacy bodysuit, wine-red. "And even though I don't approve of the male gaze per se . . . I do want my husband's gaze on me."

I pictured him drinking in the sight of her, desire sharp in his eyes.

"Do you think it would suit me?" There was a doubt in her voice that surprised me.

"Of course—you'll look gorgeous!" I feared the compliment sounded too generic so I added, "I do think red would suit you, I've only ever seen you in black."

"It would look good on you too." Sophia held it up in front of my body. Then she frowned. "No, maybe not." She picked up another. "There."

I stared at my reflection, the sexy lace overlaying my clothing. We both smiled.

Temptation tickled, but Adam had recently taken to recording all our expenses in a spreadsheet. I knew his thriftiness was wise if we wanted to save up for a deposit on our own place, but I watched Sophia go up to pay for the red bodysuit with a slash of envy.

Yesterday I'd glanced out of the window and seen Finn passing. Our house was on a main road into the Village, so I figured it was by chance; still, I'd savored watching him through the net curtains as he spotted Lyra in the front garden and bent down to stroke her. A man who liked cats: how cute. He had lingered, looking at our house. I had been tempted to run out, offer him a coffee—but just as I'd summoned the nerve, he strode off.

I wondered if Sophia would head home now, keen to see Finn as soon as possible, so I felt a flare of pleasure when she suggested we grab some drinks.

We found an outside table at the Dog and Fox, bathed in the fading light of the setting sun. I texted Adam that I was going to be late home. He'd probably be pissed off; this morning he'd been joking about whether I had a Sapphic crush, with an edge to his voice. But we'd stayed in so much recently, and before Sophia had come along, I'd been craving more fun nights out like this.

We chatted about our university years and then Sophia fell quiet, tracing a finger along the edge of a drinks mat. Suddenly she said: "I can see you're attracted to Finn."

I flinched, instantly flushing. The other day she had come into the café and his image had been on my screen; I'd only just slammed the laptop shut in time. But maybe, maybe she had seen it.

"No—not really. I mean, he is attractive—obviously."

"He *is*," Sophia agreed, a little smugly. I tensed: did she want my desire for him, my jealousy?

"But you're my friend," I emphasized, "so I would never . . . you know . . . I mean, I've not thought about him at all since we had dinner," I lied.

"I see women going crazy over him all the time. Sometimes they blatantly flirt with him, right in front of me. Others are more subtle, though I can see them sizing me up, wondering what I've got and if they can compete. It used to drive me mad—now I find it amusing. I've got used to it."

"Adam and I are very happy," I asserted, mortified that she might have put me in a box along with *those women*.

"Yes, I can see that," Sophia agreed, and her eyes softened.

"So please don't think I'm a threat . . ." I was relieved when she looked reassured.

"How long have you and Adam been together?"

"Oh, forever. Well—seven years."

"And you're happy?"

"It's like we're still in the honeymoon stage," I lied. We were stagnant as hell, but at least it was a happy stagnancy.

She smiled, nodding, but then confided: "When we were living in Cornwall, we had all these problems with a stalker. It was one of the reasons we moved, actually. This woman—Meghan—just got *fixated* on Finn."

"Oh, God, how awful."

"She still writes him letters. *Long* ones. They're embarrassing—about how badly she wants him. She seemed so normal when I first met her . . ."

"I'd take it as a compliment," I tried to flatter her, but Sophia just looked uncomfortable, so I divulged: "I've had other women chase after Adam too—there was this woman at his work, Lorraine, who had a crush on him."

"Really?" Sophia looked intrigued.

"Luckily she ended up moving to New York, but there was a period where she kept texting him. So I know just how you feel." I put my hand on her arm.

I was glad Sophia had been honest with me, offloaded her fears. It showed we'd bonded in some way, but I was relieved to change the subject. I told her about the holiday Adam had recently booked for us: a week in Nice in August. Sophia told me how jealous she was, saying she loved France. I didn't add that, because we went there year in, year out, I had grown a little bored of it.

An hour or so later I headed home, feeling tipsy and still a little uneasy. Adam greeted me in a slightly sulky manner, but then we settled down in front of the TV with a glass of wine and cuddled up in mellow warmth. They lingered, those words—*I can see you're attracted to Finn*—like a splinter under my skin.

Over the past seven years, I'd suffered minor crushes from time to time. A handsome Croatian guy at the local Costa near our old flat; my ongoing adoration of Sean Connery when he was a young Bond. So had Adam. I knew being attracted to other people was natural; I was loyal but realistic. But not like this, not like I was with Finn: a lovesick teenager unable to focus, lusty with fantasies, obvious when she thought she was being discreet.

I imagined Sophia and Finn sighing and laughing over my embarrassing crush, and my cheeks burned.

Later, as Adam went into the bathroom to brush his teeth, I opened my laptop and quickly removed all references to Finn MacInnes from my search history.

7.

NOW: ELENA

Whilst Adam is talking to his mum on the phone—or rather, *listening* to her—I creep upstairs again.

In our bedroom I open the notebook that Sophia gifted me and check the list:

Lightbulb
Perfume
Mobile
Rucksack
Alarm
Back door

From the back of the wardrobe, I pull out the rucksack of clothes hidden under the empty travel bags, go to the bathroom, shove it in the airing cupboard behind some towels.

I cross *Rucksack* off the list.

I can't risk staying up here any longer. I hurry back down to the kitchen, where the mugs of tea I made have cooled to lukewarm; I quickly make fresh drinks.

On the dresser is a framed photo of Adam and his dad, taken by his aunt Mary. They're in an autumn field, gathering up leaves and throwing them into the air. It's a picture that makes me feel sad.

There are no photos of Adam's mother in this kitchen.

Adam is finally wrapping up the call: "Mmmm . . . yeah . . . sure . . . okay. Bye, Mum."

He comes into the kitchen, frowning. His tone is much sharper, aggressive, as though he's channeling her: "D'you want to finish this episode or not? We can just go to bed."

I shrug, feeling hurt. It's as though he digests her poison and then injects it into me.

"Whatever you like."

"Well, let's finish it then. Come on. Stop faffing around."

I roll my eyes at him. Any guilt I've had about tonight has been extinguished. *He deserves this.*

As I exit, my eyes fix on the kitchen clock.

Two and a half hours to go.

8.

THEN: ELENA

Shit!" Adam was cursing every other minute. His road rage had amused me early in our relationship. I'd laugh at his impatient put-downs about cyclists and "those mad idiots on scooters," in part because they seemed at odds with his usually sunny nature.

Tonight I wasn't smiling: he was tooting, swerving, overtaking, and I wanted to say "Slow down," but feared he'd explode.

The call had come in just after we'd had our Indian takeaway. I was in the living-room with Lyra on my lap, googling Rotten Tomatoes ratings for films, when Adam entered with tears in his eyes.

"It's Mum," he said.

For one chilling moment I thought she had died. As I jumped up and hugged him tight, he told me that she'd had a fall earlier today after suffering a stroke. She was left lying at the bottom of the stairs for six hours until her housekeeper arrived in the afternoon and called an ambulance.

Now we were speeding toward the hospital in Windsor. I felt mute with sadness. Adam's mum, Hilary, was seventy-two and lived on her own. She was vulnerable and called him often. I thought of my own parents, in their little cottage in Shrewsbury. It had been a week since I last rang Mum; I was seized with the urge to call her, to make sure she was all right.

At the hospital, Adam blasted into the main reception and I ran after him. We were directed toward the stroke ward.

The nurse there informed us that his mother was having an MRI scan to assess the damage. Hilary had suffered a mild stroke, aggravated by the effects of her fall. She had severe bruising and may have suffered a concussion when she hit her head on the stairs.

We sat in the waiting area. Adam bought a Coke. We both googled stroke symptoms and aftermath and the list looked frightening: numbness, weakness in limbs, slurred speech, blurry sight. Plus, a mild stroke was often a warning sign that a bigger one could be on the way.

The nurse came back, smiling awkwardly: "She says she'd like to see her son."

I clenched up inside. It was a polite way of saying Hilary wanted to see Adam but had no doubt specified that she didn't want to see me.

He gave me a sheepish kiss and followed the nurse. When he came out twenty minutes later, he looked shellshocked, saying he'd never seen his mother in such a bad state. There was nothing we could do but head home; Hilary would probably be here at least another week before she'd be discharged.

We stopped off at her house to feed her chihuahua. Adam wanted to take it back to ours but I pointed out that Lyra wouldn't be happy; we needed to arrange a pet sitter tomorrow morning.

On the journey back we were quiet, the windscreen wipers whirring away the rain. I turned on the radio but Adam switched it off after one song. I gazed at his profile, trying to decode him. When it came to his mother, I never fully understood their relationship, no matter how hard I tried. If I'd suffered Adam's childhood, I'd have cut her off and never reconciled; part of me felt angry that he was even bothering to go to the hospital. That he was showing her such love given how little she had ever shown him.

Home. We could hear voices and for one scary moment we were worried a burglar had struck, that we'd forgotten to lock up properly. It turned out we'd left the TV on in our panic. I felt sad, looking at the cold cup of Earl Grey that I'd brewed before we went out, sitting on a coaster by the sofa, when we'd been about to share a lovely evening together.

It was past midnight. In the bathroom we watched our reflections clean their teeth in the mirror and then we collapsed into bed.

Adam pulled me in tight, our ribs crunching against each other. We'd not made love for a while and I was shattered, which was the excuse I'd used the last time he tried to initiate sex a few weeks back. I could feel the rawness in his kisses, taste the desperate sadness. He wanted to lose himself in me.

And so I pushed away the thick tiredness, and responded with enthusiasm. He rolled on top of me. Normally Adam was attentive and gentle, but tonight he just wanted me and there was something selfish and a little brutal and urgent that I found arousing. I found myself closing my eyes, imagining a man with dark hair above me. *You're attracted to Finn*, Sophia's words slapped me. Adam entered me, climaxing quickly, and I was close, much closer than I usually was.

Hilary was sitting in a wheelchair when we arrived at the hospital to collect her a week later. I wondered if, with the general scarcity of beds, they were discharging her a little early.

I was used to seeing her in silk blouses, her short hair coiffured, her features harshly emphasized with makeup. Now I was shocked by her frailty. She looked ten years older, gaunt and haggard. One side of her face was drooping and slack.

The nurse passed her a form to fill in, rating the NHS on the stay she'd just had. She suggested I could fill it in for Hilary, given that she was left-handed and the stroke had affected that side.

"'How likely are you to recommend this hospital to a friend?'" Hilary read loudly in her clipped, posh accent. "I think I will say no, I would certainly not. From now on, I'm going private."

I cringed, but the nurse took it in her stride, just smiled and nodded in a professional manner.

"They've saved your life," I said to Hilary, "and I think they've worked hard, looking after you—"

"Mum's just stressed," Adam overrode me, grabbing the wheelchair handles, though he gave the nurse a sheepish grin. As he pushed Hilary into the corridor, the form went floating out of her hands and landed behind her on the floor.

I picked it up and put it back on the table. Then I grabbed a Biro, giving the NHS ten out of ten for everything, leaving the form behind for the nurse.

It wasn't easy, transferring Hilary from the wheelchair to the back seat of our car; Adam and I cupped our hands underneath her, panicking that we might bang her head on the doorframe.

"Careful, careful," she kept saying, and I saw sweat breaking out on Adam's forehead. "Sorry, Mum, I know you've had a long day. We'll be home soon."

But our drive back to Windsor was delayed by heavy traffic. She grumbled all the way.

It was nearly five when we pulled up at her large house, bought from the proceeds of her third—or perhaps her fourth—divorce.

Hilary had turned down a care package from the local council in favor of hiring a private carer. She turned up on time at 6 p.m. A woman in her forties with white-blonde hair, she seemed warm, brisk, and capable.

I eyed her with sympathy. I couldn't say that I would ever want to be in a situation where I was having to look after Hilary.

9.

THEN: ELENA

So sorry I'm running late, I messaged Sophia, willing the bus to move. Instead, it sat and shuddered in traffic and impatient horns tooted all the way toward Wimbledon Village.

We'd arranged to meet for a drink at seven; it was all Adam's fault that I was late. This afternoon I'd been in the Vicomte, in the middle of a proof-reading job, when he had called out of the blue. His voice was high and terse. He said it was an emergency. His mother was alone, scared, vulnerable. I asked where her carer had gone and he muttered something about her failing to turn up.

"But—I'm working," I stuttered. "I've got a deadline. For five today."

"But if I go, I'll get fired," he cried. "I've got meetings all afternoon. Come on, please, Elena, it's not as though you've got a proper job."

"What?" My face turned hot. He backtracked quickly, saying my work was *flexible*, which I knew meant *female*. The words stung all the way over on the train from Wimbledon to Windsor. When I arrived, my anger softened; I felt sorry for Hilary, and there was a touching moment when I brushed her hair for her and it felt as though she was a child. When I took her to the toilet, she wept a little, perhaps from the humiliation, and I thought, *I never want to get old.* Then the sniping began. The tea I had made her wasn't as good as when Adam made it. I was clumsy. She wanted him. It soon transpired that she had fired her carer for "incompetence" and it was this that had created the emergency.

On the train back to Wimbledon, I saw an email from my client who was asking for a twenty percent discount because I'd requested a deadline extension. Just when I was getting my business going and starting to get recommendations. In the meantime, Adam was up for a promotion, which he would no doubt get because he hadn't had to take an afternoon off work. I knew I ought to cancel the drink with Sophia but, fuck it, I was fed up. I didn't want to go home to Adam and have it out with him. At the same time, seeing Sophia now carried a trace of discomfort, ever since the *I can see you're attracted to Finn* thing. I hoped that had been forgotten.

By the time I arrived at Hemingway's, I'd received a WhatsApp from Sophia saying she was running late as well. The waitress led me to a table. Noticing a few cat hairs on my tights, I picked them off. I suffered a longing for my old crowd of friends in Walthamstow. I could've relaxed and moaned with them; with Sophia I had to strain to be my very best, as though my personality now had a filter like the Instagram photos I fretted over.

"I'm so sorry I'm late!" Sophia was flushed, her perfume laced with city smog, cigarette smoke.

She sat down in the booth opposite me. I noticed a faint tremor in her fingers as she picked up the menu. We were both clearly in need of a drink.

"Oh—look at you—you're gorgeous!" She'd noticed my new haircut. In the direness of the day, I'd forgotten it myself and now I touched it, self-consciously. "Dominic did such a good job."

The Wimbledon hairdresser she'd personally recommended normally had a months-long waiting list but she'd somehow got me in. It had blown half my budget for the week. I did love the cut and highlights, even though I now realized it was a bit too similar to Sophia's style.

Suddenly there was a guy standing right next to us, swaying slightly, eyes bloodshot. He was youthful and handsome and he knew it.

"How about you beautiful ladies let me buy you a drink?" he suggested.

"How about you just fuck off and die?" Sophia retorted, in such a hostile tone that I was taken aback. I'd never heard her swear before. It was actually quite funny.

Realizing he'd already lost the game, he took the piss: "I hear there's a new Trad Wife movement starting up—want to be my Trad Wife?"

Sophia gave him the most withering stare I'd ever seen. "No."

He paled and walked off.

"Men!" Sophia hissed, and I grinned, agreeing, "What a dick!"

Our conversation resumed, skating on the surface, Sophia going on about how successful her art was, me boasting about how well my proofreading was going and how Adam was up for a promotion and we were oh so happy and wonderful. I felt overtired, unable to relax; just one more drink, then I'd make my excuses.

Next to my glass, my mobile began to sing and vibrate.

ADAM flashed up on the screen. I hesitated.

"You're not going to get that?" Sophia raised an eyebrow.

"Um—yes, of course," I muttered. I picked it up, avoiding her gaze, staring at the table.

"Hey," he said softly. "How are you?" Then, before I could even answer: "What happened this afternoon?"

"I went over, like you asked," I replied in bewilderment. My headache sharpened with the unease that crept in. "My client wasn't all that happy about me delivering late."

There was a loaded silence and then he replied in a quiet, sad voice: "Mum said you bullied her. I know you two have always had some issues but I thought this would be a chance for you to bond . . ."

"Bullied her?" I could hardly get the words out. "I—*helped* her—to the toilet—and I made her tea. Adam, you can't seriously think I would do that . . ."

Silence. "Okay."

"Okay? What does 'okay' mean?"

"I'm still at work—I know you're out for a drink but I'm having a really busy day and I have to go. We can talk about it later tonight."

I hung up, staring at my phone in shock. *The bloody bastard.*

"Everything okay?"

"Oh, fine," I said, forcing a smile. Sophia's chatter became distant, muffled. How embarrassing, this prickle in my eyes and throat; I took a big gulp of my cocktail, then began to choke on it. As Sophia soothed me, I found that the tears streaming from my eyes wouldn't stop. Sophia's mouth became an O.

"Oh my God, what's wrong, Elena?"

"It's nothing." I picked up a napkin, blowing my nose. I hated crying in front of other people.

"Oh, come on," she chided me gently. "It's not nothing. It's very clearly something. Is it . . . Adam?"

It all came out little by little. Hilary's stroke. Her difficult behavior. Sophia pointed out that when people became ill, their personalities can really change and it wasn't necessarily personal but due to their pain speaking through them.

So I rewound, back to the beginning. We'd been dating two years when Adam reconciled with his mother after a long time apart. I felt excited for him, touched by the idea of their reunion. He met her several times on his own before introducing me to her. I remembered him fussing about what I was going to wear. He rejected my entire wardrobe from jeans to Oasis dresses to black trousers. In the end, he bought me an awful flowery thing from M&S. It didn't quite fit. I wore it there, my stomach in pain from the strain on the zip. Eyeing up my bright lipstick, Adam offered me a tissue; I crumpled it defiantly. He seemed anxious, like a little boy being called in to see the headmistress. I felt buoyant. Generally people liked me; I was friendly and enjoyed socializing. Hilary was charming, that day, but I noticed a beadiness in those eyes that seemed to be constantly analyzing me, as though storing all my data, seeking out weakness. And yes, her eyes did flit to my bold lipstick with a flash of disapproval.

The odd behavior started slowly. Little snipes, little digs. I felt concerned that I'd offended her by mistake, so my intense cooking phase began. Whenever she came over, I'd make three-course meals, inspired by my Nigella cookbook. She would declare it was delicious but call up Adam later saying she had a runny tummy, my kitchen hygiene wasn't up to scratch. Once I even overheard her saying that our place was a pigsty. So I cleaned it obsessively but the truth was, I was messy, and Hilary would come over, spot me beaming with pride at the hoovered floors and gleaming surfaces, and find that one corner I'd missed, pointing out a cobweb, a sliver of dust. She started bringing over her own food, delicate sandwiches that her housekeeper had made for her, wincing when I passed her a plate, as though it would pollute her to eat off it.

"She's one of those toxic people who are so awful that in the present, you can't really take them in," I said to Sophia. The napkin was a tight ball in my palm. "But there's this aftermath—you know what I mean? Afterward all the little digs stay with you and you feel rotten for a day. And the only time Adam and I argue is after seeing her. I can't keep up the pretense that I like her, that we've bonded in any way. She's the fatal flaw in our relationship, our arguments are constant repetitions. Usually we only see her twice a month, and I can survive that. But now . . . now she's ill the thought of her is there all the time, poisoning us . . ."

"But why did she take such a dislike to you?" Sophia looked puzzled. "I mean, you're so lovely, Elena. You're a mother-in-law's dream."

"Well . . ."

"Hold it—I need the Ladies like mad." Sophia got up, looking apologetic. "All those cocktails." She patted my arm reassuringly, then hurried off.

Her timing was handy because I wasn't prepared to tell her the full story. How I had met Adam seven years ago when I'd seen his profile on Tinder back in 2015. I was tired of idiot men with Team Jordan Peterson hashtagged in their profiles. Adam's photos had been attractive: floppy blond hair, ripped jeans, a rough and ready look. One of the pics showed him leaning over a car wielding a spanner, looking like a mechanic. He was twenty-seven then; three years younger than me. His profile had words like "feminist" and "Marxist" in the title. He'll be like me, I'd thought, from a similar background.

Then we had dinner. I fell for his gorgeous Scottish accent, sunny manner, witty jokes, and confidence. However, it transpired that he worked in a bank, having failed to become a film-maker. His father had been a professor at Edinburgh University; his mother owned an upmarket boutique. He'd been educated at Westminster College and rebelled against his "bourgeois" upbringing. At least I hadn't felt embarrassed about my parents (as I had been made to feel at Cambridge)—Adam loved that my dad was a retired printer and my mum a cleaner and school dinner-lady. When I introduced him to them, she fawned over him as though he was royalty, while my dad—who really was a Socialist—was a bit cheeky, dropping sarcastic remarks about champagne Marxists, and I had to tell him off. In the bedroom, Adam played on our class differences as a sexy joke, calling me his wench while he was my lord. He was the aristocrat seducing his naughty maid. When we'd met his mother, she'd picked up on it at once. Just a sly observation: "You don't pronounce your Gs, Elena. You said singin' instead of sing*ing*." I hadn't even noticed; Cambridge had poshed up my accent, I had thought. Usually when we met people for the first time, they assumed I was the privileged one and Adam from a lower socio-economic background, a deception we both enjoyed.

A few times a year, Hilary would host a cocktail party in her home. I found it embarrassing, watching her fawn over anyone titled, with the desperation of a middle-class social climber. Adam moaned about having to attend but he was able to make easy conversation with everyone whereas I felt perpetually uncomfortable, especially on one occasion when Hilary tried to get me to serve drinks and play waitress. (I politely told her where to go.)

When Sophia came back we ordered more cocktails and she asked me a different question: "Can't Adam see how awful she is?"

"It's all so weird and complicated. You know, when he was a child, she would openly tell him that he was an accident."

"No!"

"Yes. Adam's dad was a wonderful man, by all accounts, but Hilary was always having affairs. He just pretended they weren't happening, put on a stiff upper lip. Then, when Adam was eight, she fell in love with a millionaire and walked out on them both."

"Dear God."

"When Adam was a teenager he hardly even saw her. Luckily, he had a father who cared for him. But he died when Adam was only twenty-two . . . I feel so sad that I never got to meet him."

"I bet he would have loved you," Sophia insisted.

"Thank you," I said gratefully. "Adam says the same. But, you know, Hilary didn't even turn up to the funeral! I mean, he was in his late twenties when she came waltzing back into his life—and maybe if his dad hadn't passed away, he wouldn't have felt so vulnerable. She just seems to cast this spell over him, he turns into another person when he's with her . . . If Adam and I hadn't been solid by that point, maybe she would have broken us up before we'd even had a chance, that's what scares me. I'm sorry, I've been going on and on . . ."

"No need to apologize!"

She had been such a good listener, and without judgment. She was kinder, more open-minded, than I had realized; despite idolizing her, I had actually underestimated her. Suddenly a rush of gratitude filled me and I leaned over, pulling her into a hug. *A mistake*, I thought, feeling her tense, but she returned the embrace.

"Thank you for listening, it's really helped—and you've saved me from spending the evening filling my diary with mad ramblings."

"You keep a diary!" Sophia held up her palm for a high-five and we laughed drunkenly. "I keep mine hidden in plain sight, so Finn can't find it—it's wrapped in a Georges Simenon cover."

"That's risky," I giggled. "But I like your old-school style—I type mine up and have it password-protected."

"That's hilarious, I bet Adam spends his life trying to guess it!" she cried, her eyes gleaming. "Let's order more cocktails! Sod our partners!"

"And how are you and Finn?" I asked tentatively. I didn't want to be narcissistic and just talk about my relationship, but I was worried she'd think I was looking for weaknesses. "I'm sure Adam and I could learn from you—you have such a perfect marriage."

Sophia's laughter was bittersweet. "Far from it. But that's a story for another day."

"What about Meghan the stalker?" I asked cautiously.

"Oh, as batshit as ever!" Sophia seemed less fraught about her than she had a few weeks back. "Sending Finn love letters, even a poem that rhymed *love* with *dove*. You can imagine . . ."

Three more rounds of cocktails later, Sophia generously put down her card for the bill, fobbing me off and declaring it was her treat. We weren't far from home, but she was still nervy after her bag theft and insisted on ringing Finn, waking him up. It was now nearly one in the morning; he pulled up in his Jaguar looking grim-faced. Sophia got into the front; I slid into the back. She kept singing drunkenly. In the rearview mirror, I saw a smile twitch across his lips.

Suddenly his eyes met mine in the mirror; held mine, for too long. Something burned between us that felt as intimate as a kiss. *I can see you're attracted to Finn*, Sophia's words echoed. Was he toying with me, taking the piss?

Finn drew up in front of our place and I got out in a tipsy panic, glad that Sophia didn't seem to have noticed; she was blowing me blurry kisses goodbye.

I slipped in quietly, saw Adam's jacket on the peg. He would've been home long ago. I discovered several cross texts on my phone asking me what time I planned on turning up. I tiptoed upstairs, saw that he was in bed, snoring. He had pulled the curtains but not the blackout blind and I yanked it down, then got into bed beside him, the darkness a relief.

10.

NOW: ELENA

Adam and I sit up in bed together, pillows puffed behind our backs. I'm in a cotton nightie; Adam in boxers and a T-shirt. It feels odd being back in the double bed. I've been sleeping in the spare bedroom for much of the past fortnight. I've grown to enjoy having my own space. Now we're stiff, self-conscious, like I'd imagine a Victorian couple would be.

I yawn loudly, as though I'm much too tired to read. Adam ignores me, reaches out, clicks his bedside lamp.

He frowns. Clicks it on–off.

On–off.

"Fuck. I'm too tired to get another bulb."

I think he's hinting for me to go down and get one from the kitchen drawer. I roll my eyes, bite back a retort about laziness, and mutter that the glow from my lamp is enough for both of us. He opens *The Hound of the Baskervilles*, which he must be reading for the twentieth time. I sense his eagerness to escape his cares and sorrows, to enter another world where he can align himself with a clever hero.

Irritation crackles between us. Arguments, unspoken, too late to be unraveled, cloud above us.

I pick up *Wuthering Heights*. My eyes skate across the words. I picture

Sophia over in her house, her rucksack also filled with clothes, tucked under her bed. I picture her praying for Finn to fall quickly into a deep sleep.

Then, my mobile buzzes.

"You didn't ask how Mum is," Adam says.

"Sorry?" I'm itching to pick up my mobile. It must be a message from Sophia.

"Mum. She called up. When we were watching the crime thing."

"Yes. I know."

Distracted, I grab my phone. It's a WhatsApp from Sophia. **Finn suddenly went out for a walk. Sorry. He NEVER does at this time of night.**

What does it mean? Are we on or are we off? Won't he come back soon? Can't we delay? Or is she just making an excuse? She has always been so confident and assertive that we could do this, but I've never been a hundred percent sure she would go through with it.

Do you want to cancel? I message back.

I slump with disappointment. Desire has been humming through my body for days, the note becoming more and more soprano. The thought of waking up tomorrow next to Adam, back in the same rut, is so depressing.

11.

THEN: ELENA

The Ivy Café was one of the fanciest restaurants in Wimbledon Village. Sophia had offered to treat me to lunch to cheer me up. As we ordered, she rejected my choice of elderflower fizz, insisting we get some wine. God knows how much work I was going to get done that afternoon, but eating out was a rare luxury; Adam preferred staying in with a cozy takeaway.

"How are things?" Sophia asked, her eyes tender.

"Great," I replied but my voice was so flat, we laughed at my inability to sound convincing. "Awful. One minute I was labeled a bully by his mum, the next Adam was backtracking like mad and ringing me up to go over there after another carer crisis. Plus, he's now canceled our holiday in Nice because he doesn't feel we can desert Hilary for a week. But I don't want to spend our lunch moaning." I insisted that Sophia tell me some good news.

"Well, I've just become a godmother to an eight-year-old," she said. "A friend of mine, April—she's also an artist—just got round to having him christened, and asked me out of the blue!"

"Oh, congratulations!"

She related how much she was enjoying taking her godson to kids' films and reading to him: "It's making me feel quite clucky, actually." She gave a soft sigh.

"Really?" I was slightly taken aback, because Sophia hadn't seemed the maternal kind.

"Who was your favorite author when you were a kid?"

"Oh, Enid Blyton—except, she's *persona non grata* now, isn't she?" I said; we both laughed. "The Famous Five—I did love it, but it was so sexist. There were those two brothers, what were their names?"

"Dick! Dick and Julian!"

"And there was Anne, the quiet one."

"Yes," Sophia said angrily, "and whenever there was an adventure, they said to Anne, be boring, stay behind, play with your dolls, while we go off being manly and save the day."

I snorted laughter-bubbles in my drink. Sophia was such a tonic: I was cheering up already.

"My favorite was Roald Dahl," she said. "Seriously, J. K. Rowling has nothing on him."

"I loved Dahl as well! *Charlie and the Chocolate Factory. Danny the Champion of the World*—I longed to have a father like his," I added wistfully.

"Oh, yes, me too."

This surprised me: I'd pictured her as a daddy's girl, with a wealthy, indulgent father. I nearly asked her what he was like, but held back, a little shy.

"Dahl's short stories were good too," I mused. "The one about the woman who kills her husband with the joint of lamb!"

"And what about that story in *Switch Bitch*!" Sophia exclaimed. "Where those husbands secretly sleep with each other's wives."

"Oh, my goodness!" I cried. "Yes, that was juicy, that one. How did it end? Did the wives find out?"

"I can't remember," Sophia replied, her finger circling the rim of her glass. "I think it was first written for *Playboy*. It's a male fantasy really, isn't it? But it's one of those stories that makes you think it'd be so much fun to try it in real life—it'd be wild, but doable."

"What—you want to wake up next to another man in your bed?"

"No!" Sophia laughed. "I mean, the reverse. The feminist version." Her eyes flashed. "Where the women trick the men and sleep with them without them realizing."

I frowned, wondering why on earth she would want to sleep with anyone except her delicious husband.

"Did Finn like the underwear you bought?" I blurted out, without thinking.

She looked taken aback and I wanted to kick myself. Now she was going to think that I'd been imagining them in bed together.

"He . . ." She swallowed.

"Sorry—I was being really nosy."

"Oh, not at all," she insisted, but she seemed to be holding back, and I felt pervy, intrusive. "I—just haven't had a chance to wear it yet," she said, averting her eyes.

An awkward silence.

I had succeeded in neutering my crush on Finn; just about. The only slip had been a dream about him the other night. I had found myself falling off the wagon, googling him again.

"You know," she said slowly, "we're the same height, the same build."

"Yes . . ." I wondered if she was about to suggest a clothes swap.

"Just like the men in *Switch Bitch*."

I looked up abruptly at her. I had thought that she was berating me for desiring her husband.

Now I realized that she had another agenda all along.

"Are you suggesting . . ." No, she couldn't be.

She's drunk, I thought, as she smiled at me impishly. *She's joking. Surely.*

"Why not?" She shrugged.

"Uh-huh."

"I'm serious."

"You want *me* to sleep with Finn, and you to sleep with—Adam?"

"In the dark, without them knowing. In secret."

"They'd know!" I exclaimed. "It'd be impossible to pull off in real life. I mean, it's just a story."

"But you have a blackout blind."

When had she seen that? When they'd come for dinner? Had she been plotting, thinking about it, even back then?

"If it's pitch-black, how could he ever see?" Sophia went on. "I could get one installed too. I could say to Finn that I got the idea from you, that we'll enjoy beautiful sleep."

I laughed out loud at the outrageousness of it all, wishing I wasn't so tipsy, my intuition blurred. Was she testing me in some way? Was this all another game to find out if I wanted Finn?

"For a start," I pointed out, "Adam knows my scent. It's a very *particular* thing, the scent of someone's body. And then there're all the little habits, the way I sleep, the way I breathe when I sleep—everything."

"The scent part is easy," she asserted, her pupils dilated. "It's an amalgamation of perfume, body wash, shampoo, food, washing powder. That would be easy to fix."

I started, realizing that she'd been thinking this through. I pictured her slipping into bed beside Adam, her mouth on his, and felt a cut of jealousy.

"I just can't believe he'd be fooled," I said firmly.

"But don't they say that the perfect crime—"

"Crime?" I laughed.

"—crime," she laughed too, then added in a deadly serious tone, "the perfect crime is just about attention to detail? If we considered every little possibility, wrote a list, ticked them off . . ."

"I don't think it would work, even then," I said in a high voice.

"I mean—if you were to, say, slip into my house, which is only— what?—five . . . seven minutes' walk from yours—and I left the back door unlocked, and you went in and tiptoed up the stairs . . . Finn would be fast asleep, and you'd slip in and wake him up and he'd enjoy it. He likes surprises. And you could kiss him the way I kiss him, softly at first, and then firmly, winding your fingers through his hair . . ."

Her description didn't sound convincing at all, more like she'd pulled it from a romance novel, but I couldn't help it: the blood pulsed in my cheeks and a fire beat between my legs. I took a big gulp of wine.

"But you and Finn must have an amazing sex life," I challenged her. "Why would you want to throw it all away?"

"It's not about throwing anything away. It's about spicing things up."

"You're not . . . happy?"

The waitress came up, setting our main courses down in front of us, and I came to. It was nearly one o'clock. We were sitting in a nice restaurant, surrounded by posh people, having a conversation that belonged to the night.

Sophia sighed. "After ten years, things are a little—flat—between us. Perhaps you're in the same boat?"

I was still gaping. *Flat?* And here I was, thinking they were the perfect couple, who shared goodbye embraces in the mornings with a frisson, and celebrated their sex life with lingerie.

"It is a bit flat, but he makes me feel safe. I feel I can depend on Adam. But we don't . . ." I stopped myself, feeling disloyal to him. Perhaps I needed to start sobering up.

Sophia had been looking for a crack in my defenses, and now she'd found it: "So it's not great between you? The sex, I mean."

"God, I can't believe you've asked me that!" I cried.

"Sorry." She pointed to her wine glass. "I just thought, as I'd told you about mine . . ."

"It's actually pretty fantastic," I told her forcefully. "Before Adam came along, I was wasting my time on bad boys and wankers. Gradually I realized I deserved better, that nice guys weren't boring, and that being with someone nice meant valuing myself. Once I believed I deserved to be treated as someone special, I got Adam."

"I know, I know." Now Sophia wore the soothing expression of a therapist who isn't going to judge. "But let's face it, no guy is the perfect package, no relationship is ever completely fulfilling, is it?"

"Right," I said.

"You look as though you think I'm patronizing you. I'm not—"

"I didn't—"

"What I mean is that all women are fed this bullshit, from a young age, and this story of The One—a perfect man whom destiny delivers—is stupid. It takes a while to figure out reality. No guy can ever fulfill all our needs, just like we can't fulfill all theirs. You gain and you lose, you make a choice based on some sacrifices. You go for the nice guy and get stability and friendship but perhaps the sex isn't perfect. Me and Finn—we got married far too young, and I find him old-fashioned at times. And the sex—it's not great anymore. And maybe for you it's not great either."

Indignation flared inside me. Then I looked into her eyes and realized we were on the same side. For the first time she seemed human and flawed, and even if I didn't want to take her up on her mad proposal, I could still confide in her.

I set down my knife and fork and confessed: "I fake my orgasms."

"Of course."

"Actually, I don't even know if I fake them." I cupped my chin in my palms. "I sort of do and then they seem real, kind of. It's complicated. And now we're in a rough patch so we've stopped having sex altogether . . ." When I looked up, the intensity of her gaze was unnerving, but then she leaned in and said in a low voice: "I'm with you there. I fake mine too."

"Seriously—you fake them? With *Finn*?"

"Of course I do!" she laughed. "We've had sex about ten thousand times. No, more probably. You know, monogamy suits people in theory. Emotionally, it's very hard to share. But sexually, we're all polyamorous by nature—we all fancy other people, we're all tempted. I mean—take a bull. You put a bull in a paddock with a cow and after a few goes he gets bored; you put in a new cow and he goes wild with lust. That's biology. And so every person in a relationship is fighting a battle between their heart and their biology. We condemn so many people for picking 'the wrong option,' but it's hard. It's really hard."

She sounded as though she was quoting articles now and I pictured her flitting through Google searches, mining blogs, trying to find theories that gave flesh and shape to her anxieties, and felt sorry for her. *Isn't life a sod*, I thought, *that she got the man everyone lusted after and she didn't even want to go to bed with him?*

"Maybe it won't be such an issue as we get older," I mused. "I mean, me and Adam reaching the peak of sexual boredom might coincide with the menopause, and then we'll be grown up and boring and sex won't matter so much." The very idea of the menopause made me shudder, though, and I wanted to see it as far, far off in the future.

"But we're in the here and now," said Sophia. "We can't live for the future. And, the thing is, a switch could save a marriage. It's a controlled experiment. It's not like a real affair. It's a game, it's danger made safe."

We were back in shark territory again.

"Safe?" I exclaimed. "And what happens if one of them were to reach out in the middle and say, 'I want to see you,' and switch on the light?"

I expected her face to crumple, but Sophia replied calmly: "Before the switch, we'd remove the bulbs from the bedside lamps. Or just unscrew them a few notches so they don't work. Like I said, for a perfect crime, every detail has to be thought through."

"You sound as though you've done this before."

"Just spent a lot of time thinking about it all," she said. "And yes, I admit—I do want to try it. For me, it would satisfy this restlessness, this boredom, this longing for something else. I'd get it out of my system— and Finn and I could go on side by side for another ten years."

My eyes flitted to the crucifix gleaming at her neck, which she wore from time to time: it seemed incongruous with all this talk of the perfect *crime*. "But there's a big elephant in the room here—isn't this really rape?"

"Rape?" Sophia looked incredulous.

"Well, yes," I said uncertainly. "If they don't know, then they're not consenting, are they?"

"Oh, you really think they'd complain? If they knew, which they won't," she added hastily, "they'd be *thanking* us, over and over. Men *love* sex. Statistically, they think about it seven times a minute. This is their dream come true—only they don't have to face the guilt in the morning. They get to have a secret sexual adventure with no consequences. What man wouldn't want that? We're doing this for them as much as for us . . ."

I wasn't entirely convinced by this, but I carried on engaging with the idea.

"But . . . would you ever tell Finn? If you found another couple to do this?" I emphasized the word *another*.

"No. He doesn't need to know. As I said, I'd want to protect his innocence—let him enjoy this without the burden of knowledge. It's a controlled thrill. It's the infidelity equivalent of—of a rollercoaster." Her eyes flashed again. "You get to scream and go to the edges but nobody's going to get hurt."

"It still seems to me like there are so many risks—like, what if the other woman freaks out and tells her husband?"

"I'd deny everything. Besides, there has to be some risk or there would be no thrill."

"Well, I hope you're successful in finding someone to do it."

Sophia bit her lip, deflated, disappointed; and I felt sad, sensing the desperation behind her crazy bravado.

"Sorry," I said, putting my hand on her arm. "It's flattering of you to suggest this, really, but Adam would never forgive me. His mum wasn't faithful to his dad, like I told you . . . and Adam's always been so principled about fidelity." I paused, thinking about his work colleague, Lorraine, but that wasn't something I wanted to go into detail about right now. "He'd hate to feel I was betraying him."

"It seems to me that you think a bit too much about how Adam feels about everything and not enough about *you*."

She wasn't the first friend who had said that. But this was all becoming too much for me: the force of her personality, normally so beguiling, felt like knuckles pressing against my skin. If we sat here another hour, God knows where the conversation would go. I checked my watch and was genuinely surprised by the time.

"I have to run—I've got a meeting in Vauxhall at four," I lied.

"You don't want dessert?"

"I—I really have to go."

Sophia was still leaning forward, her eyes fierce on me—then she sat back, sighing in defeat.

"Sure," she replied coolly. She hailed the waitress for the bill and, in that moment, she was the usual Sophia again, charming, saying how delicious the food had been, adding a generous tip.

"I really appreciated the lunch," I said. Suddenly I felt anxious that this was going to be the full stop on our friendship.

"It was my pleasure." She smiled and for a moment all was forgotten. "Hey. We should . . ." She fished out her phone and gestured for me to lean in, snapping a selfie of us, adding the hashtag #creativesatlunch. We parted company and as the afternoon went by, her words circling round and round my mind, I received a constant flurry of Instagram notifications and new followers as the photo was liked again and again and again. Later that evening, I scrolled through the comments underneath: you are both such gorgeous women and Sophia who is your lovely friend? and looks like you had so much fun . . .

12.

NOW: ELENA

I check my phone for the umpteenth time. I'm going crazy over Sophia's failure to reply. Is Finn back? Is the plan in place? Are we on or are we off?

The time is now eleven-fifteen. We're getting too close to the wire. I sigh quietly.

It seems like it's off.

Adam yawns. "Ready for lights out?"

I nod. He tucks a bookmark into his paperback. I click off the lamp. Pitch-black: the blackout blinds really work. Our plan was so perfect, down to every detail. What a waste, what a stupid waste.

In the old days, before sleep, he used to say, "Good night, wench," and I'd reply, "Good night, my lord," and we'd giggle into the darkness.

While neither of us are in the mood for affection right now, I wait for him at least to say good night.

Perhaps he's waiting for me.

The silence bristles between us.

"You did set the alarm, didn't you?" he suddenly asks.

"Yes. I did," I reply in a small voice.

I roll over, surreptitiously pick up my phone, shielding it with my hand: we have a rule of no phones after lights out.

Another message from Sophia.

My heart leaps.

He's BACK! PHEW! We're still ON!

13.

THEN: ELENA

Sophia was there in the Vicomte Café, the morning after making her proposal, frowning at her laptop, a half-drunk latte beside her.

I panicked. Flashed her a vague smile. I found myself walking past her and sitting down two tables away.

A faint hangover was throbbing at my temples and I felt frayed, incoherent, waiting for the paracetamol to kick in. We'd drunk a lot in the Ivy Café and later that evening I'd opened another bottle of wine at home. I could feel shocked hurt radiating from Sophia in waves. I knew I was being a bitch and she would completely misunderstand why.

"Hey," she said softly. She slid down the leather banquette until she was close to me. "Can I buy you a tea?"

The pleading in her voice sounded so alien. The power balance between us was shifting. That she'd come crashing off her perfect pedestal was both a relief and a disappointment to me.

I said that I wasn't really thirsty.

Then I said that I wouldn't mind an Earl Grey.

"Listen," she said, "I'm so, so sorry about the mad proposition yesterday. I called my therapist for an emergency Zoom session afterward. She guided me to realize that I'm attempting to resolve my marriage problems through you because I'm scared of facing them directly."

Once it would have surprised me to hear she was in therapy, but not anymore. I frowned, wondering if, in turn, I was projecting onto her. By putting the faked orgasm issue into words I'd made something vague much more vivid, giving it weight and force. I ought to discuss it with Adam, really, but it felt odd, after seven years of being together.

But imagine if this goes on for ten years, I thought. *Twenty. What then?*

"I hope we can just pretend it never happened," Sophia pleaded. I was shocked to hear a catch in her voice.

Antonia brought over my Earl Grey. I tore open the sugar packet, poured in the milk, stirred it, took a sip.

"But . . ." I trailed off. I didn't want to admit that the reason I'd freaked out, that I hadn't been able to sit next to her, was because I'd spent the night in torment.

That, although I was shocked by her idea, and wildly jealous at the thought of her and Adam together, though I felt sick that I had confided in her that I faked my orgasms, though I wondered about her bizarre motives, I was tempted. Fantasies of how Finn might kiss, might caress, had begun a slow burn in my mind.

And I had felt so freaked out that I hadn't wanted to sit with her and admit, "Yes—maybe I do actually want to try out this crazy plan!" Because there was so much at stake, so much that could go wrong, and I might throw away everything that Adam and I had. Yes, we were going through a bad patch. But this was no way to resolve it.

"Let's just get some work done," Sophia said, getting out her sketchpad.

I enjoyed our shared concentration, the unity of discipline. She didn't mention the switch idea again and by the end of the day it had already begun to fade, like the memory of a drunken evening that feels blurry, that you're not entirely sure happened.

A week later, I discovered that the seed had been growing shoots, seeking light. I was on a train on my way to see Hilary.

She was getting on well with her new carer, a twenty-something Lithuanian, but today he had failed to show up. "It's the last time I'll ask you, I promise," Adam had pressed me when he called me up in desperation. All the way there, my blood boiled and I argued with him in my head. It reminded me of the early days of our relationship, when I'd ended up doing twice as much housework as him despite the "feminist" declaration in his dating profile. Adam was always so tired in the evenings, worked longer hours than me, but there was feminist theory, which I believed in, and there was practice. Sometimes being human transcended ideology. It was an act of love to wash someone's dishes, to make them a cup of tea, to put their socks into the machine. I hadn't done those chores for him feeling resentful. And yet, there had been pressure on me too: he was paying two-thirds of our rent on the Walthamstow flat. Without him, I'd be renting a room, not a flat.

My phone buzzed with a notification. I checked my gmail. A client was demanding a major discount on my proof-reading work for them; I'd handed it in a day late last week when another sudden caring duty had thrown my schedule off-kilter.

I exploded then. I was a woman who always handed in her tax return six months early, who kept her deadlines, who ticked her lists.

I sent the WhatsApp message to Sophia suddenly and spontaneously:

Let's do it. The switch, let's just do it. Exx

And I was surprised when I sent it, because it hadn't been sharp and bright in my conscious mind at all. Or so I'd thought.

Hilary was meek when I arrived, but it wasn't long before she started griping. Why hadn't Adam sent her flowers this week? Shouldn't a son send his mother flowers? Freesias, her favorite? Had I talked him out of sending her flowers?

Because I had sent Sophia the message, I felt light and breezy and oddly invincible. The switch was chaos; it laughed at ordinary life and its boundaries and structures. I almost felt drunk. Late in the afternoon, when Hilary moaned at me having to take her to the toilet, I let slip a giggle. Her eyes narrowed; they fell to my belly and I realized she was trying to work out if I was pregnant.

On the train home, as I was imagining Finn's lips on mine, drowning in the solace of fantasy, a text came through from Sophia. It was like a punch in the gut: **I've been thinking—maybe it isn't such a good idea. Let's discuss. Sxx**

Oh, shit, I thought. She'd never been serious. Now I felt like a complete idiot. And a little angry with her, as though she'd tripped me up.

Home. I sobered up.

In the kitchen, there was a surprise gift for me on the table. Adam had left me a box of Dairy Milk. Opening it up, I breathed in the scents of cocoa, vanilla, sugar, marzipan. I shouldn't be so easily appeased by the sight of glinting milks—but I was.

Whenever Adam felt he was in the wrong, he would buy me a box of chocolates rather than actually saying sorry. And sometimes he'd be too easy on himself in thinking that sorted everything, that we didn't need to discuss the issue, he'd made the effort and that was the full stop on it.

"Adam?" I called out.

No reply. Lyra came padding into the kitchen and I picked her up, kissing her, suddenly irrationally worried. What if Sophia had called? What if she had told Adam about the switch and he was dumping me?

I found him in the living-room, crashed out asleep on the sofa after work. TV images danced across his softening jawline. I saw him afresh, as Sophia might: tall, muscly, looking tired with bags under his eyes, but such a cute face. When I had texted her, I'd felt as though I didn't need to worry anymore, but I'd just been side-stepping the current problems, creating a wild distraction, because facing them felt so hard.

I'd told Sophia that Adam and I had been together for seven years, but I hadn't told her about our six-month break in the middle, back in 2018. I'd returned to Shrewsbury to live with my parents. It had felt like a regression, being back in my childhood room in a too-small bed, animal posters on the walls, old board-games like Snakes & Ladders and Careers in boxes held together with Sellotape. Mum, who'd been so proud of me escaping the life she had, with a good job in the capital and a fancy middle-class boyfriend, had urged me to patch things up. As far as I was concerned, Adam had betrayed me and I wasn't about to forgive him any time soon. In rebellion, I'd gone out and partied and rejoined Tinder. But a brief flurry of one-night stands with younger men had been disappointing; they were endearing but sex always seemed to revolve around their pleasure, not mine. A few months on I'd felt lost and lacking an anchor and Mum's words had worn me down. When Adam had come calling, begging me—*let's try again*—I'd caved in. And it had felt good, being back together: comfortable, secure.

I didn't want us to break up again. I didn't want to end up slithering all the way down the snake to square one, back at my parents', starting over, at the age of thirty-seven. But how long was this bad patch going to go on for? What if it wasn't just a patch? Hilary was in her seventies; she was surely only going to get worse; what if this was going to be our life for the next decade or longer?

I sat down on the sofa, gazing around the room, at the possessions we had accumulated over the past seven years, and sadness slowly swept over me.

14.

NOW: ELENA

Is Adam asleep yet?

After several nights of insomnia, my body, with perfectly timed irony, has suddenly decided to pay back my sleep debt. I blink hard, force my eyes open.

And then I hear it: Adam's tell-tale snore.

It's time.

I slip out of bed, tiptoeing across the carpet, using the edge of the mattress as a guide, feeling for the wall and the door handle. I open it, then remember: *the mobile*. The little blue wink of his iPhone by his side of the bed; I unplug it from the charger.

Outside, on the landing, it's easier to see: a murk of shadows and streetlamp seeps through the window. In the bathroom, I remove the rucksack and pull out a pair of silky white knickers and a wine-colored nightie. I put them on, gazing in anxiety at my reflection, imagining how the nightdress would look on Sophia, how her curves would complement it. I pull on jeans and a jumper, and I get an odd feeling of déjà vu, of that sense you get when you're going on holiday and you wake and dress at a weird time for a flight.

I pull out my little notebook from the rucksack and consult the list once more:

Lightbulb
Perfume
Mobile
Rucksack
Alarm
Back door

The perfume—of course! I put it in one of the side-pockets of the rucksack; now I spray it on, breathing in that gorgeous smell of rose and jasmine. "I get it from Penhaligon's—I just adore their perfumes," Sophia once confided in me.

It's silly, putting on makeup when he's never going to see my face, and yet I find myself doing it, for my confidence: applying eyeliner, a little eyeshadow.

Finally, I take out a crucifix, identical to the one Sophia usually wears, and do up the chain so that it hangs at my throat.

Half an hour to go.

15.

THEN: ELENA

I know this is all really . . . *personal*," Sophia said. "But are you on the pill? The coil? Or . . . ?"

She was blushing but I could tell she was also enjoying herself. Knowing we needed to concentrate, we were both sipping on mint lemonades, sitting on the terrace in her back garden. Finn was out at work. There was the faint drone of her help, Séverine, hoovering upstairs in the background. We were giggly, edgy, self-conscious.

"We use condoms," I said in a low voice.

"Oh, right." Sophia looked surprised. "I was actually worried that . . . you might be trying for a baby."

I wondered why, but figured I was at that age, late thirties, where everyone reminds you it's your last chance to go for it.

"On the contrary—we've decided not to have them for the time being," I declared.

To my surprise, Sophia looked almost shocked. While Adam's mother was furious about the lack of any impending grandchild (we hadn't even told her of our decision), most of my friends hadn't blinked an eyelid about it.

"Right—okay." Sophia wrote down *Condoms* in her elegant, flowing script, inside the pretty Matthew Williamson notebook. Knowing how much I liked lists, she'd bought one for each of us. They had peacocks sparkling on the front.

"So will Adam have a supply of condoms?" she asked.

"He keeps them in the cabinet by his side of the bed, the top drawer," I said. "I'll definitely make sure it's stocked up for next week."

Next week. Only seven days to go until the assigned night.

May 5.

A Thursday.

Gulp.

How surreal this all was. I still couldn't quite believe we were really going to do the switch. And I was wary. I wasn't sure if this was all just a dress rehearsal for a performance that would never take place.

Sophia had changed her mind slowly. We'd been for drinks, a lunch, a movie trip, when suddenly, in the middle of the film, Benedict Cumberbatch earnest on the screen, she'd said: "You're right, we should do this." And I felt exhilarated but odd, as though the whole plan had been *my* proposal, my idea.

I had visited her house; she had visited mine. We had given each other perfume samples, bought each other's shampoos. My Head and Shoulders versus her Philip B Peppermint and Avocado. We practiced climbing each other's staircases and recording where the steps were creaky. Sophia had had a blackout blind installed. We'd set a date—April 28— but Adam had fallen ill three days before that, so we burned that plan.

Now we were trying again. We were at Sophia's house, plotting and planning.

"And you and Finn?" I asked, suddenly fretful. "Are you on the pill?"

I was convinced she must be, which made me worry I might have to go back on it. It didn't seem to agree with me; I couldn't handle the side effects.

"No, I'm not," said Sophia, "but there's no need to worry about that.

It's difficult for Finn to have children, so . . ." She stared down at her notebook.

"I'm really sorry," I said quickly. Finn looked so healthy, so utterly *vital*, that the revelation shocked me.

I saw the pain knotted into her forehead. *Gosh,* I thought, *they really have had problems as a couple*—was this a good idea? We were all so fragile: what if we shattered?

"It's fine," said Sophia, gathering herself together. "Sometimes I think that I'd quite like to adopt at some point . . ."

"You wouldn't consider IVF?" I suggested tentatively.

She grimaced. "No, I really don't like the idea of that. I guess it's being brought up Catholic . . . the idea of a baby made that way, it's just not for me."

I raised my eyebrows, though it didn't entirely come as a surprise. I had noted the crucifix she wore, the Catholic iconography that decorated their home: a wooden cross on her bedroom wall, a picture of the Virgin Mary in her studio. In some ways, I found it quite reassuring: though Sophia liked pushing boundaries, she must have a moral compass somewhere inside her.

"What about you?" she asked. "Would you ever adopt?"

I sensed she might be angling again. Maybe to her we seemed foolish, selfish, when we had a gift that she lacked. In truth, I had accidentally got pregnant a year into our relationship and miscarried a few weeks later. We were both sad and guilty and relieved; Adam said that he hadn't felt ready to be a parent, that we should go traveling, embrace adventure together. I'd looked online each night, jotting down places to go, dreaming of seas and mountains, different languages and customs. But later that year, he had got a promotion, the travel plans had been put on hold; they'd been on hold ever since and somehow the years had slipped by. From time to time, we discussed the baby issue and came to the "not yet, not ready" conclusion.

"I think we're happy as we are," I said quietly. "We might rethink in a few years' time."

"So things are better between you?" Sophia inquired. "I'm just asking because—well, if things are pretty bad at the moment—will he find it surprising that you want to make love?"

Make love? I wondered. Surely this is all about sex? The ultimate one-night stand.

I told her that despite everything, Adam had tried to initiate sex yesterday, but I hadn't responded, not with this knot in my heart. I'd told him to go wank. "Adam's always up for sex," I concluded, and we both laughed.

"How did you first meet?" Sophia's eyes became dreamy, as though she wanted to hear a romantic fairy-tale.

It surprised me, given that she normally seemed so cynical about relationships. I felt dull, telling her that it was just a Tinder thing.

Then I recalled: "The funny thing was, I'd knocked three years off my age. It was a bit awkward, having to tell Adam I was an older woman."

"Oh, by all of three years! So now you're thirty-seven, he's thirty-four?"

"Yes, he used to joke that I was his Mrs. Robinson." I knew I ought to tell Sophia about the way he called me "wench" in bed too. She might be shocked if he came out with that in the middle. But I just felt too embarrassed.

"When was the moment that you realized he was special?"

"There was no lightning flash," I said. "It was gradual, slow. We went on holiday to Nice—it was so lovely, swimming in the sea together every day. The trip seemed to put a frame around us, make us whole. That's why we love going back each year . . . except we won't make it this year with his mum being ill," I added glumly. "What about you and Finn, how did you meet?"

"I lived in France in my early twenties," she said. "In a bar in Ville-franche, I met this guy who seemed perfect—young, gorgeous, rich. I thought I'd met the man of my dreams."

I recalled her and Finn speaking in French at the first dinner party they came to at our house. Now their use of the language made sense.

"I moved in with him because I was young and stupid and I didn't see the signs." She lowered her eyes, fiddled with her straw. "Day after day, he was abusive to me . . . He broke me down. I couldn't escape. I thought I would never get away. It was Finn who saved me." She gazed up at me, her eyes raw, and I exclaimed, "I'm so sorry."

Another click of understanding: so this explained why she could be so hostile to men, like that guy who tried to chat us up in Hemingway's. But now I was confused: if Finn was her savior, why would she want to cheat on him?

"I looked up to Finn so much," she said. "He was like my father figure, my hero. We moved back to the UK and I healed. But—you know what it's like when you turn thirty. You're a mature adult. Finn is used to being in control, making all the decisions, but I'm not some broken kid anymore. I'm a grown woman now, and it drives him mad."

"I see," I replied uneasily. Every time she said his name, I felt a guilty tingle of excitement ripple over my skin.

"Let's get back to the list," Sophia said.

"I've thought of something . . ." I swallowed, reddening.

"Go on." Sophia nudged me.

"Should I know anything about the position you and Finn normally . . . um . . . adopt?"

"Good question," said Sophia, nodding, twirling her pen. "He likes it from behind. And Adam? Don't tell me—missionary?"

"Oh, God, are we that predictable?" I sighed.

"Not you, my darling—but Adam, a little." She smiled and wrote it on her pad. And my heart fluttered again: *just a week to go, a week to go . . .*

We were silent for a moment. Séverine appeared, hovering by the French windows, said she'd finished. Sophia went to get an envelope of cash for her. It made me feel awkward; reminded me of the cleaning work my mum used to do.

As Sophia returned, I thought of a crucial topic we ought to be conferring on. I was so embarrassed I started laughing.

"What?" she asked, bemused and amused.

"I've just thought that . . . sorry . . . but . . . our partners will be used to . . ."

"To . . . ?"

"Our . . . you know?"

"Breasts?" Sophia frowned. "I think we're roughly the same size."

"No—the other place—down there. I mean, whether we're bushy or shorn." I was laughing like a schoolgirl now but it was infectious; Sophia caught it too. A relief after our confessions. The more we tried to sober up, the more we set each other off every time our eyes met.

"I'm . . . quite shorn," Sophia said finally, wiping her eyes.

"I'm not," I said. "And I'm very attached to my bushy bush, so I'm afraid you're going to have to grow yours."

Sophia's eyes widened. Then she realized I was joking and we collapsed into laughter again.

We jumped at a sudden appearance, a figure at the French windows.

"Hi, ladies." It was Finn. He wasn't supposed to be back from work until six.

I sobered up immediately while Sophia only laughed even harder. She shut her notebook, went up and kissed him on the cheek.

"What's so amusing?" Finn smiled, looking over at me, and I flushed scarlet.

"Nothing," said Sophia airily. "Just a private joke."

"I need the bathroom." I closed my notebook, fretful at leaving it behind. What if Finn happened to flick through it? Being in his presence was unnerving. It made our abstract plotting seem real, too real.

Upstairs, I used the toilet. The room was tiled with exquisite blue mosaics. There was quilted toilet paper and an old-fashioned chain you had to pull. It was so posh it felt wrong even to use it. It was always easier to come to Sophia's for a plotting session; at mine, Lyra had to be shut away in the dining-room and she'd rip at the carpet scratching to be let out. I made a mental note to shut her away for the switch, a detail I must add to the notebook.

I preferred being at Sophia's, enjoying the grandeur and beauty of her house, though its interior was darker and more brooding than I had expected, with antique furniture and oils on the walls. There were framed photos of Sophia and Finn dotted everywhere, holding hands, nuzzling, looking sickeningly gorgeous in each one.

On the landing, I hesitated. I knew exactly which door led to their bedroom. We'd rehearsed that a few times. I tiptoed toward it again, imagining the steps I'd take on the night.

Adam had once teased me for being a "sticky beak." Yes, I was a bit nosy, I had to admit. Other people's lives fascinated me.

The door was ajar. Inside the room smelled of air freshener, products from the recent clean. There was a newly installed blackout blind at the window. On Sophia's dresser was a pile of books. I recalled how she'd confided in me that she concealed her diary in a Georges Simenon dust jacket.

I'd been updating my laptop diary too, especially now that life was so interesting. A tingle of temptation came over me. I was itching to see what she had written. How strong was her attraction to Adam; how much did it motivate her? When I tried to pin her down, she was elusive.

"Hey."

Finn was in the doorway, right behind me.

"Sorry," I said, gazing at him in embarrassment. He looked so good in his suit; his tan against the white of his shirt, the black of the cloth matching his hair; the solidity of his body beneath it. "I just wanted to go to the bathroom."

"And you got lost?" he said sarcastically.

"Sorry." I bit my lip, waiting for him to move so that I could get past him.

He remained standing, drawing out the torture.

"So, what were you doing—casing the joint?" he asked tersely.

"Of course not!" I cried, and then I saw his eyes were crinkled with laughter.

He rubbed my arm. "Who hasn't wanted to nose about in a friend's house?" he asked good-naturedly.

Finally, he stepped to one side, but I found myself frozen. He frowned, his gaze boring into mine. I felt as though he could read my mind, see into my fantasies, unaware that they were about to become real. Blushing, I hurried past him and into the hall.

Three days before the day, May 5, I was in the Vicomte Café, reading through the notes I'd scribbled about Finn:

He wears pajamas at night. Silk, navy, patterned.
He tends to dominate in bed.
He is romantic.
He can be a restless sleeper. Sometimes he goes downstairs to
make himself a drink in the early hours so we need to be
careful.

And suddenly I panicked. I could see how it was going to play out: Finn would find me in his bed and immediately feel revulsion for me, an inadequate substitute for his goddess of a wife. The men in *Switch Bitch* have such self-assurance with their big male egos; not a shred of doubt. I wasn't sexy enough for Finn, no matter how "flat" things were between him and his wife. I called up Sophia: "I just don't know if I can go through with it," I said.

Her voice was firm, with a touch of impatience: "If you believe it's going to go wrong, it *will* go wrong. Confidence is vital. You know, when I was first trying to make it as an artist, I used to lie and blag all the time, and by making myself sound like a success, I became a success. You fake it to make it. If you get nervous, our partners will sniff it out like dogs."

She was always using animal imagery to describe men. But what if she was underestimating them, reducing them to clichés driven by their cocks?

"But we still don't have an emergency plan for a worst-case scenario," I said. "For one of them realizing. I mean, I've been thinking about it, and we should say we have . . . er . . . sleepwalking issues . . ."

"That will sound ridiculous. There's no worst-case scenario."

"But it's like we're going to jump out of the plane without a parachute."

"Let's enjoy the fall."

16.

NOW: ELENA

I tiptoe down the stairs, carrying Adam's mobile.

I leave it on the downstairs hall table so that he can't reach out for it in the dark.

I take my coat and pull it on over my jeans.

I go into the kitchen, not turning on the light.

The clock says ten to midnight.

I check the alarm. I lied to Adam earlier when I said that I'd set it up. It covers the downstairs rooms. I must make sure I remember to put it on when I come back from Sophia's. It's one of those crucial touches that will help to convince should anything go wrong: how could anyone have crept in and pretended to be me if the alarm's been on all night?

I feel a sudden presence by my ankles and I jump. I pick Lyra up, smiling, burying my kisses in her fur. Then I shut her into the living-room, settling her into the comfy armchair she normally favors, hoping she sleeps rather than scratching wildly at the door.

I check my mobile once more, rereading her message:

PHEW! We're still ON!

I make myself a cup of coffee. Normally I can't handle the caffeine but I tell myself I need it; then, as twitchy paranoia sets in, I regret it and remember why I always opt for tea.

I keep waiting for a new WhatsApp, a cancellation, but nothing comes in and now it's two minutes to midnight and I have to go.

17.

NOW: ELENA

The streets outside are still. Luminous pools from the streetlamps on the pavement. There is the distant sound of a few passing cars; then silence.

I walk down Church Road until I come to the roundabout at the center of Wimbledon Village. The empty shops and restaurants are a little eerie. I pass the Ivy Café, where Sophia first proposed the idea; cross the road past the Dog and Fox.

I walk up past Carluccio's and the Giggling Squid, past the indie bookshop, up to the Common, where horse chestnuts look majestic against the night sky. The ducks and swans are quiet, sleeping around the rim of Rushmere Pond.

It's here that I see Sophia.

She's a little late, just emerging from Murray Road. She too is dressed in jeans, as agreed, so that we look normal, don't stand out. But I know that, underneath, she's wearing the white cotton nightie Adam bought me as a birthday present last year.

She smiles at me—a wobbly, nervous, thrilled smile. Her face is dappled with leaf-shadow. "See you in an hour," she whispers.

For a moment I picture her with Adam and then push the thought away. I knew that the only way I could do this was to forget about that element of the story, and focus only on my own.

I walk down Murray Road, past the huge houses. At number 186 I enter Sophia's front garden, walk up the path between the perfect flower-beds and go through the side-gate, taking care to close it after me quietly. I just hope there are no nosy neighbors watching who might mistake me for a burglar.

When my hand curls around the back-door handle, for a few seconds I'm convinced that I will find it locked, that Sophia is already heading home to say she changed her mind.

As I turn it, panic flutters. This is not a joke. This is really happening.

In the kitchen I close the door very quietly behind me. It's spotless, all shiny surfaces, knives on the wall in an arpeggio of sharpness. The clock's tick seems thunderous; a drip from the tap makes me jump. I silently release a huge breath.

I remove my coat and jumper, and fold them neatly, followed by my trainers and jeans. I put them on a kitchen chair, push it tight against the table so my clothes are hidden. Now I'm wearing only a floaty wine-colored nightie.

Five-past midnight says the clock. I have fifty-five minutes left.

I'm about to enter the hall when I remember—*socks*. Cursing myself for being so stupid—I can't afford to make a single mistake—I pull them off and add them to the pile. The hall carpet is soft beneath my bare feet. I face the stairs.

I can still back out now. I picture myself chickening out, heading home, standing outside in the cold, forced to hear the faint cries of Adam and Sophia having sex.

I put my foot on the first step.

How dry my throat is; I wish I'd got a glass of water in the kitchen.

Two steps, three steps—

Skip the creaky fourth.

I'm hurrying now—five, six, seven . . .

Oh, God, I nearly forgot that the eighth is creaky too. It lets out a faint squeak as I draw back, pausing, waiting, then carry on up steps nine, ten, eleven, twelve, thirteen.

The landing is faintly lit by the glow of a streetlamp, seeping through the bathroom and onto the carpet. Four doors; the one to the far left is the bedroom. It's slightly ajar. I creep in, closing it behind me. Pitch-blackness. I can't hear his breathing. I reach out, feel the hard edge of a cabinet, the softness of a duvet, and slip into bed on the right side, just as Sophia instructed.

18.

NOW: ELENA

I lie frozen, convinced I've got the wrong room.

There's no warmth, no human body beside me—

The noise of a flush, from across the landing. He got up and went to the loo just as I was creeping into the house.

What if he turns on the hallway light and floods the room?

In a panic, I pull up the duvet right over my head, heartbeat frantic. I hear running water, splash of hands, footsteps on the hallway carpet, the door opening, closing. A rush of cold air as he lifts the duvet. Then the solid presence of his body next to me. A long, deep out-breath, tingling warm on my skin. The darkness is reassuringly thick; the blackout blind shuts out all light.

"Sophia?" he says.

I lie stiff, hardly daring to breathe.

"Sophia?" he whispers. "I'm sorry about earlier."

I'm frozen. I'm just going to lie here, I decide, until he goes to sleep, and then slip out. I can't do this, it's too terrifying.

"Sophia?"

Oh, God, he's not going to relent. I reach out, my fingers banging his nose. Fuck. I trail my fingertips against his cheek, as though in apology.

He grabs my hand, lacing his fingers into mine. Heat dances through my hand, up my arm, finds my bloodstream. I hear myself let out a faint gasp.

The warmth of his breath on my face, the prologue to a kiss. My lips are rigid against his. My shocked body is a statue.

"So you're not really in the mood?" he whispers, but his voice is playful, as though this is a challenge rather than a turnoff.

He smooths a finger over my lips, then pushes it between them. Spontaneously, I bite. He draws in a breath.

His fingers trickle over my collarbone, dance against the crucifix, circle past my breasts, edge down, very slowly, my stomach flinching with each tickle, down a little more, reaching my thighs, shifting as though he might—but then they move again, circling my hips, smoothing my thighs, parting them, hovering. I hear a noise emerge from my lips, entreating him. Faint laughter, triumphant; and his lips press down hard on mine. I return the kiss, fiercely. Sophia's instructions are jumbling in my mind. Wasn't I supposed to be reaching up, furrowing my fingers through his hair? But when I reach out, he puts my hand back down with a tut and a warning tone: "Sophia."

I'm jolted for a moment, remembering that this intimacy is theater.

His palms are back on my thighs, his strokes leisurely. Slowly, he tugs down my knickers. His little finger splays out, catches my wetness and I let out a cry. He returns to his teasing. I can hear him smiling in the darkness.

I want to say his name. I want to beg him to stroke me properly. But my voice will betray me and I hold the words thick in my mouth.

Finally he breaks, stroking me, kissing me hard, and a burning rushes up inside me. I'm used to my intellect trying to stoke up my desire, but tonight I feel as though my reason has been drowned in lust; I can't think anymore, only ache and yearn and pulse for him. He pushes a finger inside me and I'm gasping now, helpless, dizzy, and just as I'm on the brink, he pauses. I gaze up, wishing I could see his eyes. "Finn," I whisper.

He moves on top of me, parting my legs, and I open up to him. There is none of the usual initial pain that I experience with Adam, that takes a few minutes to get past, and my desire recedes in consciousness of my betrayal, but then Finn's mouth is passionate on mine, my neck, my cheeks, and he rocks in a frenzy, his control lost, and the heat builds, builds, and breaks. Not long after, he breaks too, head collapsing onto the pillow next to me.

"Sophia," he sighs, withdrawing from me.

In the aftermath of climax, reason is harsh and cold. I think of Adam, my dear Adam. I'll never be able to undo this; there'll always be this crack in our history; a secret to carry. What possessed me? Revenge?

My body replies, raw, still tingling with sensations I've never experienced before. This is all too much.

I need to get out of here.

My fingers fumble, seeking out my nightie, but his hand curls around my wrist, cuffing it.

He pulls me over into a tight hug. I want to fight him off; but I want to hold him tight too. I surrender and sink against him, wondering at how well our bodies fit together so that even a simple hug feels so perfect, my cheek against his chest, his chin on my head, his arms strong and warm and secure. I love the way he's stroking my hair. His fingers trail down my spine, stubbing the bottom notch, and I shiver.

No, I want to say. But his lips are already moving down, seeking mine, his fingers tipping up my chin.

He pushes my head down, and I take him in my mouth. I suffer none of the revulsion that I do with Adam, that I have to stifle and steel myself past, only a hunger to please him in the way he has sated me.

His sounds of joy spur me on and then he pulls me up, turns me onto my front, strokes my spine, thighs, building another climax of teasing, this climax still shuddering with echoes of the last. Then he enters me from behind. His kisses on my neck have teeth, his cries ragged in my ear.

We lie there, breaths slowing back down.

"What time is it?" I whisper, having lost all sense of it. What if Sophia is already out there, waiting, shivering, furious?

Finn says, "Time to sleep, my darling," and pulls me in tight.

A few minutes later, he's out, snoring, and I slip out from the cage of his arms.

I'm panicked now. I can feel a fabric bunched up under my ankles—my knickers. I slip them back on. But I can't find the nightie and my fingers curl around something, only to realize they're his pajama bottoms.

I can't waste any more time. I slip out, hurrying naked down the stairs, flying past the creaky dangers, pulling on my jeans and top and shoes. When I open the back door, I find Sophia outside, hissing, *"You're late."*

"Sorry," I whisper.

I search her face for clues about the encounter but she merely says, "Goodbye," goes in and locks the door. I go to wave at her, but after all we've done, it feels flippant, ridiculous, and she disappears, leaving the kitchen in darkness. I picture her heading up the stairs, into the warmth of his bed, and my envy hurts.

Back in my house, I let Lyra out and creep upstairs. I nearly enter the bedroom in my jeans, then stop and undress, remove the crucifix and ball up my clothes, tiptoeing in, shoving them into the washing basket, slipping into the bed still warm from her body.

19.

NOW: ELENA

I wake up. My mobile says it's only five-thirty. I think I can smell her scent on my pillow, and jealousy surges inside me—before I remember that I am wearing her perfume.

Next to me, Adam is sleeping deeply.

My body is still on heat, swollen with it. Mediocre sex would have been easier than this: sex scored deep in my psyche, sex I will never forget.

I feel the horror of disloyal longing—the ache to be back in Finn's bed, to wake up beside him, to examine the beauty of his sleeping face, and as the dawn rises, to raise the blinds, feel the sun pour over us, make love once more. I'd skive off work and pretend I was sick; he'd do the same. We'd spend all day in bed and he'd call me by my name . . .

I roll over and find relief in slipping back into the blackout of sleep.

20.

NOW: ELENA

When I wake again, Adam is staring down at me, dressed in his work suit. I let out a gasp.

Does he know does he know does he know—

He's smiling. There is a sparkle in his eyes. Affection in his face.

"Nightmare?" He touches my cheek.

I can't help flinching, and, seeing his surprise, I improvise: "Yes—it was awful!"

We used to share our dreams in detail and I am about to conjure an old one, when Adam's eyes widen.

"God, look at your neck!"

"What?!"

"I must've . . . last night." He laughs, leaning down to kiss me, nuzzling his nose against mine. "Didn't mean to. Your boyfriend is a vampire."

I'm desperate to jump up and run to the mirror, but I lie and wait for him to leave. He's humming; how disconcerting. Sophia obviously made him happy.

But he hasn't guessed what happened. He wouldn't be able to put on an act—Adam is too straight. He thinks we've made love. He thinks we've shared makeup sex.

In the mirror, I examine the round plum-colored bruises on my body. I remember Finn's teeth breaking my skin and shiver.

I can't wear a rollneck in this hot weather. How long will they take to fade?

My body looks wired. My lips are scarlet; my cheeks flushed; there's a glitter in my eyes. But inside I'm hazy, hungover with tiredness. I want nothing more than to sink back into bed. And I'm scared of seeing Sophia in the café, fearing I look too raw, that she'll guess how good it was—and then what?

I find myself taking the lid off the washing basket, pulling out my jeans from last night. I bury my face in them, catch a whiff of his scent, my new favorite drug.

After showering, I put on chinos and a white Victorian blouse with a high collar. I find a floral floaty scarf in my drawer too, slightly musty from not having been worn for months.

Adam calls up that he's bought croissants for us, his voice jubilant. It's quite a contrast to the last few weeks, where we've often shared breakfasts in hostile silence, him listening to a film podcast, me scrolling through BBC articles.

There are a few messages on my phone. One is from an unknown number: **Hi Elena, I was wondering if we could meet up for a quick chat about some possible proof-reading for my company. I hear you come highly recommended. Thank you, Finn.** *What the hell?*

Downstairs, I take a bite of croissant, and the almond sweetness soothes me. Adam puts his plate in the sink, kisses my head, and hurries off upstairs.

I reread the text message, interpreting it a dozen different ways. He knows, he doesn't, he wants me, he wants me not—

"Have you seen my watch?" Adam is back in the kitchen again. "I can't find it anywhere."

"In the bathroom?" I say. It's not like him to lose anything.

"No, I looked there—but can you look too, just in case I missed it?"

I feel far too tired for all this, but I check the bathroom shelf, the cabinet, under the rug. Then we hunt through the bedroom, drawing back the sheet in case it got tangled up. It's precious to Adam who inherited it from his father. But—nothing.

"It will turn up," I promise him. "I'll have another look today while you're at work."

"Thank you, I should be home by seven tonight." He hugs me. "And Mum's carer has definitely turned up today." He gives me a quick, hopeful smile. "By the way, you forgot to set the alarm last night."

"Oh, shit, I'm sorry."

"No worries." He gives me a kiss goodbye.

In the Vicomte Café, I stare at a single line on my laptop screen for five minutes. I hail Antonia and order a latte, adding, "Just one shot, please." Coffee is normally off my menu but not today.

The buzz is recuperative, though soon I'm regretting it, feeling jittery, eyes flitting between the door, the clock, wondering why Sophia hasn't turned up. I check my messages again. What if she sent the one from Finn herself? What if it's a test? But that makes no sense: all this was *her* idea . . .

Maybe she's waiting for me to message her. Endlessly checking her mobile and wondering what went on.

I decide to reply to Finn: **I'd be happy to work on proof-reading for your firm. My rates are on my website. Could meet for coffee later today, or else on Thursday.**

His reply comes back right away: **Today would work actually—5 p.m.?**

Why so keen? Surely he's a busy man? I remind myself that this is my career. I need to control my paranoia; I can't risk being unprofessional.

Can we meet near your offices? I text back. The last thing I want is us chatting here and Sophia walking in.

Caffè Concerto on Piccadilly?

Yes, I text back. **See you there at 5.**
He knows he knows he knows.

21.

NOW: ELENA

"Hi, Elena."

As he leans in, kissing my cheek, a trembling takes hold of me. My body is still wild for him, imprinted with his kisses and caresses. My "hello" is too loud, too exuberant, before he ushers me into the café.

We sit down. Classical music is soft in the background; it's a quiet, expensive place. Slowly, I raise my eyes to meet Finn's.

"Are you okay?" he asks. I can't detect any teasing in his tone. "You seem upset."

"Sorry." I sit up, getting a grip of myself. "I'm just a bit tired—I didn't sleep much last night."

"Is your insomnia back?"

My eyes flit over his face, seeking a tell-tale twitch, but there's no hint of double entendre, of flirtation.

"No—yes—yes, actually," I reply. "Just when I thought I'd got it under control. And I went and had a coffee this morning, which was probably a bad idea."

He smiles for the first time that day. The effect is dramatic, his naturally stern expression opening into softness and radiance, and I catch my breath. Suddenly I'm afflicted by a crazy urge to lean over, press my lips to his and kiss him, here and now, and then he'd know who was with him last night; it would be like that moment in *Cinderella* where the prince slips her foot into her shoe, the revelation of a perfect fit.

I'm relieved when the waiter approaches. Finn orders coffee and I ask for a tea.

"More caffeine!" he says and I smile.

"So, what can I help you with?" I ask formally, regretting the necessity of adopting my business mode.

"I was wondering if I could use your proof-reading skills—the company website needs a going over, not to mention all our recent publicity materials."

I feel relieved, a little stupid. So he really does want to employ me.

He takes a sip of his espresso. I stare into his eyes, swallowing. The punch of it: what was amazing sex for me was just a normal night for him. My life has been irrevocably shaken but his hasn't changed by a fraction.

"Maybe you're busy," he interjects, confused by my silence. "I'm sure you've got many clients."

"No—no," I say, staring into my tea. "I'd be very happy to work with you." I push aside the fact that I'm cutting back my workload now, with all the time I've spent on Adam's mother. "My rate's thirty pounds an hour."

"I'll double that."

I look up at him sharply.

"You're undercharging," he says generously. "And I hear you're excellent."

"From Sophia?"

"Oh, no," he smiles. "I think my wife might be a bit biased on that front—she thinks the world of you. No, I'm friends with James Pulford from Everard International and he said you were meticulous. And the fact is, I'm a perfectionist. I'm sure Sophia has complained about it to you—it drives her mad in many ways. I can't bear sloppiness. I only want to work with the best, and the last company I worked with let me down."

"I will do my very best for you."

"That I know. It's great to be working with you."

He raises his espresso cup and I chink my teacup against it. Then he hails the waitress.

"Would you like to order something sweet—to celebrate?" he asks. "I remember you have a sweet tooth."

I flush, touched by his attention to detail.

"I'd love to," I say, and feel pleasure emanating from him as he watches me scouring the menu, weighing up cake hedonism, and finally settle on the strawberry gâteau.

"So, how are you enjoying your life in Wimbledon?" I ask, forcing myself not to look at his hands.

"It's very different from waking up and walking along the cliffs in Cornwall."

Oh, yes, Cornwall; I remember Sophia mentioning that Finn had that awful stalker there—Meghan. I wonder whether to be bold and bring that up, but he asks: "And you—how are you both enjoying Wimbledon? How long have you lived there?"

"Oh, about five months." I pause, wondering whether to admit to the housesit. Then I improvise: "We're renting, actually. We're saving up to buy somewhere."

"It's tough for everyone right now, with prices shooting up all the time. And as for the younger generation . . ."

The gâteau comes and he watches me take a first bite. The sugar rush is a comfort, calms me a little. Smiling, he orders another espresso. Half of me is flattered, the other half panicked. I want to stay here with him forever and I want to run away right now.

"So," he asks casually, "how is your midlife crisis going?"

I smile. This is like the post-coital chat we didn't have last night.

"It's still an issue," I say, "but I'm working on it."

"But why did you move?" he asks again, tentative. "Was the crisis something to do with it?"

"We needed a fresh start," I say.

He hesitates, as though anxious that it would be inappropriate to ask any more questions. The irony: he seems interested in getting to know me, unaware that less than twenty-four hours ago he was bringing me to the most amazing orgasm of my life. I feel bittersweet as I hear him ask for the bill.

I'll pay you double. I enjoy a warm glow of confidence. Whereas Adam has trivialized my career, Finn has given me the boost I should have got from my partner. Indignation hardens and then I remind myself of what I've just done and wonder if my anger is a way of deflecting my guilt. Still, Adam has been unfaithful to me too.

Finn tells me that he has to return to his office, while I head home. The Victoria line is busy but when I change at Vauxhall, I manage to get a seat on the train back to Wimbledon. Exhaustion comes over me. I resolve to skip dinner. I'll leave a note for Adam and curl up under the duvet. Sleep will put everything behind me, purify the day.

Back home, however, Adam greets me with a big grin on his face. He's wearing his apron, the one I got him a few Christmases ago with a cartoon mustache on it.

He's made a mess of the kitchen—there are pots and pans everywhere. But I'm touched by the effort he's put in; when I enter the dining-room, I see the table has been laid. He must have left work early.

Adam brings in a plate, setting it down before me with a pantomime flourish: "For madame. The first course. *Bon appétit.*"

I wish I wasn't still stuffed with gâteau. But I grin and eat the toast with pâté and it's lovely.

"How was your day?" he asks.

I fight back a yawn. "I met a client—I've got a new job, a big one. He's going to pay me double." I feel twitchy, half expecting Adam to say I don't have time, I need to be on call for his mother.

But he enthuses: "Brilliant."

I'm taken aback.

"It means I won't have time to drop my work for anything unexpected," I add, in warning.

"Rightly so," Adam agrees. "I spoke to Mum today. I told her that we can't keep relying on you to drop everything and run over to Windsor. I was firm with her. I said she can't fire her current carer without speaking to me first. And she came round."

"Well, that's good news," I say, in relief, though a cynical little voice warns me: *he made that promise before.*

So, after weeks of rows, we're finally moving in the right direction. Was the sex with Sophia really that phenomenal? Oh, the irony: it seems that it was so good that it has dissolved some of the strain in our relationship.

"And I was thinking," he goes on, "that maybe we could rebook Nice?"

"That would be lovely." I think we more urgently need to sort out where the hell we're going to live after this housesit when it runs out at the end of August, a problem we've so far neglected—but I don't want to burst the bubble.

Following a delicious main course that has my stomach groaning, he brings in the dessert: a big trifle from M&S.

"I wish I wasn't so full up," I wail.

"But you've *always* got room for dessert," he teases me and watches me take a mouthful, in much the way Finn did earlier today. I feel slightly sick now but I force it down, making *mmmm* noises.

"Now we're done," Adam jokes, "who's going to spend the next three hours washing up?"

We both laugh.

In the living-room, we cuddle up on the sofa together, Adam's arms curled around me, my back against his chest.

"Did you find your watch, by the way?" I ask him.

"Not yet." He sounds anxious. "Can you help me look again later?"

"Of course." I frown, wondering if Sophia picked it up by accident.

He lifts the scarf I'm wearing and starts kissing the back of my neck.

"Sorry," I say gently. I'm about to add that I'm really knackered after last night, when my stomach turns over and makes a groaning noise as it struggles to digest.

"Sorry," Adam suddenly says. "I gave you all that food and forgot the pill makes you sick, doesn't it?"

"What?" I ask.

"The morning after pill," he says. "After last night—you did take it, didn't you?"

"Um, yes," I reply, glad I'm facing away from him. My heart is thumping hard. *Morning after pill?* So they didn't use protection? But I told Sophia that condoms were a must.

I feel the itch to jump up, message her, demand to know what happened between her and Adam. No wonder she wasn't at the café this morning. She's broken the rules and now she's hiding.

Maybe the condom split. I try to think of a way to word things so that he will reveal what went on, but my mind is too foggy.

"Are you okay?" Adam whispers, kissing my ear.

"Definitely. Just worn out—from last night, from the pill."

He asks softly, "Did you enjoy it?"

I realize it's a rhetorical question. I lift up his hand, his fingers entwined with mine, and kiss his knuckles.

"Before last night . . . I'd sometimes thought . . ." Adam's voice becomes small and hesitant.

"Yes?" I whisper, suddenly full of dread.

"I'd felt recently that you were . . . not really there when we were . . . I thought you were faking it with me."

I tense up, about to gabble a protest, when he says: "Be honest with me, my gorgeous wench." He tries to sound jokey but I can hear the tension in his voice.

I swallow. "Sometimes," I agree softly. "Sorry. Sometimes I haven't always managed to quite—it's harder for women to . . ."

I'm wary of his hurt, his offense, but his arms curl more tightly around me. "I know, I know," he says, "and I didn't want to embarrass you by bringing it up, ruining the mood. But last night—it felt like we got the old magic back, it was like our early days again—didn't you feel that?"

No, would be an honest response. But I can't say that I'm not convinced there's ever been much magic, can I? That would be so cruel. For me, it's never been about the sex, but about friendship, security, supporting each other.

"Yes," I reply finally. "I don't know how it happened—the chemistry just came back, didn't it?"

"It damn well did!" Adam kisses the back of my neck. "It's okay—I know you're too tired. We'll go to bed soon, right? Get an early night."

The happiness sings in his voice. And I'm suddenly conscious of a hazy knowledge becoming sharp, shifting from foreground to forefront: that our relationship hasn't been right for quite some time. I've attributed it all going wrong to his mother, but that was just a challenge we didn't rise to because we were already weak. I'd assumed that faking my orgasms was no big deal, but perhaps we've been stagnating for too long, too many problems left unaddressed. The fact that he had such great sex with Sophia hurts: does that mean the problem lies with me?

I feel overwhelmed with emotions.

Guilt.

Jealousy.

Panic.

Lust.

Confusion.

Suddenly I'm so tired, so lost, that I find myself bursting into tears.

"Hey!" Adam clutches me tight. "Did I upset you? I thought it'd be okay to discuss the orgasm thing now we've—cracked it!" He curls his arms around me so tight I can hardly breathe. "Elena?"

"I'm sorry." I rub my cheeks. "It's not you—it's just been a long day. Sorry. I think it's the pill," I improvise. "It's upset my hormones . . . I need to go to bed."

We get up and he surprises me by suddenly picking me up in his arms and carrying me, like an old-fashioned groom with his bride, which makes me laugh. He puts me down on the bed and I get ready quickly, hungry for blackout, but knowing that tomorrow, when I wake, nothing is going to be any easier.

22.

NOW: ELENA

The next day Sophia reappears. She messages me to ask if I fancy a walk in Cannizaro Park. It turns out to be a hidden treasure in Wimbledon that Adam and I have so far missed: a gorgeous green space with a Japanese garden, a rose garden, and a grand house at the top with a fancy café/restaurant.

We arrange to meet by the entrance on Wimbledon Common. I feel odd as I approach her, butterflies giddy in my stomach. She's wearing sunglasses, her hair tied back, and she looks pale. But when I hug her, she holds me tight, and when I try to pull away, she hangs on.

"We did it!" she whispers in triumph. "We did it, we did it, we did it!"

I pull back, laughing nervously.

"We did get away with it, didn't we?" A faint panic on her face. "Adam didn't guess?"

"Oh, no," I reply quickly. I have a sudden vision of them together, sharing their phenomenal sex.

We buy some takeaway coffees from a van and stroll across the grass toward the woods. All around us are dog walkers, their expensive breeds racing about, barking and sniffing each other's genitals.

"God, I still can't believe they fell for it!" Sophia is exhilarated. "Men are so stupid!"

What is it with Sophia and men? I've admired her for being a feisty feminist, but now I wonder, I worry, if she simply hates them. Because of that abusive relationship she was trapped in?

I bite my lip. "Well, Adam is actually really smart . . ."

"You're right, you're right. What I should have said is: what clever women we are. We pulled off the perfect crime because we took care of every detail."

Perhaps it's better if she jeers. Better that than her getting too attached to Adam.

"So, how did it go with Adam?" I ask tentatively. *What did you do*, I want to ask her, *that was quite so amazing? And why the hell didn't you use protection?*

Rhododendron bushes line the woodland path, their pink and red flowers like brilliant clusters of jewels.

"I made one mistake," she says, lifting her sunglasses. Her eyes are so pretty, close up; lashes as thick as fur. "I'm sorry—I hope you'll forgive me—but we didn't use condoms. I looked in my notebook afterward and realized I'd written down that they were in the top drawer of Adam's bedside cabinet. But in the heat of it all, I simply forgot . . ."

"But surely Adam would've wanted to use them? He would have got them himself?"

"I think we both just got carried away . . ." she says. "And he did reach out—but with the bulb out, it was hard to see."

But the cabinet is right next to the bed, I think. Adam must have reached for that drawer a hundred times over. And he is sensible that way, especially given that we did once have that accident.

"Anyway," she says, her voice becoming louder, more assertive, "I took a morning after pill. Sorry, that's why I was so quiet yesterday, I know I should have messaged you back. I felt really sick and spent the afternoon in bed."

"I'm sorry to hear that," I say quietly.

"It was inevitable that there would be one slip, one detail that went wrong," says Sophia. "But it's fine. It was sorted out."

She passes by a fuchsia bush and the light falling through patterns the colors of the flowers in her hair. I want to ask her about the watch but I can't; there's no way I can word it without making her sound like a thief.

"And how was it with Adam?" I ask again.

"Look." Sophia suddenly reaches for my hand and gives it a squeeze. "I've been thinking. We shouldn't tell each other anything about what happened in bed, not a single detail. Otherwise we'll drive each other mad and get jealous and—this should be our secret."

"Oh. I see . . ." On the way here I'd been fretting about how to relate my experiences with Finn, downgrade them from great to good. At the same time, I'm itching to know if he said anything, if she had to endure what I have, her husband telling her that last night was amazing.

"Our friendship is important to me," she says. "And we didn't do this to make each other jealous or to compete, did we?"

"No—you're right." I smile at her, squeezing her hand back. I'm frustrated, but relieved too.

"Besides, it's already becoming distant . . . Doesn't it already feel dreamlike?"

Sophia breaks off as a dog walker enters the path, her Jack Russell racing ahead.

No, I think, *it feels more real than ever.* And as we walk on in pensive silence, I'm so close to suggesting that we do it again. Since breakfast, I've been musing on casual ways to broach it, to say something like, "Didn't the men in *Switch Bitch* keep on playing the game?"

But then Sophia muses: "Well, it was a one-off, a risk that we can't ever repeat, but it was pretty damn amazing, wasn't it?" That look of euphoria on her face again; meanwhile, my heart crumples. "Now we have to get back to work, to boring old everyday life. Come back to mine for a coffee first, then we can work in the café?"

I manage to nod and smile. Back at Sophia's house, we're sitting at the pine kitchen table when Séverine brings her a cream envelope. I'm surprised when Sophia rips it open; it has Finn's name on the front.

"Oh, my God—it's from Meghan Roskilly! That stalker woman!" She reads aloud: "'Finn, you are like a hymn to me. Like a stained-glass window. Light falls through you and you fill it with color.'"

"She does sound . . . a bit OTT." I laugh uneasily.

Sophia reads on and her expression gradually shades to grim seriousness. She turns the letter over, reads and shudders. I'm about to ask what the rest said, but she jumps up and puts it in the bin: end of subject.

Heading home later that afternoon, a terrible sense of anti-climax comes over me. I've written down every detail of my night with Finn in my diary, and I suffer a craving to read it all through again for what must be the tenth time, but I can't risk it. Soon the words will be so familiar they will lose their power and become gray. They will read like fiction. I just can't bear the thought that I'll never share that experience with him again. Everything that Sophia has said sounds right and logical and fair. I love our friendship and I'd never want to wreck her marriage like mad Meghan is trying to. But my craving for Finn is like that of a desperate addict.

Still, my job today is my proof-reading for him. At least I'll get a chance to see him again soon, even if I can only look but not touch. I tell myself it will get easier over time. I hope . . .

PART TWO

23.

ELENA

So, this is the kitchen. There's an oven, dishwasher, hob, fridge . . ."
Adam and I stare round at the studio flat, trying not to look too
dispirited. The woman showing us around looks a bit put out.

"I've had loads of viewings today," she asserts. "There's actually a lot of
interest."

The flat is in a block in Walthamstow, back where we used to live before Wimbledon Village. It has to be a basement one for Lyra's sake, so
that she can venture outside. I gaze at the window, the light filtered through
an iron staircase, at the truncated view of shoes scurrying past on the
pavement. Then at the double bed, only three feet from the dining-table.
We've grown used to the sprawling comfort of a three-bedroomed house;
it's going to be so hard to shrink back into a small space. We've grown
used to birdsong and a big garden of greenery and a front path with a gate.

We still have over three months in Wimbledon, I try to console myself,
but I'm scared they'll rush by so fast.

"So it's eighteen hundred a month, all included," the woman sums up.

I can see Adam doing calculations in his mind. By nature, I'm a spender,
he's a saver, and I'm grateful to him for reining me in. My parents strug-
gled with money when I was a kid. They both worked full-time but their
joint income was still too low to meet all the bills. There were times when

we had to hug hot-water bottles because the heating was too expensive; times when meals consisted of making a loaf of bread last until the next pay check came through. That's partly why I worked so hard to get my degree: I don't ever want to live like that. Adam's good sense with money makes me feel secure, assured that we'll always be okay. With no rent to pay, we've been able to save a lot for our deposit and still enjoy the odd cinema trip or takeaway. Now, with this move, we'll be back to budgeting with more care.

I glance in at the tiny bathroom, which only has a shower. No more reading in the bath for me.

"Thanks, we'll get back to you," says Adam.

"Thanks very much, it's lovely." I manage a smile.

We leave the block in silence. Last night I called Mum and confided in her about the depressing move. She told me, kindly, to be grown up about it. She tends to take that tone when life gets hard, because of the sacrifices she has made. And she's right, of course: you have to make the best of things, I understand the value of that.

The switch cast a magic glow over everything, for a few weeks. Now life feels like that time after Christmas, when the glitter has gone and the world seems bleak and stark and it's hard to find things to look forward to. And so you make resolutions, desperately trying to improve yourself. I've resolved not to see Finn again. Not to read through that diary entry. It's easy enough to see Sophia without him, and I've finished the proof-reading job.

But now I look at Adam and wonder: is this how life is going to keep playing out? A tiny flat, a freelance business that I'm struggling to make work? Or am I being self-destructive, taking the safety net of our relationship for granted? But what do I want? For a moment I'm at a loss.

"Shall we go get a coffee?" he suggests.

We go into a nearby Costa on the High Street. Unlike the Vicomte Café, it's overcrowded. I pull out a tissue, wiping away crumbs from the table.

Adam sips his coffee before he says, "We don't have to do this, you know."

"What?" I break out of my glum mood.

"Move into that flat."

"But we can't afford Wimbledon Village, can we?"

"I mean—if you don't want to carry on living with me . . ." he says, hurt raw on his face. Sometimes he can become melodramatic in his insecurity.

"Adam!" I reach over and grab his hand, which is tucked under his folded arms; I unfurl his fingers and stroke them. "Of course I do. I'm just going to miss Wimbledon, that's all. I've fallen in love with the place. You know that."

"Fallen in love with Sophia, more like," he mutters.

"She's my closest friend now! That's all."

"Maybe we should look for a bigger flat, get two bedrooms. We've saved a ton on rent."

"But we need to save for our deposit . . . And the flat we just saw, it was pretty nice." I try to sound enthusiastic.

"The trouble is, now Sophia's infected you with her bourgeois inclinations—"

"Bourgeois inclinations?" I echo him, smiling.

"Yes, bourgeois inclinations, you've gone all fancy now." His tone is tragi-comic. "You'll be wanting to hang out with illustrious artist types, not a boring old banking guy like me."

"Nonsense!" I fire back. "I'm just a simple wench who's happy to be with her lord."

Adam laughs and I rub his hand again. He's always needed lots of reassurance, which I think stems from his mother's neglect, a fear that love might be suddenly withdrawn. And he must sense I'm not quite there at the moment, no matter how hard I'm trying, which makes me feel perpetually guilty.

A buzz on his phone. I see it's a text from his mum and repress a wince. It's another sign of her meanness, I ponder, that she has never given Adam any financial assistance despite her wealth. She could easily help with the deposit, but no: she only wants to take, not give.

After we head out of Costa, I spot someone I know across the street.

"Hey, Anil!" I call out, but he's in a hurry and doesn't see me. He's a good friend of mine from uni; Adam and I used regularly to hang out with him and his partner when we lived nearby.

On the Victoria line home, I feel a little cheered. Seeing Anil has reminded me of all those fun nights we had as double couples, getting takeaway together, playing card games, drunkenly dancing in the kitchen. At least socializing with Anil again is something to look forward to.

Adam kisses my cheek and whispers in my ear, "After dinner, what shall we do tonight?" And I blush, smiling seductively, panicking inside.

Home. Even though I'm tired, I offer to cook. Adam looks boyishly pleased; he loves it when I mother him. I kiss his forehead and he sits on a stool, watching me prep.

"I can't wait to get dinner over and done with," he says, coming up behind me and curling his arms around my waist, his erection pressing hard against my back.

"Oh, thanks a lot," I reply playfully, "my cooking's not that bad."

Adam laughs. "You know I love your cooking." He kisses my temple. "But . . . I can't wait for you to do . . . *that thing* . . . that you did . . . before . . . on our magic night."

"*That thing?*" I trail off, my panic rising. I stir the wooden spoon through the risotto, steam rising into my face. "Which is . . . ?"

"Ha-ha," says Adam, sounding hurt.

I twist my head, silencing him with a kiss. "Oh, yes," I murmur, "we'll definitely do that."

Five minutes later, a reprieve: Adam opens up the fridge and suddenly realizes we're out of wine. His aunt doesn't keep any in the house that we can borrow and replace. He tells me he'll go get some from the fancy wine shop in the Village and—after giving me a passionate kiss goodbye—adds, "I'll get some extra condoms on the way!"

As the front door bangs with his departure, I exhale a long breath. *Oh, God.* My hands trembling, I add more stock to the risotto, then turn it down to a simmer. **I know we said we'd keep details quiet,** I message Sophia, **but I really, really need to know what special "thing" you and Adam did.** It's breaking the rules, but this is an emergency. In the living-room, I sit on the sofa, chewing my nails, checking my phone every few seconds for a reply. I slip my hand down into my knickers. I feel completely dry. Adam's going to go mad.

The last time I caressed myself was a few days after the switch: brief and frantic, locked in the bathroom, reliving my night with Finn. Now I touch myself a little, closing my eyes, tipping back my head. I rewind to an early memory of Adam and me making love. We'd just begun to sense that his mother disapproved of me and before it became a rift it added a frisson, as though I was forbidden, dangerous. There was that night where we were in mid-sex and his mother banged on the door, asking if he wanted hot milk for bedtime . . . But to be honest, he was far more excited by the whole scenario than I was: so scratch that. I find myself slipping back to thoughts of Finn. The thick darkness, his lips pressing down on mine, the heat of his body, his teasing fingers. Then, as a slight pain ripples across my abdomen, I frown. I pull out my fingers, taken aback—and do a doubletake.

I run upstairs to the bathroom, checking, confirming. Then I grab some sanitary towels. Three days early. Sometimes luck takes your side.

I head back down to the kitchen. Still no reply from Sophia. When Adam returns, he looks flushed, jaunty, whistling as he uncorks a bottle with "Château" on the label. I'm taken aback by the price on it; it's not like him to splash out.

"I saw Sophia," he says. "I bumped into her in the wine shop."

I jump. The wooden spoon slides into the risotto and I pull it out, drying the handle on a tea towel. I gaze at Adam, his back turned to me, suffering flickers of suspicion. I've been so fretful that Finn might have guessed, I never considered that Adam might be playing with me too. I picture how the night might have unfolded: Adam switching on the light, shocked to see Sophia, then making love, making a pact. Maybe he gave her the watch as a gift, a memento of an amazing night, and made up the story about it going missing as a cover.

"So . . . what do you think?" he asks, sounding impatient.

"What?" I mumble, realizing he's been speaking for some time.

"Dinner?" he asks. "With Sophia and Finn."

"What, tonight?"

"Pay attention, darling! Next week." He rolls his eyes. "I tried to fob her off but she was very insistent." Pause. "I know she's your friend and everything, but—she's a bit artificial, I think. You can't trust her."

I feel relieved then. I can't believe he would feign such disdain, he's so honest in his opinions of others. He tends to be very black and white: he either loves someone or he takes against them.

We sit down to eat. Adam looks deflated when I tell him about my period. After a brief sulk, he gets pissed and starts doing la-di-da impressions of Sophia. Soon I am tipsy and laughing hard and then we're cuddling up on the sofa, warm and cozy, trying out a new detective show.

Still no text from Sophia. The sex issue might have been deferred but it's on the horizon. Sex was never that great during our early days but, back then, I did fancy Adam like mad; he was mysterious to me, and discovering each new layer of his personality was a thrill. As intimacy set in, love and lust seemed like a seesaw. The more tender I felt with him, the harder I found it to open up to him sexually. He could sometimes be a bit rough with me, early on, pretending I was a lusty wench he was taming, but what had felt sexy as strangers seemed vulgar when we became a couple. If we argued, I couldn't open up to him physically; conversely, if everything was good between us, lovemaking could feel mechanical and flat. And energy was a big factor: we were often too tired after work or cinema trips or dinners out. We shifted from sex every night to sex on Sunday mornings. But sometimes even that drifted as we went out for indulgent breakfasts in Wimbledon Village.

And yet: I do love him. It's not a wild passion; it's a warm, steady, familiar feeling, but I'm not a teenager or a foolish romantic. I don't need lightning bolts. My earlier restlessness has passed. I need to count my blessings. Sitting here, on this sofa, warm in his arms, I know I want to be with him, whether in Walthamstow or Wimbledon.

So I ought to make an effort. To turn the switch into something positive instead of destructive. After all, that was the point, wasn't it? To improve our relationships, not fray them.

Later on, when Adam's in the bathroom, I check my phone: finally, a reply from Sophia: **So sorry, but I can't tell you! We made a pact!** I roll my eyes, feeling irked—does she have to be such a stickler? And: **I'm so looking forward to our dinner.**

I'm not sure if I'm looking forward to it. I'm fond of her and she's become a dear friend. But there's something about being around Sophia and Finn that makes me feel as though my life is a snow globe, usually calm but in their presence wildly shaken up.

24.

ELENA

Adam and I stand on the doorstep of Sophia and Finn's house. My mind wanders back to the night I tiptoed across their road in the eerie dark and crept inside. It was only three weeks ago. It feels like months.

The climbing rose above their front porch is still in bloom. Adam lifts the old-fashioned knocker and bangs hard.

I practically had to drag him out tonight, he was so reluctant. I've made an effort with my appearance, putting on my favorite red dress, curling my hair, applying my deepest scarlet lipstick. Fortunately Adam just thinks I'm trying to compete with Sophia.

"So d'you think we're going to get sucked into an orgy later?" he whispers, laughing in my ear.

"*Shhh,*" I hiss back, laughing.

I haven't told him about the switch, of course. But carrying this secret has felt so heavy that something did slip out last night. We were watching a Louis Theroux documentary about swingers in America. Without thinking I said, "Like Sophia." Improvising, I quickly added that she and Finn secretly enjoyed bed-swapping with other couples at parties.

"At the end it'll be car keys in the bowl," he goes on and I dig my fingers into his ribs.

Finn opens the door and we quickly straighten up. He shakes Adam's hand, greets me with a kiss on the cheek.

Immediately I feel color pulsing beneath my skin. I tell myself to get a grip. I have to get used to being in his presence without behaving like a teenager.

It's the first time Adam has been in their house; I follow his enquiring gaze. The hallway is old-fashioned, decorated in green William Morris–style wallpaper, with an antique table and a vintage black telephone with a dial. A shoe rack; I find myself eyeing up a row of Finn's black, shiny shoes.

Suddenly, there is a piercing sound from above us.

"Don't worry," says Finn cheerfully. "It's just the smoke alarm. It usually goes off at least twice when Sophia is cooking." And he winks at me.

"*Darling,*" Sophia calls from the kitchen. An hour ago I saw a photo she'd posted on Instagram of herself wearing a sexy apron, captioned "Domestic goddess."

"I'll get it," Finn calls back.

He grabs a chair, climbs onto it, and pushes the alarm. The horrible noise stops.

In the dining-room, the cherrywood table has been laid with a lace cloth and engraved cutlery that looks heavy and ancient. Adam has brought a Chilean Sauvignon Blanc as a gift, but Finn opts instead for a Château, which he pours into exquisite glasses. When I take a sip, it tastes like silk. I suffer that habitual pinch of anxiety as I gaze at it all: those little flourishes and touches that belong to another class, that will always elude me. Who has the wealth, I wonder—him or Sophia? Adam and I have speculated. It's not as though Finn's business is that big. One of them must have private wealth, an inheritance.

As Sophia enters, carrying a roast chicken, I'm a little surprised—and relieved—to see how stressed she looks as she coos hellos and kisses. She sets down a serving dish. The food looks . . . *burned*?

Sophia and Finn bring it all in: the roast potatoes, the sprouts, the peas, the carrots and parsnips. It seems like far too hot a night to be eating a roast, but I say how nice it looks, trying to ignore the slightly charred smell.

As we sit down to eat, Sophia and I exchange glances, sharing the delicious oddness of the moment, of *we know something you men don't know.* Then we discuss the weather and how lovely it is, with temperatures set to rise at the weekend. More wine is poured; I want to get drunk to cope with Finn's presence, but I'm also scared of letting something slip.

Frowning, Adam saws at a potato. They are the worst of all, patchworked with black, greasy skins. He gives me a raised-eyebrows look but I pretend not to notice.

"Do you like it?" Sophia asks anxiously.

"Not particularly," says Adam, as I say, "Delicious."

Sophia's eyes flit from him to me to him.

"Adam can be rude," I apologize in horror, making eyes at him.

"I'm honest," he banters back at me.

"It's fine." Sophia breaks into a smile.

We all carry on eating, the silence thickening with awkwardness. She turns to Adam. I dread a barbed remark, but to my surprise, she says: "I was on YouTube yesterday. And I saw your film."

He looks taken aback, the potato forgotten. "I've not seen that myself for years!"

I blink. "Adam used to be into film-making before he worked in IT," I explain, rather superfluously, realizing I must already have told Sophia this before.

The film is one I watched a lot when we were getting together. It's a twenty-minute short about rival gangsters who bump into each other on a train; soon the buffet car becomes a war zone. It won several prizes at indie festivals.

"It was so good!" Sophia exclaims.

"You think so?" Adam is blushing red.

"Finn and I enjoyed it so much. Really, given your talent, why did you stop?"

I can see Adam's struggling with himself, trying not to be charmed by her, but he can't resist.

"I wanted to be the next Tarantino, the next Martin McDonagh . . ."

"But why didn't you pursue it?"

"Well, the first film did well, but the second wasn't such a success," Adam confesses.

"It was a bit too experimental," I interject, but nobody seems to hear me. All eyes are on Adam.

"And my third script is just sitting on my laptop, unmade," he says. "Nobody was interested. Anyhow, it was so time-consuming, trying to raise funding all the time—you wouldn't believe how many hundreds of thousands you need just to make a good short. I sold out. I got a good job in the City." He raises his hands sheepishly. "But I don't regret it," he asserts, even though I know he does.

"You ought to go back to it—even as a hobby," Sophia says.

"Well, I'm pretty wiped out by work, and besides, we're saving up now for our house—"

"Now we're going on holiday." I talk over him, giving him a look: he's not meant to disclose that we're housesitting. Adam gives me a look back that asks: *Why do we have to put on an act?*

"Oh, lovely, where are you going?" Sophia asks.

"We still want to go to Nice this year," I interject.

"Nice is glorious," Sophia says. "We're thinking of going to Ville-franche."

The town next to Nice, only more classy and expensive.

At least the conversation has been diverted, though soon it winds back to Adam's film projects. And it's odd, how the pattern repeats: just like that very first dinner we had, Sophia and Adam form a little bubble. Sophia's charm works its magic. He seems to have changed his opinion of her; he's chatting away with enthusiasm. I would be jealous if it weren't for Finn and the chance to speak to him.

I turn and smile at him. His smile is so sexy, but a little bashful around the edges. It always surprises me, those flashes of shyness that I see in him, little cracks in his confident manner. I find them so endearing.

"You did such a fine job with our proof-reading," he says, echoing the glowing email he sent me. "I've recommended you to several others, by the way."

"Thank you so much," I reply, touched.

I notice his eyes sweeping down my arm and I jump at the sight of several cat hairs clinging to my sleeve, despite the lint remover Adam rolled over me before we came.

"How's your cat?" he asks. "I wish we could adopt, but Sophia hates them . . ."

"Oh, you're cat deprived," I smile, thinking of that time I saw him stroking mine. "Lyra always makes me feel better if I need cheering up . . ."

"My father didn't like cats either. I was desperate for a pet when I was a kid, but he said no. In felines, I have been thwarted. I did adopt a stray for a term when I was at uni, though."

"Did you study business?"

"No, I actually did English Lit, at Edinburgh," he replies.

"Oh, wow—I did English too. Any favorite reads?"

"I like the Russians." Finn surprises me again. "Dostoevsky—*Crime and Punishment, The Idiot*."

Interesting: I find them too heavy, too gloomy.

A silence, slightly odd; as though he's finding it hard to answer these questions, as though they're deeply personal rather than light conversation. He starts to caress his glass, which distracts me.

"Have you been to the opera recently?" I ask.

"I'm still waiting for *Lady Macbeth of Mtsensk* to be scheduled. We were listening to that in the car—do you remember? It's one of my favorites."

I'm finding it increasingly hard to look him straight in the eye. My gaze dances to his lips, to his neck, to the sharp lines of his starched collar. I am sliding, back, back into that night with him, remembering the way he tugged my hair gently as I held him in my mouth. His pupils seem dilated, but perhaps it's the wine. His lips on my neck, the delicious pain of his teeth on my skin . . . Is his knee pressing against mine under the table deliberate?

"I haven't seen much opera," I confess. Like the theater, it wasn't something we could afford when I was a child.

"I've often thought about taking a box there with a woman." He lowers his voice. "Closing the curtains, making love as the music soars below . . . The intensity of it."

I swallow, my eyes dropping to the tablecloth, a pattern of lace. This is beyond flirting. Maybe Sophia's made a slip, like I did. Maybe he's suspicious, guessed something, is probing . . .

"Time for dessert!" she announces gaily.

She returns from the kitchen with a plate of pastries. I know they've been bought from the delicatessen on the High Street, though she doesn't correct Adam when he bites into one and says, "Wow, this is good. Nice job, Sophia!"

I'm aware of Finn's eyes on me again as I bite into a creamy chocolate-topped pastry; as at our business meeting, he seems to be extracting pleasure from watching me eat.

"It's so hot in here," he says, going to open the French windows so that the perfume of night-scented flowers enters on the breeze.

He sits back down beside me, too beautiful and terrifying for me to cope with anymore. I get up abruptly, nearly knocking over my chair, saying that I need the bathroom.

"Let's have coffee," I hear Sophia saying as I leave. "And cigars! Finn has these gorgeous ones shipped over from Cuba . . ."

At the bathroom sink I want to splash my face with cold water but it would ruin my makeup. My reflection shows starry eyes, flushed cheeks; I look just like I did the morning after our tryst, so alive. How does he do this to me? In his presence I feel as though I am slowly being unraveled, layer by layer, losing all sense of boundaries and common sense.

I'm more drunk than I realized; I nearly trip on the landing and knock a heavy oil portrait out of place on the wall. I correct it.

There's the bedroom door. The place where it all happened.

Temptation calls.

I slip inside, shutting the door behind me. The blackout blind is up, the sunset streaming in, and the room looks too civilized for me to recapture fully the sensation of that night. I bend down, push my face into Finn's pillow and then it strikes: I'm shocked by the burn of memory. But, as I lift my head, I detect another scent lacing his, polluting it, and I realize it's Sophia's perfume.

I feel nauseous. I want to pull down the blind and lie on the bed and fully relive the experience. But I need to go, this is all too risky.

Just as I'm about to leave, I spot it again. Sophia's diary. Wrapped in the Georges Simenon cover.

25.

ELENA

I grab my chance before my conscience can dissuade me. I pull it from the pile, flick it open, past pages of her spidery black-ink handwriting, to the latest entry. It's dated May 6—the day after the switch.

Then I hesitate. Yes, I need to learn about this secret *thing* she shared with Adam. But I might end up reading about how amazing the sex was, or even a confession of love. If I bite into this apple, I'll never be able to forget what I learn.

I can't resist:

We did it! We got away with it. Everything went according to plan. I crept into the house, followed all the rules—and it went okay. Enjoyable, at times, discovering Adam's fetish, having him at my mercy, a slave to desire. I knew it was just a case of paying attention to detail. Finn was very happy today. Will it be enough? That's the question.

What an odd, underwhelming, elusive entry. *Okay. Enjoyable.* And there are no clues about his fetish: oh, this is so annoying! Still, I light up as I reread: *Finn was very happy today.* So he did enjoy it. *Will it be enough?* What does that mean?

I want to read more entries, find out when she first picked on me for her plan, but I think I hear a creak on the stairs. I flinch and nearly drop the diary. Something flutters out onto the floor. I pick it up.

It's a newspaper clipping, old and delicate; I unfold it with great care. It's in French, so I can't understand much of it. The date is October 21, 2006. I stare at the photo of a beautiful, dark-haired teenage girl. *Une jeune fille est morte*, says the headline. *Morte* means dead, I know that. The *jeune fille* is called Claudine Lambercier.

Anxious now, I quickly slot it back in and ease the diary back into the pile. Is that the right place? I fret. Was it above the Anthony Trollope or below?

I hurry out onto the landing, shutting the door. Maybe I can risk another look later.

There are footsteps on the stairs.

I turn as though leaving the bathroom.

It's Finn, holding a glass of wine, with a slight sway to his approach that suggests he's drunk, perhaps very drunk.

"Elena." He stops on the top step. His eyes travel over me slowly, inappropriately. "You look very beautiful this evening. Red suits you. Your lipstick is . . . it looks good."

"Thank you." I remind myself that it was the dress I wore for Adam on our first date.

He steps forward until we're side by side, and I feign interest in the portrait on the wall.

"One of your ancestors?" Examining it more closely, I notice there's a familiar look captured in the oils, the heavy brows, the dark eyes. But there are also qualities Finn doesn't possess: a malice in the man's expression, a nasty curl to his lips.

"Yes," Finn says. "My father."

He looks grand, aristocratic.

"You've had a privileged upbringing, by the look of it," I say.

"I was lucky. Life was always kinder to me than it was to Sophia."

I squint at the signature and realize Sophia has painted it. I'm surprised at how unflattering it is.

"What were her parents like?" I ask, for she's not revealed much about them yet.

Finn smiles down at me. "What were *your* parents like?" he asks.

I flinch, wondering if he's like Adam's mother, implying my background is too humble, not good enough. But when I stare up at him, I find myself unable to speak. He leans in. His pupils are dilated and bloodshot, his breath laced with wine and cigars. I lean forward, just a little. Our lips are so close—

He pulls back, shaking himself. "Sorry," he mutters. Then, stepping away: "They're waiting for you. I just came up for a slash." Another step backward. "How's proof-reading?"

I let out a shrill laugh, feeling dazed.

"Um, fine," I murmur. "I finished your job, if you remember."

"Did you receive payment?"

"Ah, not yet. But I only invoiced a week ago."

"Well, I'll chase that up on Monday. I'll email the accounts department."

"Right—thanks. So—I'll just go down now . . ."

"Glad we cleared that up." He disappears into the bathroom.

Downstairs, I encounter an odd sight: Adam and Sophia are on the patio, sharing a cigar back and forth. Usually Adam loathes smoking. But I'm too dazed to really care. The near-kiss has left my body screaming for Finn. All the way down the stairs, I very nearly went back up and grabbed him.

I need to get out of here, I think. Before something happens.

Something's already happened, a small voice inside me points out.

But not in real life, I argue back. *Not consciously, not properly.*

I'm about to say that we should go now, it's been a lovely evening, when Sophia comes up and takes my hand. "Come with me."

Adam makes to rise from his chair, but she insists: "No. It's girls only."

She leads me down through the long garden. At the bottom, we pass through a wooden arch, wreathed in jasmine, the scent heady and seductive. Trees arch over us, forming a dark green cave of leaves, filtering the moonlight.

Sophia sits down on the edge of a raised rocky bed, her glass tilting between her fingers. Drunk, she is both softer and harder: blurry in her speech, more prone to laughter, but with steel in her eyes. "Are you thinking what I'm thinking?"

"What?" I say, carefully. I can sense what she's about to say and excitement fizzes inside me.

"You know." She cocks her head to one side. "Shall we do another switch?"

I hesitate. "I do want to, I want to so much, but I'm really freaked that Finn might know. He's been—he's been really flirty just now."

Sophia lets out a terse laugh. "He doesn't know anything about the switch. I can assure you."

"Really?"

"If Finn had thought that anything like that had gone on, he would have *made* me tell him. He'd have broken me down."

She makes him sound rather cruel, given that it was he who saved her from an abusive relationship.

"He's flirting because he's attracted to you," she goes on. "Which is why I chose you for the switch. Finn doesn't like many women."

"Really?" My voice is sharp with eagerness. In my drunk state, I'm giving too much away; I want her to persuade me.

"I know how much you want him." She shrugs. "I understand. And of course he wants you. You're my beautiful Elena."

"Well, you want Adam too, don't you?"

She smiles, crosses her legs. "So . . . Are we going to?"

"But . . ." I try to sound detached, citing the risks that have sprouted worries in my mind over the last few weeks: "The trouble is . . . if Adam or Finn felt there was anything odd about that night, they'll have dismissed it initially. But if a pattern develops, then they might start to get too many pieces of the puzzle. They'll wonder more, ask more questions."

"You're right." Sophia sips her wine with relish. "The stakes are higher and we need to pay attention to detail even more than before. But . . . you must, surely, surely, be tempted?"

I break into a wild smile and she holds my eyes, smiling back.

"We're mad, aren't we?" she says.

"Totally mad."

Sophia stands up, plucking a flower and threading it into my hair. "Queen Elena." She kisses my cheek.

And I realize I've made a mistake; I shouldn't have agreed to it until she told me what the special *thing* is that Adam loves in bed.

But Sophia is already waltzing back up the garden, singing.

26.

SOPHIA

I always wake up on the morning of a switch with a tingling sensation all over my body. Anticipation is the best drug. Elena must be feeling it too, because it's not even seven and she's sent me a WhatsApp.

Today's the day!

I message her back, smiling: **Don't clean too much. Adam will guess.**

She will, though. She'll be changing the sheets and pushing the Hoover nozzle into every corner.

When he's at the gym later I'll just change the sheets, she replies with a rolling-eyes emoji. I smile: I knew it.

I'm so glad I found Elena and Adam. The other day I went back to my diary entry of January 22 and checked out the shortlist I made, in the early days of moving to Wimbledon:

Mary and Jonathan
Anjali and Ross
Evie and Kieran

Mary turned out to be too suspicious; Ross was too ugly; and Evie and Kieran were *fous*. I was starting to feel a little frantic. Finn and I were going to parties, socializing a lot, but it's important to pick the potential couple with care—or was I being too fussy?

Then fate stepped in. I met Elena in a café after my bag was stolen and I felt it in my gut at once: she was perfect.

She's pretty but not the sort that you notice at first. More a slow-burn attractiveness. The more you look at Elena, the more you notice the sheen of her hair, the blue of her eyes, the classic beauty of her cheekbones. Good-looking, but not enough to be a threat. And not sexy either. That bright lipstick she dons looks garish to me, rather than hot. That she's having problems in that department with Adam doesn't surprise me. It's hard to picture her having an orgasm, which sounds harsh, but she just doesn't strike me as the sort of woman who takes great pleasure in sex. For her, the joys in life are books, films, proof-reading, and her cat, which she dotes on and I loathe.

She's smart. Warm-hearted. Eager to please and polite, but not a pushover. She has her opinions, her ideas. She has a sweet tooth. Enjoys making lists. Can suddenly surprise you with a witticism, a wicked joke.

And yet.

I haven't entirely sussed Elena out. I sense she's cautious, a little nervous of intimacy, of fully opening up. She has a mysterious air, at times. There's an insecurity I can't quite place. Given that she was at Cambridge, has had such a privileged life, with two loving parents, it surprises me. There seems to be an issue with Adam's mother that I can't fathom—why on earth would anyone disapprove of Elena so vehemently when she's so inoffensive?

I'll figure her out in time. I need to understand her fully for the switch to be successful.

When I was a teenager, my favorite book was *Les Liaisons Dangereuses*. The tale of two scheming aristocrats, Merteuil and Valmont, who plot to ruin a virgin for revenge, and seduce a married religious woman for the challenge of it. They're such wicked souls. Or perhaps they're just products of their era. Marquise de Merteuil is a feminist, ahead of her time. She records how she invented herself, putting on a feminine mask to please society while being far more canny underneath. One detail from the film that has always stayed with me: she taught herself to hide emotion by pushing a fork into her hand when she was sitting at the dinner table and not showing a flicker of pain. Of course, it's easier for women now, but the battle hasn't been fully won. I have the scars to prove it. If I'd been born a man, I wouldn't have these marks on my body. I wouldn't suffer recurring nightmares that he's got me trapped . . .

When I join Adam in his bed tonight, I won't put on Elena's perfume and nightie and act like a woman dressed in borrowed clothes. I will become her.

It's similar to that feeling I get when I'm painting a portrait and I'm so lost in a face that I melt into those features, morph into that person. When I'm Elena, I age from thirty to thirty-seven. I feel those extra years, the weight and the wisdom of them. I become shy. I become a woman living with Adam to whom I feel loving but am not in love with; a woman who is cared for but not fully supported, who is repressing a wild side she's trying to hide from everyone. It's not the sex that excites her, I can see that. It's the gathering up of her life and putting it all on the roulette table: the mad gamble, the thrilling risk.

Adam's a good choice for me too. Handsome, tall, athletic. His energy is much blunter than hers, more sexy, more overt. I'm not convinced by his supposed "Marxism" and "feminism," but he is smart.

I've realized recently that I'm sapiosexual. That was the trouble with the last switch, back in Cornwall, with Scott and Meghan. Scott wasn't all that clever and he worked in insurance, which meant having to put up with all those anecdotes about selling on doorsteps, feigning interest over dinner. At least Adam's creative. When I heard about his films I feared he'd be some lame Tarantino wannabe, but he does seem to be genuinely talented, and the films are a way to get closer to him.

A clever man is more likely to suss things out, however. I know that switches can go horribly wrong—oh, yes, I do. Cornwall is still raw in my mind. Scott and Meghan and the games that went too far. And those sad, awful days, and the blood everywhere, and the tragedy.

Wimbledon is a fresh start. The rent is eye-watering and Finn sometimes worries we should downsize, but why not enjoy his inheritance? I love this huge house on an exclusive road of millionaires; I hope we can put down roots here.

I'm pulled out of my reverie by another text from Elena.

It's a picture.

Of condoms. Two packets. Fetherlite and Mutual Climax. Stuffed into the top drawer of a cabinet already overflowing with them.

With a message: **Just so you don't forget this time.**

I let out a laugh, it's so pointed. Then I swallow. This is humiliating.

I've half a mind to cancel, but then I control myself. I need to stick that fork into my palm. So I send back a smiley **of course** message. I remind myself that Elena's attention to detail is a good thing. Her proof-reading mind is an asset. We can't wake up tomorrow to a potential breakup. We need to stay sharp and on the ball.

I take a few snaps of myself for Instagram in front of a portrait-in-progress. I was due to have my roots done yesterday with Dominic, but didn't dare. I feared that the strong dye smell would linger, that Adam would pick up on it. I don't look my best, but with some plucking and a filter, I manage to take a shot that looks casually glamorous.

Like. Like. Like like like. Fifteen, thirty, a hundred likes.

I feel soothed. Everyone likes Instagram Sophia; I like her too, better than the real me.

Ten o'clock, chimes the grandfather clock.

Fourteen hours to go.

27.

ELENA

I got Finn to bed on time. All going to plan.

I glance at Sophia's text surreptitiously, then oh-so-casually put my mobile back onto my bedside cabinet and flash Adam a smile. We're sitting up in bed together, reading.

The morning after that dinner with Sophia and Finn, Adam and I woke up declaring that we were getting far too old for hangovers of this caliber. And then I remembered with a jolt of shock: *we agreed to a second switch!* Oh, God. Oh, fuck. I drafted texts to Sophia requesting we cancel and then drafted texts confirming we were on. Every hour I fluctuated between opposing emotions as temptation whispered and my conscience fought back. Anxiety versus the thrill of risk. Desire versus restraint. Indulgence versus responsibility. Anticipation versus dread.

And—here we are. The days have gone by and anxiety and restraint and responsibility and dread haven't been enough to stop me. I feel as though it's happening to me rather than me making a decision, which I also know is a way of absolving my guilt.

I keep thinking hard about why we got away with it last time. I don't think it's all just down to the details. Unlike me, Adam's always emphasized the value of reason over intuition, so even if he'd felt a bit uneasy, he would have railroaded the emotion with logic: who else could have been in the bed that night? Who else could have worn my exact nightie, washed their hair with the same shampoo, worn my perfume?

The risk is greater this time. The more anomalies he notes, the greater the risk he'll ignore the prompting of reason. It's all very well Sophia saying that we need to plan every detail, but she never wants to acknowledge just how much we can't control. Though, I have to admit, that's also part of the secret thrill . . .

These summer days are getting dark later and later. The sun set around nine o'clock this evening. Finally, the night is drawing in.

Just as I'm about to get up and switch on the main light, I'm aware of Adam, his hand stretching out to his bedside lamp—

Déjà vu. The switch doesn't work.

He tries it again.

And again.

"It was only a few weeks ago that I put in a new bulb," he says.

He frowns, leaning forward, investigating.

"Just leave it," I say, gaily. "I'll change it myself in the morning."

"No. *Look*." Adam holds up the bulb. "It's been unscrewed—that's pretty weird."

"Maybe we have a poltergeist," I reply. Yesterday we were watching *Don't Look Now*. We've been joking about ghosts and hauntings ever since.

Adam laughs and screws the bulb back in. I'm smarting. Damn. I can always just unplug it at the wall, but it's not easy, the socket right behind the bed; I'll have to crawl under it in the dark and fiddle about after he's gone to sleep, in the pitch-dark.

Adam switches on his lamp. "There. All fixed!"

"Great," I enthuse, seething inside.

I push a valerian tablet out of its packet and pass it to Adam, then pretend to put one in my mouth. I swallow a mouthful of water, pass the glass to him. He sips and swallows while still reading.

I've been giving him valerian the last few nights. He's been restless, not sleeping as well as usual. I'm sure it's because we still haven't sorted out the new place to live; we're being far too picky because neither of us really wants to move.

"So," says Adam, putting down his book. "Are we having sex tonight? I figured we are, 'cos you did another big clean on the bedroom. The last time you did that, it meant hot sex."

I freeze up, then improvise playfully.

"I'd suggest you go to sleep and see if you get lucky in the night."

"Oh, so it's going to be like that, is it?" Adam laughs, his pupils dilating.

For a moment, the splinter in my heart throbs again: am I so uninteresting that he can't even tell when I've been replaced by another person?

"Wait and see."

I'm scared he might pounce on me, but he picks up his book, smiling. "And I saw you filled the drawer," he adds. "There are . . . what? . . . at least twenty condoms in there."

I go back to my book, a coy smile at my lips.

We still haven't done *that thing*, still haven't had the glorious sex he wants, which remains a tension simmering between us. Sophia's return tonight will solve the problem. But I feel like bursting into terrified laughter at the realization that every time Adam wants amazing sex involving some mysterious fetish, I can't keep calling her up. This is a short-term fix that is creating a long-term problem.

It's now nearly eleven: our usual lights-out hour. I get up to pull down the blackout blind, when Adam says: "Leave it up."

"What?"

"It's nice, now it's summer, letting some light in. I feel like a vampire with that blind down all the time. And it's hard, getting up in the mornings . . . Your insomnia's better, isn't it?"

"No, not really! It's only because of the blind that I got better." I feel irrational with nerves: why is he being so difficult on tonight of all nights?

"We've just taken a ton of valerian."

"We've taken *one* tablet."

"Yes—but what about later?" Adam winks at me.

"Huh?"

"It's nice—to be able to *see* you—when you suddenly pounce on me and wake me up."

"Oh. Okay." I shrug, too panicked to think up a protest, drawing the curtains instead. They're far too thin, slender white fluttering things that let in street-light.

We switch off our lamps and I lie rigid in the murky light, my mind scurrying over the bulb, the blind, the complete failure of my set-up. I consider texting Sophia, calling it all off. Then I think of Finn and the flickering ache that has been the backdrop of my days and weeks. By going to bed with him again, I can gain a much clearer picture of the chemistry between us. I can see if the first switch was a one-off or something more special. I'm inclined to think it's the former, that I've exaggerated the memory since, idealized it, shaped it into spectacular fantasy. As much as I'm yearning for Finn, I'm also hoping that tonight will burst the bubble.

I dread that Adam might leap on me but soon he's snoring. Finally, I slip out of bed and go to the window.

I tug the blind cord gently. *Squeak.* I hadn't even noticed it made that noise before.

Squeak.

Squeak.

Squeak.

I pull, I pull, heart hammering, blackness filling the room—

"Elena?"

I've woken up Adam.

"I couldn't sleep," I hiss, pulling it right down.

"Okay." His voice is sleepy, resigned.

I stand there, hovering in the dark. Then I hear the sound of a snore again. Oh, thank God. I pick up my mobile and feel my way to the door.

I reach out, feeling the edge of his lamp. The bulb still carries a faint warmth. I try to turn it with one hand but Adam's screwed it in tight. I hold the base and use more force and to my relief it untwists noiselessly. I just hope it's enough.

In the bathroom, in my notebook, I write a reminder: *screw bulb back in when you return.*

I dress. In the mirror I watch my reflection brushing her hair. I wanted to grow it longer but I had to cut it back to the exact same length as Sophia's, one that suits her but doesn't flatter me. I reach for her perfume and hesitate. I'm almost tempted to leave it off, to give him some clue, some hint, that I'm not her, that I am me.

I give myself a sharp talking-to and spray myself liberally, dressing in the same uniform as I did before: jeans and top over my silky nightie, fastening the crucifix around my neck. As I make my way downstairs, I see that I'm a little late. I shut Lyra into the lounge, then hurry out. I'm a few minutes down the road when I realize that *I locked the back door on autopilot* and I race back, unlock it, sweating now, my heart telling me we should call it off, something doesn't feel right.

But on I go, through the silent moonlit Village, toward Murray Road, toward Finn's bed.

28.

ELENA

I open the bedroom door, sidle in, close it behind me. Darkness, thick as oil, and the nervous sound of my own breathing.

I lift the duvet, see Finn's sleeping form, and slip under the covers next to him, heart hammering. I've been dreaming about this for days but reality is scary. I tell myself: *You can do this, you did it before.*

I'm wondering if I need to wake him up when he reaches over and kisses me. The last time we kissed it was slow, tentative. This is feverish and frantic. Desire licks up inside me. His fingers hurry down to my knickers. "You're soaking," he whispers and I want to tell him that I've been thinking about him all day but I just reply with a sound of lust.

Suddenly he moves fast, pulling off the nightie, stripping down my knickers, thrusting inside me. He kisses me hard, opening my mouth up with his tongue as he comes quickly.

He stays inside me for a while, breathless, shaking, while I lie there, smiling, enjoying the weight of his body. My relief is sweet: I didn't climax, it was all too fast for me, but I took pleasure in his pleasure and just being with him, the feel and scent of his skin, is so good. I can enjoy this. And I can go back to Adam without carrying an exaggerated fantasy that multiplies in my imagination day by day.

Finn withdraws and lies beside me. Now his kisses are soft around my mouth and cheeks and neck. He trails them down my body, kissing my breasts, stomach, hips, circling down, brushing them over my thighs, playing that teasing game he did last time. This time he's more controlled. He draws out the torture slowly. He tells me to imagine we're in a box at the opera. *Lady Macbeth of Mtsensk—*

I freeze: is he playing me? No, no, I recall, Sophia too has mentioned how much he loves that opera; he would have shared his fantasy with her.

He goes on: we've drawn the curtains; we're on the floor; we can't help ourselves. The solo rises to a crescendo, not loud enough to drown us out. People might be able to hear us, sense what we're doing. "Oh, please," I risk a whisper. And he teases me back, "Are you sure you want this?" When I climax, wave upon wave of pleasure breaks over me, leaving me stunned. I've never had an orgasm so dizzying and beautiful before. He climbs up, pressing his lips onto mine so I can taste me on him.

He pulls me up, inside me now, both of us upright, face to face, my breasts against his chest, his fingers splayed across my spine. I feel lost, deliciously defeated. Whenever Adam and I have gone to bed together, I've had to constantly break the spell by guiding or instructing him. My body has always felt clumsy and heavy in his hands. Finn seems to have such a natural ability to translate my every moan, to sense my every wish. He knows when to be gentle, when to be firm, when to be tender, when to be wild. As he guides me to a crescendo, whispering a fierce *Sophia* in my ear, the sound of his climax thrills through me and I break too. He says *I love you* and I whisper it back to him.

We're lying alongside each other, in a dream state, kissing now and then. We've made love again, this time even more intense than the last. I've lost track of time. I feel as though I am existing purely in the present. I want to stay in this room, in the dark, with him, forever. His fingers brush the crucifix on my neck, travel down, stroking my thighs once more, and I have to whisper, "Please . . . stop." He whispers back, "You can't handle any more?" and I nod. My mind is floating but my body is spent, shattered by the feast of pleasure. He laughs, kissing me, saying, "We can wait a bit but I'm not finished with you yet, Sophia."

Sophia: that cut, every time he says her name, especially when I am so vulnerable, every part of me opened up raw to him.

I lean over and kiss him possessively and he sighs, melts into me. We lie there for a while, lazy and sleepy, and I indulge myself in the fantasy of imagining what it would be like to be in his bed every night. I picture us living together. He'd be at work all day; I'd proof-read. There'd be less worry about money. No budget plans, no frugality. Kisses hello; dinner; to bed. Would it ever become flat between us when our chemistry is so amazing? Surely we have something special—certainly something I've never experienced before. I picture us taking a holiday in Nice together, lying on a beach, and the scene blends into a dream. We're in the sea, kissing, and the sky is so blue above us—

Suddenly Finn is sitting up. The duvet falling away from us, cold air rushing in.

"Did you hear that?" he asks. "Someone's in the house. I heard the back door."

My heart clenches. I picture Adam. He's found out, he's raging, he's charging up the stairs to confront us—

"There's someone here." He reaches for the lamp, tries to click it on. "Fuck. They've taken out the electricity."

Someone in the house?

I did leave the back door unlocked. That was our plan.

Finn gets out of bed. I pull the duvet up, terrified that he's going to turn on the light, but he just says, "Wait here."

He leaves the door ajar; light from the streetlamp outside the house trickles in. I search for the nightie, suddenly conscious that I've lost all sense of time. It's one-thirty. How could the hours have gone by so fast?

The person downstairs is surely *Sophia*, coming back, wondering where the hell I am. She'll be furious with me—and what if he encounters her? Oh, my God . . .

I find my knickers and the nightie at the bottom of the bed, pull it on; a strap breaks and I curse. My hair has tangled with the crucifix chain and I have to wrench at it to get it free. I sit still for a moment, my mind frantic. I knew this was going to be a bad night; it seemed ill-omened from the start. I shift on the sheet, feeling dampness beneath my thighs, the stains of our pleasure, and already regret and shame are seeping through me.

I want to slip downstairs, grab my clothes, flee. But it's too dangerous, he's bound to see me—

Unless there really is a burglar down there.

And what if he has to call the police?

My mobile is downstairs in the kitchen. I can't even message her to formulate a plan.

I listen hard. What's Finn doing? Brandishing a baseball bat like someone in a movie?

Then I hear his footsteps, coming back up the stairs.

I lie down, on my front, my face in the pillow, pulling the duvet up over me. Finn slips in beside me. I'm conscious that he hasn't closed the door fully, that a little light is stealing in.

"We forgot to close the back door before bed," he says. "It was swinging open. But there's nobody down there, we're safe." He rubs the top of my back. "Maybe it was a fox or the wind or something."

I imagine Sophia, freezing to death outside in the night cold.

His hand slithers down my spine. "Why did you put this back on?" He tugs at the nightie. I feel my body responding to his touch, then tensing.

"You okay?" he asks, immediately alert to my body and its subtleties.

"I got scared," I whisper, and he says, "Oh, Sophia. Come here." He pulls me over, into his arms. He likes to play the paternal role, I think, and I feel so safe with him, my head against his chest, his lips on my hair.

I want to stay, but the clock reminds me I must go. As he falls asleep, I ease oh-so-slowly out of his arms and hurry downstairs, dreading Sophia's ire.

In the kitchen, I see my clothes, still folded into a carrier, which I shoved under the table and concealed by pushing in the chairs. I'm lucky Finn didn't spot it.

I yank on jeans, top, trainers, over my nightie. I go to open the back door—only to find it's locked. Finn locked it, of course.

I panic, then tell myself to calm down; Sophia told me the keys are in the cupboard to the left. I open it, yank down a few, try them. They won't fit, they don't work, I'm locked in.

I put them back with trembling hands, let out a breath, take the one with the blue tag. I'm praying now—and then, *yes*, it turns in the lock. I leave the door unlocked, hurry down the garden, calling her name softly.

I can't see Sophia anywhere.

There's a faint drizzle outside. As I reach Wimbledon Common, I hear the distant yelling noise of what sounds like a drunk, and my walk becomes a run, pounding hard on the pavement, until I burst in through my back door.

No clothes, no shoes, no sign of Sophia.

Upstairs in the bathroom, I see a condom poking out of the little silvery bin. When I ping it open with my foot, there's another coiled inside— good. So they did use protection.

I can hear the faint sound of Adam's snores coming from the bedroom.

I think of Finn, asleep in bed, with a wistful ache.

You okay? I send Sophia a WhatsApp.

I remember that I need to check my notebook. The sensible tick list is stabilizing. I go downstairs and set the alarm, punching in the code. Back in our bedroom, I pick up the bulb lying loose and gently twist it back into the lamp.

Next to me, Adam is deep in sleep, looking entirely wiped out.

The duvet is rumpled. It feels uncomfortable, slipping under it, knowing she's rolled and turned and twisted and fucked on this mattress. I hear my mobile vibrate, shield the light with my hand. What happened to Sophia?

29.

SOPHIA

My period was due this morning but there's no sign of it. I know it's far too early to get excited but I can't help it. The day has taken on a hue of hope.

In Cannizaro House there's a restaurant with full-length windows that overlook the park. I sit down with a Lady Grey tea and experience one of those rare moments of calm. Some days I wake up feeling like I'm barely able to get out of bed. *His* voice is a snarl in my mind, telling me I'm damaged, I'm worthless. Finn will hold me and stroke my hair, tell me the past is past, make me breakfast, remind me of portrait commissions I have.

But today is a day when I feel how normal people must feel.

As I sip my tea, I watch mothers and fathers with their children, holding them so tightly, such pride and love and tenderness on their faces. I know we live in a cruel and vicious world where even God cannot always intervene. But I swear that if I have this baby, I will love and look after her—I know it's a her, I just know—and protect her and give her the happy childhood I never had.

Elena was starting to suspect, after the first switch. I shouldn't underestimate her. The *we forgot condoms* was a lame excuse, and the morning after pill suspect.

Elena said that Adam was fooled because we appeased his logic with attention to detail. But I think he's sexually frustrated and desire blurs his judgment. Early on, he whispered to me, "I'm so glad the naughty Elena is back, I was scared you'd gone for good." He slipped on a condom; I let it come off when I gave him a blow job, and whispered that it was back on; he was too turned on to register. Then there was a break, a phone call. We fucked again and this time he whispered, "Are you sure it was on last time?" He insisted we doublecheck before he entered me. So I had to improvise. The moment he fell asleep, I went into the bathroom, thrust my fingers into the condom, pushed them inside me, then lay down on the lino for a minute, legs high, door locked. Praying. Could it work? Was it really true that you can take sperm from a condom, or just one of those internet myths? Doesn't it die the moment it's in there, killed by the spermicide that lines the latex?

I spread the rest of the sperm between two condoms. Then inspiration struck: I rearranged one, leaving it hanging out of the bin for Elena to see. As I hurried downstairs, I realized it was one-thirty and I was late.

Outside, I ran down Church Road toward the roundabout, adrenaline coursing through me. There was a drunk nearby, and his shouts arrowed toward me; I gave him the finger and hurried on. When I got home, I could see a light on upstairs, feared the worst. I prayed and prayed. Through the kitchen window, I spotted Finn looking about. Then he locked the back door and went upstairs. I scurried down to the bottom of the garden, hiding behind a trellis, shivering. What the hell was going on?

I saw Elena unlock the door and hurtle out. A few minutes later, a WhatsApp came through from her, saying Finn had thought there was an intruder, but all was well.

We'd pulled it off, just.

I messaged back, emojis with tears of laughter: **Finn nearly saw me and I had to hide. I saw you go. It was like a French farce!** And she texted back the same emojis and we had a giggle together.

I keep thinking about the phone call. Adam and I had just had sex and we were lying breathless in the dark when he heard the faint ring of his mobile from downstairs. He muttered, "It could be Mum." I crept onto the landing, listening in, as he paced the downstairs hallway. It was his mum; and what I heard was shocking. He spoke in a low voice, and I sensed that Elena wasn't meant to hear, so I tiptoed back into the bedroom as he rang off. I lay in the dark and prayed he wouldn't turn on the main light. A tingling excitement enveloped my whole body. He slipped in, made some excuse about the call, but I shut him up with a kiss and soon it was forgotten. Now I know what his fetish is, he's putty in my hands.

The phone call has certainly given me more insight into Elena, though not all of the pieces of her puzzle are in place yet. People are always full of surprises, so complex—you think you know them, but there's always so much going on beneath the surface.

I wonder if I should tell Elena what I heard. I feel a tug of loyalty to her. She's become like the older sister I always wanted. Then I remind myself that soon, once my pregnancy is confirmed and I start to show, I might need to distance myself.

I jump when I hear a shrill scream. A child outside has been climbing a tree and he nearly falls; his mother rushes to his side. Oh, God. His cries slice my heart.

Suddenly my calm feels fragile. I try to relax and enjoy the thought of my little baby girl taking shape inside me, but instead I find myself fretting over the plan. I've gone through cycles of faith over the years, phases of wearing a crucifix, going to Mass; phases of shoving my crucifix in a drawer, relishing freedom, turning my back on the Church. I have to admit, I only tend to become religious when I feel desperate. What if my inconsistency has canceled out any hope of a divine boon?

Elena's not religious. She wouldn't understand that I can't use a sperm donor, that some baby concocted in a test tube from a random stranger's sperm is a big no-no for me. I try to think it all through. Even if she did object to the pregnancy, even if she guessed it was Adam's, what could she say to me? "I gave you permission to sleep with my husband and now I'm upset that you're carrying his baby." It would be too hypocritical and embarrassing for words. There is the risk of Adam finding out and fighting for paternity rights, which scares me. But would she tell him, blow her whole relationship? Surely the switch gags her, traps her too?

Besides, they can easily have kids—and yet they want to throw away that golden opportunity. They are restless, their relationship is empty, but still they can't see how much it would enrich them. Surely it is a kind of divine justice that Elena was put in my path? That I can have the baby she doesn't want?

The child who was climbing the tree walks past and I hear his mother say, "Oh, my, Adam." My heart leaps. It's too odd to be a coincidence that he has the same name; it has to be a sign.

A sudden sensation of peace envelops me.

I'm on the right track. I will be blessed with a child. It has to happen.

30.

ELENA

There's a hair on the sheet. I'm just making the bed when I spot it. A pubic hair, nearly black, much darker than mine are. I quickly brush it off and then, with obsessive anxiety, I scour every inch of the Egyptian cotton. Another hair, on the pillow, longer and dyed blonde. When I hold it up to the morning sunlight streaming in through the window, I can't tell if it's mine or hers. I unpop the duvet buttons, then pause: I've only just washed it in preparation for the switch. Adam might get suspicious. But I hate the sensation of lying on the bed she's slept in with him. I know there must be stains dried into the sheets. The memory of their lovemaking imprinted into the cloth—

I yank off the bottom sheet, put it into the washing basket. I'll tell Adam that I spilled some tea, blame Lyra for knocking it over.

I'm dazed after last night's switch: sleep-deprived, oversexed. At least there are no love bites to hide this time. I haven't showered yet. I don't want to remove his essence from my skin, even though there's a risk that Adam might pick up on it. I'll wait until this evening, when I get in.

In the Vicomte Café, I open my laptop. My body is still raw, a slight pain in my groin, a heat lingering; yet I also feel peaceful, strangely calm and happy.

There's an odd sense of expectation hovering over me. As though I'm waiting for the guilt to descend. I think I feel guilty about not feeling guilty enough. It was definitely sharper the first time round, which means maybe I'm getting used to being a bad person. But how can it be wrong to feel this good?

The bubble bursts when a text comes through from Adam. I was sleeping deeply this morning; I didn't even hear him leave the house for work.

Last night was hot stuff, my wench!

A tremor in my calm: that first pulse of unease, the prospect of consequences I will have to face.

I'd never dreamed that sex of this nature was possible. I went to see the *Fifty Shades* film with Adam; he said once was enough, so I dragged Anil along to the sequels. I enjoyed them but thought that the phenomenal sex they shared was risible. I believed that books that included metaphors about sex being "earth-shattering," or invoked other environmental disasters, were fantasy—sometimes silly, sometimes titillating—a case of art and life being quite separate.

Finn has shattered all my cynicism. He's proved that the fantasy can come true—only my prince is already married and has no idea of what we've shared. I don't think it was just the dark or the danger that bonded us. We have chemistry of a kind that is once in a lifetime. But now what? I keep looking at that photo of him online; the firework whoosh inside never fails to accompany it. This morning I sneaked onto their road, watching him kiss Sophia goodbye. I've played opera on my iPod. I don't want to break dear Adam's heart. I don't want to disrupt a marriage and I have a feeling Sophia would cut me into pieces if I tried. She's happy to loan me her husband but she certainly doesn't want to lose him.

We could keep on with our switches, but the odds are not on our side. Sooner or later, we'd get caught. I can't imagine Finn or Adam would forgive us. Or would they? It's not as though Adam's always been the perfect partner. I try to imagine what Finn would say. Surely this euphoria isn't just mine? If he knew, would he be shocked? Or would he want more of me?

Such terrible thoughts. If Sophia notices, she doesn't show it.

We're sitting out on the patio in her garden, chatting. She suddenly got the inspiration to sketch me and now her pad is balanced on her knee, her pencil sweeping and darting over the page, her eyebrows knitted in concentration.

When I hear a noise from inside the house, I jump.

"Oh, Finn's home early," Sophia says, setting aside her sketchpad.

She smiles, traces her finger across my wrist, as though to say gently: *Calm down, dearest.*

Finn looks shattered; I want to run up and hug him, but instead I have to watch Sophia embrace him.

"Long day?" she asks.

He grimaces, then gives me a nod hello. "I need a drink."

I am too overwhelmed to say hello back. I rise as though to excuse myself, but Sophia flaps her hand, tells me to sit back down. I'm quivering all over, my stomach somersaulting, my cheeks scarlet. Finn comes back out with a glass that clinks with ice. He starts telling Sophia the problem: something about an investment that seems to have fallen through, though he's not entirely sure, there are rumors flying about . . . I think back to the night that we came for dinner and he flirted with me. I've been convincing myself that his desire for me exists in the day, not just the anonymous dark. Tonight, he is cool by comparison. Maybe that dinner was just a case of him being drunk.

The sound of his voice inflames me. The deepness and the grit of it. *I love you.* That's the moment I replay the most, hearing him whisper those words in my ear with his cock hard inside me. The pleasure and pain of them.

Sophia suggests that I might stay for dinner and the look on his face is like a punch to my heart. He's tired. Not in the mood for entertaining. *He doesn't want me to stay.*

"Oh, God," he says.

I flinch—is that directed at me? Then I realize that he's holding another letter; I recognize Meghan's handwriting. Sophia bites her lip and takes it from him, then slowly tears it in half.

Oh, God indeed. Maybe I'm just as pathetic as his stalker. I turn away, fixing my gaze on a green parakeet that's just swooped into the garden. I mustn't cry, I tell myself fiercely, stilling the tremor in my chin. This deceit hurts me more than it hurts him. We've created an affair that has none of the usual dangers: I don't have sexy texts coming through that Adam could see at any moment or a man pressurizing me to leave my partner. But here he is, sitting a foot away, oblivious, and it all feels so ephemeral, as though it's a fantasy I've conjured up that never happened.

"I have to go," I say, standing. "I want to cook Adam a special dinner, I've got a new recipe book . . ." And I add some crap about a Jamie Oliver I've just been gifted.

"Oh, by the way," Sophia says, "we'd love to chat more sometime about Adam's films. Maybe we could help with financing."

I'm taken aback: "Well, it's really just a hobby he abandoned long ago, so . . . I don't know if . . ." I glance at Finn, who couldn't look less interested.

I say my goodbyes and leave.

He's ruined me.

Twice.

First with amazing sex that I am convinced I'll never find again, and now by breaking my heart with his careless indifference. I'm so cut up: tears tumble as I walk down Murray Road. I smear them away quickly, so that by the time I reach the Common I'm presentable again. Home, then. We'll have a lovely evening in together. I have to repair the relationship I've got, because Finn is a silly fantasy. I've been a fool; now I'll play the role of a perfect partner.

31.

ELENA

*E*lena!"

Adam and I are sitting in the Curzon Wimbledon café when Sophia comes in through the swing doors.

I get up to give her a hug. It is good to see her, though I needed a week's space after my last visit to her house, making the excuse of a severe cold. Being in her presence evoked too many painful memories of Finn. I'm not sure if she senses what I'm going through and, in that respect, I'm grateful for the pact we've made not to share details.

Finn is currently engrossed in an ongoing work crisis, leaving Sophia feeling lonely, so the three of us agreed to watch the latest art film together. She buys a coffee and returns looking flushed, as though she's harboring a secret. *What's going on?* I wonder uneasily.

"Adam, I have a proposition for you," she says, and when he raises a cheeky eyebrow, we all fall about laughing. "No," she rolls her eyes, "not like that. I want you to make another short film and I want to be the exec producer on it."

I'm taken aback; Adam too. He looks awkward, then dubious.

"Why? You've never produced a film before," he says with his customary brusqueness.

But Sophia won't let it go. She raves on about her mother's friendship with Audrey Hepburn and all the film tips she picked up from a young age. She tells us that one of her closest friends is Jackson Green. Adam's eyes light up then: he's a well-known producer. When I check him on IMDb on my phone, I see he's alternated between big Hollywood block-busters and daring art films. As Adam starts to thaw, enthusiasm danc-ing in his eyes, I feel a bit thrown: what game is Sophia playing? Is this a set-up for another switch?

By the time she's finished her pitch we realize the film has already started and we have to muddle through the dark to find our seats, ending up out of sequence—me on one side, Adam on the other, and Sophia sit-ting between us.

Sophia joins me again the next morning. I need to visit Hilary and she offers to come along for "moral support."

Hilary's still getting on well with her Lithuanian carer. But each week he has a day off and Adam looked surprised when I volunteered to fill in. While I don't think I can ever become best friends with Hilary, I do want at least to make more effort. Guilt is probably a motivation too—I've be-trayed Adam and I want to make it up to him.

Normally on that train ride from Wimbledon to Windsor, I suffer a gradual, intensifying dread. Sophia cheers me up today, dilutes my anxi-ety. She starts playing around with an Instagram selfie she wants to up-load, asking for my advice on different filters, lights, hues—"I can sometimes spend an hour editing a pic before it goes up," she confesses. I can't hide my surprise that anyone would waste so much time and energy and she laughs, "God, I'm so vain!"

I warn Sophia not to take it personally if Hilary is offensive and un-grateful. She nods cheerfully but when we get off the train, she insists on stopping at a florist's.

When Sophia presents her with the bouquet of roses and freesias, Hilary gives them a long, hard look; then she does the same to Sophia.

She is making all the mistakes I did when I first met Hilary. The more you try to please her, the more she twists the thumbscrew.

"I'll put them in water," says Sophia in a dejected tone. She looks taken aback that her usual charms have failed to work.

"I think they're lovely," I say, pledging my allegiance. I feel furious with Hilary and I've only just got here. I must calm down. "Would you like a cup of tea?" I try to sound patient but it comes out as though I'm offering her a drink of acid.

Hilary sips it, staring out of the window. Her eyes look misty and sad. Sophia hangs back while I rummage in a cupboard and find some Duchy biscuits, spreading them over a plate.

"I've only just had lunch," Hilary objects when I offer her one. "Now they'll only go to waste."

I bite into one with a loud crunch.

"Adam's a very talented film-maker, isn't he?" Sophia tries again. "Finn—my husband—and I, we're going to help exec produce a short film by him. We have some friends in the industry."

"Adam's keen," I say. I must admit, I'm still taken aback by the offer. When I pressed Sophia, she claimed it had nothing to do with the switches: she just wanted to help.

Hilary immediately picks up on something in my voice. A trace of jealousy, I must admit: I've never been able to help Adam with his film career, beyond reading his scripts and proof-reading them.

Her eyes travel from me to Sophia, assessing. Suddenly she gives Sophia a big smile back. "Oh, really? That's awfully generous of you."

And soon they're talking about how talented Adam is. In the past, Hilary has always dismissed his film work as a time-wasting hobby.

Sophia is too thrilled with the success of her charm offensive to see how I'm smarting at being left out. I know Hilary's playing divide and rule but it's hard not to react to the bait. I offer to take her chihuahua out so it can poo in the garden. *This is why I'm a cat person*, I think, wincing as I scoop it up into a plastic bag.

Through the window, I watch them chatting together. Maybe Hilary is winding me up, but I'm also conscious that they're from a similar class background. Hilary would be much happier if Adam ended up with someone like Sophia.

A buzz from my phone. It's an email from Finn, offering me more proof-reading work. I find it a wild turn-on and a huge put-down when he sends me formal emails. *I was in your bed a few weeks ago,* I draft a reply, *and so, yes, I'd love to proof-read your work. I mean, why not, when we've shared a wild night of passion that I'm now working hard to forget?* Then I press delete, telling myself to get a grip.

I'll rewrite and craft it a dozen times before I send back a perfectly formal and polite reply.

I go back inside, declaring that the dog seems restless, so I'm happy to take him out for a proper walk.

Sophia says she'll join me. Hilary looks disappointed. I'm glad that Sophia has sided with me, but as we wander out to the local park, she falls into a troubled silence.

"Elena . . . there's something I need to tell you. About Adam. About that last night with him."

My heart starts to speed up. "What do you mean?" *She's going to say that Adam has fallen for her, is leaving me for her.* "I thought we made a pact," I add fearfully.

"Oh—don't worry, it's not about that. It's about something else."

"Go on . . ." I say cautiously.

"After we had sex, Adam got a call. I mean, it was half-past midnight but he ran downstairs to get his mobile. I could hear him speaking in the hall. He was talking to Hilary. I think he thought I was asleep. I know I was being nosy but I listened in."

"Oh," I say, confused. This sounds a tiny bit implausible. Hilary does sometimes selfishly call in the middle of the night when she has insomnia and wants a "chat," but usually Adam goes into a downstairs room or else the bathroom, rather than risk me being woken up and hearing.

"Adam was having a go at her about having to leave the housesit and go back to Walthamstow. He was saying that you both would've been able to stay in Wimbledon if it wasn't for her."

I flush, embarrassed. So Sophia knows about the housesit. She must think I'm pathetic for having pretended.

But the look on her face isn't judgmental, it's one of concern.

"The thing is—from what I heard—Hilary promised him some money to get his foot on the housing ladder. A big lump sum. And judging from their conversation, it's been on offer for years."

"What, like a trust fund or something?" I ask in bewilderment.

"Adam was saying to her: 'I shouldn't have to break up with Elena to be allowed to have it.' It seemed as though, right from the moment you two started dating, she laid down that rule, forced him to make a choice—you or the money."

"Oh." I'm winded by the revelation. "Oh, my God."

"But if you think about it," Sophia concludes, "it's actually really romantic. The point is, he chose you. He made a sacrifice."

I'm stunned, unable to reply. This explains why, a few weeks ago, Adam got this bee in his bonnet. He kept saying that we might be able to stay in Wimbledon, rent a place. It made me wonder if he had secret savings. Later, I found a lottery ticket in his pocket as I was sorting out his clothes for the washing machine. I felt sad and affectionate; I thought he was being a fantasist. Now I feel sick at the realization he was hoping he might change his mother's mind. And he failed to.

"Fucking hell," I burst out, trembling. "Fuck! Fuck! Fuck!"

"I'm sorry," she says, touching my arm, looking fraught. "I really debated whether to tell you or not, I didn't know what the right thing to do was."

"I'm glad you told me," I say, though I'm suffering from a touch of shoot-the-messenger. I force a brave smile. "I don't think I can face seeing Hilary, though. I may just throttle her. Could you take the dog back?"

"Of course." Sophia takes the lead.

We head back in silence and I wait outside the house, arms folded, pacing about. *What did I do to this woman that was so wrong?* I want to shout. I got a fucking degree from Cambridge, and I got that from being a total square and scoring As for every essay. I have been kind too, made an effort, looked after her far more than Adam has, remembered birthdays, made her cakes, cooked for her despite her bloody accusations of food poisoning! And *still* I'm not good enough. Because I don't pronounce the *ing*s on the ends of some words. Because I'm not some vapid *Tatler* blonde nepo baby who's mates with Kate Middleton and has a rich mummy and daddy. Dear God. And right now Adam and I could be staying in the place we love, instead of packing up all our things into boxes and scouring for crappy flats. I feel like setting fire to her lovely house, seeing the bricks crack and blacken. And then I start to feel mad at Sophia because she's been in there for a good fifteen minutes. How can she fuss over Adam's mum when she knows the truth about her? And why the hell did she buy her flowers?

Sophia emerges, looking apologetic, saying that Hilary insisted she take her to the toilet and help prepare things for dinner.

We sit on the train home in awkward silence. I still feel so embarrassed that Sophia knows I pretended we were renting our house in Wimbledon. Now she'll be thinking it all through—those awful dog ornaments she hated, the dated furniture in our house—all those moments where I lied and covered up. Like Hilary, she'll be secretly thinking I'm not good enough.

"You know, Finn's father never liked me," Sophia confesses, startling me. "He really had it in for me, in fact."

"Really?" I wonder if she's just making it up to reassure me, but the pain on her face seems genuine.

I cheer up as she elaborates on how stern he was. She would find herself smiling until her cheeks ached in the hope that she might coax a smile from him, but he would only grimace at her. She could never measure up. I ask her about her own parents, wondering what her background is, but she changes the subject: "I'm just sad that you and Adam are going to be moving."

I'm touched by how upset she looks.

"I'll come back and visit," I reassure her, but she sighs.

"It won't be the same."

I sense her subtext: there'll be no more switches. But as much as I will miss Sophia, I'm glad the switches will finish. Another night with Finn, opening up those floodgates to longing and obsession, isn't something I can face again. I'm only just sobering up from the last one, coming back to earth. Only this time, I'm determined that reality shouldn't be disappointing. From now on, I'm going to focus on treasuring the relationship I have.

32.

ELENA

The doorbell rings. Adam and I wince and stare at each other. We're in the hallway, pulling on our shoes, ready to go out.

I open the door. It's Sophia.

Fuck, I think. I'm not prepared for this. The house is a bit of a mess. It's been a week since that visit to Adam's mother, when Sophia revealed his secret, and the sight of her again stirs nausea and anxiety in me.

Today is a day off for us both. We have plans.

"Hey!" She greets me with air kisses. "I've got some film news—I was going to call, but then I thought I could just drop by."

She hugs Adam too. I grin uneasily. I'm still getting used to his shift from loathing Sophia to thinking her the next best thing.

"I showed Jackson Green your old short films, Adam, and he *loved* them. He says you're a great talent and he'd like to meet you."

"Wow!" Adam beams with delight.

"That's good news." I hug Sophia too; their excitement is infectious.

"Let's go over the script again right now," she enthuses.

"We were—" I begin.

"About to go out," Adam says at the same time.

We've planned a boat trip. One of a list of things we want to enjoy before we leave Wimbledon. It's mid-July; the days are flying by and we've only got six weeks left here. I've been looking forward to that lazy boat ride from Kingston to Hampton Court, to ice creams and the long walk back.

"But you've got an appointment with Dominic, haven't you?" Sophia interjects, glancing at me. "At two?"

"Do I?" I have no memory of that.

She pulls out her mobile, checking the details. "There's a confirmation email . . ." She flashes the screen at me briefly. "I got you booked in a while back, you must have forgotten."

It's not like me to forget: usually I scribble in appointments on the calendar *and* tap them into my phone. Then I catch sight of Adam's expression: his eagerness to excuse himself from our day out. I bite my lip, pushing away disappointment; I'm pleased to see how excited he is about his script. To see that passionate creative side of him—flattened over the years by his job—waking up. Ever since Sophia's revelation, I've been overwhelmed with fury against Hilary, but my feelings for Adam have become more tender. I can see now why he's been prickly about the subject of his mother; a lot has fallen into place. He made a sacrifice for me. I want to support him in return.

"Well . . ." I relent, running my fingers through my hair. "I do need a cut."

"Oh, thank you, my darling." He hugs me. "I'll remember you in my Oscar speech!"

"Ha-ha—see that I'm the first person you mention!"

I leave them chatting on the patio. The image of them leaning in together, poring over a scene in Adam's notebook, lingers as I walk down into the Village. Initially when Sophia declared she wanted to produce his film, I wondered if she was just name-dropping, that it was all hot-air enthusiasm. But she genuinely seems to be putting in time and energy and connections. Does she really want to help him, or is there something more insidious going on?

The switches might have unleashed feelings beyond her control, ones that she might not even be ready to acknowledge. Finn still invades my dreams at night but I've reverted to my previous plan of avoiding him as much as I can. Sophia, meanwhile, is doing the reverse. She's spending more time with Adam, building intimacy with him . . .

The trouble is, what can I say? If I play the killjoy and tell her to back off, it will hurt our friendship and might damage the film project. He keeps saying over and over how this could be the restart of his film career. I want him to succeed too.

I realize that I've been so churned up I've walked straight past the salon and quickly backtrack. When I was a kid, Mum used to arrange for the neighbor to come in and do our haircuts, then tidy up the wonky bits later. Coming here feels like a guilty pleasure.

There's a woman ahead of me making a theatrical fuss about when her next appointment will fit into her "insanely" busy schedule. As I wait, I fiddle with my phone, wander onto Instagram. This morning's search is still on the page.

Lorraine Parker.

Adam's old work colleague. Her full name is actually *Lady Lorraine Parker* but she doesn't use her title. She's in New York now, so her feed features a stream of ballgowns at charity events and posh weddings involving huge and elaborate hats. I get that clenching feeling in my gut. I used to look her up every day, then gradually, as the wound in my heart healed, less and less, every week, every month. It's rare that I bother to check up on her these days. It just struck me this morning that Sophia looks a bit like her: the same eyes, perhaps, or the upturned nose.

I wonder if my friendship with Sophia will survive the move or fade over the months. Maybe it's for the best, I muse, and then remind myself: *don't shoot the messenger.* I'm glad she told me about Hilary, but I can't untangle that moment of revelation from feelings of resentment, of inadequacy.

Finally, the queue clears and I step forward.

"Oh, sorry, we don't seem to have a booking for you." The receptionist's nails tip-tap on her keyboard.

"Oh! My friend made it—it might be under her name, possibly—Sophia MacInnes?"

"Sophia . . ." She looks again, shakes her head. "Sorry. We have a waiting list for months ahead." She scans her computer screen. "The earliest we could fit you in would be September the twelfth at nine a.m.?"

I frown. "Are you absolutely sure you've got no booking?"

A woman with silver foil in her hair has turned to glance at me. She shares a surreptitious look with her posh friend. Suddenly I feel like some desperate wannabe trying to get into an exclusive club, pleading with the bouncer. A blush throbs in my cheeks.

"D'you mind if I call my friend? Just to check if there's been a mistake?"

She gives me a sympathetic nod as I ring Sophia. She's not picking up.

"Um, okay—I'll take the September slot," I say in a high, strained voice, and hurry out of the salon. I decide I'll head home—but shouldn't I give them space to work on their project? Feeling panicked, I call up Adam. I imagine them in bed together, his mobile ringing downstairs, unnoticed—but he picks up right away.

"You okay? I thought you were having a haircut."

"I was," I say. "But it got postponed." I wonder if I dare rant about her when she's in the room with him.

"Okay. By the way, you didn't tell me that Sophia and Finn are going on holiday at exactly the same time as us. Sophia was saying that we could all go to Villefranche together rather than Nice, and stay in the same hotel?"

"What?" My voice is sharp as a whip. I tell him we can chat more about it later and hang up.

A joint holiday? How am I supposed to handle a week with Finn? And why has Sophia mentioned it to Adam and not me? She's supposed to be *my* friend.

Is she my friend? I've been so dazzled, so grateful to have gotten close to her, that I've ignored a growing unease for some time, ever since she "forgot" to use condoms. The switches have entailed such a depth of trust. But even though I've worn her nightie, sprayed on her perfume, slept with her husband, how well do I really know her?

Her recent behavior has been so careless.

She should have asked me about the joint holiday before suggesting it to Adam.

She should have revealed *that thing* she and Adam shared in bed.

And she bloody shouldn't have made up a fake hair appointment as a ruse to get me out of my own house and have my partner all to herself.

I feel like the switches have been our pact on one level, but there's another shadow game here, some long-term play underneath, that I can't quite grasp.

I decide that I really must head home to confront her—when another idea grips me. I know it's risky and I know it's wrong. But even if I do talk to her, I bet Sophia will just give me gloss and smiles and pretty re-assurances. I have a better plan: I head for the Common at a swift pace, turning off at Murray Road and hurrying up toward number 186.

I check the driveway: there's no car. I ring the bell and peer in through the window. From across the street, a neighbor pruning his ceanothus glances over at me with suspicion. I'm relieved when their help, Séverine, appears.

"Sophia's not in," she says.

"She told me she would be," I say gaily. "I'll just wait in the back."

She shrugs, confused, and offers me a drink. While she makes the tea, I tell her that I need the toilet.

I don't have much time. The script meeting could end any minute. Séverine looks permanently bored. She seems unlikely to care enough to tell on me, but then again Sophia does inspire loyalty in people and I don't want to risk this getting back to her.

I hurry into the bedroom, grab Sophia's diary from the pile of books, and upend the whole lot, cursing.

I leave them be for now and flick forward through the diary pages.

Temptation tickles me. I know that what I'm doing is unethical, but I'd rather be unscrupulous than naïve.

Here it is:

We did a second switch and only just got away with it. It felt good to turn him into a slave to desire, hear him humiliated and begging for more. He's starting to annoy me recently. All this talk of his "feminism" when he's got Elena doing all the cooking, and while his script is good, the sole female in it is a blonde gangster babe who shoots villains while dressed in her lingerie.

Annoying? Really? You wouldn't guess that from the way she charms him. And it's easy for her to jeer at me for cooking but not all of us can afford a help to do it for us.

In bed with him, I get my revenge. I make him my slave.

This fetish—is slave meant to be a metaphor or is it literal? Does she order him around?

I still have his watch. I like to stroke it, to hold it in my palm and close my eyes and feel the faint vibrations of generations past.

What! That watch is worth enough to finance his bloody film, which would be a lot easier than her sorting out a producer.

I always suspected that she had taken it; I couldn't work out why. It doesn't sound as though her motives are mercenary. Has she fallen for him? Yet she finds him "annoying." Nothing makes sense.

The noise of a horn tooting on the road outside reminds me that I don't have forever to do this. I feel torn between wanting to seek out the watch and reading more of the diary. I flip back a few pages, coming across the newspaper clipping again. The one about the dead girl: Claudine Lambercier.

I spread out the delicate paper on the bed. I'm running out of time, so I snap a picture with my phone.

As I fold up the article, I make a slight tear—fuck. I quickly slot it back into the diary, resurrect the pile of books. I'm sweating, nervous, confused.

I hurry downstairs. Séverine says the tea's getting cold, and I take a polite sip. I tell her that I've spoken to Sophia and realized that she's busy doing something else, so there's no need to mention that I dropped by.

In the Vicomte Café, I sit down with a cup of Earl Grey. I'm still freaked out by my discoveries. Then I take a look at the article on my phone and scrawl a shaky translation in my notebook, using Google Translate.

A fire broke out at Maison Aubert, Villefranche, which has resulted in the tragic death of fifteen-year-old Claudine Lambercier.

The fire occurred around 11 p.m. on the evening of October 20th. Fortunately, other members of the household were able to escape. These included businessman Monsieur Charles Aubert, his son, Alain, and his staff. Claudine was locked into an upstairs bedroom. Staff attempted to break down the door and were forced to exit the house due to the risk to their own lives, leaving the teenage girl to perish. She is survived by her mother, Annie Lambercier, who previously worked as a nanny for the Aubert family.

I note that there are no details of her funeral, though maybe it's not the French way to include them. When I google the paper, *Le Villefranchois*, I discover it's only a local with a small circulation, and I can't find any other articles about the Lamberciers.

I enlarge the image of Claudine's face on my phone, but it's low-res and the pixels begin to blur. *How did Sophia know you*, I wonder, *and why has she kept the clipping for all these years?* The longer I look at Claudine's eyes, the more I feel an uneasy sense of familiarity, as though I know her from long ago, though I can't think why.

33.

ELENA

I wake up in the pitch-black, my heartbeat frantic. It takes a moment to realize that I'm at home in bed, in Wimbledon. Adam is snoring beside me. Two thirty-seven, says my mobile. It was just a nightmare.

I slip out of bed, head downstairs, make a hot chocolate. Lyra curls up on my lap in comfort.

When I try to go back to sleep a little while later, I can't drop off. The past is churning through my mind.

Adam wakes up at eight, all jazzy with nerves and excitement. Today is his Big Day: the meeting with the film producer. I help him pick out his outfit. We settle on a Hugo Boss suit with a dark shirt, the one I bought him last Christmas. He puts a tie on, then tears it off, declaring he wants to look like a creative, not a banker. I suggest a cravat, but he ends up looking like a posh poet and we both crease up with laughter.

Sophia comes by to collect him, dressed in a black power dress. She seems to sense my mood, giving me a hug and saying we should go for a drink later, "just us girls." I give Adam a flurry of kisses for good luck, then run upstairs and watch them from the bedroom window, walking down the road together, looking like such a glamorous couple.

————————

Adam and I had been dating three years when I found Lorraine's messages on his phone. He had lost his mobile and I found it down the side of the bed; as I fished it out, I saw the message flash up on the screen: **I want you back in my bed.** What the hell? I punched in his code and read the exchange. Lorraine was asking him to fuck her again, while Adam's messages were scared and contrite. **Please stop messaging me. I have a partner. It was a drunken mistake. I've never been so pissed in my life. I can't even remember much about it.** I read and reread them, hands trembling, piecing it all together.

It had happened the previous weekend. A one-night stand in Norfolk. After a funeral. Adam had been devastated when his boss had suddenly had a heart attack; he'd been something of a substitute father. I'd come down with the flu, which had forced me to stay home, so Adam had gone alone, stayed overnight after the Saturday service. He returned on Sunday evening looking red-eyed, haggard, hungover. Then I found the messages. For all my fury, I understood that he might have got wildly drunk, drowned his sorrows, lost control. But—with Lorraine? Lorraine who was *Lady Lorraine*, the colleague in his office whom he moaned about each day, who was *bourgeois, privileged*? I'd thought he hated her.

For the three years before that, Adam had been the jealous one. Anxious I'd run off and meet someone, as though I might repeat the sins of his mother. I'd had to reassure him constantly, or tell him to back off when he got suspicious of my close male friends like Anil. It felt like both a pressure and a comfort: jealousy showed he cared, I told myself. But after all that, he was the one who'd been unfaithful.

It was this discovery that had prompted our breakup and my six-month return to my parents' cottage in Shrewsbury. Adam spent most of that time texting me, calling, weeping, begging me to come back, swearing it would never happen again. As the months went by, I came to realize he was sincere. And I caved in, believed in his promise to be faithful. But now, thinking about it, I wonder if the switches have been a way of controlling a potential infidelity. If I orchestrate it, then I'm in charge. Yet I've set something in motion that feels increasingly out of control.

A call comes in on my phone.

I stir; it's Adam. He's nearly due to go into his film meeting, so I hope it's all okay.

"Elena?" he begs me, sounding breathless. "Can you do me a favor?"

Two hours later:

"I can't believe you did that!" Adam's only just opened the door but he's already ranting. His Scottish accent always sharpens when he's angry. "Elena? Elena? Where are you?"

In the kitchen, I nurse my mug of Earl Grey. Sensing tension, Lyra's ears prick and she slithers off my lap, padding off to another room.

This morning we were friends. Now, in the space of three hours, we've become enemies.

"It was my only chance to impress the producer," he rants and rages. "And I asked you to do me *one* favor!"

"We had a pact!" I flare up. "You said before that there'd be no more sudden calls where I had to drop everything and go look after her! You said she wouldn't be allowed to fire her carer without permission—your words, Adam, your promise. I had a deadline, I couldn't do it!"

"When you said you wanted to give up your job and do your proofreading, I supported you." Adam's voice becomes bitter. "Then, when I need you, you let me down."

I feel stung. Is that really the way he sees things? From my perspective, it's a completely warped version of events. "You don't take my work seriously—remember that dinner, when Sophia and Finn first came over, and you said, *some of us get to sit in cafés every day drinking coffee.*"

"What? I never said that!"

"You damn well did."

"Well, I was joking. I was just trying to ease the tension, they were new acquaintances."

"It didn't sound like a joke."

"But, seriously, this morning was so important—"

"I thought you still made it to the meeting," I say in concern. "I thought you went in."

"Yes, but once you said you couldn't go, I wasn't able to concentrate. I kept imagining Mum going hungry. I couldn't give it my best shot!" Adam's voice rises, angry tears flashing in his eyes. "You know how many years I've had to get up and commute to that stupid job so that we can have a good life, while you get to do what you enjoy—and let's face it, a café is a much nicer place to work than a bloody office. Maybe you just don't want me to succeed. Maybe you're jealous."

I gape at him in shock. I knew he found his job boring and tiring but I hadn't realized quite how much he hated it, how he had become resigned to that hate.

"Of course I want you to succeed. But I got upset about—your mum—and—the way you are with Sophia, it's like Lorraine all over again."

Adam blinks, taken aback by this curveball. To be honest, I'm surprised too. I hadn't meant to bring her up.

"What the hell has Lorraine got to do with this?" He regains momentum. "It's bullshit. You're bringing up something that has absolutely nothing to do with this issue, to distract from your crap behavior—"

"But actually I think it does—"

"Oh, fuck it," Adam says. "I'm going for a walk."

I start to protest but he storms away and there's the slam of the door and its echo in the silence.

I return to the kitchen. The argument spins and spins in my mind. When Adam called, it was the same old story: "There's no one to cook lunch for Mum, her carer's gone off in a huff, please can you go? Please, please, Elena . . ."

I did try, I really did. I set off down the hill, heading for Wimbledon station. It was starting to drizzle; I found my footsteps slowing. The thought of that long journey, of entering her luxurious house, making her tea like a servant while she sniped and snapped, reveling in the knowledge that she was holding back a huge sum of money—I just couldn't do it. My anger felt wild, animal. Here we were, spending weeks flat-hunting, finally settling on an ugly basement to move into when we handed back the Wimbledon house, when we could be paying a mortgage on our very own place. I was scared I'd shout at her, confront her. And then what?

So I turned back. I went home and made a cup of Earl Grey. I opened the window and listened to the birds and felt the summer breeze waft in. The minutes ticked by. I knew I needed to call Adam and let him know, but his call came through first.

What could I say to him? "Oh, by the way, I found out all about your mum's nasty secret because Sophia overheard when she was having sex with you." I could say that his mum had let it slip, but she might refute it or spin a conspiracy story around how I'd managed to find out, like I'd been snooping round her house. I suppose I could say that I simply overheard him on the phone that night, but I felt nervous, not actually being there, not knowing the details, relying on Sophia's blurry memory.

So I sent him a quick message saying I couldn't do it, but he should just go into his meeting and forget her for now. Hoping that he wouldn't see it until he came out.

Now, sitting in the kitchen with my cooling mug, I feel a sadness sweep over me. Our relationship has become both stronger and weaker since Sophia's revelation. Yes, Adam has chosen me over a big chunk of money and that overwhelms me at times. But any day now he could surely think to himself: *Well, if I just gave up Elena, I could move into a lovely house, find myself a posh blonde Mum likes, have a much nicer life.*

I thought I'd forgiven him for Lorraine. But perhaps a thorn has been left in my heart that's been festering steadily over the months, the years.

34.

SOPHIA

I'm standing in the sitting-room behind my easel, working on a portrait of Annabel Hamilton, when I feel a growl of pain low down in my abdomen. I frown. I pause. It ebbs away. I pick up my brush again.

Annabel is one of our neighbors. She saw my work on Instagram and offered a small fortune for me to paint her. She's a brunette in her early forties with a hook nose and strong cheekbones, but I haven't quite captured her essence. Then I realize what's wrong and I want to laugh. I've started to blend Elena into her features. Which triggers a memory, suddenly: last night I dreamed I'd had my baby and she was wailing in her cot. I picked her up, cradling her, only to look down in horror and see her face was Elena's, a grotesque adult head on a baby's body . . . And in my shock, I dropped her.

Get a grip. I mix a little more Burnt Sienna into the white, refining a tone for her skin.

I love painting. I love losing myself in strokes and colors and forgetting my cares. But my concentration is poor today. I'm thinking a lot about Adam and Elena, about whether I've made wrong moves, created a stalemate. Elena's withdrawn recently and I miss her. The film project was meant to tangle us all up, bring us closer together, not cleave the two of them apart. She seems suspicious, wary. I don't think she liked me finding out her fatal flaw, the lower-class background that she hides. It's useful to play on, but for now I want her to trust me.

She's been odd with Finn too. The morning after the second switch, he didn't say anything to me. So I figured it was mundane; missionary sex, most likely. But Elena came over and she seemed overwhelmed in his presence; minutes later, she was composed and saying polite good-byes. Maybe she, too, has a streak of Merteuil in her.

Last week, I faked a hairdresser appointment to get her out of the house, then paid Adam a surprise visit. Elena once mentioned that she wrote a diary on her laptop. While Adam was downstairs, I pretended I needed the bathroom, crept into their bedroom and flipped open her MacBook, found the file called *Diary 2022*. I sat on the bed, hammering in password after password—her date of birth, Adam's middle name; I'd done my detective work, having got him gradually to disclose all these details over the past few weeks. None of them worked. I was left frustrated and tantalized.

What might she have written about Finn? I'm used to women going crazy over him, but I don't want Elena for a rival. Then there's our group holiday in a fortnight: our accommodation and flights have been booked, but Adam says they might have to cancel because he and Elena have had a huge row. I've pushed him to resolve it, but he goes into a cagey sulk whenever I bring it up.

Perhaps it's better if it does fall through. France, the Riviera: a place where memories will hiss and hurt. Claudine Lambercier; scars from the past; pain and sacrifice.

Another flicker of discomfort, sudden and stabbing. The paintbrush slips and I blur a carefully composed contour.

"Annabel—excuse me, please," I say. She looks relieved to release her pose.

And then, in the toilet, I see the blood.

No.

I press the paper against myself, harder.

A period.

But—I'm a week late. The test was negative but I thought it was just too early. How, *how* can I be having my period?

As I wash my hands, my reflection sobs back at me, mascara streaking in black rivulets. That's it, I think dully. My baby girl wanted to be with me, but she couldn't find a seed. I feel as though she's been waiting, pressing to be with me. *I'm so sorry*, I tell her silently, *I'm so sorry*.

Now what? Adam and Elena are moving after the holiday. We can't do a switch if we're in Wimbledon and they're in Walthamstow. And I can't go back to square one; the thought of picking another couple, testing them, playing the game, is so tiring.

Adam is the one. Life confirmed it with a sign. It's got to be him.

Or maybe there's no hope for me. Maybe God is punishing me. Jeering at my uneven faith. My sobs become overwhelming, wracking my ribs.

"You okay?" Annabel's knock on the door is tentative.

How long have I been in here? Ages, no doubt, for her to come and try to find me in my own house.

"I just need five minutes," I manage.

"Of course."

I wash my face and half my makeup comes off. I open up the bathroom cabinet for a fresh supply. I pat on foundation. As I try to kohl my eyes, my fingers are trembling so hard and tears start to slip again, but I force them back, put the eyeliner on, smoky eyeshadow, lipstick. A Hitchcock blonde: that's the look I'm going for. Or do I just look like a clown?

I comb my hair slowly; I find it soothing. Breathe out. Unlock the door. Tread downstairs. Put on my mask again. Paint a smile on my face.

I hear myself making a teasing joke about how Annabel's not allowed to look until it's finished, telling my anecdote about how I learned portraiture directly from Tracey Emin. My fingers pick up a brush. I suffer a sudden wave of hatred for Annabel, mother of two bratty children. I feel like plunging the brush into red and smearing it across the canvas. I take control, dab it into the cream base I've mixed, smooth it over her obliterated cheekbone. In the act of repairing the damage, I lose myself again. For a few minutes I am oblivious.

Until I remember and the hurt stings again.

My darling baby girl. I want her so badly. She is a ghost before she has even been born.

Villefranche: it's our last chance. It might be a place of traumatic memories, but if I can just engineer one last switch, there is still hope. I have to persuade Adam to make up with Elena, and he must persuade her to go.

35.

ELENA

Meghan Roskilly: I'm on Instagram, seeking out Finn's infamous stalker. It might be a long shot, but I want to connect with her and see if I can find out more about Sophia.

Yet Meghan isn't showing up when I run a search in Sophia's list of followers. Sophia definitely mentioned that Meghan sent her messages on Instagram, so I wonder if she has a private account.

I'm sitting up in bed, scrolling, when I realize it's ten o'clock—nearly time to sleep. I yawn, then freeze at the sound of a key turning in the front door: Adam.

We've been living separate lives this past week, ever since our huge row. I'm sleeping in the spare bedroom at the front. I linger in bed in the mornings until he's left the house; in the evenings I eat early and head upstairs to my room before he comes in late from work. If we do pass each other, the silence is stony. Sometimes I feel like grabbing him and shouting that *he* should be the one to apologize. Normally when we fight and play this game, I'm the one who breaks first. Well, not this time.

Yet the sounds of him getting ready for bed, the whir of his electric toothbrush, fill me with sadness. This feels more lonely than being on my own. It's all so petty. Perhaps I should go to him, hug him, heal things: after all, what right do I have to be angry, after the way I've betrayed him with the switches? Sometimes I tell myself they were entirely justified, Finn for Lorraine, tit for tat; sometimes I wonder if what I've done is far, far worse.

His bedroom door slams. Soon I can hear faint rumbles through the wall. Normally his snoring annoys me but now I miss lying beside him, being aggravated.

At two a.m. I wake up with worries buzzing through my mind. We're due to move into that basement flat at the end of August. Will it still happen? And what about our holiday next week—I don't even know if Adam's canceled it.

I suffer an unexpected pang. I miss Sophia: being able to call her up, confide in her, meet for an emergency discussion in the Vicomte Café. Putting distance between us has been the right decision but the loss has left a void.

I pick up my phone again, even though I know the polluting light will only worsen my insomnia—and then an idea hits me.

I check Sophia's Instagram. The latest pic is a selfie of her wearing a new summer jacket: 356 likes. I can't see a like by Meghan, but maybe it's too recent. What about a post from last year, when Sophia and Finn were in Cornwall?

I scroll back to one from 2021, a photo of Sophia standing by the sea, her hair windblown. A comment, right at the top: **You look gorgeous as always X.** Meghan Roskilly—it's her! Her account is private. I follow her, praying she follows me back.

In the morning, when I wake up, I can hear Adam getting ready to go to work. The slam of the front door. I peel back the curtain. As though sensing my gaze, he suddenly turns to look up at me. Our eyes lock. I can't tell what his expression means. I quickly turn away.

I pick up my phone. An Instagram notification—Meghan has followed me back. I take a look at her photos. Shots of her with her dog, her husband, going on walks by the Cornish sea: she looks normal enough. I message her: Hi, I'm a friend of Sophia MacInnes. I think you knew her back in Cornwall? I love the portrait she did of you.

There is no portrait. I figure that if Meghan really is a stalker, she'll be curious and immediately message back.

A tentative tap on my bedroom door.

It's only five in the afternoon: Adam is back from work early.

"I've . . . got a present for you," he stumbles over his words. "It's downstairs. I mean, it's a present to say sorry."

Relief swims over me, though I keep my expression neutral as I follow him down into the kitchen. I'm suspicious: will it be more cheap chocolates? Having wanted to make up, I feel a resistance inside me: will this change anything?

Then I see the Penhaligon's bag. Expensive perfume! It isn't like Adam to splash out. I squirt the spray into the air. Adam sees the look on my face and becomes alarmed.

"I did get the right one, didn't I?"

I breathe in the beautiful blend of rose and jasmine, checking the label. *This is Sophia's perfume.*

Is he trolling me? For a moment I imagine him and Sophia together, concocting this wind-up, laughing at me.

"Are you mad at me?" I whisper.

"I smelled it on Sophia," he says.

Oh, God.

"And I realized she wears the same as you, the one you've started wearing recently . . . so I asked her where to get it." He frowns, seeing that I'm silent and trembling. I gaze straight into his eyes: does he know? Is this a game?

"Bloody pricey," Adam adds. "But God, it is a nice smell. Don't you like it?"

I think he's sincere. And it makes sense. My perfume was weak; hers much stronger. I delayed showering after the last switch. I've created a Pavlovian response: he must associate its floral sweetness with sexual fulfillment.

"You've spoiled me," I chide him gently.

"I . . . I'm sorry about everything. Sophia says the film meeting went well and there was no need for me to worry. She says I'm being unfair on you."

"Since when has Sophia been our marriage guidance counselor?" I say, my temper flaring.

Adam grabs the perfume and apologizes for forgetting to remove the price tag—as though keen to remind me how much he's spent on trying to make up—then squirts it onto my wrist playfully. I breathe it in again and a memory floods back, primal and visceral: Finn inside me, his mouth raw and hot against mine, his hands on my body.

"Let's have dinner."

I frown. A memory of Sophia's diary entry stings me: *All this talk of his "feminism" when he's got Elena doing all the cooking.* I shake her words off: this is my relationship, not hers. And yet I hear myself snapping, "I'm not in the mood to cook . . ."

"Let's eat out," he says.

"Okay," I enthuse, surprised. Up in my room, I change into a slinky black dress decorated with Japanese flowers.

Outside, Adam loops his arm through mine, a warmth flowing between us, a desire to forgive, as we stroll down toward the Village. He guides me into Carluccio's, a lovely little Italian on the corner. It's a place I've often wanted to dine at, but Adam's always said, "Too expensive." Now I smile at him, feeling appeased.

I say I need the Ladies. I scrub my hands several times, trying to override the scent and its associations, and give my phone a quick check. Meghan has read my message but there's no reply yet.

Upstairs, we sit at a candlelit table and Adam clasps my hands.

"I don't want you to be jealous of Sophia. You're the one who's been saying for months how great she is. She's married, El! She just thinks I have talent, that's her motivation," he adds in a hurt voice. "This is nothing like the Lorraine thing—you know that. That was just a one-off . . . years ago."

And he looks so sincere and contrite that I relent and touch his cheek.

"I'm sorry," I say. "It's just that—Sophia reminds me of Lorraine."

"Really?" Adam looks genuinely surprised. "I can't see that. I swear, I just want to work with her on the film."

"She is very beautiful," I mutter. *And I'm the one who put her in your bed.*

"You're the beautiful one," Adam replies. "You're my wench."

And he is looking handsome, I muse; better than he has in some time. There's a sparkle in his eye, a happy glow to his face. This film means the world to him, and yet . . .

"Have you thought any more about the holiday?" he asks tentatively. "Sophia's really keen for us all to go still."

I frown uneasily and he adds, "No rush. But it is next week . . . We can still get something back if we cancel, or maybe book a place separate from them?"

I pleat a napkin, refusing to commit.

"By the way," he changes the subject, "I'm planning to tell my boss that I want to go down to four days a week."

"What? But *why?*"

"So I have more time for film-making," he says. "Don't worry, we can still save for the deposit—I'll make it up with the money from the film. Sophia thinks it's a good idea and once the short is a success, they'll want a script for the full feature."

Sophia's diary haunts me once again, her verdict on Adam: *He's starting to annoy me.* A horrible fear has been worming its way into me recently: what if the switches were never the end goal, but a distraction from a con? What if they're scammers? What if Adam is the target and I'm just a vehicle to get to him?

"Adam," I say cautiously, "I remember that when you last did scripts, you got paid for just doing a treatment—it was about five K, wasn't it? Surely they should have paid you for the work you've done so far?"

"I will get paid when I've finished the script revisions the producer wants," he says. "But it's been a spec script up to now, 'cos I've been out of the industry for years. I've had to prove myself all over again."

"They have a huge house in Wimbledon and they're not even paying you up front? Adam, this is business."

"Sophia's put me in touch with a top film agent," Adam insists. "He's going to sort my contract—why would she do that if there was anything weird going on?"

"Okay," I sigh. As the waiter comes to collect our plates, I notice a string of message notifications has appeared on my phone—*Meghan has replied.*

I'm itching to look. I force myself to be patient.

"God, I love that perfume on you." Adam's pupils dilate. "Shall we bother with dessert or just go home for makeup sex?"

I smile, biting my lip, but then he whispers, "We could do *that thing* again . . ."

Oh, fuck. The second switch must have temporarily sated him, but now his hunger is back. I'm never going to escape this.

Adam gets up, declares he needs a slash.

Damn Sophia. I try to reassure myself that before the switches, I often put off sex with excuses of tiredness, headaches, my period. Sighing, I grab my phone and read through Meghan's replies.

> Sophia is not my friend.
> I don't know anything about a portrait.
> If I were you, I'd steer clear of Sophia & Finn.
> They're not to be trusted.

What the hell! This is supposed to be the woman who's *stalking* them and this is what she has to say about them? I think back to those letters Sophia received—were they fakes? Or was Meghan besotted before she gradually realized, like me, that Sophia seems to bring conflict and trouble with her? I try composing a reply: **Have you ever been asked to do a switch?** No, no, too risky. Instead I type: **Could I give you a call?**

Adam comes bounding up to the table and I put on a bright smile. We both order fig panna cottas and then I tell him, "You know, I think this holiday is a good idea. We should go."

"You do?" Adam looks delighted. "That's great!"

It is great, because I'm going to use this chance to find out everything I can about them. I'm tired of feeling lost and helpless, trying to work out what Sophia's game is: I need to act. If this is a scam, we could end up losing our flat. We could end up bankrupt. There's no way I can persuade Adam to back out of the film project without a cast-iron reason; I need to show, not tell. Evidence—that's what I must root out. And let's face it, it's easy to put on a glossy veneer over a dinner or a meeting, but a holiday means constant exposure. We'll be seeing them day to day; the cracks will show; they're bound to slip. I'm not about to let Sophia screw our lives up. I'm going to find out what her game is.

PART THREE

36.

ELENA

Finn and Sophia arrive in Villefranche a few days before us. Sophia's Instagram stream lights up with gorgeous photos of beach-paradise and bikini shots. There's still no sign of Finn in any of her photos. Perhaps she feels she's more promotable if she looks single, Adam jokes when I show him. **We can't wait for you guys to join us**, she keeps messaging me, signing off with exuberant streams of hearts and kisses.

On the flight over, Adam and I drink some wine, though I can't quite relax into my usual dreamy holiday mood. I keep thinking about Meghan.

The morning after our dinner, I found she'd deleted all her replies and unfollowed me. I sent her a tentative message; it remains unread. Now I feel deflated. I'm starting to wonder if perhaps Sophia was right, if Meghan is unhinged, or maybe suffering from trauma.

I want to enjoy this holiday but I'm still wary. Why did Sophia take Adam's watch? And then there's that strange article about Claudine Lambercier that disturbs me: Villefranche should be my chance to find out more. My French is very rusty, but I've been brushing up on it, re-learning the basics. Though I'm still pretty clumsy, it might be a useful tool.

In Nice, we catch the tram to the station, chugging past the rows of palm trees, the blue, blue sky. Then a train to Villefranche, where we descend

at the small station, perched in the hills. Our hotel, La Fiancée du Pi-
rate, is a little further up. As the taxi drives up the winding roads, we
catch glimpses of the dazzling sea below, rolling turquoise waves reflect-
ing the cloudless sky like a mirror.

The hotel wows me: it's much plusher than the usual flat we rent for
self-catering. I'm surprised Adam was willing to splash out, just as he did
on the perfume and the meal.

On the fourth floor we knock on the door of room 413. There's no
reply from Sophia and Finn. We're next door, in room 414. Inside, we
dump our luggage, open the windows, and enjoy the view from the
balcony.

A WhatsApp from Sophia: **Would you like to join us for an early dinner? At the Brasserie du Col—it's just a minute's walk away.**

When we arrive at the restaurant, she jumps up from the table, causing
the other diners to turn their heads.

"Elena! Adam!" She engulfs each of us in a hug.

She looks tanned and beautiful in a green sundress. Finn's wearing a
button-down shirt and linen trousers, sunglasses tucked into his pocket.
His deeper tan makes him look more delicious than ever. It's been some
weeks since I last saw him; he stands and kisses each of my cheeks the
French way. The feel of his arms around me is so solid. I resist the auto-
matic pulse of desire that he invokes, determined that my mind should
win out over my body, but it's not easy: he has such a powerful effect
on me.

We share dinner in a lively mood, though I feel stiff and wary at first.
Adam chats with enthusiasm about his current rewrite following some
edits from the producer. I watch him and Sophia closely, but she doesn't
flirt with him—unless she's being cautious in Finn's presence. As I get
tipsy, I make a silly joke punning on Monet and money that makes Finn
roar with laughter. It annoys me how much his reaction pleases me.

"Have you guys heard from Meghan recently?" I ask, during a lull in the conversation.

Finn starts. Adam looks confused for a moment, and then says: "Oh, that stalker woman you had trouble with."

Sophia takes a sip of wine and shrugs. "She's gone quiet recently, thank God."

Finn nods and they change the subject. *They're not to be trusted*, Meghan's words echo. Tonight, I notice, they're not being tactile. No kisses, no caresses, no hand casually brushing an arm, a thigh. Toward the end of dinner, Finn puts a hand over her glass: *"Assez*, Sophia."

Sophia's mentioned how controlling he can be, I muse uncomfortably. Her next suggestion, then, seems like a rebellion: she insists that we should all go swimming—it might be eight o'clock but the water's still warm. Finn shakes his head but the three of us clamor and override him, as though we're kids with a strict headmaster.

When the bill comes, I notice Adam looking at it a little anxiously and I narrow my eyes—but Finn immediately slaps down his card: "It's on us," he says, and Adam looks quietly relieved.

We get our costumes and towels from our rooms. On the beach, I feel self-conscious as I strip to my red swimsuit. Sophia's wearing a filmy black robe over her bikini. When she removes it, I catch sight of her skin and do a doubletake. As we wade into the water, I try not to stare at the red scars studding one shoulder and across one breast: they look like burns made by a cigarette. She must airbrush them out of her perfect Instagram photos, I realize.

Finn looks so beautiful in his black trunks, exuding Cary Grant cool. I can see the faint hairs on his tanned chest that I caressed during our nights together. I see Sophia watching me watch him, and I quickly look away.

The waves swirl around us; we splash each other, laughing.

"Don't go out too far," Finn says, as Sophia starts to swim away hard and fast.

So controlling, I think again, but then I see the look in his eyes.

———————

Later that night, I lie awake and analyze that look. The raw fear in it. Like a father concerned for his child. Not controlling, I correct myself, but over protective. Those scars: her last partner must have been such a bastard. That's why Finn is in the habit of looking out for her. That's why their relationship might have become stale: a responsibility for him, a safety net for her.

Next to me, Adam is snoring lightly; I push my earplugs in and cuddle up against him. The darkness is thick and dense; the hotel sports blackout curtains. I fall asleep with my head on his chest, but Finn invades my dreams and turns them red-hot . . .

Breakfast the next morning is jarring. Finn looks brooding; Sophia's mouth is a bunched rosebud. Both of them are wearing sunglasses and they speak in monosyllables. When Finn asks Sophia to pass the salt, she sulkily pushes it one inch toward me with her little finger, so that I have to pass it to him.

I feel unsettled and intrigued. I've never seen them like this before.

Adam raises his eyebrows at me across the table, looking uncomfortable.

"So," he says in a faux-cheerful voice, "Elena and I have made plans today to go to Antibes—we want to have lunch, see an old friend there. So we'll be off but see you guys later for dinner?"

"Sounds lovely," Sophia replies, pursing her lips. Are we being cruel, deserting her? Over the past few weeks, I've built her up in my head as a scheming bitch, but those scars have reminded me that she is still human. I wonder if I should offer support, but Adam is already strolling off impatiently, so I follow him. Back in our room, I send her a message: **Are you okay? Do you want to chat?**

"They clearly need some space," Adam says. "And we don't need them, do we? We don't have to talk film stuff all the time, we're here to have fun too."

I nod my head, checking my phone. My message has been read but she hasn't replied. Now I feel frustrated: I wanted to make progress today on unraveling what Sophia's intentions really are. I make a firm resolution that I'll have more success tomorrow.

Antibes is heavenly. We visit every year, but I always forget how exquisite the light is around here. After a few days on the Riviera, the medicinal cocktail of sun and sea and bliss begins to take effect on me. I relax in a way I never can elsewhere.

I remind myself that even if I'm planning to do some digging into Sophia and Finn, I do want to enjoy myself too. Our house move is set for a fortnight after we get back and summer will be over for us; this should be our Roaring Twenties.

We make our own fun and it's just like our traditional holiday. We swim in the sea, dry off in the sun, and head to a restaurant for an early lunch, where Adam has grilled tuna and I have a Salade Niçoise followed by Café Gourmand. Then we laze back on the beach, occasionally taking dips in the waves when it gets too hot. I stare out at the horizon, following the path of a distant ship, enjoying the lullaby shush of the sea.

It's the deepest moment of calm that we've shared for some time. But, as often happens in our relationship these days, our Eden doesn't last. At around two-thirty, we head back through the old town, the sunlight slanting through the narrow streets, and Adam checks his mobile. He realizes he's missed about half a dozen calls from Hilary. I make a thoughtless remark: "Can't we just have one holiday away from her?"

"She's my *mum*," Adam emphasizes, as he's done a hundred times before. "I can't switch her off."

I roll my eyes.

"It isn't her fault she's vulnerable," he hisses, and we're back repeating the same old argument, and I'm so close to telling him that I know about the money she's withholding—but I swallow it back.

On the train to the hotel, the sun pierces through the glass at a headache-inducing pitch. Countryside, beaches, little stations roll past.

Inside, we pass room 413. A *Do Not Disturb* sign is on the handle.

Adam opens up the doors to our balcony. Finn and Sophia's voices stream in. They're talking in French, their voices terse and sharp.

Adam frowns, taking out the wet towel and his trunks from his bag, hanging them up over the bath. I pull off my sandals with relief: they're too new and stiff and I'm getting slight blisters. I make a mental note to buy some plasters.

"*Oublie-là, c'est du passé!*" Sophia's voice is rising to a shout. "*Je ne peux pas,*" he replies. "*Laisse tomber,*" she says, three times over. I frown, picking up my phone, wondering if I should ring her.

Suddenly: the violent slam of their balcony door.

Then, from within their room, a bang against the wall.

And another. As though someone is punching it.

Adam and I stare at each other, wide-eyed, united in our shock, our own tensions trickling away. Silence: more shouting in French—

Bang! The violent noise is accompanied by a scream. As though someone has been thrown against the wall.

"What the . . . ?" Adam exclaims. "He's murdered her or something."

"Or her him," I say in shock, because I know Sophia's no damsel in distress.

"I'm going to check on them," Adam asserts. He's got that look on his face that signals he's going to play the hero, which I normally admire.

"We should," I agree, though I'm anxious, the full meaning of their French phrases eluding me. I know Sophia was telling him to forget something but I didn't catch much else. *What if he's found out about the switches? What if that's what they're arguing about?* I picture Adam storming in there and Finn telling him everything . . .

37.

ELENA

I listen to Adam banging loudly on their door, calling: "Sophia, what's going on?"

I dart out into the hallway, edging behind him as their door opens.

Sophia looks wild, disheveled, her hair like a scarecrow's. There's a nasty scratch, beaded with blood, on the left side of her face. She's breathing very hard.

"Sophia?" Adam touches her arm, and she flinches violently. He steps backward. "Sorry—but—are you okay?"

Behind her, Finn appears. He's dressed in shorts and looking far worse than she is. We drink in the scratches slashed across his chest and the black eye, red and swollen.

My eyes fall to the ironing board lying on the floor, one leg dented. So that's what he—or she—threw against the wall.

Finn's eyes are on me. There's no accusation in them. They are filled with pain, fear, remorse. I look away in shock.

This isn't about the switch, I realize. But what on earth are they arguing about, that it could come to this?

"Are you guys okay?" Adam asks again. "It's pretty claustrophobic in these rooms, isn't it? We could all go to the beach and chill out there."

"I think they might need some first aid," I say quietly.

"No, we don't!" Sophia bursts out angrily. "We're fine. We just got too hot. The air con's not working properly—and then it becomes so hard to *think*."

Silence. Broken by the audible hum of their air con, blasting out icy air. I feel stung, upset to have upset her further. They're both jittery as wild animals, bristling and ready to bite.

"Well, let's go to the beach," I say brightly. "Cool off in the sea."

"Right," says Sophia, trying to take control of her voice. She smooths her hands over her wild hair. The floor is littered with things that were flung in the fight and she picks up her hairbrush, the one with boar's bristles that she told me is the very best kind you can use. She pulls it through her hair slowly. The action seems to soothe her. She switches on a smile and suddenly she is Sophia again—the mask back on.

"Well, then. Let's all go. We'll be ready in twenty."

Back in our room, Adam and I pack towels and fresh swimwear into our bag.

"That was awful," I say in a low voice.

"I feel sorry for her," Adam whispers.

"He had worse injuries," I point out.

"But maybe they were made in self-defense," Adam hisses. "I've a good mind to go back in there and black his other eye!"

"Sshhh!" I hiss. "We don't know what's going on."

"It's not very feminist of you," Adam reprimands. "Taking the man's side."

"I'm not taking *any* side," I say. "All I know is that Sophia used to be in an abusive relationship, and Finn saved her from an evil guy. So I don't think he'd do that to her."

Adam looks a bit shocked as he digests the news. Her abused past is a secret I've kept from him so far; he's struggling to align it with his view of her as a happy, successful woman.

"Unless history is repeating itself," he says at last. "When was she with the abuser?"

"Oh, I don't know," I snap, picking up my phone. I search for Google Translate but I'm struggling to remember the exact phrases they spoke. There was one phrase that Sophia kept repeating, though, which has stuck in my head: *Je ne veux pas la* . . . What was it? *Voie? Voire?* That comes up as *I don't want to see her.*

Who is Sophia avoiding? Who would Finn want to make her visit? A relative? An ex? My questions keep mounting, and I need to start finding answers. But I can't help feeling deep disappointment. Knowledge is power, but knowledge can also be painful. It's hard to face the fact that Finn, beautiful Finn, might be an abuser.

The late-afternoon sun is more gentle after the daytime burn. On the beach, I sit down next to Sophia on a towel and give her a side-hug. The urge to mother her comes over me; in her vulnerable state, I'm suddenly conscious of the age gap between us, how much younger she is than me. She leans her head against my shoulder and I glance up at Finn, who's standing staring out to sea. "You okay?" I ask in a low voice.

She nods.

"D'you want to go get a coffee, talk about it?"

"Not now—but thank you." Her façade is up again: end of discussion. Adam strolls past Finn, bristling with hostility, walking down to the water.

Sophia takes out her sketchpad. I watch as her eyes flit between me and the page; she captures so much with a few strokes. She doesn't notice when Finn gives me a beseeching look, as though he's trying to say, *I'm not the villain here.* I observe how the act of drawing calms her. By early evening, we've all softened and I admire Sophia's sheaf of sketches. There's Finn, looking troubled, and me with a strained smile, but mostly they are of Adam: Adam in the sea, Adam shielding his face from the sun, Adam lounging on the beach, licking an ice cream, smiling, saying her name.

The next day, I propose a girls-only outing to the Picasso Museum. The thought of Adam and Finn having drinks together makes me feel a little nervous; I dread the start of a conversation that might speculate on strange happenings at night. But I want to get Sophia on her own, do some delving.

She's quiet on the train to Antibes, cooling her face with a white lace fan. Yet I can sense a growing agitation in her and she suddenly bursts out, "I hate being back in France!" I start to press her, ask if it's evoking bad memories, but the train pulls into Antibes station and Sophia changes the subject. "Did you know that when Lucian Freud met Picasso, Picasso told him that he liked to make women cry?" she says, her voice souring.

I wonder if she might declare we should boycott him altogether, but we carry on, walking round in uneasy silence. If we rejected all art by misogynists, I muse, the galleries and museums would be nearly empty.

In the museum, we climb the stone steps to the top floor. We sit down on the bench in the middle of a room full of his paintings and faun sculptures. I'm about to ask her about Finn when Sophia suddenly suggests it. The third switch.

My first thought is: *no way no way no way.*

"But what about Finn . . . is he hurting you?"

"Of course he's not," she laughs. She adjusts her sunglasses, which are holding back her hair. "We just needed to let off steam. All couples do."

Hmm. When Adam and I let off steam, we don't end up with scratches and bruises. I've been wondering if this is what the switches have really been about: a chance to escape Finn, secretly undermine him, a silent revenge.

"I'm fine. Please don't paint me as some tragic figure," she sighs. "If anything, Finn is too much of a gentleman."

"Okay," I say, relieved, but worried that she's just telling me what I want to hear, that Finn is not a bad person. "But what did you fight about?"

"An artist." She sighs again, as though the subject is tedious. "She's up and coming, she has an exhibition locally, he wants me to go . . . I said no."

"But who is she? His ex?"

"God, no! Finn doesn't have exes," Sophia asserts, which makes me dubious: how can a man that handsome not have exes? I wonder if she's attached to the idea that she's the only one true love he's ever had.

"So . . ." she cajoles, giving me a look. "What about the switch?"

"Well, we're moving," I reply. "We'll have to start packing, to get ready for the move."

I feel sad at this thought—it's too soon. I'm going to miss Sophia and Finn. But I'm also relieved to have a get-out. Life will be duller without them, but it will also be peaceful and sane again.

"But we can do it here," she says urgently. "It's easier—no creeping out in the night. We just swap key cards. The rooms are dark enough, aren't they? The rooms have blackout curtains."

Oh, fuck. Is that why she chose this hotel? Was she scheming that far back?

"But . . ."

"And look, if we take our key cards with us, the lights won't work, will they? They need to be in their slots for everything to come on. That's actually much easier than having to mess around with lightbulbs."

"I . . ."

"It will be our last chance," Sophia presses me.

I pause. Oh, God. I can sense she wants to persuade me but I'm not going to give in. I'm still trying to rebuild my relationship with Adam, and the risk of a third switch, with little proper planning, is way too dangerous. I'm on this holiday to observe them, not get tangled up in more games.

"I'm sorry," I reply. "But I just don't think it's a good idea."

38.

SOPHIA

Elena is resistant to my suggestion. I'm surprised: I thought she was hooked on the switches.

"But why?" I dig, softening my tone, playing therapist now.

"I . . . I just found them hard-going."

Hard-going? With my gorgeous, skillful husband?

"I thought I could compartmentalize them, but then I found I couldn't . . ." She trails off, a blush creeping up her cheeks.

"Because of Finn?" I nudge her gently. I can see from the look on her face that he means a lot to her, that just the mention of his name erodes the guard she's trying to put up.

"No. Well—yes. I . . ." She's conflicted: carrying a burden of angst, but not wanting to share.

Why has she stopped trusting me? I think back to that night we shared in Hemingway's in Wimbledon, before the switches. To Elena confiding in me, her eyes shining with such admiration, her hanging onto my every word.

"Why don't we go to the pub?" I suggest. "There's a good one just round the corner."

The Blue Lady Pub is a traditional English cozy place. Initially Elena opts for a Coke, but I persuade her that we're on holiday, we should be indulging. We order gin and tonics and text Adam and Finn to say we'll be a while longer. They send back a picture of them sunbathing together. Elena smiles, looking surprised and pleased that they've bonded.

"I'm sorry if things have got a bit weird between us," I say, knowing that "weird" is a word Adam tends to favor when describing things going wrong with Elena. "Honestly, I'm just working on the film with Adam because I admire his talent. That's all. And look, I'll admit—after the second switch, I did get a bit jealous. I mean, Finn came down the next morning and he was so euphoric . . ." I smile wistfully. "I don't know what you did to make him so happy."

I see her face light up in shock. *There: I've got her.*

She does care for him. More than she wants to reveal.

"But . . . he . . ."

"What?"

"I remember . . ." She hesitates and I give her space to fill with words. "Not long after the last switch, we were sitting in your garden, Finn came home from work—and it was obvious he didn't want me there. It felt horrible. I know it was just one night, but God, it was like being a teenager again, and you kiss some guy who says you're his goddess one day and the next he's with his friends and he ignores you. Yet it was stupid. I realize Finn had no idea."

"But he just had a really stressful week!" I improvise. "You're projecting, that bad mood had nothing to do with you. Listen. The morning after the switch, he gave me a good-morning kiss and said, 'Last night was incredible.'"

"Really?" Elena is fighting to control her elation. Then she frowns. "Well, Adam finds sex so good with you, I can't live up to it!"

I hear the barb in her voice. *Now we're talking.*

"He thinks I'm deliberately toying with him, withholding," she confesses.

I can't help but feel a flash of delight; she sees it. I quickly compose my features, berating myself: it's sheer vanity on my part. It's odd, though, that after seven years together, Elena has never discovered his latent fetish. It shows such a lack of imagination.

"There's *that thing* you do to him," she persists. "You won't tell me what it is, and it's made things hard."

"But I'm not sure what it is," I say. "I can't quite zone in on any specific act—I think he just means the overall mood of the night."

"Hmm."

I lower my eyes, feeling sheepish. By holding back, feigning ignorance, I still might win at this game. If I tell her, then she'll have all the cards in her hand. She and Adam might have amazing sex and then she'll lose her hunger for Finn, who has clearly made more of an impact on her in the bedroom than I realized.

Elena takes a big gulp of G&T and suddenly blurts out: "Doesn't the guilt get to you?"

It's such a silly question. Why do people want life experiences to be nice and simple?

"I think it's wrong to assume that switches are just about the joy of sex," I reply. "That's reductive and it's idealistic. I think it's about the pleasure and the pain and the guilt and the agony, a whole gamut, like all great life experiences are."

For the first time since we started our debate, I feel that I've penetrated her defenses. She looks thoughtful as I take a sip of drink, enjoying the challenge of persuading her. I love to play devil's advocate. In the story of Adam and Eve, I always admired the snake, inviting Eve to embrace experience rather than being cloistered in a garden. Since arriving in Villefranche, I've been unraveling. Now, with the burn of adrenaline, I'm feeling more like my real self.

"Have you ever read *Les Liaisons Dangereuses*?" I ask.

"Um, yes," she says, looking taken aback. "In translation. And I saw the film."

"My father hated me reading that book. I loved it. I read it over and over. There's that moment where Madame de Rosemonde is giving advice to Madame de Tourvel, who is heartbroken. She says something like 'we can't hope to be made happy by love. Men are made happy, we're made happy by the happiness we give them.' And that was the female lot of that time. Look at you right now. Adam's about to have this great film career, he's soaring, while you're pining over Finn and feeling sad despite the fact you had amazing sex."

Elena laughs in outrage. I've succeeded in riling her. "I'm not pining," she declares. "I'm on holiday, having a good time."

She's proving to be more stubborn than I expected. Now what? I suddenly feel lost and that fraying sensation returns.

"Damn it!" I burst out. "I can't believe you'd turn down such a great adventure. You always struck me as being sensible on the outside, wild underneath, both sides fighting it out. Don't let the boring side win."

A flash in her eyes: I've hit a nerve. But still, she remains unyielding, defenses up. She smiles, her finger circling a wet drinks mark on the table, as though she knows my game but she's just not going to play.

I offer to buy us more drinks, taking a moment at the bar to mull it over. I dissect the conversation, trying to find ammunition. Finn: that's all I really have to use as a weapon.

I return to our table with the drinks and say: "If you won't do the switch, can I ask you another favor?"

"That depends." She gives me a wary smile.

"Tomorrow, Finn is going to visit a woman, an artist," I say. "I was wondering if you could . . . follow him."

"Like a spy?" She laughs it off. "Or I could just offer to go with him?"

"No. If you do that, he'll cancel altogether. Just follow him. And look, if it doesn't work and you lose him, that's fine. But please, please can you try, just for me?"

"But why? Who is this artist?"

"Someone from our past. Someone I don't want to see and Finn does. I can't say any more—I'm sorry. It's kind of . . . personal."

Elena looks irked. Her eyes dwell on the scratch still healing on my cheek. I reach up, self-conscious, stroking the thin line of darkening scabs.

"I need to know more," she insists.

I recoil slightly. "This woman—she's someone Finn has known all his life, pretty much."

"But you don't want to see her yourself?"

"She's a bad person!" I blurt out, then swallow and fix a smile on my lips. I didn't mean to disclose that. "Well, maybe that's a bit harsh. I . . . would find it difficult to see her."

"Have you done something to her?" Her tone is almost goading.

"She's the one who's harmed someone!" My voice has risen again and Elena's face is bright with curiosity. Damn this. "Look. Please. Just follow him, if you can. I'd be so, so grateful—just to make sure Finn is okay."

"But what harm has she done you?"

"Let's drop this." I'm feeling sorry I ever brought it up—I'd expected a simple "yes" from Elena. "It's traumatic . . ."

"Okay," she relents, "I'll do it."

I'm so relieved that I lean over and give her a hug.

"Are you feeling better after yesterday?" she asks. I can hear genuine concern in her voice.

"I feel better around you," I say, and she squeezes my hand.

"You're sure that Finn isn't . . . giving you a hard time?" she asks.

I frown—is that what she's worried about? That they'll climb into bed and he'll beat her? Oh, for fuck's sake!

"Finn saved my life!" I cry, with a vehemence that makes her eyes widen. "He was the one who protected me from that—that bastard."

"I guess it must be hard, being back here with all those bad memories," she says.

Why is Elena so inquisitive, all of a sudden? Anyhow, we're not going there. As I keep reminding Finn, the past is past.

"Finn is a good person," I emphasize.

"So, when I follow him tomorrow, what should I look for?"

"I want to know where she lives, what she looks like," I say, unease mixing with the alcohol in my stomach, coalescing into pain.

There's a brief silence and I dread Elena's going to start digging again, when suddenly she asks, out of the blue: "How's Meghan? The woman who was stalking you?"

I shrug, wondering why she's brought that up for a second time. "Like I said—she's been quiet lately, thank goodness."

"That must be a relief." She bites her lip and I feel bewildered.

"Has she tried to get in touch with you?" I ask quickly.

"Oh, God, no," she replies and I feel a little reassured.

We're interrupted by Adam and Finn entering the bar, saying they've been missing us and we're having too much fun without them.

Immediately the mood changes. Elena gives Adam a kiss; with him by her side, she seems more relaxed. Finn is in a jovial mood; he gives me a warning look, as though to say: *behave.*

We order more drinks. I laugh and joke along with them, but I don't feel on top form. I'm deflated that I couldn't persuade her to do another switch, that I lacked subtlety, that I used such blunt arguments. Elena might seem weaker than me on the surface, but underneath she's stronger than I've realized.

She's warming to Finn, though. As he makes a risqué joke, she roars with tipsy laughter. It gives me hope. I see her gaze skirt his black eye. I shouldn't have done that. Being back here has been such a strain, waking up the ghost of Claudine, surrounded by the French language, memories stirred. It feels like we've lost the plot.

I ponder the sadness of repetition: why does life fall into the same patterns? People always like me when they meet me. At first sight, I'm gorgeous, glamorous, talented, charismatic. Sophia with her 6,000 followers and her house in Wimbledon and sexy husband and nice manner. But, at some point, sooner or later, I turn them off. I'm not always even sure when it happens. They see a crack, sense darkness, realize I'm a lot more fucked up than I first appear. And I become resentful—why can't they allow me to be human? I don't know anyone who's endured anything as bad as I have.

Our "great couple" act is fraying too. We kept it up in Wimbledon but here we keep forgetting the script. Perhaps, despite all these years of honing our act, we can't sever the past, form new selves, and expect them to stand up.

"Did you enjoy the Picasso Museum?" Adam is asking.

"Sophia isn't very impressed with him," says Elena and I smile, repeating my thoughts on him. Adam grins and nods in sympathy, though I roll my eyes because I can tell he's thinking *are there any white men left that I'm allowed to like?*

The conversation swims on, into chats about Matisse, tide times, good local restaurants, and I find myself falling quiet again.

Did I make the right decision, asking Elena to follow Finn when he goes to see N. tomorrow? I am enlisting her to be my proxy, to face what I cannot. The thought of Finn with her suddenly makes me want to cry, and I excuse myself. I return from the restroom with a smile on my face, and we drink into the twilight and order some food, and carrying on chatting and laughing, two happy couples on holiday.

39.

ELENA

I know that Sophia is a Catholic, but I've never seen her faith on such ardent display before. I'm sitting in a pew inside Église St.-Michel in Villefranche. It's one of those ancient stone churches, with stained-glass windows and a cool, hushed interior. An odd mixture of old-fashioned and kitsch. There are candles to light for prayers and a garish statue of the Madonna, her face painted in primary colors.

Adam is outside, taking photos of the view; as an atheist, he wasn't keen on hanging around. Sophia is on her knees, her head bowed. She's muttering, as though praying feverishly. Finn sits beside her, staring ahead. Confusion fogs my judgment again: just what sort of marriage do they have? What does she want so badly that she needs divine intervention?

In the early afternoon, I tell Adam that I have a headache and need to lie down. Adam says sure, he'll go with Sophia to the beach—they can chat more about the short.

Finn left a few minutes ago. We finished lunch and he said he needed to go for a walk. Sophia gave me a glance that signaled: *now*. She gazed at his retreating figure with a look of quiet fury.

And so I go after him. He's heading up the hill, walking the narrow, winding roads that characterize Villefranche.

I enjoyed standing up to Sophia yesterday. Her attempts to manipulate me were so transparent and I had to let her know I wasn't a pushover. If she wasn't going to tell me about the special thing she shares with Adam, I wasn't going to give a thing back. I'm glad I stopped confiding in her, didn't tell her everything about Lorraine; God knows how she might have used that ammunition to undermine us.

At the end of our chat, though, when she asked me to follow Finn, she suddenly looked so vulnerable that I felt an unexpected rush of affection for her. Secretly, I was pleased she'd asked me: it was a chance to find out more. But I knew that she wanted to feel she was in control, so I feigned reluctance, let her think she was coaxing me into it. I recall her words: *You always struck me as being sensible on the outside, wild underneath.* She's right. I am excited about following Finn.

At least I managed to get her to disclose something: her anger about this mystery artist who has done her "harm." I wonder if there really is traumatic history there, or if Sophia is just jealous. Maybe she sees her as a rival, another Meghan type.

I picture the artist as young, blonde-haired. I imagine Finn knocking on the door of her villa, her greeting him in paint-smeared clothes, giving him a flirty smile. They'll kiss wildly . . . Now I'm the one who's jealous.

I tell myself to calm down. Be cool, be detached.

If he sees me, I have excuses prepared: *I got lost, I caught sight of you, I thought you could help me work out where I am.*

But Finn doesn't look back. He just walks on, stopping to wipe his forehead, to take sips from a bottle of mineral water. There's something almost dogged in his steps. As he walks past the church, through the narrow, stone streets, up winding pathways framed by beautiful villas and abundant gardens, he seems to slow down even more, until finally I see him stop at a small black gate.

I'm at the bottom of the road and quickly step backward, hiding in an entry by a whitewashed wall. A little boy passes me, wheeling a bike, and I smile at him. I crane my head forward, peering at Finn.

He stands by that gate for some time before he opens it.

I edge closer, watch his figure move away through the greenery. The rap of his fist on the front door. A woman dressed in white lets him in. I strain to see her face—but she closes the door.

Feeling bold, I push open the gate. The garden is overgrown with trees, beautiful flowers wild in the long grass. The villa is small and it doesn't look as glossy as the others here, the white render a little cracked, one shutter broken.

I can hear voices; they're out in the back garden. I risk a look through a window, into a cozy sitting-room, praying there's nobody else inside. On the wall are numerous framed photographs. One catches my eye, of a small boy with dark hair and a gappy-toothed grin. Is that *Finn*? For a moment I contemplate creeping into the villa, but that would be going too far.

Their voices grow louder, higher. Intrigued, I follow the path—little slabs of stone that peek through the grass—round to another wooden gate that leads to the back garden.

I pause. If I open it, it'll creak, they'll hear—that's no good.

Finn is speaking French. The woman's voice sounds odd, wavering, as though she's weak or ill. Maybe he is bullying her in some way.

I realize that there's an easier way for me to watch them. The fence surrounding the villa is run-down and straggling; I circle back and follow it round, ducking my head to wriggle beneath a tree bearing wrinkled pears. Leaves and twigs brush my hair. I find a gap, a few broken slats that I can peer through, hoping they don't spot me.

The sight before me surprises me.

A woman is sitting on a wrought-iron chair on the terrace. She's not what I expected.

She's elderly, perhaps in her sixties or seventies, her tanned skin wrinkled, her white hair in a bun. She's wearing a white cotton dress. Is she the artist?

Finn is kneeling before her, his head in her lap. She strokes his hair softly, muttering in French. I hear her say the name "Alain" a few times as well as "Finn." He lifts his head. I can see from his profile that he is weeping.

I walk away hastily, the sight of them imprinted on my retinas. Pushing back through the greenery to the path, I hurry down to the main track. I stand by the black railing at a viewing point, staring out over the beach at figures swimming in the sea, bright costumes and trunks like darting fish, the cries of joy and excitement.

Who are you, Finn? I wonder. *Who is that woman? An ex-lover? Your mother? A relative?*

After some time, I turn and see Finn slowly walking down the path from the house. I set off downhill before he can see me—but then I hear his footsteps quickening, his voice calling my name.

I turn and feign surprise.

"Elena." He manages a smile.

"How are you?" I ask him, swallowing.

"I'm fine," he says, his voice frail, as though he has aged by decades since the encounter.

An awkward silence.

"Would you like some ice cream?" he asks. "There's a place just along here. Let me treat you."

"Sure," I say. We go to a little kiosk framed by bougainvillea and stop to eat our cones by the railing. The ice cream is delicious and our silence seems companionable. I'm about to delve and ask if he has a relative here, or if there are any local artists he admires—but when I glance over at him, I see that he's staring out to sea and tears are rolling down his cheeks. He smears them away, carries on eating his ice cream, refusing to look at me. Halfway through, he abandons it, tossing the rest of the cone into the vegetation.

All my anger toward him dissolves. I want to hold him. *Oh, Finn.* I want to kiss him better.

I finish my ice cream and, with great control, touch his face gently, careful of the bruising around his eye. "It looks sore."

He gives me a broken smile. "We should never have come here," he says. "I told her we should never have come."

Back at the hotel, I sit on the bed, blinking back tears, feeling oddly emotional about Finn's mysterious meltdown. Adam's texted, asking if I'm okay, and I need to reply. I'm just opening up a fresh box of plasters to re-line my sandals, when suddenly it hits me—I heard the old woman say *Alain*. I've seen that name before.

I pick up my mobile, flipping frantically through photos. Here it is: the article I found tucked into Sophia's diary, which detailed the death of Claudine Lambercier. I cut and paste it into Google Translate again.

> The fire occurred around 11 p.m. on the evening of October 20. Fortunately, other members of the household were able to escape. These included businessman Monsieur Charles Aubert, his son, Alain, and his staff.

I sit and ponder: surely there's a connection? Did the old woman know Claudine, the Aubert family? Is this connected to the "harm" Sophia thinks she has done? I could speak to Finn about it, but he and Sophia are so evasive. Maybe I should pay a visit to the artist myself . . .

40.

ELENA

I'm in the sea with Finn. He splashes me playfully and I dash water right back at him. The sun threads gold glints into his dark hair, shines on the beads of water on his chest. I feel his eyes on me, traveling over my navy swimsuit, his faint blush as he catches me noticing. His next splash is harder and I nearly go under. "Whoah!" he laughs, wading over, his palm on my back as he steadies me.

I don't so much want to kiss him as shake him. I want to whisper, "You're flirting with me and you've no idea what we've shared. We've made love in your bed; you've told me you love me."

"It's so lovely and warm!" Sophia joins us, sporting a tiny pink bikini. The moment has passed.

After swimming for a while, we head back to the beach. Sophia mouths, "Private chat." We go to get some ice creams.

"I did follow Finn," I say, and I relay how emotional he became after seeing the old woman. It feels like a betrayal, describing his private moment, but I want to see how Sophia reacts. Her face remains a mask but something flashes in her eyes that I can't quite pinpoint—fear? Unease?

"I told him that going there would make him sad," she sighs. "Finn is in love with ghosts." There's a barb of jealousy in her voice.

"Which ghosts? What d'you mean? What did that old woman do to you?" I press her, but Sophia doesn't reply. She's turned to look at Finn; I follow her gaze. My hunger for him overwhelms me. I want him like I've never wanted anyone before.

"Let's do a third switch," I say impulsively.

To my surprise, a brief look of envy darkens her face. Her expression changes so fast I wonder if I imagined it. A moment later she's all beaming smiles again, and replies exuberantly, "Okay—let's do it!"

As she hugs me, my own sense of insecurity rears its head: is it ridiculous to let her spend another night with Adam? Yet, as I gaze over at Finn in the water, I realize that my desire for him outweighs my jealousy.

Sophia is back on top form tonight. We're all out drinking together; she sparkles with beauty and vivaciousness. I'm subdued. I keep holding Adam's hand tight; I can't look at Finn. I can't pretend this time, as I did with the last switch, that I've been persuaded, trying to blur my guilt by shifting responsibility onto Sophia.

I made the decision this time.

I want this. I want Finn. He's a drug I can't give up.

I keep repeating what she told me to try and reassure myself: *it will be our last chance.*

The following night, the fourth night of our holiday, I slip out of my room just after midnight.

Sophia and I meet in the corridor as planned. She gives me an impish smile. We've both got our hair tied up because mine has grown longer than hers over the last month. We're wearing identical hotel robes. Underneath mine I'm wearing her white silky nightdress, while she's borrowed one of my T-shirts and a pair of my knickers. The same perfume dances from our skin; Sophia was amused when I explained Adam's recent gift. She's carrying condoms in her pocket; I made sure of that.

It's all been planned at such short notice, without our notebooks, without our lists to tick, and I have this nervy feeling we've forgotten something.

Shaking, I put my card into the door of 413, wincing at the buzz as it unlocks. The triangle of light from the hallway is lost in blackness as I shut the door behind me.

I fumble, find the card in its slot, and remove it. Now I have both key cards. I wait for my eyes to adjust to the dark when suddenly there's a noise—

The bathroom door opens.

A figure comes out.

I let out a scream.

"Sophia? The lights suddenly went out." Finn's fingers curl around my shoulders.

Is that "Sophia" ironic or genuine? It's too dark to see the expression on his face.

I feel him prize the key cards from my hands. My heart is racing, my hands clammy. If he reinserts the key card, I'll just make a bolt for the door and run.

But the dark remains and there's just the sound of our breathing and suddenly he's kissing me, pushing me against the wall, hard up against me. Oh, it's so good to feel his mouth on mine after months of wanting him.

"Sophia," he whispers, voice ragged in my ear. I feel myself melting against him, my confusion no longer sharp but blurry, desire taking over. He seizes one of my hands, tugs me forward—I nearly fall and he grabs hold of me tight, whispering, "*Fais gaffe.*" I realize he is steering me toward the bed. I hear the rustle as he tugs away the duvet; I lie down on my back. The bounce of the mattress as he kneels beside me, pulling me up the bed, and—oh, God—one of my arms is being stretched backward, pinned in place by some kind of tie.

"But . . ." I try to protest.

"What?" he whispers, biting my ear. "You said it was what you wanted, Sophia. You told me it was your fantasy."

I can hear my breath coming fast and shallow. I feel helpless as he pulls my other arm back taut, tying that too. And, oh, fuck, my hairband has come loose, my hair falling down around my cheeks.

Then: his breath is on my cheek, his fingers at my throat—and I realize *that I forgot to put the crucifix on*. What if Sophia's gone into Adam's room wearing hers?

"Where did your crucifix go? I hope it's a sign you're still feeling liberated and sexy?"

I moan and he pushes up my nightie, stroking my thighs leisurely.

"How come you were outside in the corridor?" he asks. "Did some other man catch your eye?"

"No," I whisper.

He leans in, kisses me possessively. "Are you sure?"

"Yes," I whisper. "I just . . ." I'm scared my voice is going to give me away any minute. *I need to get through this before he realizes*, I think in panic. *Just make it happen quick and get out of here.* My fear is now sharper than my desire. I arch up, giving him a kiss, and he lets out a groan of pleasure.

He starts caressing me, playing that delicious, unbearable teasing game he played last time.

"I'm not going to untie you until you come," he whispers, brushing his lips over my thighs.

But each time I'm close, he pauses, until my whole body is flooded with heat, my wrists rubbing against the ties as I writhe and squirm. *"Please,"* I beg him. I try to think of the French: *S'il vous plaît.* Fear kicks in again, censoring me: I stop speaking and just moan.

Finally, he relents, flickering his tongue against me, bringing me to climax. He comes up to the pillow, kissing me fiercely, my breath fluttery against his. I no longer want to escape. I'm back in that place only he can take me to: one of complete surrender, where I feel I would do anything for him.

I tug at my ties. "Untie me?" I whisper.

"No. Not yet." His mouth curves against mine in a smiling kiss. "We can negotiate. You offer me a reward for untying you, and I'll see if it appeals."

The silence burns. I'm dizzy with desire, fraught with anxiety, terrified of the risk I take every time I speak.

"Come on," he teases me.

I think of our first night together, the way he pushed my head down.

"I could taste you," I whisper.

"You could do what?" He brushes his lips against mine.

"Taste you." I raise my voice.

Silence.

"Elena," he says softly.

I freeze. He runs a palm up and down my right thigh. He's recognized my voice—oh, God, oh, God. I yank at the ties, cry out in pain.

"I'm not Elena." I attempt to mimic Sophia's voice, failing miserably.

I hear the creak as he rises from the bed, his footsteps. What's he doing? The sound of his return, a click—and suddenly, a shocking flood of light. I freeze up. He must have re-inserted the key card. We stare at each other, blinking, shocked. My nightie is curled up around my waist—I want to pull it down, suddenly embarrassed by the harshness of the glare, of what it reveals. I'm expecting Finn's anger, but instead he looks amused. I realize he's not surprised to see me there.

"You know," I say.

"I know," he says.

"You mustn't tell her," I cry, because he can't know, surely, that I am in his bed and she is in Adam's. "Sophia doesn't know. She's gone for a drink. She texted me and said she couldn't sleep," I improvise. "She's in the downstairs bar."

"I'm sure she is," he says, but I can't tell from his tone if he believes me or not.

I want him to untie me, but I have a feeling he won't agree to it until

I've answered all his questions. The tying, the teasing—is it all his punishment of me?

"How long have you known?" I whisper.

"Since the first night you came over," he replies. "Back in Wimbledon."

"The first night?"

What the hell? Is he serious? He's had me completely fooled . . .
I've been in bed with him three times and on every single occasion *he's
played me.*

"I enjoyed it very much," he whispers, stroking my leg with one finger.
I shiver; in the light his movements seem much more potent. "I didn't
want it to stop."

"But how did you know?"

"I saw something in Sophia's notebook that looked odd. And then I
saw her creep out on the first night. I got up to go to the bathroom—only
to catch sight of you coming up the stairs. Then I realized what game you
two were up to." His tone is reasonable, even affectionate. "I knew I had
to make a quick decision, so I decided to play along."

My mind gallops through all our past interactions, all my nerves and
angst and guilt. There were clues, I suppose: the way he flirted with me at
the dinner at their house, the *Lady Macbeth* fantasy. But he played it so
straight I didn't see it. I feel such an idiot for thinking we'd tricked him.

"You've tricked us!" I burst out and he laughs.

"That's ironic, don't you think?"

"Ha . . . so . . . you know she's with Adam?" I ask nervously.

I picture them next door, half scared Finn will jump up and bang on
the door and drag him out.

"I accept it," Finn says, frowning.

"But does Adam know?" *Are the men in this together? Turning the tables
on us?*

"I have no idea," he says, and I *think* he's being straight with me. "It
would seem not."

"You're not jealous?"

Finn smiles. "Well, I get to be with you, so that makes the exchange worthwhile." He brushes his lips against my neck. "You're a beautiful woman, Elena."

My heart is singing with his words, but I say: "You must untie me now. Please."

"I'm enjoying having you here, under my power," he says, his eyes traveling over me, the wicked bastard.

"Finn."

He sighs, then undoes each tie, and I feel relief as I rub my wrists, pulling down my nightie.

"You're free to go," he says, his voice colder.

But I can't leave. Not like this, not when so many questions are whirling in my mind, memories being rewritten. He said *I love you* knowing that I was me: did he mean it? Or was it just part of the game, fooling me back? He ignored me knowing that it was me too. And there's an excitement tingling inside me: that chemistry between us, that connection, wasn't the result of him imagining I was his wife.

It was real. It was us.

"Are you mad at me?" I ask warily.

His face softens, his voice becoming quieter now. "Of course I'm not. I got to spend three nights with you."

We stare at each other, nervous, guarded, with no darkness, no lies to cover up feelings.

"I'm guessing you must have liked it too," he whispers, circling my collarbone with the tip of his finger. "If you came back for more."

Telling him that it was the most amazing sex of my life will make me vulnerable. All I can manage is a nod.

"That second night—it was particularly special," he goes on. "I remember that, a few days later, you came to see Sophia. I'd just come in from work." His eyes are still fixed on his finger, still circling my skin.

"You ignored me," I say quietly. "You'd had a really stressful day, you said."

"I was pretending," he said. "It was all too much for me. You were the stress. I wanted to walk over and kiss you and—take you right there." Suddenly he looks me straight in the eye. "But Sophia would have killed us both."

A wild joy begins to beat in my heart.

"I've been wanting you ever since," he goes on, moving closer. "I've been willing Sophia and you to do another switch. The weeks kept going by. It was agony. I thought we'd never get another chance. This morning, in the sea, I just wanted to grab you."

"I've been fantasizing about you too," I say, and I almost laugh, it's such an understatement.

He leans in to kiss me but I put a finger to his lips.

"Hang on, what about the night of the second switch? You said there was an intruder. I nearly had a heart attack . . . what was that all about?"

Finn is unabashed, his eyes glittering with wickedness.

"So you were just winding me up!" I give him a cross, playful slap on the cheek—and he flinches dramatically. I gaze at his bruised eye, mortified. "I'm sorry, God—sorry!"

"I'll forgive you if you give me a kiss," he says solemnly. I press my lips to his. As his hands roam over my body, I ask him softly if we can turn off the light. I crave the liberation of anonymity, the loss of inhibitions and cares. There is a fleeting regret: I loved us being strangers, the freedom and danger of the game. Now that we both know what we're doing, the betrayal seems greater.

At the same time, his caresses feel much more intimate now that I know they're intended for me, not his wife. He kisses me feverishly, entering me, and our lovemaking feels more ecstatic than ever. As we climax together, my head fills with stars. I want to say out loud, *I love you, I love you, I love you.* He stays inside me a while before withdrawing; we clutch each other tightly, breathless and wondrous that it can be this good.

"Why did you and Sophia fight?" I ask tentatively.

Finn pauses. I feel his guard coming up.

"Why did you follow me when I went to see my friend?"

"Who was that woman?"

"Answer me first."

He and Sophia seem to have turned the deflection of questions into an art form. Well, two can play at that game: I'm not explaining either. "It was painful, seeing you cry." I gently kiss his cheek, his eyelids, his bruising, his lips.

"Sophia and I fight like that once or twice a year," he relents. "Everything builds up and we just explode, I guess, and go a little crazy. It's purifying. Cathartic."

I frown into his chest, a little jealous that their relationship could be so passionate.

"I didn't hurt her, by the way—the scratch was self-defense. I was trying to push her away. I'd never hurt her. I've always protected her, I always will. Sometimes it's easy to forget what she's been through. Some people would have ended up in a psychiatric ward, or in prison."

Prison, I think sleepily. Why? Is he implying she's committed a crime? I feel chastised. Perhaps I've been hard on her, cooling down our friendship. Perhaps she means well.

"Will you tell Sophia that you know I know?" he asks.

"What do you think?"

"I think it's best to keep it a secret between us," he whispers, and we seal the pact with a kiss.

"I don't think Adam's guessed," I whisper.

"Can't tell the difference between his lover and a friend—more fool him," Finn says curtly.

"Oh, that's cruel," I say, with a stab of guilt, but Finn looks unrepentant.

"I saw a photo of you," he changes the subject. "When we were over at yours—the one on the kitchen noticeboard, of you as a little girl, with your mother on the beach."

"Oh, that one." I realize that was the dinner they came to the first night we met. I feel warm again, realizing he was interested way back then.

"Is that where you grew up—by the sea?"

"That was just a holiday we went on. I grew up in Shrewsbury . . ."

"Were you a good girl at school or a bad girl?"

I laugh. "Both."

"How?"

"Well, I was pretty wild for a while. My parents didn't earn much . . ." There's no point in trying to pretend; Sophia will have told him. "I was going out partying with a bad crowd all the time, my grades were sliding. Mum gave me the talking-to of my life. She told me that if I wasted this opportunity now, I'd end up like her, stuck in a rut. So I changed overnight. I think I suddenly saw my future, two possible paths, and I became a total square, worked really hard, got into Cambridge. My mum cried the day the letter came. I think she was prouder than I was. Getting in was better than being there . . ." I trail off, thinking of all the privileged, posh types I grated against.

"I grew up in France," Finn surprises me by saying. "Here it's not like the British class system where you can literally place someone's class within a few sentences. The French language isn't as cruel."

"But which region?" I ask softly. "Near here?" I think of the old woman, eager to know more, to ask him a hundred questions, but he gives me a dreamy kiss, distracting me.

"You're my smart Elena," he says, and I nearly die at that *my*. "My smart and kind Elena. The way you looked after Sophia the other day, on the beach—it was touching." He strokes my face. "How long do we have left together?"

I check the time: the night's gone so fast.

"Not much," I whisper sadly.

Finn rolls on top of me, biting my ear. "I'm torn between wanting to make love to you and wanting to fuck you." He sighs. "I just wish you were in my bed every night." We begin again and this time he stares very intently into my eyes, savoring every degree of my desire as he guides me into complete abandonment . . .

41.

ELENA

The next day I wake up next to Adam feeling euphoric. I found him sleeping deeply when I slipped back into the room last night; I think we got away with it. I'm nervous about breakfast, of maintaining an act in a group. I'm not like Sophia and Finn; I'm not great at hiding my feelings. I plug in my earphones and wander down to the beach. Opera unfurls as I watch the sun rise in a blaze of beauty, tentative at first, then glorious and radiant. My heart feels softened, all my senses refined, and every so often a smile breaks across my face.

At lunch, I put on sunglasses but my face keeps flushing. Thankfully it's a hot, sticky day, 89 degrees. Adam keeps yawning despite a lie-in. Sophia must have tired him out.

Beneath the table, I feel Finn's bare ankle rub against mine. He gives me a secret smile and I smile back.

"By the way," Sophia says casually, putting a possessive hand on his arm, "Finn and I are going to do our own thing this afternoon, if that's okay with you guys. We need some us-time."

"Sure."

Adam and I end up sitting on the beach together. I furrow my fingers through the sand, my euphoria flattened. I feel ridiculously jealous that Finn is with Sophia, and as weirded out as ever: why is she behaving so competitively when she's the one who suggested the switch? Is it a game between them and I'm just the subplot? Something to jazz up their lives? And who was that old woman Finn went to visit, who has a link with Claudine? He told me nothing last night and I was too distracted by ecstasy to care. Now I feel pissed off.

"I need to go for a walk," I tell Adam. "I want to go by myself."

"Okay." He shrugs, looking a bit sulky.

"Hey, I won't be long," I appease him.

I wander up through the hills. It takes me a little while to find the villa. I follow a few wrong turns and curse in frustration; then, doubling back, I realize it wasn't as far up as I remembered. It's turning into a scorcher of a day; the burn of the sun seems to be intensifying by the minute.

Here I am, at last. Standing at the gate.

A cat is here this time, sunbathing on the grass. I reach down and stroke his dark gray fur, warmed by the heat, and he purrs.

I go up to the door, muster my courage, and knock loudly.

There's a long pause before the elderly woman appears. Up close, her face is like an old apple, creased with wrinkles.

"*Puis-je avoir un verre d'eau, s'il vous plaît?*" I learned the phrases on Google Translate on the way up, but the syllables slip and slide uneasily in my mouth.

"*Pardon?*" She looks utterly bewildered.

"I was wondering if you had a glass of *eau*—water? I am really thirsty— *j'ai soif.*" I wave up at the sky; it's such a hot day that surely it isn't entirely crazy of me to knock and ask this?

Though her forehead is creased into a frown, there's warmth in her brown eyes. I'm sure I recognize Finn in their darkness, in the length of her lashes, and I break into a smile. It seems to reassure her. She says, "Wait here."

As she heads for the kitchen, I feel sheepish, for her steps are slow and doddery. I step into the cool villa, scanning my eyes around. Where is the room with the photos? I want to see that one of the boy who looked like Finn.

The cat slinks in and sits in the doorway, gazing at me with huge yellow eyes.

The woman returns with the water, looking startled to see I've entered. I give her another big, reassuring smile and glug back half of it.

She watches me; the cat watches me.

"I . . ." Nerves kick in; I wish my French wasn't so basic. "I'm *une amie* of Finn's," I say at last.

At his name, her eyes widen.

"Do you know him well?" I manage. "Finn—you are close—*proche?*"

Now she looks a bit suspicious, as if to say: *If you're such a good friend, why are you asking me this?*

"*Je suis en vacances.*" I parrot some of the useful phrases I learned. "*Avec . . . avec Finn. Je suis* Elena."

"*Elena!* Oh! You are his *amie* Elena!" she says, her face lighting up. So Finn has spoken to her about me. "I'm Annie."

Annie. Could she be Annie Lambercier, the woman mentioned in the article?

"Is Finn . . . your *ami?*"

"Like a son to me," she replies. "I was his *nounou.*"

"*Nounou?*" Is that a term of affection? I start to type it into Google with one finger when she interjects:

"Nanny. I have some English," she adds hesitantly. "I used to be very . . . *courant* . . . fluent, but I'm a little out of practice."

A pause between us: as if she's mulling over whether to usher me out of here or to be polite and invite me in as a guest. I have to seize the moment. Through an open door, I can see into the lounge and the sweep of photographs on the wall.

"Oh, that looks like Finn when he was a boy!" I push aside my natural shyness and enter boldly.

She follows me in and I point at the photo: it *is* Finn. Finn in school uniform, next to a little girl in a white dress. Behind them, looking grim-faced, is a man with a mustache and a cruel mouth.

"Finn," she says, nodding. "Alain."

"Oh!" It's then I realize what Annie means: *Finn* is *Alain*. My heart flurries. So that's why I can't find out much about his past on Google. He must have used both names.

"*Ici.*" She sits down, patting the sofa, growing more friendly by the minute, as though pleased to have company. "Would you like to see more?"

"I'd love to—thank you!"

She shuffles over to a cabinet and rifles around, pulling out some faded brown A4 envelopes. Sitting next to me, she pulls out sheafs of photos, sorting through them, checking the dates scrawled on the back. There are more pictures of Finn, which show him evolving into a handsome, sulky teenager. There's a girl, a few years younger, always by his side, clutching his hand or gazing at him with such deep admiration. She looks familiar: those dark eyes, the halo of black curls around her shoulders.

I start. Is she *Claudine Lambercier*? I wish I could check against the article on my phone, but I'd swear it's her. "Claudine," I murmur quietly, seeing how Annie responds.

Her whole body tenses up.

Silence. The moment feels so delicate, it seems best to wait. My heart is beating: am I right, am I right?

"Has Finn told you about her?" she asks.

"He's confided in me a little," I lie.

Annie raises an eyebrow in surprise, then nods. I tap the photo of the stern-looking man and ask her who he is.

"Monsieur Charles Aubert. *Mon amant.* Finn's father."

"Wow."

"That's me next to him. Wasn't I *jolie*?"

"*Très belle.*" She does look gorgeous and glamorous in a pink dress, her dark chair coiled in a chignon.

"I fell in love when I was *vingt-huit*. Monsieur Aubert was wealthy, a businessman. It was a big error. I wish I could tell my old self not to be so *idiote*."

"He was a bad man—*mal*?" I ask.

She purses her lips. "*Un méchant.* He had a wife."

"Finn's mother?"

She nods, then looks guilty, guarded. "She died when Finn was still a boy. I felt *vraiment désolée* because I had been with her husband. And Claudine was inside me."

"Claudine was your daughter?"

"Yes."

Which means she was Finn's half-sister. No wonder he looked so haggard yesterday, no wonder he was weeping. To lose your mother, and your sister too: what a weight of grief to work through.

"We went to live with him, Claudine and I . . . and I became Alain's *nounou.*"

I wonder how Finn felt about that, having his mother usurped by a new woman, one who had been having an affair with his father. And yet the photos suggest that he might have loved her like a substitute mother: in one picture Annie's arms are wrapped around him, in another they're smiling at each other.

I look at the photos of their home, a big white birthday cake of a house with grand gates and a sweeping drive.

"Did it burn down in the fire?" I ask carefully.

She shakes her head. "Just Claudine's room."

"I'm sorry for your loss," I say at last.

"I miss her *tellement*," she says, her voice trembling. "I think of her *tous les jours*." In her emotion, she slips back into French, speaking rapidly, and I hear her mention "Sophia." I sit up.

"Sophia? Has she been to visit?" I ask her.

Immediately her face darkens. "I doubt I will see her again." Annie can't hide the note of bitterness in her voice. Suddenly her tone shifts from natural to strained.

"Why? Are things, um, *mal*, between you?"

Annie purses her lips. "She is happy to live a life of lies," she sighs. "And Finn goes along with it."

I open my mouth to ask another question, when I hear a rap at the door. Annie rises, and when she returns, Finn is with her. I freeze in guilt.

He looks surprised to see me here. And clearly angry.

"I wasn't expecting this."

Annie looks confused. The cat strolls up, purring against Finn's legs and then mine. In my fraught state it's a consolation, as though he's reassuring them I'm to be trusted. I pick the cat up. I tell them both that cats love me.

But Finn is shaking his head and warning me that Laurent won't like it. It's too late: he's already swiped my face with his claws. He struggles out of my arms, landing on the floor, hissing. I gasp, touching my cheek.

"We should get that seen to," Finn says.

Annie returns with a bowl of water, adds a ribbon of disinfectant to it. Finn takes the cloth from her and dabs my cheek; I wince with the sting. I hear his breath catch, feel the simmer of his desire.

For a moment we gaze at one another, memories of last night tender between us.

"If you wanted to meet Annie, you could have just asked. I would have introduced you. Now you've intruded."

"*Je suis désolée*," I say to her.

She smiles. "*Moi aussi*—about my cat! And it was no problem—I liked your company very much."

I smile too, sensing how lonely she is. Finn notices the photos spread across the sofa and frowns.

"We should go," he says sharply. Annie cuts in in French, and I'm sure she's saying she's happy for us to stay longer, but Finn is guiding me toward the front door and I call a hasty "*Au revoir*."

As we walk down the road, heat blasts us and I feel the charge of his anger.

"I'm sorry," I lie. "I was just passing—I was thirsty—and then she was being chatty and friendly, saying she was your nanny, showing me photos."

Finn pauses and I'm ready for more evasion, but to my surprise, he turns to me and confesses: "I lost my mother when I was only six years old. It was . . . terrible . . . having Nounou helped."

"I'm so sorry."

"It was—an accident. My mother fell from a bedroom window."

I picture Finn as a frightened little boy, the world suddenly vast and lonely. I stop and draw him into my arms, my face in his chest.

"I love you," I whisper into his shirtfront. His arms tighten around me and I feel him kiss the top of my head. We stand there for a while, the sound of seagulls above, a faint breeze caressing our hair. It's dangerous to embrace like this, in the open, when Adam and Sophia might come looking for us.

As he pulls back, I try to explain: "I find you so hard to get to know. We've had these nights together where we've shared so much physically . . . I've just wanted to understand you better."

"You don't have to do it by sneaking around," he says, brushing his lips against mine. "You can ask me."

I did, I think in frustration, *I did ask you.*

I feel my phone buzz in my bag and suddenly become conscious of how long I've been gone. Adam must be wondering where the hell I am.

I ignore it. I feel as though I've caught Finn like a butterfly, beating between my cupped palms: he's about to open up to me, I can sense it.

"Tell me about Nounou," I coax him. "Tell me about your childhood."

There's a strange look on his face, as though he's tempted. "I'd like to tell you more . . . but Sophia's expecting me back."

"Perhaps we could go for a walk tomorrow—or Friday." Then I realize that on Friday Adam and I are heading home; I feel dismayed at how fast the days have gone.

"Tomorrow," Finn promises. "We'll walk and we'll talk. I'd like that very much."

———————

Back at the hotel, Adam looks cross as I enter our room.

"You were gone *ages*. I finished my script and came back here. I wanted to go for a swim but, like I texted, I thought I'd wait for you—" He suddenly stops ranting and notices. "What did you do to your face?"

"It was a stray cat," I say. "I made friends with him on my walk."

"Clearly he didn't reciprocate." Adam's tone sounds jeering and hurt.

I examine the scratch in the mirror. It's in nearly the same place as Sophia's, which makes me feel foolish, as though it's a cheap carbon copy of her original. It reminds me of the way I unintentionally picked up one of her gestures when we first became friends, the habit of tucking my hair behind one ear that Adam pointed out.

I turn back to him, still feeling strange, as though I've spent the afternoon in an eerie dream and can't quite come back to reality.

"Let's go swimming, then," I say, and Adam cheers up. But I can't stop thinking about Annie's confession. What was she going to tell me about Sophia, before Finn interrupted? *She is happy to live a life of lies.* What did she mean by that? I remind myself that there are two sides to every story. Sophia claims Annie's the bad person who's done her harm. Yet Annie seems benign to me. So many questions: I hope my talk with Finn tomorrow can yield some answers.

42.

SOPHIA

We're sitting on the plane home. I picture Elena and Adam, still asleep in their hotel bed. We got to Nice airport early this morning, changed our return tickets, managed to pick up a British Airways flight to Gatwick.

I left them a brief note: *So sorry, family emergency—see you back in Wimbledon. Enjoy the rest of your stay. Adam, let's be in touch about the film.*

Finn keeps fiddling with his mobile, as though impatient for airplane mode to finish so he can check his messages. Business or her? The bruise from the black eye I gave him is fading. I remember how I used to examine my own bruises every day in the mirror, the way the colors shifted from rainbow to pastel. Finally the day would come when my skin was shiny and new and clean. And I would feel a pang: the proof of what I had endured had gone too.

In the early hours of this morning, I woke up, my mind ablaze. Would the switch work this time? Would the Virgin Mary bless me? Had my baby girl entered me? On the night of the switch, I could have sworn that Adam saw me fleeing the room as Elena came in. But there were no awkward questions the next day, and the excuses I had formulated in case of emergency were unnecessary. As for Finn and Elena: judging by the looks on their faces, their switch had been bliss for them.

So I woke Finn up. He got angry. I told him that yesterday I'd gone for a walk to look for him and spotted Elena and him, up in the hills, kissing. He said she had sussed out that he knew about the switches. But she didn't know the whole story. He assured me that she wasn't a threat; he was keeping her sweet.

Something snapped inside me when I saw them together. I felt sure he was lying. Finn is the only person in the world I can trust. And if he's lying to me, then there's no stable ground, only a black dancing chaos. I threw the hotel lamp at him. I didn't mean to hit him, just to shock him. To say: *This is me, not some idiot woman you're fooling.* His hand flew up to shield his face and the lamp caught the side of it, making it bleed. He started weeping. I ran over, kissed him. I said, "Let's just go. We've done the switch. I can't stand another two days here. I can't take it." He protested, saying a sudden departure would look odd, might break their trust. But I insisted.

When we were sitting in the airport lounge, Finn started shuffling his feet, looked wistful. I queried it and he told me he was tired, he'd hardly slept from our row and the early check-in.

At first I thought it might be from the trauma of seeing Annie. We've always made a pact that the past is a foreign country. It was a time of different rules; we don't revisit it. By seeing her, he was opening up a door into an attic, climbing up into bad memories and dust and pain. He said she was old and frail and lonely, and keen to see me too. I said no.

But now, sitting here on this plane, looking into the clouds, I feel regret. And so I tell myself to toughen up, reminding myself that she betrayed Finn, betrayed Claudine, and she should never be forgiven for that.

But perhaps Finn isn't just sad to be leaving his *nounou* behind. Or moping over memories of his beloved Claudine. Perhaps there's another reason for his melancholy.

It feels so good to be back home. I underestimated how much our routine holds me together. Séverine bringing us breakfast, coffee and croissants; sitting outside on the patio; writing my diary; my painting. Finn's wounds shame me. I tell him I'm sorry, kiss him, but he seems distant. He gazes down toward the bottom of the garden, and jumps when I brush a croissant flake from his lips.

"Have you done a test?" he asks.

"It's too soon," I reply.

"Well, fingers crossed." He sounds glib. But I don't want another fight. I sense that he hasn't forgiven my bad behavior.

I can't go back to those days of wild, obsessive hope, because if I fail then the crash is too painful. I'm just trying to let go, say my daily prayers, stay calm, and let my baby girl come when she's ready. I'll try not to think about it until my period is due in a fortnight. Then I can do a test.

"I've been thinking," he changes the subject, "we need to sort the house." We've been saying this for months, but his tone sounds more urgent. "We can't keep putting it off."

"It'll take ages," I sigh. "And that drive down to Cornwall takes forever."

"There's a lot we can throw away. All that junk in the attic—the books. Photos of Claudine, old clothes."

I nod. The past is past. To keep those things hanging around is dangerous. I picture flames licking through the photos and shudder.

Finn falls quiet. His mobile buzzes, again. And again. He checks it, and I swear a look of euphoria crosses his face for the briefest moment.

I get out the compact from my handbag; in my eyes I can see panic. I know that Finn needs the switches as much as I do. When I first came up with the idea, three years ago, we were on holiday in Italy. Just the two of us. We were sitting on the balcony of a villa on the coast of Puglia, cocktails on the table, reading together, moonlight and the stars above. That's what I love about life with my husband: that we can enjoy doing simple, quiet things together. I looked up from my Roald Dahl short-story collection, *Switch Bitch*, and said, "Finn, have you ever read 'The Great Switcheroo'?" Yes, he said. I remarked that it would be so funny to exchange husbands instead. He remarked that they'd be easier to fool than women. It was as though he'd lit a touchpaper.

He was dubious about the idea, at first. We debated it for days, weeks, months. For me, it meant a baby. Finn felt anxious that the child would never really be his. "Of course she will be," I argued passionately. "The man we pick will just be a vessel, a vehicle for us to achieve our dream. She'll be *ours*. She'll grow up loving you as her father and we'll never tell her otherwise." That he couldn't give me children made Finn brooding and sad; I think he felt threatened that I might leave him for the real father. I had to reassure him we'd be together always. Besides, I know that the idea of the women appealed to him. He has a strong sex drive.

In the game of the switch, they're just supposed to function as a treat. A succulent dessert. He doesn't need any more than that. I'm his wife.

But the women can be a problem. When we decided to dispense with Scott and Meghan in Cornwall, she couldn't cope. We'd shared three switches; three is about the maximum you can get away with before it becomes too risky. I told her it was time to give up and she cried her eyes out. I had to explain to her that Finn loved me, that he would never leave me for any woman. Full stop. She was devastated. It's one of the reasons I don't put up pics of him on Instagram. Every so often I'd get a whiny message along the lines of *How is Finn? I'd love to see you both . . .*

She worships me still, which means I can control her, but only to a certain extent—she's an unpredictable one. If she starts to get out of hand, I have to resort to blackmail: threatening to tell Scott about the switches. That soon simmers her back down.

Her stalky letters are irritating but knowledge is power: I'd rather be aware of what's going on in her unhinged mind than not. Fortunately, they're forwarded on from the caretaker at our Cornish place; she doesn't know our new address. That she hasn't turned up in Wimbledon seeking us out is a consolation. I think she's satisfied in some strange way simply to wallow in her unrequited obsession.

After the last switch I caught Elena staring at Finn, wide-eyed and vulnerable with lust and perhaps even love. I feared she might be another Meghan in the making.

Now I worry that something far more troubling has happened.

I keep thinking about that moment when I saw them together. Finn had his back to me, but he kissed her with a passion that was palpable. Our switches have always been mysterious, night-time plays that we never discuss; it's best not to make each other jealous with details. It was the first time I'd ever *seen* Finn kiss another woman. It made me feel very strange.

If Elena is beginning to steal his heart, then I'm in trouble. I suddenly feel frantic for the next two weeks to pass. If I can just achieve this pregnancy we both crave, then it will bind us together. Finn and I will have accomplished the goal and Elena will be forgotten.

43.

ELENA

Hi Elena, I'm so sorry we had to depart suddenly—family emergency.
I hope you and Adam enjoy the rest of your stay. Btw,
I didn't tell you the thing you asked me about ☺.
Adam's secret fetish: he likes to be spanked like a naughty boy :); I hope you have fun with that. Kiss kiss, Sophia.

I sit up in bed, reading through Sophia's message, barely digesting the words. It's Finn I care about. He left without saying goodbye. I suppose if there really was an emergency, it couldn't be helped. But—oh!—I'd been looking forward to a little more time with him: swimming in the sea, subtle flirting, illicit kisses.

It's only been twelve hours since I last saw him, but I miss him. I miss his smile, his dark eyes, the way they change color when he's aroused. I miss his moments of shyness, his teasing. The way the wind ruffles his dark hair; his strength when he swims in the sea; the fast, confident way he walks; the way he will suddenly glance at me, in the middle of a conversation, and hold my gaze and burn me with his.

It was so intense, learning about his boyhood yesterday. And he'd promised to confide more today. I ache to hear everything. Now I wonder if I ever will.

"I can't believe they'd just take off like this." Adam is disappointed too.

We head out to Antibes. At the start of the holiday, it was a relief to escape them, but now we feel strangely pastel without them. We take it in turns to swim in the sea or stay on the beach looking after our stuff. I gaze out into the water, remembering how Finn caressed me under the waves. What if our time together was just a holiday fling for him? A game, an extension of the switch?

Later that morning, Adam and I return to Villefranche for a walk in the hills. I see the church where Sophia prayed. I keep thinking about that article on Claudine. Why does she keep it in her diary? *Finn is in love with ghosts*, Sophia complained—is she jealous of the bond he had with his sister? When I get back to England, I'll have to find out more about what happened between her and Annie. Before the holiday, I was certain our friendship was over, but now I've realized she's a bit fucked up, that she's human too, I've thawed. She spoke about her plans for Adam's film in enough detail for it to seem legit. And at least she's finally shared "that thing" with me, which I appreciate.

Knock *knock*. It's afternoon and I bang on the door of Annie's villa. I'm hungry to see more photos, chat further, but there's no reply.

I sigh and head back to join Adam in a café on the seafront. He jots down script ideas; I idle with a book. It feels weird between us, disconnected; maybe I'm more conscious of it now we're on our own. I think of Finn and how present he is, the full weight of his attention on me. Yet here we are in one of the most beautiful places in Europe and Adam's lost in the world of his script. He's stopped shaving and has a faint, fair beard; he's slightly pink from the sun.

I notice that the cover of his notebook is a Matthew Williamson design, decorated with peacocks. Just like the one Sophia bought me for notes about our switches. A drawing of him is poking out.

I tug it out, examining it. Adam gives a self-conscious laugh.

"Something odd happened the other night," he says. "Just after we had sex, I thought I saw Sophia coming out of the bathroom."

"Seriously?" I can't look him in the eye. I wonder if it was me he saw, or her; as I crept in, she slipped out.

"I swear she was watching us, which is pretty kinky really. Maybe it's her fetish or something." He laughs uneasily, and I shrug, as if the idea is absurd. Then I picture Sophia with Adam across her knees, her hand coming down against his backside. I wince, pushing the thought away: urgh.

We wander back to the hotel room. My post-coital euphoria has totally worn off. Before Finn, I never realized sex could be such a drug. I crave a text message from him, anything to confirm it meant something to him too.

I'm standing in front of the mirror when Adam curls his arms around my waist. Suddenly he's present again. "Darling wench." He kisses my neck, his beard an irritation on my hot skin. "The other night was very, very sexy, wasn't it?"

Finn's words echo in my mind: *can't tell the difference between his lover and a friend—more fool him.* But that's unfair; I set this game up. Suddenly my guilt is overpowering. I push him away, telling him I need the bathroom first; I pee and clean my teeth. Worry is starting to pulse inside me again, as though it's becoming a habitual twin to my desire. I tell myself not to be silly. Even if I can't do *that thing*, Adam and I have had sex hundreds of times. There might have been some fakery, but there have been plenty of genuine moments. I just need to be myself with him.

We lie down on the bed. Kissing. *Finn and Sophia*, I wonder, *are they home now?* I'm distracted by the thought of them back in Wimbledon, of whether they're unpacking, having sex—then push it away. I need to stay in the present, feel with my body rather than thinking with my head. It's different with Adam than it is with Finn; there's no dramatic surge; desire tiptoes in slowly, softly. But I can't help feeling a sense of betrayal toward Finn. It makes no sense, but he has possessed my body so completely, taken me to such intimate places, that I feel I belong to him. The conflict arouses panic: Adam is my partner. I can't forever put off sex with him. I have to get through this, I have to try and enjoy it.

The heat is rising when Adam whispers, "Please, do that thing again, please." I whisper *sure* but I hesitate. I'm surprised that Adam likes to be dominated, given the power he enjoyed in our wench/lord routine. This must be a new predilection; I'm annoyed and ashamed that Sophia's discovered it. Maybe this is why he went for Lorraine; maybe I've lacked imagination in the bedroom. Can I really spank him? I'm just not a natural dominatrix.

I improvise. I climb on top of him, position myself. He looks anxious, but as I roll on a condom, he nods with relief. As he enters me, I realize this is too soon, I'm too dry, and I can't help a wince of pain. Adam sees it and I quickly bend down to kiss him, but his lips barely move against mine. I rise up, and feel—to my shock—him slipping out of me.

He's gone soft. Limp. What the hell? Adam's normally so permanently hard and hungry for it. I reach for him, but, feeling his eyes on me, my fingers falter.

There's nothing else for it. I've got to do that thing. I sit up on the bed and adopt a sharp tone.

"I think it's time I put you over my knee."

"What?" Adam sits up on his elbows, looking taken aback.

"Come on," I order him. "Over my knees."

Adam obeys and I feel lost again, staring down at his bare back. What do I do now? Pull down his boxers? Maybe it's better to keep them on, then progress. *Bang!* I bring my hand down onto his backside. Am I being too hard or too soft? *Bang! Bang! Bang!*

"I'm really not into this!" Adam wriggles off my lap. "Can't we just do that thing?"

"I . . . I just thought you'd like the spanking thing," I say in confusion. His look is one of betrayal. I roll over and lie down next to him in defeat. "Why are you doing this?" he bursts out.

"I'm sorry," I protest. "I wasn't in the mood for the thing, it doesn't mean I didn't want to . . ."

"You're so—so Jekyll and Hyde! One day we're having amazing sex and you're all over me and we have our special thing . . . and the next you're barely there. If it's a game then I'm not turned on!"

He gets up, yanking his shirt on, doing the buttons up the wrong way in his temper. I sit up, pleading, reaching for him with my outstretched hand, but he shakes his head.

In a matter of minutes, our bonding moment has been destroyed; if we climbed a ladder then we've slithered straight back down the snake to square one.

I hide in the bathroom. *Oh, God. Oh, God.* I think back to the past holidays we've shared. Even if it's become a bit lackluster, returning here year after year, they've still been so relaxing: lazy, dreamy, drifting days. How have we lost that peace, that fun, that friendship? Am I just too ashamed to admit that it's over between us?

I take my phone out of my handbag, re-checking Sophia's message. She did mention spanking. Did she lie to me deliberately? Things might have cooled with our friendship before Villefranche, but I can't believe she'd do that. We just did a switch together; rebonded; made a fresh pact of trust. I've been naïve—*again*.

My heart stops when I see that I have three new messages *and they're from Finn*.

Immediately, Sophia is forgotten.

I'm sorry we left so suddenly. Sophia was taken ill.

No family emergency, then? I wonder. But joy quivers through me as I read on.

I miss you.

I hope we can meet as soon as you return.

A euphoric smile breaks across my face; as Adam rattles the door handle, I quickly push my phone into my bag, feeling heavy with guilt and confusion.

PART FOUR

44.

ELENA

Finn and Sophia are standing by the Dorfman Conservatory bar in the Royal Opera House. Sophia is wearing a long, shimmering backless black dress; Finn's hand is casual on her bare back.

As they turn to greet us, Sophia gives me an exuberant hug. Finn's smile is thin.

"Such wonderful news about the film!" she exclaims. She's back to her old, polished self again.

I manage a smile. It's been a month since we got back from Villefranche. I've not seen much of her since, not after that lie about Adam's fetish. Oh, she tried to apologize, bluff away the confusion, but I know she set me up, humiliated me. I should never have trusted her again.

But I have to be polite. For Adam's sake. To my surprise, his film funding has come through: the short is definitely going ahead. So Sophia wasn't bullshitting or playing him. There's a lot of excited chit-chat about potential stars who could be cast. I'm proud of him, but the names being bandied about are getting more and more A-list and ridiculous—Tilda Swinton, Carey Mulligan, Alexander Skarsgård. I zone out, aware of Finn's presence: dark suit, cool demeanor, hand in his pocket. When we got back from holiday, he was texting me ten times a day; a week ago, they stopped altogether. The last one he sent was decidedly cold.

You'll never hear from me again.

I refocus my attention to hear Sophia finishing off an anecdote about how she and Finn first met. They were both walking through Villefranche one evening when an unexpected storm erupted; they sheltered under the ineffectual protection of a palm tree and bonded in the thunder and lightning.

What? It's an entirely different anecdote from the one she'd told me a few months earlier, one that Finn confirmed and echoed. The one where she was in a bar on the seafront, had forgotten her wallet, and Finn was the knight who stepped in to pay. For a moment, their charisma drops away and they seem the oddest couple: is anything about them true? *She is happy to live a life of lies*, Annie's words echo in my mind, *and Finn goes along with it.* What do they have to hide?

Then my gaze shifts back to Finn and my cynicism melts. He looks so beautiful in his suit. Noticing, he looks away curtly. His rejection stings like a slap.

Sophia leads the way into the auditorium. Adam sits beside her, which leaves me sitting next to him, and Finn forced to take the end seat. As he sits down beside me, I risk a sidelong glance but he stares hard at the stage.

The lights dim. *Lady Macbeth of Mtsensk.* As the first act begins with Katerina's unhappy marriage, I struggle to concentrate.

Finn's texts began the week we got back from Villefranche. As Adam and I filled boxes and suitcases for our house-move, they came through in an incessant stream. **I need to see you. I need to kiss you. All over.** And: **I can taste you in my mouth, still. I want to taste you again. Now.** And: **Why aren't you replying? How can you be so cruel?** I was replying, but only sporadically, nervously, sheepishly, imagining Adam's face if he saw them, deleting them immediately. Then came the cross ultimatum: **I need to see you. If we don't set up a time and place within the next hour, you'll never hear from me again.** I sweated, dithered, the hour went by and that's when he cut off.

I'd yearned for him secretly for months but he'd been so elusive; having his passionate interest was overwhelming for me. The conversation with his nanny gave me a rare insight into him, but he left Villefranche before giving me his own account of his childhood. Even the constant stream of texts surprised me. For all the passion we've shared at night, he's always seemed a cool character.

On stage, Katerina sings of her lonely marriage to Zinoviy, falls for the handsome Sergei, has an illicit affair. Early in our relationship Adam was so convinced I would leave him or cheat on him that I began to feel like some heroine in a Greek tragedy, doomed to play out his worst fears. I feel sad that I've become the scarlet woman he always feared I would be. Then I remind myself of my years of loyalty and how he repaid that by sleeping with Lorraine.

Beside me, Finn tenses. He seems agitated by the plot twist: Katerina dispenses with her evil father-in-law by feeding him poisoned mushrooms.

Then I feel his touch.

The back of his hand against the back of mine. A kiss of skin. A reconciliation. An interval begins: the lights go up and I see the burn in his eyes.

We go back to the bar and I feel panicky. When he was rejecting me I felt hurt, but now he wants me I don't know how to handle it. I join a long queue for the Ladies. I'm at the door when announcements overhead warn that we should be back in our seats. Suddenly Finn is by my side.

"Come with me," he whispers in my ear. He draws me through a door marked *Private*, leading to an empty staircase. "These lead to one of the boxes. We're safe."

And then he kisses me. We kiss and kiss and kiss and I feel his hands claw my hair, cup my face, range over my body. I'm wild with excitement, nearly ready to embrace abandonment and make love in a stairwell— then I picture Adam and Sophia eyeing our empty seats. I turn my face to one side; he trails kisses across my cheek. "Finn, we need to get back," I whisper, and he relents.

We hurry back in the dark. Sophia gives us a hawkish look, Adam a puzzled one. The opera unfolds. Finn gives me a shy but dangerous smile and I feel a sudden surge of love for him. I let my hand fall to the edge of my seat and the back of his hand presses against mine, his little finger caressing mine. The second half is tragic. Tears well up in my eyes and I see Finn's become liquid too, and the touch of our skin becomes a comfort.

It is two weeks since we moved into our new flat in Walthamstow and it's still an obstacle course of half-unpacked boxes. Lyra is restless, eager to go out and explore her new territory, but we want her to settle in first.

We take off the glossy clothes we put on for the opera and climb into bed.

"Well, that was fun," Adam says. "I just wish Dad was alive to see the film going ahead."

It's then I remember with a jolt: today is the anniversary of his dad's death.

"He'd have been so proud of you," I reply, feeling wretched for forgetting.

We lie in the dark. Since the big row we had on holiday, we've stopped having sex altogether. Adam hasn't laid a finger on me beyond the odd, affectionate kiss. I've actually felt frustrated, but haven't dared initiate anything.

I gaze over at the haphazard silhouettes of our furniture and belongings. We haven't unpacked half our things; bubble wrap still clings to ornaments. Whenever we've moved into new places in the past, Adam has got stuck into DIY, erecting shelves, arguing with me over the best place to put our big leather sofa. This time round, he hasn't seemed interested in where anything should go. The carpet desperately needs a hoover; I've decided that it's time we evened up the housework, but I'm not sure Adam has even noticed.

"Night, wench," he says softly. It's the first time in a while that he's resorted to our old routine.

"Night, my lord," I whisper back.

Soon he's snoring while I lie awake, turning the night over in my mind. Why does Finn have this effect on me? Yesterday I met up with my old friend Anil and confided in him. We've known each other since Cambridge, and he makes his living as a successful therapist now. "Elena, you dark horse," he laughed when I told him about the switches. He echoed my own guilt back to me, pressed upon me that I should make a decision one way or another. But I have no idea if Finn wants an affair or a relationship—is that even on the cards? I need time to get to know him before I make the leap, but I'm also conscious that dragging it out is so unfair on Adam.

Is lust a strong enough foundation for a relationship? The sensible part of me has always believed in companionship. Isn't that the advice you always hear: that once the fire has burned away, it's the friendship that counts? But if that hasn't been enough for me and Adam, then perhaps I've got it all wrong. Perhaps that burning fire is important for the survival of a relationship, perhaps it can hold two people together. On those three precious times that I went to bed with Finn, the aftermath was so euphoric, it felt like love to me.

I turn to look at Adam's sleeping face, soft and boyish. I'm not even sure if he wants to be with me anymore, which makes me sad despite everything. We seem to be slipping away from each other, a little more each day. Should I accept that this relationship has never been perfect and give up on it, or should I fight one more time to save what we had? Sooner or later what's unsaid between us is going to erupt. I need to be honest with him: I owe him that. But how much do I reveal? If I tell Adam about the switches, it's going to destroy him.

And, of course, there's Sophia. I think of the black eye she gave Finn in Villefranche, and I feel afraid. She wouldn't let her husband go without a fight.

Mr. MacInnes is ready to see you." Finn's secretary stands up and opens the door to his office.

I go through. I'm dressed as though for a professional meeting. His beautiful, drawn face lights up at the sight of me. I've ached for him during every moment of the three days since we were last together at the opera. We kiss and he bites my ear and says, "I've booked a hotel room."

I pull away, frowning. Finn strokes his finger under my chin, sensing my change of mood.

"That sounds tawdry," I say. Is this how it's going to be from now on—from secret switches to dirty sex in hotel rooms? "I can't."

"But I need you, I want to be inside you," he says, caressing my face. "I don't want the time constraint of a switch, I want hours with you."

My breath quickens with the thought, but I bite my lip and say: "I can't do a hotel."

"No?" His fingers trace my lips.

I want to ask *what is this between us?* But I dread I will sound heavy and he will call it an affair when I want to call it a relationship.

"Don't you feel guilty?" I blurt out. "What would Sophia say if she knew I was here?"

"Sophia isn't a—we don't have—we don't have a conventional relationship," he says at last.

"You mean you have an open relationship?" I ask.

"No." He chooses his words with care. "Just—not conventional. We're . . ." He fingers his ring. "Please keep this to yourself, I'm trusting you with this secret—but—we're not actually married. We don't sleep together. This ring is for commitment, though."

"Oh." I feel lost, that sensation of vertigo returning: who are these people? Is he just offering up the usual clichéd lies of a married man? "So Sophia really wouldn't mind?"

"Oh, she would!" he says. "She doesn't know anything about this."

"Right." I swallow. "So that doesn't make much sense."

He kisses me again, successfully distracting me, until I pull away once more.

"I'm sorry—I've just—got—too many questions." I hardly know where to begin: *Why aren't you married? Why are you never on her Instagram? Why did you change your name from Alain to Finn? What's the rest of the story about Claudine?* "You were going to tell me about your past," I burst out. "But you left Villefranche so suddenly."

Finn curls his arm around me tight and kisses my temple. "Why don't I tell you about all that later?"

"No," I assert, finding the resolve to do it despite the heat of his lips and hands. "I need to hear everything first, before I agree to go anywhere with you."

I see him withdraw and start to regret my stance: I don't want to lose him. Maybe I can live with the lies and the mystery if I have to, I want him so much. But then I hear him pick up the phone and instruct his secretary: "I'm leaving for today. Can you cancel my meetings?" He turns to me, holding out his hand, smiling nervously. "Come on then, my darling."

45.

ELENA

On Piccadilly, we pass by Caffè Concerto, the place we went to earlier this year, the day after the first switch, when Finn asked me if I wanted a proof-reading job. He played me so well back then. Should I trust him now?

To my surprise, he steers me across the road to Fortnum and Mason's. A doorman welcomes us. My senses are dazzled by the plushness and beauty; Finn takes me up to the Diamond Jubilee Tea Salon, where we order delicate tea and fancy cakes.

There's the murmur of polite, posh chit-chat around us. Finn brushes spilled sugar crystals across the table.

"So . . . your mother died when you were six," I trail off, biting my lip, wondering if I should reveal what I gleaned from Annie. "And you changed your name from Alain to Finn."

"Yes."

I speak in a reassuring tone: "Tell me everything. Start wherever you like. I won't judge you."

"I think you will," he says at last. His tone is pleading, almost boyish. "By the end of my story, you won't want to be with me."

Just how bad can it be? I gaze into his dark eyes, sensing how fragile he is beneath his outer show of stoic reserve.

"Does Sophia know?"

"Yes. She's the only one."

"If she can handle it, so can I," I reply, but my heart is beating quickly.

He begins with short, halting sentences. He tells me what Annie told me in Villefranche: that his mother died, that his nanny moved in with her daughter, Claudine, that he learned the girl was his half-sister.

He pulls a photo from his wallet. "My father—Charles Aubert."

"What was he like?"

"He was loved by all the locals. He was a wealthy businessman, wining and dining within local society. He was the patron of a homeless charity, he took in a penniless nanny along with her daughter. Or that was the story he fed the outside world." Finn's voice is acidic. "So often I've gone to tear this photo up, but in the end I always decide to keep it. To remind myself never to be like him."

I watch Finn closely, remembering that Annie also called Aubert a bad man.

"He betrayed my mother. She was barely in the grave before Nounou moved in."

"What about Claudine, did she get on with him?" I ask.

"I was the golden child, she was the black sheep. At least I got to go to school. But she . . . was home-schooled." Finn's face looks haunted. "My father's motto used to be *La vie est un jeu*—'Life is a game.' Claudine would be locked in her room all day, told to pretend she was stranded on a desert island. Later, he'd tell me to take her up a tray of food."

"He locked her up?"

"Frequently. I got used to taking her meals after school, smuggling in presents, tutoring her. We became very close. But my father was ashamed of Claudine. She was living proof of his cheating. My mother—she was an aristocrat. My father acquired a great deal by marrying her, even more so when she died . . ."

"And Annie—your nanny?"

"Nounou was beautiful, and kind—but he soon tired of her, and began to despise her for being from a lower class. I loved her. She was warm and funny but, as the years went by, she grew harder, sadder . . ."

"She must have wanted to get Claudine out of there."

"I think Nounou felt trapped. She had little money—and his hold over her was tyrannical. She became prone to having 'accidents,' and I noticed welts on her arms that she could never account for. Eventually I stopped asking."

"That's terrible—I'm so sorry you experienced this." I look down and notice that I've been anxiously crumbling pieces of cake on my plate.

"I confronted him once about the abuse and he denied it—because I was a teenager, it was easy for him to gaslight me and claim she was *hystérique*," Finn confesses. "But my hatred for him grew. In the evenings I'd be forced to dine with his fat-cat friends while Claudine was locked in upstairs."

"How did he get away with it?" I ask, appalled.

"Oh, he had everyone in his pocket—including the local Commissaire of Police." Finn manages a smile. "But he underestimated Nounou. She fought back."

"She went to the police?"

"She poisoned him."

"Poison?"

The waiter comes over to check we're happy. We both flash him stilted smiles.

"I was eighteen when it happened. I'll never forget being woken by screaming, seeing my father on all fours in the hallway, vomiting violently. Nounou was trying to flee down the driveway, but the police had already arrived."

I remember how weirdly Finn reacted during the opera to the poison plot on stage: now it makes sense.

"Did she go to prison?"

"No. My father told her he wouldn't press charges but in return she had leave—without Claudine."

God, Annie must have felt terrible, in a no-win situation: a cell or exile.

"And your father survived?"

"Just. He needed an operation and dialysis for the rest of his life. When he came out of hospital he'd aged ten years."

"And Claudine?" I ask tentatively.

"She died a few years later in a fire. The official report was that she lit some incense, caused it herself. But I really don't know . . ."

"What—you think it wasn't an accident?" I ask. "Who would have done something like that?" I don't like where this is going, but I have to hear him out. I have to know how this ends. I reach for his hand and squeeze it gently, prompting him to continue.

"I ought to have acted." Finn stares intently at me, confirming what I'm thinking. "That's what still haunts me. Instead, I deserted Claudine. I went to university in Scotland—Edinburgh—at the insistence of my father."

I'm stunned, still processing this information.

He looks down, becoming self-conscious again, and I ask, "You must have missed her?"

"Oh, God, yes. Before I left, I remember holding her so tightly and promising that I'd come back for her. I also told her that in a year she'd be sixteen and legally an adult, free to do as she pleased. During my first term I wrote to her every day . . . but that's when the fire happened . . ." He stops, too emotional to go on.

"So it was your father's revenge? Annie poisoned him and, in some kind of terrible tit for tat, he took Claudine's life?"

Finn doesn't reply, his eyes cloudy with grief.

"I'm so sorry." I rub his arm gently.

"Nounou never recovered from the pain of it," he says.

"She must be glad that you've stayed in touch." I pause. "I heard her call you Alain—when did you become Finn?"

"At Edinburgh, after Claudine died. I wanted to free myself from the name my father chose for me. And MacInnes was my mother's maiden name."

"When did you meet Sophia? Was there anyone else before her?"

"Well, during my Edinburgh days, I could tell girls liked me . . ."

"Oh, I'm sure they did." We both laugh, grateful for some light relief to the tension.

"I was scared of getting into any relationship. I was glad to be free from my father, but afraid I might end up like him."

"But you're not like him!" I assure him. "Do you think . . . you were drawn to Sophia because you wanted to save her from an abuser? The guy she got into that bad relationship with?"

"Yes," he replies quickly. "I wanted to help her because . . . I failed Claudine."

I think of the black eye Sophia gave him in Villefranche and Finn seems to read my thoughts.

"She only lashes out at me from time to time because she couldn't fight back before."

He is very patient, taking that on, I muse. Patient and kind. At the same time, on holiday I also witnessed him wanting to control Sophia, even if the impulse is protective; and that must echo his father.

"Did Sophia ever get to meet Claudine?"

"No." Finn shakes his head, and I think of her complaint: *Finn's in love with ghosts.* In her own way, Sophia is also haunted by Claudine, through Finn's past.

"Sophia told me that your father didn't like her." At the time, I had wondered if she was just making it up, given how shiny and perfect she seemed. Now I understand.

"No." Finn gives a bitter laugh. "My father did not like Sophia. He used to call all women *hystérique*. He's dead now and I don't mourn him."

"What about Nounou—does Sophia get on with her?" I ask.

"Not that well," says Finn warily. "There's a—a—rift between them.

It's complicated. I often feel torn between them: Sophia wants me to be Finn, my nanny wants her Alain back." He looks guilty. "To be honest, I've neglected Nounou, hardly seen her in recent years. I feel bad about that."

That sheds some light on the issue, but it doesn't explain the "harm" Sophia felt Annie had done her. But there's another, more pressing question on my mind, even though I'm afraid the truth might hurt:

"If you saved Sophia, then how can your marriage be a sham?"

"Our relationship isn't a sham," he says quickly. "We exchanged rings to show our commitment. We felt we didn't need a piece of paper to legalize it."

"I see," I reply, feeling crestfallen.

"I think we've both realized the limits of our relationship," he says. "We can't entirely make each other happy—we realized that in Cornwall. Wimbledon was supposed to be a fresh start."

"And then you found out Sophia was organizing secret switches," I say wryly.

"I guess she wanted to spice things up," he jokes, and then bites his lip as I wince. "Have some more cake," he says, suddenly, pointing to the tier of delicious-looking sponges, filled with cream.

I want to laugh. "I doubt that even sugar can make me feel much better."

Finn looks scared. He reaches across and holds my hands. "I knew that telling you all this would be a mistake."

"No," I reassure him fervently. "You have no reason to feel ashamed or guilty. Listen: I'm glad you told me. I mean—I don't know anyone who's had a perfect childhood . . ." I trail off musing that, while that's true, I don't know anyone who's had it quite as bad as Finn. "It's just all so . . . It doesn't matter. I care for you."

He holds my hand, circles the tips of his fingers around my palm.

"You've let me rant on," he says, blushing, "and now I want to hear everything about you—your childhood, about how you met Adam. Everything."

"I will tell you," I promise him, "another day."

"Come to Cornwall for a weekend," he says. "We've still got our old place there, I can send the caretaker away. I don't want you simply to be my mistress. I think—I think I'm falling in love with you."

He says those last words quietly, shyly, so they're almost throwaway. The waiter approaches, asking if we'd like anything more, and Finn requests the bill. He sits back, crossing his arms, staring at the table, and I feel too overwhelmed to reply.

46.

ELENA

My train pulls into Wimbledon and I step onto the Underground platform. For all my nerves, I feel as though I'm coming home. I walk up the hill, past the flats, the glorious trees, the benches, the war memorial at the top. I pass the house that Adam and I stayed in before I circle back up to Murray Road.

I wanted to meet Sophia in a café for the quickest of coffees, but she insisted I should come to her house. She said she had exciting news to share with me. When I told Finn in a discreet call last night, he promised me he wouldn't be there. He accepted that I wouldn't be able to sustain any sort of façade in his presence. Then he added, "I don't see why you can't still be friends," which I thought was as naïve as you could get. Sophia might have created and legitimized our affair, but, as we surely both know, she'd kill me if she found out we are meeting independently of her. Still, as Finn also pointed out, "If you cut yourself off, she'll suspect." And I have to admit, my curiosity is piqued.

I check my phone again. It's been five hours since he texted me; two blue ticks confirm he's read my last message. It's an uneasy contrast to the relentless flurry of the past few days. I am finally allowing myself to trust him, open up to him. Last night I messaged him **I think I'm falling in love with you too**. I can hardly wait to be with him in Cornwall. After that, I tell myself guiltily, after that I'll speak to Adam. I make a promise to myself.

I'm not sure that I know what the outcome of that conversation will be. I just know I have to be honest. A phrase that Finn used has stayed with me: *we've both realized the limits of our relationship.* An odd way of putting it, but it's resonated with me. I think Adam and I have hit those limits too.

I go up to the door of Sophia's house and knock.

"Elena!" She looks thrilled to see me and I feel my guilt sharpen.

Inside, their house feels even more brooding than I remember, with its old wallpaper and those oils on the walls. Everywhere I look, I can see signs of Finn's presence. His shoes in the rack. His coats on the hook. His umbrella in that stand.

"Come up," Sophia says. "Come and see my latest paintings!"

Her portrait of Finn's father, hanging on the wall on the first floor, makes me start now I know the story of the man behind that cruel face. Isn't it something of a taunt for Sophia to hang it here? I'm becoming convinced she's too damaged to really care for Finn in the way he deserves . . .

Her studio is in the spare bedroom at the back. I manufacture some polite praise, and Sophia glows. She sits down on the guest bed, patting a space beside her for me to join her.

My eyes flit to her wedding ring as it catches the light. A moment of doubt afflicts me: is their marriage really a sham or was he just giving me a line? I suddenly notice her smoothing her hand over her belly. I saw her do that the other night at the opera and I wondered vaguely: why worry about a millimeter of fat on your stomach when you look so good? Now I frown—is it my imagination or is that a slight bump?

Sophia follows my gaze.

"I get bloating too sometimes," I say quickly. "When I eat too much sugar."

"It's not bloating—"

"Sorry." I blush at my faux pas. "There's actually nothing to see, you have an incredible figure."

"There *is* something to see. Oh, Elena. I'm going to be a mother!"

"What?" I sit bolt upright. "You're—*pregnant?*"

Does Finn know? Did he know this morning, when we exchanged those sexy texts? Yesterday, when we started making plans to go to Cornwall? At the opera?

"Sorry—congratulations," I manage. "Is Finn, um, pleased?"

"I only told him this morning. But yes, he was over the moon, as you can imagine."

The bastard. So that explains why he's been quiet over the last few hours. He's in shock. He could have told me. I guess he didn't know how.

I thought they weren't even sleeping together. I had thought Sophia was the one prone to lies, that Finn was the straight one. But maybe they're just as bad as each other.

"And you're sure it's Finn's?" I blurt out, as another shocking possibility hits me.

"Well, of course. Who else's could it be?" Then she registers the look on my face. "Oh, God, I'm sorry." She stifles an embarrassed laugh. "I totally forgot—there was that night with Adam where we forgot the condoms. But no, I took the morning after pill."

"You did," I say uncertainly.

"It is Finn's," she asserts. "I'm only six weeks, though. It's very early days."

The date of the first switch, when was it? Back in May. Five months ago. At least. I breathe out deeply. She's right—if she'd got pregnant then, she'd be showing by now.

"Congratulations," I repeat in a fragile voice. "That's wonderful!" But I'm still stunned, wary of asking: is she having other affairs? Other switches? Maybe they've been having IVF, though I thought she was against that for religious reasons.

"The joy on Finn's face, when I told him this morning," Sophia says, her eyes shining. "He's so happy, he's been like a little kid." Tears well up. "I don't want a boy, I don't want to bring more toxic masculinity into the world. I prayed for a girl. I know she's a girl."

I recall her in that church in Villefranche, eyes closed, whispering feverishly in prayer.

"I have you to thank, in part." She squeezes my hand. "You got Finn excited about sex again. Before the switch, he was barely interested . . . we'd stopped having it altogether."

"So Finn *can* have children?" I ask slowly. "It's definitely his?"

Sophia nods. "When we tried some years ago, his sperm count was too low, so we were told it was unlikely he could conceive."

"Unlikely?" My heart is racing. But I thought that they *couldn't* conceive, that it was a definite impossibility.

"But you know, we explored a whole range of remedies—with the black-out blind, Finn's been sleeping more, he went on a really healthy diet, he took vitamins."

"Uh-huh." I think of him smoking cigars, drinking wine at our dinners in Villefranche.

"And the holiday, I think that did him the world of good too. He just learned to relax. Normally he's such a workaholic and that can be a huge factor, affecting sperm count—did you know that? And, like I said, we just ended up having a lot more sex."

"Have you thought of any names for the baby?" I ask.

"I want Sienna," says Sophia. "Finn wants something old-fashioned—of course. Like Margaret. I said to him, 'Next you'll be plumping for Edith or Virginia.'"

"Virginia is good," I say, thinking of Woolf.

I can't fully digest what she's saying. There's a physical response going on inside me, which I'm using every drop of energy I have to conceal. But my mind can't quite keep up, translate this hot pain thumping in my heart.

I don't think I've ever seen Sophia look so happy. But I can't help bursting out: "I could have got pregnant! In Villefranche!"

Sophia looks anxious. "Have you had your period since?"

"Well, yes, but—"

"Oh, phew. Imagine if we both were!" she says, as though to say *imagine if we both turned up wearing the same dress.* "I didn't think there was much of a risk. I mean, it's *hard* to get pregnant, and harder when you get older . . ."

But, I want to scream, *he lied to me. You lied to me.*

I exhale and say sharply: "Finn told me you weren't married, that you don't have sex, as a matter of fact."

Sophia looks genuinely shocked and my heart sinks. *So it was a lie,* I realize. A sweetener for his mistress. Then she laughs softly, shaking her head.

"Honestly—the things men say when they want to get one over." She shrugs. "Shall we go downstairs and have a drink?"

I sit on a garden chair on the terrace, hearing Sophia humming in the kitchen as she squeezes some lemons and chops up mint. When my emotions become overwhelming, I rise and walk in a daze down to the rose bushes, breathing in their perfume. Pregnant? What the hell is going on? Why chase me, why kiss me at the opera, why open up about his childhood, ask me to come to Cornwall, if he and Sophia have been trying for a baby all along? *Because,* a scared voice replies, *he's a liar. A womanizer. He's used his past trauma to manipulate you into feeling sorry for him and he's just playing the tragic, damaged-hero act as part of a game.* I try to push the sick fear away, tell myself there has to be an explanation. But, oh God, I hate him, I love him, I loathe him I love him. The roses have a faint frill of brown on their petals; it's the start of the dying season.

Sophia comes out with the lemonades and I rejoin her and sip my drink.

"What about you and Adam?" she asks. "Do you think you might ever change your minds?"

"Oh, no," I laugh, attempting to appear normal. "Like I said, we decided against kids some time ago."

"Really?" Sophia looks almost pitying.

"We don't fancy the sleepless nights, and all the expense when we want to save for a flat . . . Besides, I have Lyra."

Sophia looks appalled and I smile bitterly. My mobile buzzes with a text from Adam and I see the time. I don't want to be here when Finn comes back from work, forced to congratulate him while my heart screams in protest.

"I should go," I say. "It's a long trek back—with the rush hour . . ."

"You don't want to stay for dinner?" Sophia looks disappointed.

"I really can't," I say. I'm about to get up but there's that charged feeling in the air, as though Sophia has more to say. And I want to hear it. I want the whole truth, even if it's killing me.

"You know," she says slowly, "I never really wanted to do those switches."

"You seemed pretty keen at the time."

"They were Finn's plan from the start. He persuaded me, I persuaded you. You're not the first couple we've played the game with. There was another, in Cornwall. Scott and Meghan—yes, the stalker woman. She got too attached. Finn's—well, he's a man. Like a bull in a paddock, he needs fresh blood, and he needs variety. And I love him, so I let him. I know I can't satisfy him. I endure the chore of sleeping with other men for him." She gazes at me, her smile bright now, bright as a balloon. "I'm just relieved we're having this baby. I know I don't always attract the best men, but Finn did save me and now—now I think he'll settle down. It's a new start for us. Oh, God—I need the loo." She smiles. "Again. It's the pregnancy," she adds, as though it's some extraordinary scientific fact she needs to explain. "I'll be back in a sec."

I watch her go into the house and then tiptoe after her. I listen to her footsteps on the stairs. I'm breathing hard, close to tears, but I keep telling myself, over and over, that I need to talk to Finn. I know by now that there can be a wide gap between Sophia's words and the truth. And yet . . . I remember those letters that I saw from Meghan and her fraught Instagram messages. That part does ring true.

I think of Sophia's diary, up there in their bedroom. God, what I'd do to seize it right now. I stand at the bottom of the stairs, trembling—and then I hear the flush of the toilet and I know the moment has passed.

I go into the kitchen. Quickly, now. I remember where the keys are kept, from the night of the second switch, when I was locked in. I find the back-door ones, yank a pair free from its hook, push them into my bag.

And then I leave without saying goodbye.

I stumble down Murray Road, reach Wimbledon Common. Under the shadow of a horse chestnut, I clutch the trunk, steadying myself. I video-call Finn on WhatsApp: I need to see his face when he responds.

"Hello—" he begins.

"Sophia told me she's pregnant."

He's on a busy street; I recognize Piccadilly. Shoppers and tourists stream past. Finn turns off by Grom Gelato, into a quieter alley. His expression doesn't look manipulative or guarded like Sophia's. He just looks panicked.

"So, were you trying to have a baby together?"

"She was."

"What does that even mean? Can't you just, for once, treat me like a human being and give me a straight answer? Don't you think you owe me that? Is the baby yours? Is it Adam's?"

"I honestly . . . don't know . . ." His face blurs, breaks up into a snarl of colored fragments: the connection's been lost.

I stand by the trees, weeping. A mum whisks her child past, embarrassed when he points to the "crying lady." Finn tries me again, but I decline his call. Instead I try Anil, but it goes straight to his voicemail. I rummage in my bag for a tissue, find an old Pret napkin, dry my face with it. I walk down to the pond, and sit by the ducks and swans. Sun and shadows alternate as clouds race across the sky. I realize how hard I've fallen for him. It's only in this moment of ultimatum and grief that my confusion clears, that the choices my heart had already made become stark. I had been ready to leave Adam for Finn. But there's no moving forward now. It's over—Sophia's won.

47.

ELENA

There's a mountain of washing-up to do; I pull on my rubber gloves. Adam's spending every last minute on final rewrites for his film; he's gradually stopped doing any housework at all. I don't actually care right now; the chores feel like penance. They're also grounding, normalizing, simple. I'm in such a state they're just about all I can cope with.

I scrub away at the dishes, the ones with the floral pattern that Adam's mum gifted us on his last birthday. Every so often, Sophia's pregnancy revelation hits me again. The shock stabbing my heart.

My mind is stuck at a path that forks left and right, A and B. It wanders back and forth, back and forth.

A: Adam is the father of the baby. Which means it's partly my fault. Which means Sophia is a nasty manipulative bitch who, instead of bloody doing IVF or using a surrogate like any sane person would, took delight in a game where she stole his sperm.

B: Finn is the father of her baby. It's both better and worse. It means that they are like a normal married couple, but he's lied to me as much as she has. Were the switches really his idea, as Sophia claimed? For what?

Fun sex? Manipulating women? Tricking them into thinking they were tricking him while he called them *Sophia* and said *I love you?*

He keeps on trying to contact me but I refuse to reply or engage. I can't even cry away my broken heart in the day, because Adam's been working from home this week; often I wake up in the night with silent tears streaming down my face, realizing, *it's over.* Sometimes I've felt so lonely and lost, I've wanted to call up my mum and tell her everything. But the parallel in our lives is stark. I know she'll expect me to make the sacrifice she did when she was once tempted.

I stack mugs and saucers onto the draining board, thinking once more of Sophia's back-door key. I haven't dared use it yet. If I were caught breaking and entering, I know she would relish calling the police, humiliating me. I think about fooling her help, Séverine, into letting me in—but can I get away with it a second time? A part of me dreads opening up that diary again, dreads what I might find. Maybe it's best just to walk away.

I pull off my rubber gloves and check Sophia's Instagram on my phone. There's no announcement of her pregnancy, though I guess it's a little early for that. It's just the same old shit: a photo of her standing by one of her paintings, wearing a floral dress that matches the flowers she's painted. Why didn't I spot how completely fake she looks, how much she strains for her likes?

I slump on the sofa, where Lyra's sleeping, and switch on the TV, keeping the volume down because Adam's writing.

I picture myself bumping into Sophia in three years' time. I imagine her with a pushchair. I imagine myself bending down, gazing into her kid's eyes and seeing the blue of Adam's in them. Their genes, intertwined. The thought fills me with horror.

Fuck.

How can Finn bear it? Not even knowing himself, at this stage? How can he?

Adam, on a break from his script, joins me on the sofa. I have a wild urge to tell him everything. This remote, weird feeling between us: it can never heal while I'm carrying this secret.

I open my mouth, then glance at his profile and lose my nerve. The truth will surely destroy us.

Instead, I blurt out: "I've been thinking back . . . to Villefranche and . . ." This is tricky: I don't want to bring up the awkward sex we had. I want to know about the sex he had with Sophia.

Adam looks anxious. His reply shocks me: "Are you pregnant?"

"What? No!"

"You're sure?"

"Yes, I had a period last week," I point out.

There's a loaded silence.

"I know we had that moment in Villefranche, where we were too turned on to use . . . so . . . I thought . . ."

What moment? I wonder.

"But since we got back, I've kind of been thinking—well, now isn't a great time, is it? I mean, I've got the short and then hopefully the feature. Once I've got those underway then we could . . . see where we're at. Reassess. D'you agree?"

This is pretty much the same sort of thing he's said on this topic over the past seven years.

"Sure," I whisper, but I still feel confused. Then I realize: he must be talking about the last night he spent with Sophia. A chill goes through me.

They didn't use a condom.

Adam looks uneasy, asks if I'd like a cup of tea. I sense he doesn't know how to close the discussion, isn't sure what I'm trying to say. We've always been on the same page about delaying kids; now he's concerned I might be changing chapter. So he goes back to his script, starts tinkering again.

I think about Sophia, rocking Adam's baby in her arms, and anger seizes me again. I pick up my mobile and message her:

I know what's been going on. I know the baby's Adam's.

Her reply comes quickly:

How could it possibly be his? We haven't slept together.

I roll my eyes and reply: **The switches.**
She replies: **What switches? I don't know what you're talking about.**
I blink, shocked. And then she comes back at me again:

**Would you really want to publicly humiliate Adam by
letting the world know what you did?
No, I didn't think so.**

I can smell cigarette smoke. I've crept down the side path, through the
back gate, to Sophia and Finn's house. Their car isn't in the drive. I know
Finn is at work. After another flurry of texts this morning, I relented and
replied, but only so that I could ask him where he was. I hope that Sophia's taken the car and gone out for the day.

Séverine is sitting in their back garden with her back to me, smoking.
I smile, because I've noticed a bottle of Merlot on the table. I don't blame
her: I'd nick their stuff too. I hope she walks off with their bloody wine
cellar.

I wait for her to put out the cigarette and go inside. Then I grab my
chance. I sprint down the lawn, hide behind the trellis at the back. From
here, I can just about see her: she washes up, sits at the table, reads a mag-
azine, does some half-hearted cleaning. I'm wondering if she'll ever go,
when finally, finally, she leaves, locking up the back door and the gate.

I wait another five minutes, then unlock the back door, slip into the
house. Silence, save for the grandfather clock and its somnolent tick.

Upstairs in their bedroom, I reach for the diary in the pile—when another thought strikes me. I open the top drawer in Sophia's cabinet. It contains notebooks, freshly sharpened pencils, a few fountain pens.

The next drawer contains makeup, most of it still wrapped in its original cellophane: spares, perhaps. Lipsticks, foundations, eyeshadows.

The next drawer contains jewelry, some of it heavy and ancient-looking. That's when I see it: *Adam's watch*. It's unbelievable: she has a house full of antiques and she can afford bottles of wine worth over £1,000. She stole his sperm, but no, that wasn't good enough on its own. She had to take his precious, beloved memento, one of the few things he has left of his father's. What a bitch.

I put it into my bag, exhaling.

Then I reach for her diary, hesitant and nervous.

I turn to the latest entry. It's dated a month ago:

France was just about as dire as I expected it to be. I had a panic attack after we landed in Nice, right in the airport, attracting attention from the customs officer, causing my passport to be doublechecked. Villefranche was beautiful but tainted with horrifying memories. I didn't want to recall the person I used to be, weak and scared and under his control. Then Finn went and told me that Annie was living close by, in some run-down villa. I had no idea the old witch was still residing there, I thought she'd left some time ago. Finn tried to get me to see her, say sorry for what I had done, but there was no way. After that I was just counting down the days until we could fly home.

Hmmm. Sophia claimed to me that Annie was the one who'd done *her* harm, but this suggests it was the other way round. No surprises there . . .

My phone vibrates: a message from Finn. **I've booked you a train ticket for our weekend in Cornwall. I've ordered in food. I'm just saying it's all**

prepared if you want it. I switch off my phone, unable to take any more of his onslaught.

> Then we did a third switch and I had sex with Adam. I didn't try to become her, not when I'm better at pleasing him than she is anyway. I was actually a bit bored this time and I made a blunder at the end, when he saw me coming out and Elena coming in. But there were no repercussions and that convinces me I'm protected. This pregnancy is meant to be. My child has been conceived as God intended—no IVF, no artificial experimentation, but through natural means.

Oh, my God.
My God.
All my suspicions have been confirmed.

The switches were a scam. She lied right from the start. Maybe the other couple, Meghan and her husband, were guinea pigs who failed her.

I ignored the warning signs. I should have jacked it all in from the moment she supposedly took that morning after pill. But there was Finn, my siren, luring me into madness . . .

As God intended. I think of Sophia praying in the church. No IVF, she claims, but I wonder if that's just an excuse to justify her love of playing games and manipulating people.

> Anyway, France is over and done with. Finn was brooding over Claudine but I keep telling him the past is past. Isn't that what we've always said, haven't we made our lives work around this? We've both suffered but I'm living the dream as a successful artist with a gorgeous husband. I can see it on Instagram every day, I feed off everyone wanting to be me. It's all behind us, I killed Claudine Lambercier, she's gone for good, and nobody must ever know. Sometimes I feel tempted to tell

Elena. Once we were like sisters but we're not as close as we used to be. If I did, I can just imagine the look on her face. As open-minded as she seems, I know she'd judge me as much as everyone else. She too loves Instagram Artist Sophia—the glossy, perfect person I project.

What the hell?
I read the line over and over again.

I killed Claudine Lambercier.

I knew it. I sensed Finn hadn't dared tell me everything. So Sophia did meet Claudine before she died, and no doubt saw her as a rival, the half-sister Finn had grown up with and adored too deeply.

This is worse than anything I've imagined. My former friend, who is now giving birth to my partner's child, is—a murderer?

48.

SOPHIA

I sit by the toilet, reaching for a tissue, wiping the vomit from my lips. Morning sickness is worse than I thought it would be, but it's also strangely satisfying, like a sacrifice for the blessing I've been given.

I wander back into the bedroom that doubles as my studio. I don't feel like painting, but the commissions are piling up. The paints' toxicity is not compatible with pregnancy. I love to use oils but I mustn't handle any turps, and I need to find a substitute for Cadmium Red. I noticed a little scratch on my finger the other day and if any of those lead-based colors leaked in—well, that would be it. I'm making lists of good and bad foods, googling the right supplements and vitamin pills. I might even stop dyeing my hair, become a brunette for the first time in years. Love and fear drive me on. If I don't make every effort I can, I fear I will be punished: she will leave me.

Finn says I'm fretting too much.

"We've waited for this for years," I cried. "We've done the switches, perfected the art of the game, taken all the risks—this is our precious moment. Aren't you happy to be a father at last?"

"Of course I am," he replied, giving me a hug.

I think maybe he's scared too. Back in Cornwall, the second switch with Scott yielded a positive test. The trouble was, it coincided with

Meghan's tantrums about how she'd fallen for Finn. I blame her for what happened then. The stress really got to me. I was lying in bed one night, suffering a nightmare that Scott had come into the bedroom and plunged a knife into my belly, yelling that he'd found out they'd been tricked. I woke up in a sweat and for a moment it seemed as though my dream had leaked into real life. There was blood pooling between me and Finn. My body had dealt with the stress by translating it into nightmare. I started screaming. I was hysterical; so was Finn. Our baby girl had fled. That day, we closed the curtains, ignored all calls, drank ourselves into a stupor of bitter sadness.

I lost her at five weeks.

But now I've made it to seven, and this time it's different. I conceived her in Villefranche, which I thought was a cursed place for me. My prayer in the church was heard. The auspicious sign was correct. This must signal a fresh start, my luck has turned. I didn't even have to persuade Adam not to wear a condom. He was in a joyful holiday mood and submissive with desire, so when I whispered, *let's just leave it off and let Nature decide,* he replied, *oh, yes,* and clasped me tight and that was that.

I remove my diary from the pile by my bed, wrapped in its Simenon cover. I notice that the newspaper article about Claudine has been torn. Has Finn been snooping? Why would he need to look in my diary when we have no secrets from each other?

I'm losing him.

We're sitting in the Ivy Café together. Finn seems so distant. He plays about with his fork. As the waitress comes up to take our order, I charm her by announcing my pregnancy, explaining that dairy seems to disagree with me.

"Oh, congratulations!" she gushes.

Finn kicks into action. He clasps my hand, puts on a smile: the happy couple.

The waitress promises to adapt my favorite dish so that it's dairy-free. I'm exaggerating the dietary complaint—I will grab any excuse to tell people. I would announce it on Instagram, but it feels too soon.

We're invigorated by her presence, playing to our personas, but the moment she's gone we both seem to wilt and fall silent. Panic begins to rise inside me again. Finn is the only man I've ever truly loved. Nobody else can replace him. We've sworn eternal love, till death do us part. So, why is he behaving like this? Doesn't he want this baby?

His phone buzzes in his pocket. He makes to reach for it—then leaves it unanswered. He drums his fingers on the table.

"How's Elena?" I ask warily.

"Elena?" He feigns ignorance.

"You know. The woman you fucked three times." I mean to sound flippant, but my tone comes out far more acidic than I intended. I bite my lip. I know he hates it when I get into these moods. Finn always said it should be us against the world, not us against each other.

"I am in touch with her, but only about a proof-reading job. We need to keep her happy and distracted. We're in a precarious situation," he says.

"I think we're in a blessed situation," I say hotly.

The waitress comes with our drinks and we flash her super-watt smiles. Finn waits for her to go, then says: "I can't just drop Elena completely when we have a professional relationship, any more than you can ditch Adam's film project. We have to keep up the act, behave normally and rationally. If we suddenly cut off the moment you're pregnant, how will it look?"

Ouch. I fall silent, fiddling with a fork. Maybe Finn's right. Elena's the smart one in their relationship. She's the threat. Adam's far too wrapped up in his film to notice anything. But surely her tongue is tied: she can't admit anything to him. As far as I can see, it's checkmate.

Our meals arrive. I pick at my food. I wish I could just press fast-forward on the next seven months and have her in my arms, warm and soft, and kiss her little face, and clutch her little hand in mine.

Then Finn says: "In a few weeks I'll go back to Cornwall. I can get the easels you wanted, and anything else you need."

Cornwall: we've not been back in nine months. Our house there with its Gothic towers and sprawling drive and those dark evergreens. The cold, dark rooms. Another place with too many memories. It was useful for the last switch, an impressive location, but Finn and I agreed recently that it would be better to sell up and buy somewhere in Wimbledon. And yes, we've been putting off sorting out MacInnes House, and I'm glad Finn's volunteered, but I sense he's hiding something. He's fingering his left earlobe, which is his tell.

Suddenly I twig. Fury fills me. I push my fork into the back of his hand, the tines creating white pressure in the skin. He yelps and freezes up.

"You're going with *her*, aren't you?"

"No." He stares at me with terrified eyes.

"I can't stand it when you lie!" I push the fork in harder.

"Okay, okay," he admits. "I have asked her."

I realize that diners at the next table are looking over. I remove the fork. There are red furrows in his skin, as though he's been bitten by a wild animal.

Finn and Elena. I thought that when I told her about the pregnancy, about Finn masterminding the switches, that she'd give up. I thought I'd won. Yes, I know *I* engineered the switches, but everything is different now that I'm pregnant, surely? Has she no respect?

"So, you're going for a romantic weekend?"

Finn turns to me and says emphatically: "I'm just playing her. Okay?"

I fall silent, tucking into my food. Am I going crazy? Are my hormones blurring my judgment? I've been happy for Finn to play women in the past. I've admired him for it. When we first began on the switches, he read seduction manuals, often with laddish titles. But they were mostly silly and we both mocked their inherent misogyny. It turned out they weren't needed, anyway. He has a natural instinct for charming women. I think his trick is that he's a good listener. Not many men are very good at sitting with a woman and really *seeing* her, into her. Society makes us wear more masks than men have to, as wives and mothers and friends and bosses. While most men are busy fetishizing such archetypes, Finn has the ability to look beyond them: it's his gift.

I look at the way he's fingering his collar. How he keeps brushing his hands against his phone. The way he's standing up now, saying he needs the cloakroom, needs to wash the blood from his hand.

In the past, he would always comfort me with touch as well as words. He would hold me tight and stroke my hair. None of this feels right. He's lying, I know it.

He returns to the table looking brighter. I realize he probably went off to call her. My food tastes like ash. The restaurant is a stage that's collapsing. The diners have faces like plates. Nothing's real, nothing's real. I stand up, throwing my glass of juice in his face just as the waitress comes up. Her expression of horror is satisfying. I storm off, leaving Finn to sort out the mess.

It's a ten-minute walk back home. I hammer up the stairs, slump on the bed. I open the cabinet drawer, seeking Adam's watch. Just holding it and stroking it, connecting with his history, always seems to calm me, and her too. It's as though she smiles and says, *Daddy*.

But the watch has gone. Who the fuck took it. Finn? Séverine?

My breathing is ragged. I tell myself I mustn't get stressed, it's not good for my darling, but I can't help feeling bereft, as though the loss of the watch is a terrible omen.

49.

ELENA

Just give us another thirty minutes. William's having a tantrum. Don't think he's happy about staying with Grandma! ☹

Adam and I are gathering up our bags and coats and pulling on our shoes when the text comes through. We peel them off again. We're going over to our friends', Angela and Anil, for the evening. I've been looking forward to it all week. I texted Anil after I found the diary: **I think Sophia might actually be a murderer—seriously.** To his credit, he didn't laugh or accuse me of melodrama. He texted, **We'll talk about it when you come.** I know the night will be therapeutic, soften the simmering tension with Adam too. We'll eat with them, laugh with them, play our game of cards, Angela will put some nineties disco on and we'll have a boogie. And then when we're all really drunk, Anil and I will find a quiet corner and I'll be able to update him on everything. I'll tell him about Sophia and Claudine. I'll tell him that Finn still keeps texting me, refusing to clarify anything, insisting I come to Cornwall, and I'm too close to caving in, and in the meantime Adam is still oblivious and doesn't seem to care about anything except his film.

I switch on Netflix. There's season two of that crime drama. We watched the first season the evening of the first switch. I think back to that night: how I thought I wouldn't be good enough to satisfy Finn, how I thought Sophia was a goddess I couldn't live up to. God, I was so naïve.

"Let's play Crescendo instead," Adam says, switching it off. "Come on, we're out of practice and we can't have Anil win *again*. He'll murder us."

The joviality in his voice sounds forced; I sense he's not really in the mood for going out. But I grin and nod and we sit down at the table. Adam deals three cards face down, three cards face up, three cards for us to hold.

As we switch in good cards for bad, Adam says casually: "Um, the shoot's been brought forward to next month. It's the only time Hoult is available."

"Uh-huh." He's told me this three times in the last week.

"Don't suppose you could check in on Mum? I mean, she's got her carer, but—you know. Just in case."

"Sure."

He flicks me a look, mistaking my sigh for simple resentment. It's not just the irritation of waiting on a woman who loathes me, it's the weird-ness of the current situation. On the surface, we're on autopilot, ticking through our usual routines, but there's constant tension simmering un-derneath. I keep thinking, *surely Adam's going to ask what's wrong. Surely he must have noticed that I'm not myself right now.* He seems oblivious, or maybe this is why he's buried himself so deep in his film: he's hurting and hiding in his obsession.

We play for a few minutes, putting down cards, picking them up, and Adam says: "If it's really, really uncomfortable, then Sophia has said she'll go."

My head flips up. "You can't let that psycho bitch near your mum!"

Adam looks taken aback by the venom in my voice.

I moderate my tone: "I just think that you should be careful around her."

"What? Why? That's a bit strong."

"I've cut her out of my life completely," I say carefully. "And look, I know you're doing your film with her, but once you get to the point where you don't need her anymore—I'd keep away."

"But—I thought you and Sophia were good friends?"

"We were . . ." I feel exasperated, hearing him defend her the way I once did. What can I say without giving too much away? I jump up and remove his watch from my handbag, passing it over to him.

"You found it!" Adam's face lights up.

"I found it in Sophia's house. In her bedroom."

Adam strokes it then straps it onto his wrist. "Well, maybe she took it by accident."

My exasperation grows. He used to warn me she couldn't be trusted; now he's behaving as though she's some sort of saint.

"She's pregnant, you know," I burst out.

"Really?" Now he does look taken aback. "I didn't know. Wow."

"Yes." My voice is high, my heart racing. I've been rehearsing this conversation for so long: I can't believe we're finally having it. I'm terrified of how he might react but I'm also desperate to be released from the weight of this guilt, which has grown so heavy.

"When did you find out?"

"About a week ago."

"Why didn't you tell me?"

"Because . . ." I put down an ace. *Say it*, I push myself, *just be honest. Say it, say it, say it.* "Because I think the baby might be yours."

Adam gapes at me in shock.

"Mine?" His tone is light. "Oh, sure, it's mine . . . only we've never slept together. She's got a husband, in case you hadn't noticed. As far as I know, you can't get pregnant from working on a script together. This isn't like the Lorraine thing," he adds, as though pre-empting any mention of her.

"No." I fall silent, losing my nerve.

"I know we've been spending a lot of time filming together . . ." Adam suddenly looks furtive.

"You have—you have actually slept with her," I confess, but he cuts in: "It was just one kiss, in Villefranche. You said you had a headache, you went off for that walk . . . we were on the beach, she was drawing me, she tried to kiss me. I said I didn't think we should mix up a working relationship with a romantic one. She was fine about it. I think it was just a heat-of-the-moment thing."

Oh, fuck. Another thing that Sophia forgot to mention. That's why Adam was so weird after they left.

"You're right—Sophia isn't like Lorraine," I assert. "Because she's dangerous. She's manipulative, controlling, and I know it's hard to see it but you're part of a very elaborate game she's playing. And I'm sorry, you might not realize it—but you have slept with her."

There. I've said it. I've said it, I've said it, I've said it.

"We were just a bit tipsy in Villefranche," Adam goes on. "We had all that wine at lunch. I guess we have got close with the film, but she hasn't even brought it up since. To be honest, I was flattered. Half the time you hardly seem interested in me, except for that one night in Villefranche . . ."

The defensive hurt in his voice reminds me of how he sounded when I first found out about Lorraine. I feel my hackles rise at the thought of him and Sophia together, on that beach—*and* after he reassured me at our dinner in Carluccio's that there was nothing between them. Sophia is such a bitch. Then I gaze into his eyes and see the pain. I realize his recent withdrawn state has been a way of masking unspoken misery. And I can't get mad at him, not after what I've done. Adam's confession is also a relief: we've both betrayed each other.

"It's a game we set up. It was Sophia's idea . . ." I hesitate: this is the hardest part. "You know that book by Roald Dahl, *Switch Bitch*?"

"No." Adam is looking very confused. His eyes are narrowed and he's staring hard at me. "Is this about Finn? You were fawning all over him at the opera."

"It was a switch." My voice cracks. "I'm really sorry. Yes, I have slept with him."

Tears fill Adam's eyes. He blinks hard. I swallow.

"How many times?" he asks.

"Three," I confess in a quiet voice.

"*Three times?* Three fucking times? Since when?"

"Since May—the night of the first switch, when you slept with Sophia . . ."

"Oh, sure, this is all me." His voice rises. "So that's why you've suddenly been bringing up Lorraine, to try to make out we're even now or something—but—but—with her, it was just this nightmare drunken one-night madness, I was barely conscious, and you—*three times*. I mean, that's . . . *that's* . . ."

"Wait. Please. Just let me explain, I'm trying to tell you—"

"Right. Go on then. Explain."

Seeing the look on his face is agonizing. For a moment I nearly backtrack, say it's all an elaborate joke. No: I have to force myself through this, get to the other side.

"Sophia got this idea that we should do a switch, without you and Finn knowing." Even as I say the words out loud, they sound so surreal. "I'd creep into her house, her bedroom, in the dark of night, she'd do the same. We'd do a—a—switch—and then creep out, so neither of you would ever know. And we did it. Three times. And I'm so, so sorry. It wasn't fair on you to trick you like that . . ."

Adam is silent. He stares back at his cards, as though unable to look me in the eye, ordering them in a hierarchy of value. Then he puts down three fours.

"Your go."

"Right." I can't even process what cards I'm holding. "So—what do you think?"

"Elena, it's bullshit and you know it is," he says in a quiet voice.

"*What?*"

"As if Sophia could slip in like that and I wouldn't notice—it's ridiculous."

"But we have blackout blinds—and—we paid attention to every

detail . . ." Seeing the look on his face, I trail off. I try again: "Look—what about Villefranche? You thought you saw her in our room. Didn't you think that was weird? It's because she *was* in the room . . ."

"Yeah, I reckon she came in to try her luck, maybe. I don't know why you're making all this up, but you've been so weird recently and this just tops it all."

"Why—why would I make it up?" I cry in disbelief.

Adam scrapes his cards against his palm.

"Sophia says you're jealous of her," he says. "And I defended you to her, but I reckon there's some truth in it. You had your hair done like hers, you copied her, you wanted to be like her, you've seduced her husband."

"She was the one who organized that bloody haircut for me," I yell. Fuck. I can't believe we're arguing about *hair*. Of course, I realize, panic rising, this is what Sophia foresaw from the start: if Adam did get fooled, I'd never be able to convince him. His ego is at stake, his judgment, his intelligence; he can't accept the humiliation of being tricked by two women.

I notice that his hands are trembling. I reach out, try to rub one of them, but he recoils.

"What's going on here is that you have slept with Finn *three times*, and now you're making up some stupid story so you can accuse me of adultery when *you're* the one who's had the affair."

"No!" I protest. "Adam, that's not what happened."

"And was it good with him?" His voice is a whip.

I can't reply.

"Or did you play games with him like you have with me, all loving and up for sex one night, and the next being icy cold? Then making fun of me, spanking me, playing games, making up lies, trying to gaslight me that I've supposedly slept with Sophia. That's abuse, Elena, that's what's going on here. We're in an abusive relationship and you're the abuser! Sophia showed me an article about it."

"I—"

"I can't do this anymore." Adam gets up, throwing his cards down on the table, a Queen whirling to the floor. "I'm sorry—I've had enough. I'm going to stay at Mum's tonight."

I jump up, trembling.

"Oh, great—go to your mum's, to the woman who's blackmailing you!" I call and he stops in his tracks. "I know she's got all this money she's hoarding, that she won't give you until you break up with me because I'm so *unsuitable* . . ."

Adam turns to look at me, his face white.

"How did you find out?"

"Sophia overheard your conversation," I say, but there's no flicker of recognition: he doesn't register that it must have been Sophia in his bed that night.

"Well, Mum was clearly right," he says. "I should have bloody listened to her sooner."

I listen to the sounds of him going into the bedroom, the bang of his suitcase on the floor.

I'm numb with shock. I can hear myself breathing hard and fast and the sound of tears catching in each exhalation. I knew that getting everything out in the open was going to be hard, that it would potentially obliterate us . . . But for me to suffer the torture of telling the truth, only for him to buy into Sophia's lies, is madness. I'd realized that Sophia is a nasty piece of work, but I hadn't seen quite how far she would go.

Suddenly the realization pierces through my shock: I can prove it.

I run into the bedroom, where Adam is tossing socks into his case.

"I can show you her messages!" I cry. "From when we were doing the switches."

Adam crosses his arms. "Okay," he says in an icy tone, but there's fear in his red-rimmed eyes.

It makes me feel ill, scrolling back through the zigzag of our Whats-App correspondence. All those friendly, cheery messages. All those times I praised her: **Wow, just saw your new painting up on Insta—it's awesome.**

Selfies of us together. I scroll faster. Back to the second switch, in June. Here we are . . .

> **This message has been deleted.**
> **This message has been deleted.**
> **This message has been deleted.**

My mouth is an O. Mine are there—but all her replies have been voided.

"Come on then," Adam pushes me.

"Hang on," I whisper.

I scroll back further, to May, to the weeks before the first switch, when we exchanged messages about swapping shampoo, perfume, clothes.

> **This message has been deleted.**
> **This message has been deleted.**
> **This message has been deleted.**

What did Sophia say, right at the start? Words which seemed a consolation at the time but I realize now were a threat: *If anyone accused me, I'd just deny it . . .*

"I . . ." My voice trails off helplessly. "Oh, God, you have to believe me—she's deleted all the evidence, just as she always warned me, but I didn't see it . . ."

"Sure," says Adam, turning his back to me, carrying on with his packing.

"She—" I want to say *she's a murderer*, but I can imagine how Adam will react.

His shoulders shake as he starts to weep and the sound breaks my heart.

The doorbell rings. I stand frozen, unable to move or speak.

It rings again.

Adam walks out of our bedroom, refusing to look at me. I hear him open the door and Anil's cheery voice booming out, saying he's called us both ten times each and he's been wondering what's going on. As he enters the flat, I feel hot tears spilling from my eyes, slipping down my cheeks. "Elena?" I hear him say. "What's going on? Are you okay?"

50.

ELENA

I wake up in the middle of the night. My mobile says it's two thirty-three. For one surreal moment, I can't work out why Adam has white hair. Then I remember that I took Lyra to bed with me for comfort and she's sprawled out across his pillow.

I get up and go to the bathroom. Everywhere I look his absence is confirmed. His toothpaste—gone. His shampoo—gone. His shaving cream—gone.

My hands shaking, I find myself calling Anil.

Even though it's the middle of the night, he's kind enough to pick up. He'd seen the state I was in earlier when he came over; but Adam had snapped tearfully, "We just need some privacy!" and I'd nodded in agreement, so Anil had backed out then, looking awkward. Now he's my hero. He says he's coming right over.

We sit at the kitchen table. The night quiet is eerie. I make him some tea and hug him for his generosity.

"I think she's a sociopath," I say. "I don't think she ever felt a thing. I was just her pawn. The way she played on the class thing, worked out my vulnerability. I think she's probably laughing now, knowing we've broken up." I picture Sophia feigning sympathy, patting Adam's arm, musing on his mother's wisdom in withholding the money, and I want to punch her.

"You know, even if you had showed those messages to Adam, would it have made things much better?"

"He would have known she was lying and I was being honest." I pause before adding, "She's bloody carrying his baby! He doesn't even know it!"

"You got unlucky," Anil says. "You should have introduced me to her back then. I'd have sussed her out."

"She took over my life—all I could think about was her." *And Finn*, I add silently. "Still . . . at least it's all come out now," I add, tears gathering again.

"Hey, you know what?" Anil gives me a pat on the back. "I've never really thought you and Adam suited each other."

Though I've sensed this, it's one of those rare things he's kept quiet about during our friendship. This is the first time he's spoken his doubts out loud. It's hard to hear him. I imagine he's going to say that Adam is some overprivileged white male, but instead he says: "You've tended to give more, Adam's tended to take. And—when I knew you at Cambridge, you were wild."

I smile through my tears, remembering how Anil and I bonded in our first term, fed up with the toffs, partying together.

"Adam's got you all reined in, somehow. The penny-pinching . . ."

"But that's sensible!" I defend him.

"Elena, he earns six figures a year. Since when have you been into sensible, anyway? He's got you stuck in a rut, and you've been too trapped in a co-dependent relationship to get out . . ."

"I—"

But Anil's on a roll now. "There's been something missing . . . some spark. Sometimes when I was with you, it was as though you were brother and sister."

"Oh, great, you have a whole *list*," I exclaim and Anil winces apologetically, as though he didn't mean to be so brutal. I know there's truth in his words, but I'm too raw to hear it right now. Everything has been such a head spin that I've lost all sense of perspective. I don't trust my judgment anymore, not after I was so wrong about Sophia. I'm not even sure if I know who I am.

The next morning I wake up late, feeling foggy. I make some tea, cuddle Lyra, pick up my mobile.

I have to stop looking at Sophia's Instagram. It's like picking a scab. I keep wondering if she's going to announce the pregnancy, if Adam will like the post.

Oh, fuck. Talk about rubbing it in. Her latest post is a drawing of him, captioned: *My latest work, soon to be a portrait. Adam is the talented script-writer on the film I'm exec producing.* I'm ready to explode.

I unfollow her.

Then a thought strikes me. I wonder if it's worth trying to get in touch with Meghan Roskilly again—perhaps she can give me the answers I'm looking for. Scrolling through her recent pictures, I notice sharp shifts in tone from one month to the next. In August she was posting pictures of dead birds, feathers dull and insides rotting; September is all shots of foaming waves, blue skies and treasures found on the beach. If she was on a downer when I last got in touch, now she's on the up.

Hey, I message her, I was just wondering how you're doing? I was thinking of visiting Cornwall—maybe we could meet up for a coffee! I've recently learned the hard way that you're right, Sophia's not to be trusted. Maybe we could chat more?

She might never bother to read it. Because she unfollowed me, it will sit in her inbox as a "Request" she needs to accept. Still, if she does bite, the trek over there would be worth it: to chat with another of Sophia's victims, to share my pain with someone who's been through the same agony.

51.

ELENA

Every morning, I get up, go to my local Costa café, and dive into my work. I'm exhausted, and my eyes feel horribly sore, but it's a way of shutting everything out. A month ago I'd been worried that my business might dry up altogether, but for the past week my inbox has been full of requests all saying the same thing: *Finn MacInnes recommended you as an excellent proof-reader . . .* I'm so moved I actually weep. I want to thank him, but don't dare get in touch.

At lunchtime, I go shopping for a few food items in Sainsbury's. Perhaps I ought to be going to Lidl, economizing. If Adam and I live separately, London's going to be beyond my salary. Anil was kind enough to offer me a spare room last night, if it came to it. But I wonder if it's too much, invading their family space. I could go home to Mum and Dad but I dread that it's going to be like it was last time. I won't be able to tell Mum about the switches and she'll nag and nag me to make up with Adam.

Mum's always been proud of me as the high-flying daughter who lived the life she aspired to herself. Now I feel like such a failure. I know she was once tempted to stray from Dad. She only ever spoke of it to me fleetingly, one night when she was drunk. But she made the sacrifice and stayed with him and me, because in those days that's what you did, she said, as though it was the 1950s rather than the 80s. Still, I know she prided herself on that decision, on her sense of duty. I've been weak where she was strong.

Back in the flat, it's so quiet without Adam. Whistling. Joking. Cracking open a Siren beer. Making cups of his Yorkshire Gold tea. Hogging the sofa. Leaving towels in the bathroom. Working on his script.

I want to call him but I feel too ashamed. Any attempt at reconciliation has to come from him, if he's ever ready to forgive me.

I picture what he might be doing right now. No doubt Hilary'll be reinforcing the breakup, telling him that he can go ahead and find a more suitable partner for the reward of her financial support. Fury surges in me again. Maybe our relationship was always doomed, even if Sophia hadn't come along.

I still feel so disturbed by that diary entry: *I killed Claudine.* I tried to discuss it with Anil, but he just looked dubious.

"What can you do?" he asked. "Play detective? You have no idea what really happened. It seems to me like the dead girl's become a distraction from facing the real issue. Forget her, Elena, and just focus on you and getting better."

So, I've taken his advice, but still, the unease lingers: what if Sophia is a full-blown psycho? How can Finn live with her when she's killed his half-sister?

The doorbell rings: Adam? I fling it open. It's a girl with short pink hair. One of our new neighbors. She says a parcel came for me while I was out.

It's a box of Charbonnel et Walker chocolates. I open up the little envelope attached, yanking out the card.

I know you're hurting but please don't give up on us. Come to Cornwall with me?

Finn.

The texts start up again soon after.

I'm sorry to hear that you and Adam split up.
If you come to Cornwall, you can have your own room. I
will respect your needs.
Just me let be a friend to you. Let me cheer you up.

There are presents too, that come in the post.

A first-class train ticket to Cornwall; he's offered to drive me there, but has said I might want to travel on my own.

A CD of Shostakovich's opera.

A first edition of *Wuthering Heights*.

I want to go. I want to be in bed with him, kissing him, drowning everything out in that delirium we create together. But I have no idea anymore who Finn is: the tender romantic bruised by a traumatic childhood, or the villain Sophia painted, a womanizer with an unconventional marriage?

Despite everything, I still have a spark of belief in him. I think that he, too, is under Sophia's thumb. He is another of her victims—I'd love to rescue him from her. I tell myself it would be for his own good, but I have to acknowledge a part of me can't help wanting revenge.

But then what? The moment I get on that train, I'm making the decision. Sophia will find out; she'll tell Adam. It will be like saying to him definitively that it's over between us, but that I'm not strong enough to do it to his face.

It feels so final.

And, as Anil tells me, I'm in no state to be making any decisions right now.

A few nights later, I'm over at Anil and Angela's flat. I'm babysitting their son as a thank you for all the kindness they've shown me.

William's tucked up in bed at nine; I read him a bed-time story, a chapter from Roald Dahl's *The Witches*.

I turn out the light and he promises to be good and go to sleep.

In the living-room, I sit on their squashy couch. Their flat is cozy, filled with their togetherness: in the photos of them up on the mantelpiece, in their slippers, sitting side by side in the corner, and, more than that: an atmosphere of laughter and love in the air. I wonder what atmosphere Adam and I created. I'm starting to hate our new flat, which has no history in it except a few weeks of bad memories.

A text on my phone from Finn.

> **I'm going to be honest with you. I'm glad you broke up. I don't think he deserved you. I don't think he knew how to make you happy, either in or out of bed.**

I'm so inflamed that I take the bait and reply.

> **Don't be so cruel. My life's fallen apart.**

Little bubbles form as he composes his answer. I stiffen, dreading that he's going to suggest a hotel room, where he can "console me" with sex and a post-coital chat full of lies. Well, I won't go.

> **I'm sorry. I know what you're going through and I just want to hold you tight.**

I didn't expect that. It's so tender, that I can't help it.
I fall.
Yes, I reply, **I'll come to Cornwall.**

52.

SOPHIA

I'm going to have an abortion!" I yell.

Finn is striding toward the front door, carrying his travel bag.

"Stop manipulating me," he snaps. Then, more gently: "You know I need to do this, and I'll be back on Monday. I'll call you as soon as I get there. Please don't get *hystérique*."

He leaves the house; I slam the front door after him.

I run into the living-room, watching him from the window. He gets into the car and programs the satnav for Cornwall. It'll take him a good six hours to reach Crugmeer. A scream tears out of me that he doesn't hear.

The house seems quiet without him, yet the ticking of the grandfather clock is thunderous. It seems to get louder and louder until I can't bear it any longer. I grab my handbag and take refuge in Cannizaro Park. I sip tea in the restaurant; rain spits against the window. I crave another sign to let me know that everything will be all right.

Sorry, I keep whispering to our baby. *I didn't mean it. I was just trying to shock your daddy. He's deserted us both.* I'm so scared that by saying those words I've jinxed everything.

I walk into the woods, trying to find solace in nature, but all I can see is rot and savagery: a dead bird being eaten by worms, trees dropping their leaves, a flailing queen bee struggling on the path. I always knew this moment might come, when Finn would move on from me. We know each other inside out, but we are stagnant. We protect each other but we hold each other back. I recall that maxim: *if you love someone, let them go . . .*

Back home, I dismiss Séverine. I try to make my own dinner. Finn has always laughed at my appalling cooking. I overcook the crab pasta and the parcels disintegrate on my plate. I hear *his* voice jeering, saying I'm no good at anything. Elena's a good cook; I wonder if she's feeding him now.

I pick up a wine glass and throw it against the wall.

How can he prefer her over me? With her drab brown hair and bright clothes and that clownish lipstick? She's a proof-reader—the most boring profession ever. With the last switch, I feared Meghan might be a threat because she was beautiful, far more so than Elena, yet Finn didn't care a jot for her. What does Elena have?

Maybe I should take revenge.

I pick up my phone and send a text: **Would you like to meet for a drink in Wimbledon this eve? Sorry short notice.**

His reply is immediate: **Love to. Name the place and time and I'll be there.**

I don't bother to sweep up the glass. I put on a little black dress, wind my hair into a chignon, apply smoky eye makeup. I smooth my hand over my belly: *Stay with me, stay with me.*

I meet Adam an hour later, at the Dog and Fox. He's dressed to impress too: an intricately patterned purple shirt with well-cut black trousers. But even in the dimmed light of the bar, he looks worse for wear: bags under his eyes, a sadness in his gaze, a smile that tries too hard.

"So excited that we've cast Nicholas Hoult for the film," I enthuse, and Adam brightens.

We talk excitedly about him for a while and then I probe: "How are you holding up? Heard anything from Elena?" I want to eke out every little detail from him as to why any man would fall for her. I was so busy seeking out her fatal flaw, her anxieties about class, that I forgot to consider her strengths:

But the moment I say her name, Adam looks crucified and says, "I can't talk about that." I smart: he's heartbroken, clearly still in love. How can she have this effect on men?

"Congratulations on your pregnancy," he changes the subject.

I scan his face: his expression is warm, sincere.

"Thank you," I say, beaming. "I'm so happy—I'm not so sure about Finn though."

"Ah, that's crap," Adam says in sympathy. "I would've thought he'd be over the moon."

"I would have thought so too."

"He doesn't deserve you," he says, his voice thick with emotion, patting my arm, his hand lingering. I see the dilation in his pupils, just as I did that day in Villefranche, when he kissed me on the beach and I felt a spurt of triumph inside.

At the end of the evening, it happens again. Adam kisses me, nervous at first—"This won't affect the film, will it?"—and then with more passion. I sense his need to seek solace in my body, let desire dilute his cares. He must be looking for a way to get back at Elena, and I'm happy to oblige. I take him home. He gasps at the broken glass and I watch as he sweeps it all up for me, taking care to find every last sliver. Upstairs, we kiss, caress, on my double bed. I just want to fuck but Adam seems to want to take his time. The burn marks on my body make him frown, just as they did in Villefranche.

"Did your ex do that?"

I don't reply and his forefinger traces the faint scarring around my belly button.

"That was from a kidney I gave away," I say, feeling more comfortable explaining that one. "Key-hole surgery."

I can't bear the pity on his face. Determined to get the upper hand, I perform *that thing* he loves: tying him up and dominating him. He doesn't actually like to be spanked, just ordered about, humiliated. Afterward I lie fretting: will sex harm my little one? He was vigorous and I had to tell him to be more gentle. Still, I gave him an amazing orgasm; I heard it rip through him. More than she could ever manage.

Adam is staring at the ceiling, looking pensive.

"You know, when Elena and I broke up, she told me this outrageous story . . . about how you and her had done these switches, where you were in my bed, and she was in Finn's . . ."

"Crazy," I echo lamely, scared by the look of realization that's dawning on his face. "I can't believe she'd make up something like that."

Adam looks confused. But what can he do? He can't prove they ever happened. I'll deny them to my dying day, declare she's being weird, melodramatic.

"But when you tied me up . . . how did you know I'd like that?"

"Because Elena told me all about it," I lie—as if that idiot woman had any idea of his fetish; I intuited myself what would turn him on. "We used to be close, we shared that kind of story. Sorry. I did think it was too much information at the time, but we were drunk."

"Right."

"I thought it would please you," I add.

Fuck this. I can't be bothered with any more games, lies, excuses. I can't spend a night in bed having revenge sex while Finn and her are no doubt making rapturous love. I jump up, drag my suitcase out of my wardrobe, start throwing in clothes and toiletries.

"Where are you going?" Adam asks, sitting up, looking stricken.

I reply curtly: "Cornwall."

PART FIVE

53.

ELENA

The journey to Crugmeer is one of the longest I've taken in years. Finn drove down yesterday; he offered me a lift. But I felt it was important to rent my own car. If things get weird, I can depart quickly. I asked my new neighbor to feed Lyra. She declared herself a cat lover and said she was more than happy to.

I'd barely slept and was suffering serious doubts about whether to go, and whether I could face Finn, when a message came through from Meghan. She's had a change of mood and agreed to meet up with me on Tuesday for a coffee. I'm not sure if I want to hang around here for that long, but if need be I can always check into a hotel for a few days and lie low. I'm desperate to talk with her and hear her story.

I set off at one o'clock after lunch, slinging my half-burned omelet pan in the sink. I've googled Crugmeer several times: it's a small hamlet near the west coast, quiet and sparsely populated, with beautiful beaches. The Friday afternoon traffic is slow, at times. For the first few hours of the drive, I keep grinding gears and taking too many rest stops, tired from weeks of insomnia.

I pull in at the Cornwall Services. I'm surprised and touched to receive a text from Adam.

How are you?

Okay, I text back. **How are you?**

Okay. It's hard looking after Mum.

I would laugh, if it weren't so painful. *So you've finally found out the reality*, I think, *months too late.*

It is hard, I reply.

I'm sorry I got angry, his next text says. **I know I had no right to. I was just as bad with Lorraine. I understand why you did it.**

I frown, slip my phone back into my bag, wondering if I'm glad to have heard from him or not. He doesn't understand. It wasn't about revenge. I'm reminded of the patterns of our previous breakup, those tentative texts of apology; I sense he wants to take steps toward reconciliation. But over the past few days I've finally realized: it's over between us.

Every so often I suffer a storm of panic, because I've relied for too long on the safety net of our relationship. I should have left him years ago, after the Lorraine affair. It's not that Adam's a bad man, and we've had so many good times together. But he is selfish and I've ended up playing the domesticated role he wanted me to, over the years; failed to notice myself slowly sinking into it. His mum made it worse, made me feel I barely deserved him, that I had to hang in there and prove that I did. I didn't use the switches as revenge, I used them to break free. I can see that now, though my guilt over what I put him through is still heavy.

I'm not taking the easy option like last time. I'm not going back to him. I have to start afresh as a single woman. First, though, I need to sort out whatever this is with Finn.

As the afternoon shades into evening, I grow impatient, increase my speed; I'm only an hour away. I've had doubts over whether I had the physical and emotional strength for this journey. But I need closure. My life has fallen apart and one of the things that drives me wild is the lack of understanding, the whys. Why me? Why Adam? I keep calling Sophia a psycho, but in quieter moments of reflection, I know that I'm caricaturing her, because I'm so frustrated by the enigma of her and Finn.

Anil has warned me against expecting every piece of the puzzle to fall into place. He said that Finn and Sophia may have spent years developing their cover stories, that it might be dangerous to threaten their narratives.

While I feel Sophia is beyond redemption, I do have a sense that Finn wants to escape their charade. Perhaps that's just wishful thinking on my part. I remind myself to stay wary as I put my foot down on the accelerator.

54.

SOPHIA

I'm just exiting the Cornwall Services when I see her.

Elena.

She's driving a ruby-red Fiat. I didn't know they owned a car. She pulls into the petrol station, tugs out the petrol hose, taking care not to spill any drops on her black and white dress. Her hair is curled; her lipstick is so red it looks like she's painted on blood; I've never seen her make such an effort.

I quickly reverse and pull over by the side of the car park, letting my hair fall over my face, slotting on sunglasses, edging down in my seat. This coincidence has to be a sign: I'm doing the right thing in making this journey.

Elena doesn't notice me. I'm not sure if she's ever seen my car before, which is normally tucked away in the garage, unused. She's concentrating hard on the road, edging forward onto the A30, hands gripping the wheel. Either she's an anxious driver or she hasn't driven in a while. I have a vision of her crashing into a car, a multiple pile-up, her throat severed by flying glass. That would be a godsend.

She pulls out; I pull out. I drive a few cars behind her.

She's heading for Crugmeer, of course, but I still suffer a mounting sense of disbelief. I wonder if Finn really did invite her, or whether she insisted that she join him until he backed down.

I turn left, following her onto the B3274.

We carry on together, a few cars apart, and I taste that first sickly scent of sea-salt in the air. It's one I've come to loathe.

A feeling of nausea rises until I have to pull over in defeat. It feels painful, letting her leave my sight. When I can watch her, I've felt in control in some way, even if it's illusory. Now I picture her with Finn, weaving her magic, her lies.

Before setting off, I'd taken the set of knives from the kitchen, wrapped them in a Waitrose bag, dumped it on the back seat. I upend the bag, with a slithering metal clash as they fall out, and vomit into the plastic.

I unscrew a bottle of spring water, glugging it back. I shiver, feeling weak and cold. I'm worried about my little girl—when suddenly I feel a kick fluttering in my tummy. A rapturous moment: my first experience of it. I call Finn, desperate to share the moment with her father. He doesn't pick up.

I burst into tears, then: angry, vehement weeping. My joy returns with another kick.

She is my gift from God.

I drive on until the roads become narrow and winding and I can see flashes of dunes, tall grasses, the sea. We're in Crugmeer now. As I approach our home, the trees become taller and denser, towering above me on either side. The outline of our Cornish house looms up. The sight of the tall turret windows makes me feel nauseous.

I park a few roads away and edge up the drive toward the house on foot, blending with the shadows. Elena must have been going slow, I appear to have arrived first.

I leave all the knives behind except for one, which I put into my pocket. I feel it shift with the rhythm of my footsteps. Just in case: I believe Elena is capable of anything.

55.

ELENA

It's seven in the evening and I've finally reached Crugmeer. I stop by the side of the road for a break. I can see beautiful glimmers of the turbulent sea and I think of Finn and me, playing in the waves in Villefranche. The sky is such a strange color with sunset alongside the threat of storm. Shades of gold and shadows of gray.

I start the car up again, the roads becoming narrower, driving until I spot the sign: *MacInnes House.*

As I turn down the graveled driveway, it becomes harder to see, the trees forming a dark tunnel.

I've made it. I check my satnav: a six-hour drive, in total. I gaze up at the Gothic-style "house," which looks more like a castle to me. Finn appears. I exhale, my stomach a shimmer of butterflies. *Here goes.* I get out of the car, breathing in the lovely salty sea air. I stretch my legs, stiff with cramp.

The look of delight on Finn's face touches me, takes me by surprise. I frown, anger stirring at the thought of all his lies, but he pulls me into a hug. "I never thought you'd really come," he whispers. He kisses my neck, face, lips.

I pull back, steely in my determination. On the way here, I made a resolution not to sleep with him until I got the full story. I need to keep a cool head, avoid the intoxication of a love-lust high that leaves me too blurred to ask questions.

"Please can we take it slowly?" I ask.

He's disappointed, but he caresses my hand. "Let me give you a guided tour."

His patter is minimal. Each room evokes a few vague mutters from him. He doesn't seem all that proud of how big and grand the dwelling is. *I'd be showing off like mad,* I think wryly, although the atmosphere isn't welcoming. In the past, I've watched haunted-house documentaries on TV and laughed at the melodrama of investigators saying they sense a bad vibe as soon as they enter. But now I get it: the air is colder in than out, and there's a grimness to the stone, as though years of unhappiness have been fossilized into them. Heavy oil paintings grimace on the walls. The bedrooms are numerous, the windows small. We pass a hallway with a small square trapdoor set in the roof, a ladder for access: an attic.

Finn guides me into a bedroom that looks lighter and warmer than the others.

"This is your room for the weekend."

There's a blue duvet on the king-sized bed and a fresh spray of ferns and flowers in a vase on the antique dresser. It's en suite too, and the bathroom has one of those glorious old-fashioned claw-foot baths.

"When did you buy this place?" I ask his reflection in the window.

"I inherited it from my father," he says grimly. "When he died fifteen years ago. He's buried in the garden."

I put a hand on his arm: a mistake. I feel it then, the electric kick between us, and quickly draw away.

"I'm so hungry," I say, keen to leave the bedroom.

"You're in luck: I've been cooking," Finn says, with a grin. It's such a change from Adam's domestic passivity that I can't help but smile.

"Sounds good."

"I realize you want to take it slow," he says, as I turn for the door, "but what about just one kiss?"

I gaze at his beautiful mouth. After weeks of feeling down, bruised by the breakup, I feel so uplifted in his presence, nourished by the attraction between us. I can see it in his eyes. For me, Finn is temptation incarnate.

"No," I hear myself say, feeling both the pleasure and the pain of my resolve.

Finn lightens the tension with a joke: "My amazing cooking will woo you," he says, with a wink, and I burst into laughter. "Just wait till you get to dessert."

As we head down the back staircase to the kitchen, we pass by a wall of photos and paintings. I notice numerous rectangular white patches left where others seem recently to have been removed.

One picture catches my eye. It's similar to the one in Nounou's villa in Villefranche: of Finn, Claudine, and their father together on the gravel drive outside the big house. They're older in this photo. I hold back, examining it. I wonder if it was taken after the poisoning. Their father looks haggard, his skin leached pale, and he's leaning on a stick. Finn looks cute; Claudine's face is shadowed by a sunhat.

"Elena . . ." Finn calls up from the hall.

"Sorry."

We pass a living-room, a lovely old-fashioned log fire burning in the grate, and step into the warm light of the kitchen. Rain spits against the windows; outside, the wind is tossing the trees into frenzied shapes.

Finn refuses to let me do a single thing to help. He sits me down, pours me water, looking a little disappointed when I refuse wine.

"So is there anything you fancy doing this weekend?" A sizzle as he flips salmon pieces in the frying pan. "What about Monday?"

It's hard to think about activities when I have so many questions that I need to ask. *Be patient*, I tell myself, *you've got the whole weekend.*

"It'd be nice to wander on the shore. Too cold to swim, I guess?!"

"Freezing," Finn laughs. "But I sometimes brave it . . . I was thinking, though, that you should be doing something *special* on Monday. How old will you be?"

"You know? I was keeping it quiet! Oh, my God!"

I had decided to ignore my birthday. Now I can't help but feel touched by his thoughtfulness.

"You have some treats waiting for you," he promises me, and he looks so boyishly sweet, that my resolve wavers: I nearly jump up and kiss him.

He serves the meal: creamy Tuscan salmon with green beans. I can't believe how delicious it is. Finn sees the naked pleasure on my face and smiles. I grin back at him. For a moment we just gaze at each other in pure happiness.

Then the past, the mess of everything, comes rushing back and I lower my eyes.

Finn looks sad. He gets up and pulls a chocolate torte decorated with raspberries from the fridge.

"You know, I have some really fine dessert wine," he says. "Want to come and choose a bottle with me?"

"Okay," I relent.

He guides me into a narrow passageway that leads to a storeroom the size of a cupboard. There's a small selection of wines and he pulls out a Château d'Yquem, strokes the bottle and tells me he thinks I'll love the sweet taste, when—

Smash!

We both jump.

"What was that?"

56.

ELENA

We hurry back into the kitchen. A broken bottle is lying in pieces on the floor, vinegar seeping everywhere.

One of the windows by the sink is open. A sharp gust of air blows in, carrying with it a fine spray of rain.

"Just the wind," Finn says quickly, setting down the wine and sweeping up the glass. I grab a cloth to help mop up, but I feel shaken. I don't remember the vinegar even being out. I suffer a sudden shivery sensation that Claudine's ghost might be watching us, then quickly dismiss it.

Finn suggests we eat dessert in the sitting-room, so we snuggle up on the sofa with our plates on our laps. I resist a yawn; the long journey is catching up with me. Outside, the storm is gathering momentum, sheets of rain lashing the windows. I take a cautious sip of the sweet wine, feeling that this self-control is too hard; it's tempting just to give in, down the glass and surrender to Finn's caresses.

Instead I force myself to ask a difficult question:

"So, how do you feel about becoming a father?"

Finn looks as though he's been punched. But we can't keep on avoiding the subject.

"The baby . . . isn't mine," he says. "Sophia and I haven't slept together this year, so it's got to be Adam's."

"Sophia claimed you were having loads of wild sex recently."

"No." Finn's voice is firm. "She's lying. We don't sleep together," he repeats his earlier claim. "Have you told Adam?"

"I tried to," I confess. "Sophia also said to me that you'd done switches before, and it was all your idea. I figured that's how you ended up with Meghan as a stalker—she's a woman you went to bed with, who got hooked on you? Which I can understand. I mean, maybe I'm just as spineless as her . . ." I break off, hearing the hurt in my own voice.

There's a long silence. Finally Finn says: "I won't lie to you. There have been switches in the past, because Sophia wanted a baby—"

"A crazy way to go about it!" I exclaim.

"Sophia has had . . . a very difficult life. I think other people scare her," he says, to my surprise. "And I think that by turning every interaction into a game, it helps her to feel that there are rules, and a structure, and she knows how to play."

There's tenderness in his voice when he speaks of her that makes me feel confused.

"But you're ruining people's lives," I reply. "You can't treat people like this. It's unforgivable."

"I know," Finn says. "I know. I don't ever want to do a switch again."

It's unbearable to ask the question, but I do:

"And what about the other women you've switched with, in the past? How was it with them?"

Suddenly I feel on the verge of tears and I blink fiercely. Finn puts down his glass and comes closer to me. He brushes his hand over mine, gently, cautiously.

"I will never, ever do another switch," he promises me. "Because you're the only woman I slept with who I've fallen in love with. And I know this is all a complete mess, but I think you and I have something special . . ."

We do have something special. But where the hell can this go? How can he walk away from her when she's carrying a baby, even if it's not his?

How can he live with a child who may grow up to resemble Adam? I can't look at Finn; I'm too raw with hurt. He strokes my hair.

"You've had a long journey, and you need a good night's sleep. Let's go to bed early—separately," he adds hastily.

He rises from the sofa, but I feel too churned up with unanswered questions to leave it like this.

"What about Claudine? I'd like to hear more about her."

He tenses in surprise.

"I know that Sophia . . ." I trail off, not quite able to say the words. "I know—"

"We have all weekend to talk about the past. We'll discuss everything tomorrow, okay?"

I nod. He's right: I'm too exhausted for any more discussion.

But as Finn goes to lock up and I climb the stairs, my mind spins into action again. Sophia has her version of how the switches evolved, Finn has his: how can I really be sure who's telling the truth? Halfway up the stairs, I stop. I can't see a light switch, so I use my mobile to examine the display of photos on the wall again. What is it about that photo of the Aubert family that makes me feel so uneasy? I lean in, gazing at the necklace Claudine is wearing.

A crucifix.

It looks exactly the same as the one Sophia wears. My heart lurches. I imagine Sophia sitting at her dressing-table, putting on Claudine's stolen crucifix, smiling prettily, taking a selfie.

Imagine what it would feel like to die in a fire. Finding your bedroom door locked; the smoke seeping in, choking you. Running to the window, finding the drop is too far; the flames tearing through the door, and then reaching your hair, your skin. Could Sophia really have done that to her? My eyes fall to Monsieur Aubert's photo. Could they have been in on it together somehow? A wild theory flares in my mind: *could Aubert have been her abusive partner?*

I hear a noise and drop my phone in shock.

Finn is at the bottom of the stairs.

"Stop there," I say, my voice thick with fear. "I know you haven't told me everything about Claudine . . ." The next words are already hovering on my tongue: *I know Sophia killed her . . .*

Finn's face is a harlequin mask of shadow and light, impossible to read.

"And if you've lied to me about Claudine, how do I know anything you've told me about your past is true? Maybe—maybe you made it all up . . . I don't know what to believe anymore."

"Of course I haven't!" Finn sounds angry now. Suddenly he comes up the stairs, grabbing my arm tightly. "Come on," he insists, "come with me right now."

I follow him down. We tug on coats and boots, grab an umbrella, hurry out through the kitchen and into the wild night. Finn struggles to hold onto the umbrella as the wind whirls around us, driving rain into our faces.

We stumble across the sodden grass toward a grave—his father's. Behind it is a small rose bush planted behind a metal plaque. Finn shines his phone onto it, highlighting the rain-spattered inscription: **CLAUDINE LAMBERCIER 1991–2006**.

I gaze up at his face, the devastation in his expression. To my shock, he attacks the rose bush, tearing off the last of the petals, wrenching off wet leaves.

"Finn—don't!" I reach for him, stilling him. He turns, looking despairing; all at once, we're kissing passionately as the rain beats down on us. "I have told you the truth," he says, "but not all of it. I'm so tired of all these lies. I'll tell you everything, I promise. No more secrets."

57.

SOPHIA

Lights suddenly flash on again in the house. It's past midnight and I'm back in my car now, parked on the driveway behind a screen of shrubs. What the hell are they doing?

Earlier on, I'd crept up to the side of the house. Rain drenched me, poured off my waterproofs. Elena had been lazing around the kitchen while Finn cooked. I gazed in through the window after they'd eaten and abandoned the room. The sight of their used plates, the smell of Finn's creamy Tuscan salmon—my favorite dish of his—drove me wild. I decided to freak them out. I pushed open the window by the sink that never closes properly, reached in and tossed a bottle of vinegar onto the floor, then ran off, suddenly feeling hysterical with laughter.

Now it just feels like a dumb, facile move. I try to drive out images of them together in bed. It's disgusting: she's only just got here. His body belongs to me. His lips, his hair, his legs, his cock: it's mine, all mine. She is a fucking trespasser.

In the meantime, I've been stuck in this car, wrapped in a sleeping bag. With the pregnancy my bladder is weak and I've had to piss by a tree twice in the freezing cold, as undignified as you can get. It nearly made me cry, having to do that—*in my own garden*.

My fingers shaking, I flip down the car mirror, applying a fresh layer of makeup on top of today's dry caked-on one. When I was a teenager, I would watch my mother spend an hour each morning making up her face, as though constructing a shield against the world and its hardships. My hair looks awful now the blonde is growing out. Last week Finn made a faux pas: "Dark will look gorgeous on you—your natural color is the same as Elena's."

I slam the mirror back up. I've had enough.

I get out of the car.

I carry weapons, in case of an emergency. In one pocket is my knife, in the other my little bottle.

Oh, God, I pray, as I strive against the rain, *please give me the strength to do whatever is necessary . . .*

Suddenly I hear a sound, like the crack of a branch—and I stop. I keep suffering the jumpy feeling that I'm being watched. I hear a rustling and turn sharply—an animal, I expect, but with a house this size, we've had trouble with break-ins before, hence the need for a caretaker and alarms.

I hope nobody else is out here. I'm probably just exhausted and anxious.

I edge up the drive, then freeze. They're in the kitchen again, both of them drenched, kissing wildly. When Finn pulls back, his expression is so loving. A look he once reserved for me.

I blink hard, suddenly despairing and helpless. God has blessed me and now God mocks me.

My resolve hardens into ice. There'll be no divine intervention. Nobody is going to help me. I have to do this myself.

I creep round to the front door, unlock it, feel the relief of warmth after the harsh rain. I remove my damp shoes and tiptoe down the passage, hiding in the storeroom behind the kitchen.

My hand curls around the little bottle in my pocket. I can hear the kettle boiling; he's making tea.

As the noise fades, I can hear their voices.

"I'm going to come straight out and say it," Elena says, sounding tense and nervous. "I know Sophia killed Claudine."

What?

"Why—why would you think that?"

"I'm sorry. I know it was wrong—but I snuck into your house and read Sophia's diary."

"Sophia would be . . . pretty mad about that."

He's fucking right I'm pretty mad. *How dare she?*

"You've misunderstood," Finn goes on quietly.

What's he doing? He's not going to . . .

"Claudine and I—we had a very special relationship . . . and . . ."

You can't tell her, you can't tell her, I can't believe you'd betray me—

Quickly, I grab my mobile, calling him. The ringtone dances out, but he doesn't pick up.

"You're right that I knew Sophia long before university."

I have to act. Now. She has no right to share our secrets. Finn doesn't get it: knowledge will be her weapon. She'll use it to destroy us.

Nothing is going to stop me protecting my man and my child.

58.

ELENA

I open my eyes and instantly the pain is agonizing.

The throb of a migraine, only multiply it by a hundred: boring behind my skull-bone, punching at my temples, weighing heavy on my lids, and I think of those old-fashioned photos of the dead with coins placed on their closed eyes to press them down. I feel more dead than alive.

What happened? Where am I?

The ceiling spins. I'm naked. Back in the bedroom, the one I was in last night. Daylight sears through the window.

I try to turn my head, but it happens in slow motion. What's wrong with my body? I can see something red out of the corner of my eye . . . but . . . everything is spinning . . .

I open my eyes again.

The room is darker now. I fight the urge to sink down again into sleep. I turn my head and start.

There's a large red stain spreading out across the white sheet. Some of it has smeared on my arm. My fingers crawl up and touch skin. Red on my fingertip. It highlights the detail of each line and whorl. Blood. In my hair too, crusty on my earlobe.

A noise wells up from deep in my chest and tries to escape through my vocal cords, but they're too sluggish to comply.

What's happened to Finn? Where is he? Did Sophia come? Would she—would she do *that* to him?

I need to get up but my body won't listen—

I've been drugged. By who?

I've read about date-rape drugs in the papers from time to time, and shuddered at the thought, but never before known what it's like to feel as though my body has lost all free will.

I can't believe they'd do this to me.

I try to cry out his name—

—but the room blurs, as though I am underwater. I close my eyes, trying to fight, but the current laps over me and I go down, down, drowning in oblivion.

I wake up again. What time is it? My head is blurry and one ear is ring-singing.

Fragments of memories whirl in my mind: the drive to Cornwall on Friday; dinner with Finn; the photos; Claudine's grave; our kiss. Finn opening up to me and my heart filling with shock. All I remember was the thought: *this can't be, he must be lying*. His voice becoming more and more distant, a heaviness coming over my limbs, him crying out, *Are you okay?* I felt him trying to grab me as I slid down onto the floor . . .

Then what? Waking up in that bed, I recall in horror. With blood next to me. Did I dream that?

But wait . . . I'm no longer in the bedroom.

Someone has moved me. I'm gazing up at a pitched wooden roof; a small skylight that lets in daylight.

I'm lying on a single mattress. The sheet beneath me is clean and white. But the crumpled blue duvet has been moved here with me and there are still bloodstains on it. So that memory was real.

Someone has dressed me too. I'm now wearing a nightie, a silky plum-colored one that looks as though it might belong to Sophia.

I try to sit up and dizziness becomes a hurricane, swirling around my head.

So I ease myself up inch by inch. Maybe Finn carried me here because it's romantic, I tell myself. Because it's private.

But as I gaze around, my heart sinks. Why would he put me *here*?

It's an attic room. One half is cluttered with boxes and junk. There's a framed Van Gogh print of *Café Terrace at Night*; a lamp and a yellow shade with the tassels half torn away, hanging by a few threads.

The other half comprises my area: the mattress and a bottle of Volvic next to a Granny Smith apple on a plastic plate.

Is this some kind of crazy sex game? I rub my ear in the hope of the ringing dimming, to no avail. Just what was he thinking?

Unless none of this is Finn's work? I have a blurry memory of waking sometime in the dark, of voices, screaming and shouting, a thump. The more I try to coax it into daylight detail, the more it eludes me, and the more my head hurts.

I'd swear this was the work of Sophia. She might have followed me here to Crugmeer. But this seems a step too far even for her, given that I could go to the police. And even if Sophia were involved, how could she have the strength to carry me, especially in her present condition?

My throat feels thick and parched. I reach grudgingly for the Volvic, as though by drinking it I am accepting my imprisonment. I sniff it—is it safe? I down a third, then cough. I remind myself that I ought to save it, eke it out.

I stagger over to the skylight. I push it hard. It rattles, moves half an inch—but it's stuck. The sky, which is pale blue with a weak sun, suggests it might be morning. *Sunday morning?* I think.

There's a square trapdoor cut into the floor which I try to lift. It's locked from the other side.

Then I notice another, smaller square cut into the wood, next to the apple on the plate. I can't work out what that's for—it looks too compact for anyone to go in and out.

A noise: *the little door is opening.*

Up comes a hand, holding a plastic plate of bread and butter.

I reach out and hold on tight.

"Finn," I call down. All I can see is his arm and a little of his chin, prickly with stubble. He must be standing on a ladder, the one I saw dangling down when he gave me the guided tour on arrival.

"What's going on?" I hear the anger in my voice, the agony.

Silence.

"Finn, just tell me why I'm here. Let me down and let's talk. I won't be angry. This isn't—it's not *you*! Is it Sophia, is she . . . mad at us?"

He tries to pull his hand away, but I hang on tightly.

"Please—look . . ." I try to think fast. "If she's jealous, then I'll go. I'll drive home, leave you both in peace."

A sound, as though he's about to reply, but then the half-formed word collapses into silence.

I hear the thump of his feet on the ladder, footsteps receding on the floorboards below . . .

"Oh, God!" I let out a cry of fury and despair. I sit there for a while, my head in my hands. That little trapdoor terrifies me. It's as though it's been specifically made for this kind of incarceration, that preparations have been put in place well in advance. Did Finn lure me to Cornwall with this intent all along?

Think, I tell myself, *think, think, think*. What did he tell you before you went under?

Back at the kitchen table with Finn: he was denying that Sophia killed Claudine. And then—then he told me something momentous. What? *What?* It's like trying to remember a dream: it slides away the moment I try to pin it down.

I glance around again—there must be something here, anything that might help me escape.

That's when I see it.

On the wall, partly obscured by the boxes: scribbled writing. I try to push them aside, but they're too heavy. I crouch down, peering at the wall behind them, and I see the words carved into the wood: *Help me! Claudine.* I swallow, shocked. Claudine Lambercier, the dead girl, was locked in *here*? Just as I am now?

This must be the place where Sophia killed her.

Claudine was once her rival. Now I am.

I picture Sophia taking a lighter, setting fire to this room, my body going up in flames, and I shudder.

Calm down, I tell myself, as hysteria mounts. The article in Sophia's diary had stated that Claudine died in a fire in Villefranche, not here. I rack my brains as I try to remember—what did Finn say?

Food might fuel my thinking. I eat the bread and butter and the apple—presumably this is my breakfast—and then lie down in defeat, still feeling hungry.

And then, just as I let go, it comes back to me.

I sit up suddenly.

Finn biting his lip, barely able to look at me, whispering. The shock of his words slaps me again as I remember: "Claudine isn't dead . . . She didn't die in a fire . . . She's my wife."

59.

SOPHIA

I stand in the kitchen, gazing out at the pale light of the afternoon sun, glinting on Elena's red car.

"Twenty-four hours she's been in the attic," Finn complains, and I turn to face him. "Tomorrow is her birthday."

I jeer at him, shaking my head. "I spent three months up there."

That shuts him up. But I see the pain lingering on his face. How was he able to dissociate from my suffering when he has such instant empathy with her? Granted, he's older now. When we were teenagers our father had him completely under his control, but still . . .

"I can't believe you told her!" I say. By the time the drug had kicked in, it was too late: I'd overheard him confessing nearly everything about our past.

"Well, she said she can't remember anything. So we're okay."

"Oh, sure," I snap back in disbelief.

Finn grimaces. He's been in a sulk for hours. After Elena passed out in the early hours of Saturday morning, I showed up. He looked shocked to see me. *"Did you do this to her?"* he hissed. I acknowledged that yes, during their midnight tea party, when I had distracted them by banging the front-door letterbox and they had hurried down the hallway to check, I had taken the opportunity to drug her tea. Finn carried her up to the bedroom; I followed him, carrying the knife I'd brought just in case. We were standing on either side of her bed when it happened. Finn misunderstood my intentions; I leaned over her to see that her pulse was okay, that the drug hadn't been too much for her; he suddenly lunged, tried to take the knife off me, suffered a small cut on his arm. Blood all over the white sheet and on her hair, like a virgin defiled. I had to bind up Finn's wound, dab disinfectant on it, calm him down. He was the one who became *hystérique*, not me.

He kept checking on her to see if she would wake, but by late Saturday afternoon she was still under. We agreed then that she would go up in the attic, just for one night. After much persuasion on my part he'd relented, carried her up the ladder and laid her gently on the mattress. He didn't lock her in; that was my doing. The old padlocks were still stored in our father's desk in his former study.

Now Finn's keen to release her but I'm more cautious. Our whole future is at stake. We need to find out just how much she remembers of their conversation.

He turns as if to storm out of the kitchen, and I run to stop him.

"Alain," I say softly, pressing my thumb against his. I stand on tiptoe and his eyes darken as I move in closer, daring him to resist. My lips brush his. He pushes me back roughly, saying, "You know we can't!"

I hear his footsteps as he hurries down the hallway; the slam of the front door.

Fuck him. My brother can be such a pain sometimes. He's the one who created this bloody mess. Now I'm the one who has to clean it up.

I sit down at the kitchen table and rub the scar on my thumb. I shouldn't have tried that: the kiss. Shame and regret are already seeping in and I feel like a kid again, on my fifteenth birthday. That night is forever seared on my memory: it rewrote my relationship with Finn.

In those days, we lived in Maison Aubert in Villefranche. I'd spent the day locked in my bedroom, hollow with despair. In the past, Maman had spoiled me on my birthdays with books, dresses, hugs, kisses. A year had passed since she'd fled, after her failed attempt to poison Father. I'd not heard a word from her since. Only Alain's daily visits kept me sane. But today he had clearly forgotten me, or else Father had stopped him from visiting.

Then, at midnight, a key turned in the lock and my heart leaped: *Alain*. We crept outside into the woods beyond the garden. By the warm light of the moon he gave me presents: books, chocolates, notebooks. It was the best birthday I'd ever had. When he kissed me at the end, it felt like a fairy-tale come true.

After our secret kiss Alain retreated for a few days and I was left feeling hurt, confused, wondering what was wrong. It was only when I confided in Marcel, our servant, saw the horror on his face, that I learned the truth. *Brothers and sisters cannot be together*, he asserted. Society outlawed it. If I got pregnant, I would give birth to monsters. When I next had a visit from Alain, I saw sadness in his eyes: he already knew. Our first kiss would be our last. And so he took my hand, sliced my thumb then his with his penknife, and pressed our wounds against each other, making a blood pact: *We can't be together but we'll always be together. We'll be best friends*, we swore, *soul-mates, survivors in life's struggle*.

I think about taking a sip of wine, longing to blur my pain, but my little girl must be kept safe. *Just get through this, Claudine*, I pep-talk myself, *work out how to resolve things*. It's funny: Claudine is still the name I call myself in my head, just as, even after all this time, my tongue still falters slightly whenever I have to say "Finn" instead of "Alain."

I watch my brother through the kitchen window, hands curled into fists, walking across the lawn to Father's grave. I remember how, when we first arrived here, the garden was an overgrown thicket of brambles, like a haunted forest in a dark fairy-tale.

The move to Cornwall was dramatic. A few nights after my fifteenth birthday, Marcel woke me in the early hours. He ordered me to follow him outside. "I'm so sorry, I'm acting on your father's orders," he whispered, before pushing me into the boot of a car. I curled myself into a tight, sobbing ball to protect myself during the journey. We arrived at a dark airfield where I was led onto a small private plane. The sight of Alain, looking pale and shocked, was a relief. Our father sat a few seats ahead of us, drinking without looking back; I heard the cold click of ice cubes. Alain whispered that we were beginning a new, secret life in Crugmeer.

The first few weeks were dreary. Father told me that it would be "a fun game" for me to stay in my room and have all my meals there. I disobeyed him once and he gave me a black eye. I screamed at him that he wouldn't be alive if it weren't for me; after Maman had tried to poison him, I had been persuaded to donate one of my kidneys to him. At the time I had thought that seeing me pay penance for my mother's sins might compel him to love me; but he only resented me even more.

After that he started locking me in. I felt as though I was becoming an ogre. Every so often I would put on one of my beautiful dresses, close my eyes, and brush my hair, pretending that Maman was doing it. He allowed Alain entry once a day to spend an hour with me. We were torn between wanting to talk and make sense of it all and needing to console each other. When we held each other tight, the sadness and the darkness of the world was muted for a while.

My memories recede: I can hear a noise coming from upstairs. Where the hell's Finn when I need him? I hurry up the stairs as another suspicious bang comes from the attic. What's she doing up there?

I need to test Elena. I need to find out how much she remembers. Then we can decide what fate she deserves.

60.

ELENA

Dear Claudine and Alain,

*I have enclosed, as requested, copies of your birth
certificates . . .*

I found this letter in one of the dusty attic boxes. After tearing off the old brown parcel tape, I sifted through the contents, trying to find anything that might help me get out of here: a weapon, a key.

But the boxes were filled with nothing but books. *The Crime at Lock 14*, *The Madman of Bergerac*, *A Battle of Nerves*, etc.—all Georges Simenon titles, covers dusty, pages yellowing. The letter dropped out of one of them, folded into a Christmas card from Claudine's *maman*. It's very moving to read it, though every time I remember my newfound knowledge— *they're half-brother and -sister*—my heart somersaults and I feel the shock afresh.

I think back to the photos of the three of them. Now I know why they disturbed me, why Claudine looked so familiar in the article about her death: those dark, haunted eyes framed by thick lashes. I was seeing in Sophia's younger self an echo of Alain. I had noticed before how similar their eyes are, but put it down to narcissism on Sophia's part, being attracted to a man who looked like her.

I've not told you everything, Finn said that day in Villefranche, with the furtive look in his eyes that I mistook for shyness.

I keep recalling the urgency in his voice when he confided in me at Fortnum's. The way he circled and circled around his story, fleshing it out more and more—but never quite telling me. For months, he's been dropping clues, phrases that have lodged in my mind, almost as though he's wanted me to twig.

What did he say after our third night in bed? About how Sophia was lucky not to end up in psychiatric care or prison, given what she'd been through?

I think of the black eye she gave him, which he'd explained away, saying she lashed out at him because she hadn't been able to defend herself before.

I think of the scars I saw on her body when we went swimming together, which must have been due to her father's cruelty.

I think of the words *Help me* carved into the beams of this attic.

I think of Sophia's bitter declaration that Annie had done her harm— no doubt devastated by the loss of her mother when she fled after the attempted poisoning of their tormenter.

I think of the way Finn looks at her, like a protective older brother wanting to make sure his baby sister is okay . . .

I think of Annie's concern that Sophia is "living a life of lies" . . .

That's why they can't have sex. They are both deprived. I remember Finn's confession, before the drug took me under, that he found it easier to connect with women sexually rather than emotionally.

That's why they haven't married. All they can do is wear rings and smiles. And IVF wasn't just out of the question because of Sophia's Catholicism. I mean, imagine the pair of them turning up at a clinic, having samples taken, the threat of DNA analysis. They might have persuaded a friend to become a surrogate—except, they would still have been left with too much to explain. And so they turned it into a game.

For several months now, I've come to feel that I hate Sophia. Yet the fragments I can remember from Finn's confession make me feel reluctant sympathy for a girl who grew up deserted by her mother and abused by her father. Who was so starved of company that she fell in love with her brother and clung to him as her only protector. Who suffered the misogyny of a father who, I think, faked the story of her death and locked her in an attic. I'm not sure if her abusive-partner story was true or a cover for her father's abuse; I suspect the latter. I've had Sophia down as a sociopath, but perhaps I've dehumanized her. Could I endure what she's endured and emerge as she has, damaged but strong, surviving in the world?

Thinking it all through gives me respite for a while from the cruelty of my own reality. My bodily needs bring me down to earth. I hate using the toilet bucket, hate not being able to wash my hands, but there's a sharp pain in my bladder that I can't ignore any longer. I get up, pulling down my knickers—

Only for the food hatch to open.

The skylight shows a smoky twilight, so this must be dinner.

I pull my knickers up, stumbling over. I'm so mad at Finn for putting me up here, but surely, surely, I can play on the repetition of cruel fate: *I'm going through what your sister did, Finn, and you must have seen how badly she suffered.*

"Oh!" I gasp, for the fingers that reach up, proffering my dinner, are pale and slender. "Sophia!"

The tray slides in.

"Wait."

She pauses. The only weapon I now possess is knowledge. She must know that I know. That's why she drugged me, panicked, went crazy. I need to bargain with her.

"I just want you to know . . . to know . . . that I understand. And I don't think it's anything to be ashamed of, we all have secrets."

Silence. My eyes fall to the letter from her *maman*.

"Look." I make a show of loyalty and honesty. "I found this letter up here. I could have kept it. But—it doesn't belong to me. It's yours."

I hear her sharp intake of breath as I pass it to her. Her fingers curl around it, then disappear, and the trapdoor slams shut with a violent bang.

Oh, fuck. I misjudged that. I can't think straight. I've had a strong emotional reaction to the revelation, but for Sophia nothing has changed. I'm still a threat. I'm probably an even worse one.

My eyes fall to my dinner. Bread, smeared with butter, slapdash and torn. She didn't even leave me a bottle of water like Finn does.

Sophia is not about to trust me.

She's inflicting the abuse on me that she suffered herself. She's pregnant with my ex-partner's child, and she's unraveling in her fear of losing Finn because he has taken a first bold step toward living a normal life. Now, to make matters worse, I know the big secret she's concealed for over a decade.

I take a bite of the bread; I feel as though I can taste her hatred. I'm in serious trouble.

61.

S O P H I A

I take the stupid letter and I rip it in two. The pieces flutter onto the hall floor.

How dare she delve into my private life and then try to turn it into some kind of girly bonding session! The shame feels raw inside me: I hate the fact that she's peeled back all my layers, found out my secrets, that I have no shield left against her.

I storm out into the cold twilight air. The trees are shedding leaves, becoming skeletal. I stop by a yew adorned with red berries. Could we grind the seeds, add them to a soup, perhaps? I feel a flash of empathy with Maman, an eerie insight into how she must have felt all those years back, desperate to rid herself of my father, seeking out deathcap mushrooms to mix with the chanterelles he so loved.

Elena might be the one in the attic but I feel just as trapped by her. I have an impulse to go back and put together the pieces of that letter, which I quickly push away. I have to work out what to do. Finn is being so naïve it's ludicrous. So we let her go, we sweet-talk her, then what? Elena loves Finn. She left her partner for him—well, I admit, I contributed to that, but she made her choice. She'll always be lurking in the shadows, looking to lure him away, to expose the truth about our marriage.

She's damaged, Father once said about me, as though I was born that way, never acknowledging that *he* was the one who did that to me.

Our baby has to have the perfect start. A clean slate. Pure and lovely parents. Elena has to go . . .

I pick several handfuls of berries, my hands pricked by the sharp leaves. I slip into the kitchen, put them into a bowl, and quickly wash my hands. Suddenly I feel exhausted from hot, frantic thoughts. The voice of reason reminds me that this sort of measure requires meticulous planning and care. I slump down on a chair. I feel weak: as though I am no longer Sophia, as though I never did fly free from the chrysalis. I am Claudine again, helpless and lost.

My father, he knew how to plot and plan. I remember the day Alain visited me in the attic, snuck in an article he'd found in Father's study. *Une jeune fille est morte.* The date was October 21—just a few days after we were flown to our new home.

"So now I'm dead, supposedly!" I cried. "I don't even exist anymore."

Alain said that they would not have been able to publish the article unless Father and the police confirmed the facts. It felt worse than anything he had done to me so far, perhaps even worse than locking me up. It was as though he had taken a pen and scribbled me out of existence.

Why? we kept wondering. *Why do this?* It was some years later that we found out, when Maman wrote us a letter.

Sophia."

It's Finn. He comes into the kitchen with the letter I ripped up. Sitting down at the table, he lays the halves out neatly, piecing them together.

He looks calmer now. I scan his face, recalling how, as a teenager, he had such a boyish, sweet visage; it was around the time Father began locking me in the attic that his habitual expression became old beyond his years, somber and stern.

"Elena found it." My voice trembles and I try to smooth it out. "She can't stop snooping."

Finn strokes my face with his finger. He pushes the letter toward me and I fold my arms. Then he begins to read, his voice gentle. And though I've read it before, years back, the words still have their power.

Dear Claudine and Alain,

I have enclosed, as requested, copies of your birth certificates.

I read of the death of Monsieur Aubert in the newspaper this morning. The obituaries state he was a kind man who did so much for the homeless via his charity, leaving behind his sole heir and son, Alain. I am afraid that I felt a sense of peace when I read the report. Thank God such a great evil has been removed from the world.

Thank God, I echo her silently. I remember that day: Alain came for me, but my limbs were weak and he had to help me down the ladder. Father was lying in his bedroom, hands clutching his chest, breathing in and out with deep, ragged breaths. Alain whispered, "He's been like this for days. I think he's really ill." It was a terrible moment, because I felt happiness flare in my heart just as Alain began to weep. I clutched my crucifix. I had spent so many hours praying that Father would die—and now I wondered guiltily if thoughts were powerful enough to have that impact. Was God finally listening to me?

I know you don't want to see me, Claudine, and I understand. I know I betrayed you by deserting you. Your father forced me to flee after the poisoning, sparing me prison but demanding custody of you. I thought I'd still be able to write to you, eventually see you, but as my letters went unanswered and I heard rumors of abuse, I wrote to him threatening to notify the authorities. Your disappearance was his retaliation. The day I saw your death announced in the papers, I nearly took my own life. I traveled to Monsieur's house immediately, banging on the door, nearly fainting when I saw that indeed your bedroom was now burned to black cinders.

Marcel opened it, took pity on me, whispered that you were alive and had been taken—but he wouldn't say where Monsieur had moved to. He told me the body of a dead homeless girl, a junkie, had been substituted for yours; the police had backed up the pretense. I think, my Claudine, that he was running scared, and this lie was his way of trying to wipe out all his own terrible actions. If he could announce to the world that you had gone, then his sins might crumble to nothing among those false ashes.

If only the poison that I gave Monsieur all those years ago had worked. If only! Going to prison would have been worth it to save you, my darling. My only solace is that all the dialysis he had to have weakened his heart, gave him the final attack that killed him. I know you feel you can never forgive me for deserting you, but Alain feels there is hope. I live in Villefranche now. After a lifetime of poverty, my maman married into wealth and, when she passed away, I inherited her villa. I miss her, and I miss you. I think of you every day; every day I wait in hope of seeing you.

I love you.

Yours,
Maman xxx

I'm staring so hard at the table, trying not to cry, but the tears spill over.

"Sophia." Finn comes to my side. He pulls me into his arms and holds me tight.

"You should have seen her when we were in Villefranche," he whispers, tears in his voice too. "I know you say the past is past . . . but sometimes it's better to face it. To forgive."

"I know," I murmur into his chest, because the raw regret did linger, on the plane home.

"We have to learn from the past too," he goes on. "We have to let Elena out."

"I just want to do what's best for *us*," I say softly; I glance at the berries I picked. "We've pulled this off for fifteen years—*fifteen*—we can't lose it all now . . ."

Finn's arms loosen and fall to his sides. We stare at each other, both of us lost, and for a moment, we're teenagers again. Alain and Claudine. I know how this has to end, but I'm not sure if he's there yet.

62.

ELENA

Today is Monday. My thirty-eighth birthday. What a way to spend it—in someone else's nightie, locked in an attic with a bucket by my mattress, hoping and praying my lover remembers to feed me.

I don't suppose there'll be any cards or presents for me today. I have to joke about these things, because otherwise I might start crying and never stop. I recall my thirty-seventh birthday, how sweet Adam was, bringing me breakfast in bed; though he also bought me a new saucepan as my main present, which seemed to be a not so subtle indication that he wanted me to keep cooking for him.

This is the third day I've spent in this attic.

Adrenaline distracted me at first. Now it's worn off, my mind is both frantic and stupefied, constantly analyzing my imprisonment, calculating how I can escape, and simultaneously too sluggish to find answers.

Wake up! I slap myself. *You need to keep brainstorming.* I found a pencil in one of the boxes; now I tear off a Simenon cover, turn it over and make a list of the people who know I'm here:

Anil
Sally (neighbor feeding my cat)
Meghan

Adam's going to be in touch with Sophia about the film, isn't he? He'll come back to the flat to collect more stuff. He'll notice Lyra's on her own.

I'm sure the neighbor is still feeding her, but I imagine my cat wandering around the flat, meowing with loneliness, and a deep ache fills me.

Mum will call with birthday wishes, and she'll expect me to call her back. After discovering what Sophia and Finn have been through, I keep thinking about how lucky I am to have two stable parents, even if they didn't adore each other. A longing fills me, to hug them and hold them tight. A fearful voice inside me wails: *Will I ever see them again?* Followed by the frantic: *I have to . . . I have to get out of here!*

What about Meghan? I'm supposed to meet her tomorrow for coffee. If I don't reply to her messages, she might start to wonder if something has happened to me . . .

Suddenly I jump—the food hatch is opening. It's breakfast-time.

A tray slides onto the floor. A variety of fruits on a plate. A bottle of water. And—an envelope.

It's Finn this time. I call out his name—

But the hatch snaps shut.

I tear open the pink envelope. Finn must have bought the card when we were in Villefranche—it has a watercolor painting by a local artist on the front. Inside, it says: *To my darling Elena, Happy Birthday, Love Finn xx*

I nearly explode. What the fuck? Lock me in an attic, but give me a card? This is insane. I pick up the plate of fruit, and notice how each segment has been beautifully cut and arranged. It tastes delicious but my stomach is taut with stress, still messed up from the drugging, and I can only manage half before it starts to hurt. I comb my fingers through my hair, which badly needs a brush, a few strands coming out. My teeth ache from the fruit sugars; I hate not being able to clean them.

The card is surely an apology. But it also scares me. It suggests Finn is trying to find some way to reassure me but that Sophia is still calling the shots. How long does she plan to keep me up here?

The terrible thought crosses my mind once again: *This isn't a punishment. This is the end. She's never going to let you out of here alive.*

Blinking back tears, I grab a box and stand on it.

For the tenth time, I try to open the skylight.

I push hard. It moves half an inch.

I can hear a slight rattling; the lock isn't welded on firmly.

I push . . .

I push . . .

I PUSH.

63.

SOPHIA

Elena's black cashmere coat is hanging up in the hallway. I rummage through her pockets, and then . . .

. . . aha! *Her mobile.*

All those sessions in the Vicomte Café together: I often saw her type in the code. I scribbled it down in the back of my diary. Just in case.

There's a flurry of texts on her phone. Fuck. Of course—it's her birthday. I reply to all the well-wishers with a standard **Thank you xxx**.

I send practical messages. To her neighbor, asking her to feed the cat for a few more days. Another to the car-hire company, requesting an extension of the rental. Another to Adam, sympathetic to his new struggles with caring for his mother; how hilarious that he's finally realized what's involved. Another to Anil, saying she's having so much birthday fun with Finn, she's decided to stay on. I read the recent string of texts between her and my husband with a flare of jealousy and punch out one to him: **I'm having such a great birthday, Finn. Enjoying my time in the attic. I wasn't expecting to have such a romantic stay.**

Impulsively, I borrow Elena's coat and stroll outside, across the damp lawn and down to the graves. There is the fake one we made for Claudine, and in front of that, a slender gravestone.

RIP
CHARLES FRANÇOIS AUBERT

I remember the week he died.

I'd told Alain I would smoke Father's cigars and dance on his grave, and he said he would never forgive me if I did. In my fury I didn't care. But when I tried to dance, after just a few steps I found myself crying, sinking to the soil. I could not understand how I could grieve for someone I hated, yet I did. Most of all, I felt so sad that he never saw who I was, never understood me, never praised me.

I started painting him. It was cathartic. I copied the big oil painting that used to hang in his study, but instead of flattering him, I captured the evil that lay behind his eyes, hinted at it in his smile. I threw the other one away and hung my version. Now the world would know what sort of man he was. In his obituaries in the French press, there were mentions of Alain. Not one mention of me. It was as though he had made me a ghost before I had a chance to live.

But now he was the ghost, and I was alive.

"And I'm still here," I tell his grave.

A week later, a lawyer came to read his will. Alain told the man that I was his girlfriend and he intended to marry me, so I needed to be present. The lawyer read out pompous words in a pompous voice, but I understood what the will meant: Alain had inherited this house, and the house in France had been recently sold, so all in all it was a small fortune.

Up in my new bedroom, I laughed and laughed until I cried. It didn't seem possible that life could swerve like this, be so bad for so long and then rain down good fortune upon us.

It was such a liberating moment, that first walk down to the village shop to buy my own food. I walked fast and hung my head down as I passed over the money. I kept expecting to discover Father was not really dead, for him to jump out and yell at everyone, "She should be locked up in her room!" But the shopkeeper gave me my change with a nod and a smile and I felt something warm flood through me.

As I walked back home, the feeling intensified. Sometimes the fear returned, and I felt as though Father was in my head, speaking poison, or watching me from the shadows, but I reminded myself that I was free. That now was my chance to become Someone.

And, once Alain stopped grieving, he too began to enjoy the possibilities of creating a new life together. We were young. Wealthy. Free.

I've never forgotten the first dinner party we held as a couple. We were so nervous, like actors on the first night of a play. Alain was to be Finn, I was to be Sophia. Our new wedding rings were shiny; we kept touching them and giggling as we laid the table. The couple were much older than us, in their fifties. Their names were John and Jean. He was a health and safety inspector, she knitted and sold luxury jumpers. I kept trying not to stare at her face because she wore no makeup, and her eyebrows were like ragged caterpillars—but there was a look in her eyes that made me want to trust her.

I was still learning how to cook. The food was a bit burned and though Alain and I made nice conversation about the weather, they seemed restless. I went to get dessert but John smiled and said, "I'm afraid we have to be off now—our daughter's suddenly turned up, out of the blue—just like they do!" I said quickly, "Oh, but you haven't heard my story about Audrey Hepburn. Did you know that my mother was friends with her?" And I related that they dined at her home in Lausanne in the mid-1990s. At the end, Jean said in a gentle voice, "I think you'll find Audrey was dead in 'ninety-three." They left and I felt mad at her. Stupid woman, with her silly eyebrows and fat lumpy body!

Alain and I sat at the table, with the burned food they hadn't eaten, sadness hanging in the air. He declared nobody would ever like us, that our childhood had scarred us for life, we were cursed to be eternal outsiders. I said fiercely, "Father is the one who is cursed! He died and we won. We have this house. We just need to practice."

And practice we did.

We sorted out my papers. Maman had doubts, at first, about us "living a life based on lies," as she berated us, but she soon relented and supported us, sending over our birth certificates. I killed off Claudine. Changed my name by deed poll to Sophia after the film star Sophia Loren. Whenever I was dealing with people and I felt shy or scared or didn't know what to say, I got into the habit of pretending I was her, mimicking her elegance and poise. I helped Alain find his look too. We started watching Hitchcock films and I advised him, "You should model yourself on Cary Grant." He blushed and said he could never imitate such an idol, but I encouraged him. He discarded his old jumpers with holes, his jeans, adopting shirts and trousers to make him look older. We decided to "refine" our ages, exaggerate the gap between us.

Finally, our moment of triumph came. A couple came for dinner and this time I overheard the woman, Mary, commenting on how "gorgeous" Alain was. Halfway through the meal, they said to him, "We heard you have a sister who lived here with you." Alain froze up but I thought fast. I excused myself and came down with the newspaper article about Claudine, explaining the tragic loss of his sister. I, meanwhile, was the supportive girlfriend who had helped him overcome his grief. I wept a little and Mary touched me on the arm. Soon the conversation had moved on and I was offering to paint her portrait for free. At the end they said they'd love to host us for dinner next time.

And as long as I could see each scenario as a game, with rules and boundaries, and the role I had to play, I could do it. I could go shopping, I could host a dinner party, I could deal with a tradesman. It was only when I was in a situation where I didn't know who I was supposed to be, or what the rules were, that I felt as if I was drowning, as if I was scared little Claudine again, locked in the attic.

The success of my life was the sweetest revenge I could have on Father. A gorgeous husband, a big house, a flourishing career as a painter. Oh, how I hope he's turning in his grave.

And it was all going so well, until Elena came along. Now I think of her, up in the attic, our impossible dilemma, and I kick his gravestone hard.

"I've won, I've won," I insist, words I've spoken to him so often before, but this time I feel as though he's laughing at me. It's as if he and Elena are in cahoots.

I storm back into the house. Finn is in the kitchen, holding up his mobile, displaying the message I sent him from her.

"I'm dealing with practical issues," I assert, folding my arms.

"Sophia, this is the real world. We have to let her out. She might go to the police. Do you want us to end up in prison? Do you want everyone to know who we are?"

Annihilation. The tearing off of our masks. For a moment, the idea has its dark, strange appeal. The relief of abandoning something that was once so much fun, but now seems harder and harder to sustain. Then I think of our baby.

"I can't have her born behind bars," I hiss.

"Exactly. And I don't want to see you there—"

"But we have to shut Elena up!" I insist. "We have to get rid of her."

Finn is genuinely shocked. He's become such a child. Can't he see that it's the only way?

"Isn't it what Father used to do?" I press him, unable to resist riling him in my frustration. "*Oh, I've accidentally killed my wife, she seems to have fallen from a window. Women are so exciting when I first meet them but then they become so annoying,*" I mimic his voice savagely.

"Don't—don't!" Finn touches his temples, flinching at the mention of his mother's death.

"*Oh, I don't care for her replacement either. Now Nounou seems to keep having 'accidents.' And what about my irritating daughter? I know. I'll start a fire, fake her death.*"

Finn frowns.

"Our father had the power to do what he liked," he says at last. "He had everyone in his pocket, he had all their secrets. We don't. We're not the same as him—and I'm glad we're not." His voice breaks with emotion. "I know—I understand you think this is all a case of survival of the fittest and we have to win at everything, but there's no harm in admitting that we've lost. We can let Elena go and catch a flight to France. We can give her money. We can sell this house, start over in a new place with the baby. We've been meaning to get rid of this bloody place."

The baby. Not *our* baby.

"So you're willing just to walk away from her, never see her again?"

I see the hesitation in him before he says yes, and my heart clenches.

"I don't want to move," I reply petulantly. "I like Wimbledon. I want our baby to grow up there." I can feel heat rising to my cheeks, tingling in my fingers. "You don't seem to understand that she's our enemy. Imagine our baby growing up, hearing rumors about us. Do you want that for her?"

Finn recoils. "Of course I don't, but . . . we can't just . . ." He won't even use the words.

"I'm not suggesting we go up there and strangle her!" I laugh. It's a shame that Finn found my bowl of berries and threw them out this morning. "I'm just saying—let's keep her up there. Maybe reduce her food for a while. Let her fade out."

Finn shudders, appalled.

"You know, for months I was locked in that attic and you obeyed our father without a word. You brought me food. You emptied my toilet bucket. You brought me down to wash my hair and then led me back up. You never called the police."

He looks distraught. "You know that I go over and over it! You know it was a nightmare and I was a child who didn't know what to do."

"You were nineteen! You were an adult."

"I didn't feel like an adult, I still felt like a frightened boy. We were both under his thumb."

"You did that for him, but you won't do this for me. You were a coward then and now you're not prepared to do what needs to be done." My voice is high—oh, let him bloody call me *hystérique*. Yes, I am *hystérique*. I bloody should be.

It's then we hear the noise.

"MEGHANNN . . . MEGHANNN . . ."

Immediately, Finn freezes in horror. The voice seems to be coming from outside.

What the hell?

64.

ELENA

I push and push and push the skylight.

Sweat dampens my forehead. I summon every last drop of energy and then—*snap!* The lock breaks and a cry is wrenched from my body.

I fall back on the floor. A gust of air breezes in. It tastes so fresh and beautiful. Of autumn leaves and bonfire smoke and sea-tang.

It tastes of freedom.

I climb back onto the box. I can see that the skylight was locked from the outside but I broke the bolt; a black metal shard tinkles to the floor. My heart sinks as I push it to full capacity. The window is too small, the gap too narrow. I can't climb out.

I try hard not to break down sobbing, not to let the despair come leaking back in.

Instead, I grab my pencil and tear off another of the Simenon book covers. On the blank back, I write: *HELP! I'M TRAPPED IN THE ATTIC IN MACINNES HOUSE.* I fold it into an airplane and aim it out. It takes off, bounces across the roof, then plummets to the gravel. The only person who's going to find that is Sophia. *Oh, God, there must be something I can do . . .*

And then I see a figure.

I crane my neck, stand on tiptoe.

There she is! Someone on the driveway, walking toward the house. She's wearing a woolly hat. Those auburn curls are very distinctive.

I think I recognize her. I think it might be . . . *Meghan?*

It is Meghan!

Oh, thank God. She's got to save me. My last hope.

"MEGHANNN!" I scream at her with every cell in my body. *"MEGHANNN!"*

She walks across the gravel, stopping and gazing up at the skylight.

"I'm—I'm Elena," I yell.

"Elena?" Meghan is startled. "We were going to meet . . ."

"Yes—I'm that Elena. I'm Sophia's friend—only—she's not what I thought. She's locked me up here, in the attic. Please, please help me get out."

Meghan looks lost and confused. Why the hell is she hesitating, chewing her lip, looking anxiously toward the kitchen?

"They've trapped me in here! You need to do something—I'm locked in! This isn't a game, it's not a joke—please, please call the police . . . Please, Meghan!"

There's doubt on her face, but then she nods, fishing in her bag for her phone, and I nearly weep, I'm so relieved: *Oh, thank God, thank God . . .*

65.

SOPHIA

Finn and I hear it again. A voice, calling out the name of our stalker.

"You wait here," I hiss at him. Finn's eyes widen: he's terrified of Meghan's mad obsession for him. For the first time in days, my brother and I are on the same page, united by fear.

I hurry to the front door and fling it open. Elena is yelling from the attic. She must have broken open the skylight; I warned Finn that the lock was rusty and old. *Shit.* I can see footsteps imprinted in the gravel. I follow them round to the back. And then I see her. Meghan.

"Meghan! Please call the police!" Elena is screaming. My mind is racing. It's typical of Meghan to sniff us out the moment we make a rare visit, but how come Elena seems to know her? I didn't see any messages on her mobile to Meghan. Fuck.

"Meghan . . ." I open my arms as I draw near, engulfing her in a hug. "It's so lovely to see you. Come in, have a cup of tea."

I spot a paper airplane on the gravel and pick it up, stuffing it into my pocket. I lead Meghan into the kitchen and close the back door firmly, muting Elena's cries.

"I didn't know you were coming to visit," Meghan says, a little coolly.

"Oh, it was a spur-of-the-moment trip," I say cheerfully, opening the cupboard and pulling out a box of her favorite Darjeeling from the back. "How are you?"

"I'm fine. It would've been nice to see Finn."

This is surreal. There's a woman screaming her name from the attic and all she can ask after is Finn.

"Oh, God, sorry, yes—but Finn isn't here today," I say.

I pass her a cup of tea and we sit down at the table. It's always painful, seeing Meghan, evoking memories of the night I lost my previous baby. The woman has seemed like a bad omen ever since. I caress my stomach surreptitiously, telling my little one to *hang on*.

She pulls out her mobile. "I've been getting messages from a woman called Elena."

"Elena. Oh, yes. Her. She's upstairs—she's a bit upset—needs her medication, her diazepam."

Meghan is gazing at me, looking unusually alert, and I feel a flutter of panic.

"How did she message you?" I ask.

"On Instagram."

Damn. She rarely posts on Insta, so I neglected it. Oh, God, who else has Elena been in touch with?

Suddenly Meghan's mood changes. Tears fill her eyes; she blinks them back fiercely. I grab a tissue and pass it to her.

"I'm sorry," she weeps. "I did something bad . . . I betrayed you . . . and now you'll tell Scott, and my life will fall apart."

The threat I used to make, to keep Meghan under control: that I would tell her husband about the switches.

"It might not be necessary," I reply, forcing a smile, trying to make it look reassuring even though I'm seething inside. "What exactly did you do?"

"A few months ago, Elena sent me a message asking about you . . . and . . ."

"And?" I try not to snap.

"I said to stay away from you." Meghan gazes at me with wet eyes. "I'm sorry. I was just jealous she might be trying to get her claws into Finn."

I pat her hand. "Meghan, she *was* trying to get her claws into Finn. You were right to be worried. Elena and I came here for a relaxing weekend together, and she started acting very strangely. She climbed into Finn's bed in the middle of the night and he had to fight her off—can you imagine?"

"God!"

"Then she confessed she'd forgotten her medication. That's why I've had to contain her, just until her doctor comes, you understand?"

Meghan can go either way. She can get angry and turn, or she can get that Labrador look on her face. Fortunately, she nods pliantly and I adopt that motherly tone that I know she finds reassuring:

"Thank you for telling me, though. I'm so grateful for your honesty."

"She wanted me to meet her for coffee when she was in Crugmeer," Meghan confesses. "I didn't expect to find her here."

"She would've tried to manipulate you, she might even have harmed you. Look—I'm sorry . . ." I check my watch. "I'd better just deal with this, but let's meet up later for coffee, okay? And as soon as Finn's back, I'll let you know."

"You promise?"

"I promise."

Meghan's face lights up and we hug a tight goodbye. I watch her head toward her yellow Mini, which she's parked further down the drive. Is she the reason I felt watched earlier? Did she see Elena and Finn together? If she saw them kissing, it will have sparked her hatred and got her on my side: good.

Back in the living-room, I show Finn the paper airplane, unfolding it: HELP! I'M TRAPPED IN THE ATTIC IN MACINNES HOUSE.

"We have to do something before she does," I gabble. "She's been messaging Meghan—did you have any idea they were in touch?"

Finn looks aghast. I'm actually glad this happened. At least it's woken him up. Finally, the realization is dawning: Elena is unpredictable, Meghan is unpredictable. We're in trouble.

He paces in circles for a bit, lost in thought, the way he used to when we were kids. Finally, he goes over to his old gramophone, the one we inherited from Father, and puts on a record. *Lady Macbeth*. Finn's favorite.

My lips tighten. If this is a romantic gesture, so that Elena can hear . . .

But then he takes me in his arms and we slow-dance to the opera. I can tell he's mulling over our options. Suddenly he seems like his old self again, strong and in control.

"Do you have any more of that drug left?" he asks me.

I nod quickly.

"This is what we'll do. I'll go upstairs. I'll give her something sweet—chocolate cake—her favorite. There's a fresh one in the fridge. We'll make a chocolate sauce, put some of the drug in that. The rest in a drink."

I narrow my eyes, staring deep into his, probing: is he teasing me? Is this a game? "And then what?"

Finn's gaze holds mine, resolute. "We put her in the boot of the car, we drive to Gunver Head, we throw her body from the cliff. It's high tide and the currents will be strong. It'll be days before she's found."

Excitement begins to pulse inside me, but I take a step backward out of his embrace.

"You're really willing to do that to your beloved Elena?"

"We have no choice," he says quietly, sadly. "The whole thing with her . . . it was just a fantasy," he adds, with a touch of bitterness. "It had no future. She would never have understood who I am, what we've been through."

"You lost your head for a while there." I feel the need to punish him, the hurt of the last few months still raw inside me. "It was scary."

"I'm over it," he says, shrugging. "Like the flu."

We both laugh. Finn's face suddenly fills with adolescent sweetness; he's back to the brother I grew up with, the one who hugged me tight, protected me.

"Oh, Finn." I feel close to tears with the relief: he's mine again. He's willing to risk everything for me. "I love you."

He presses his thumb to mine. "Always and forever, *ma petite*."

I shiver: he hasn't called me that since we were teenagers.

Upstairs, Finn climbs the attic ladder after doctoring the cake. He's up there for ten minutes or so. I'm scared she might fight back, but there are no sounds of aggression or conflict.

The creak of the ladder as he comes back down. His expression looks guilty as he whispers: "I told her we'd let her out soon."

Now all we can do is wait for the drug to work its dark magic. We sit on the sofa, listening to opera, trying to soothe our nerves. At the sound of an owl's hoot, Finn jumps and we both exhale nervous laughter; I squeeze his hand tightly.

"We should take your camera with us." My voice sounds high; my mind keeps racing, picking over every detail. "It's a full moon, you can say you wanted to take photos of the sea—if anyone were to ask why you were out driving."

"Good idea," Finn replies.

The grandfather clock chimes midnight.

"It's time," he says.

But we both sit there for a few minutes more, our palms growing sweaty.

Finally, I kiss his cheek and stand, pulling him up.

Finn goes up into the attic. I curl my fingers around my crucifix, praying frantically that the drug has worked.

The trapdoor opens. My heart leaps as I hear him struggle, groan with the weight of her as he carries her down the ladder. Her tangled hair hangs down like seaweed; her nightie rucks up, exposing her naked body underneath. Her arms swing and bang against him.

He carries her down another flight of stairs, across the hall and out into the night. I run to the car, turn the key, pop open the boot. We look around nervously: no sign of Meghan. He puts Elena's body in and slams it down.

I make for the passenger seat, but Finn stops me.

"No. We need to clean up the attic right away, remove all the evidence. Meghan could call the police still, or come back. One of us should stay here."

"Then let me go, you stay behind," I say. I'm hungry to see the moment she's gone forever.

"You can't carry her." Finn strokes my womb gently, his hand trembling.

He's right: I can't endanger our little one. He puts his arms around me and we hold each other tight as I say a prayer for his protection.

He gets into the car. Before setting off, he sits in silence for a few minutes, contemplating, before he starts up the engine. Into the night he goes, down the driveway framed with dark trees, disappearing into the black.

I stand at the bottom of the ladder that leads to the attic. Take a deep breath. It's been a long time since I was up here.

Bright moonlight floods in. Elena's presence here has recreated what it was like for me. The bucket, the mattress, the bloodstains, the crumbs on a plate, the empty bottle. I sit there, stomach churning, aching to hurry back down, forcing myself to stay. Unease inside me: Finn's hugs always speak volumes. When we said goodbye, mine gave him strength; his replied in fear. He's scared, of course: he's the one who's committing the crime, taking the potential blame . . . though they could trace me too, find me on the dark web, where I bought the GHB I drugged her with.

There is a risk. This is a quiet village, with few cars about on the roads. Finn will stand out. I just pray that fear doesn't stop him from seeing this through . . .

As for Meghan—we might need to take care of her, but it's never been hard to manipulate her, given her steadfast desire to be loyal to us, not to mention my threat to tell Scott everything unless she keeps quiet.

Elena's gone, I keep telling myself, *it's over. She can't hurt me anymore. She can't erase me. I've won.*

But I can't quite believe it: her presence in this room is still too strong. My eyes fall on the graffiti carved into the wall, which I etched all those years ago: *Help me!* I shudder, suddenly desperate to get out.

I work hard and quickly. I take down the plates and bottles. I push the mattress out through the trapdoor, see it slither down the ladder and land with a bang. Rip off the sheets, put them in the machine. Scrub the floor.

It's tiring work and I am hungry when I finish, but I don't want to eat until he's back; I want us to share a meal together.

I put the opera back on. He's been gone ninety minutes.

Oh, to be back to being us again. When life was simple. Perhaps when Finn returns we can stay here a while, cut off from everyone. Like those first months after Father died, when the world seemed an adventure, when we smoked his cigars and laughed and wept and made up our new personas. I want those days back; us against the world, so intimate together.

The sound of the owl outside.

A distant car.

It comes closer and I tense, but it fades away.

I wait for my husband to come home.

EPILOGUE

Eighteen Months Later

SOPHIA

There are times when I still have nightmares. Her drugged body, swinging against Finn, disappearing into the dark of the car boot. Sometimes I see her as a mermaid, encrusted in barnacles, sometimes as a siren who lures me down and tries to strangle me with seaweed—and I wake up in shock. The horror of that night will never leave me—of Finn returning in the early hours, looking haggard, aged by years overnight, and when I tried to hold him, he was limp, barely able to reciprocate. The panicked discussion the next morning: what to do with her rental car? And her mobile? We sent some messages to friends declaring that she was planning to go traveling, then shoved the phone into the glove compartment. In the early hours, Finn drove it over to the spot where she would have "jumped" or "slipped" and wiped away his prints, while I went back to the attic, scrubbed the floor all over again until the wood shone and my hands throbbed.

But today is a good day: I wake up, feeling fresh and cleansed from sleep. It's sunny and Finn will be back from London later.

I can hear my little one crying. I run to his nursery, lift him from his crib, shower him in morning kisses. God's irony: I had a boy. When the doctors told me, I erupted into laughter of outrage and delight, and cradled him in my arms. We called him Jean-Paul.

I never imagined that I could experience a love this wild and savage; it's overwhelming at times. Once he was downstairs when I had the French windows open and a fox crept toward him. I heard myself make a noise that sounded primal, animal. This is the price of love: this terror of loss. I know that what we did to Elena was terrible, but it was also right: Jean-Paul would never be able to enjoy this happy childhood if she was still alive, scheming against me.

Once I've fed him, I take him out into the garden. He can manage tottering steps, sometimes toppling over. We take a look at the rose bush that Finn planted in Elena's memory; he was superstitious about needing to honor the dead. I think of her, somewhere in the sea, now corroded down to a skeleton. It reassures me.

We walk to the letterbox, halfway up the drive, where the postman leaves our mail. A letter from France. Back in the kitchen, I slice it open with a letter opener.

"Look, it's you!" I show my little one the painting, but he starts to bawl. "Maman did this, your grandmother!"

There was a difficult period, after Jean-Paul was born. I came back from the hospital in Newquay to week upon week of no sleep. My mind fractured. I felt haunted. We'd opened up a crack and let in the past; with each day, it seemed to widen into a chasm. I would hear Father's voice, mocking me: *You're a murderer, you're just like me.* I heard Elena's echo: *Think you can become a mother?* I began to get obsessed with the discovery of her body. I would scour the net each day—nothing. I would drive to the cliffs where Finn disposed of her and gaze into the depths of the ocean. Sometimes I heard her voice like a siren, trying to lure me in. A gull swooped close one day, gashed my head so that it bled; I saw Elena in its eyes. When I came home that day, I found that I'd lost track of time, Jean-Paul had been crying for hours—so Finn told me furiously. I saw a doctor, took medication, hired a nanny.

At first the nanny stirred hatred in me. I realized who she reminded me of. And yet that hatred also evoked a craving in me, that grew over the days, until I had to act on it. When Jean-Paul was nine months old, we flew to Villefranche for a holiday. It wasn't easy, being back there, though returning to the church where I prayed for my baby to be born was a moving experience. And then we went back to the peeling villa, to see Maman. I was still uncertain. For the first half hour we sat and exchanged awkward chit-chat. She looked like a stranger to me, a wrinkled old hag. When Jean-Paul cried, she advised me that I shouldn't give him too much cold milk, but make sure I warmed it. Fury filled me: who was she to lecture me about being a good parent? I stood up to leave—and it was then I noticed one of her paintings, hanging on the wall. Finn had said she was an artist but I'd assumed she would be a lame amateur.

But it was a fine painting. What made my heart leap was seeing my brush-strokes echoed in hers. I recognized that my talent had come from her. I hadn't seen her in decades, yet her influence had been felt. A strange joy filled me. *I'm not like Father*, I thought. *I'm like her.*

I turned and opened my arms and she flew to me. We held each other tight and wept. Afterward, she sat holding my hand and stroking my cheek, telling me how much she had missed me. She told me how lucky I was to have Finn: it might be necessary to keep it secret from society, she understood, but he loved me, she said, and he was a good boy.

I am lucky. So everyone says. But my life is very different now. I missed Adam's film release, since it coincided with my dark depression. Still, he's back with his ex now, Lorraine, and he had her to play the doting partner. He still believes that Elena is traveling, exploring East Asia. Frankly, it's been a relief to step back, to delete my Instagram, to be released from the strain of being perfect Sophia for so many years. Over here, I have fallen back in love with Cornwall, recreated it as home, exorcised Father. And I love this simple life, my days rich and busy with Jean-Paul. Finn alternates between a week here, a week doing business in London. I'm painting more than I've ever done before, honing my landscape style on Cornish scenes. Meghan pops over from time to time. She's actually been quite helpful when we've needed a babysitter. Even she has calmed down, having realized how crass it would be to pursue Finn when we've just had a baby, and has become fixated on a new distraction, a local fisherman.

Still, sometimes I do feel a little lonely. And I look at Jean-Paul and I can't help wondering: *Wouldn't it be nice if he had a sibling?*

At five o'clock Finn is home. He's smiling, weary. He gives me a kiss, then Jean-Paul, a look of pure adoration on his face. He loves being a father, even if our son's big bright blue eyes do sometimes remind us of where his DNA comes from.

I make saffron and lemon roasted cod for dinner and Finn says my cooking is improving. I take a sip of wine and eye my husband. I think about his last verdict on the switches: *never again.*

"Did you see there's a new couple in the village? They're in their twenties, they wanted to get away from it all . . ."

"Oh, right," Finn says, smiling.

"They looked lovely. I think we should invite them over to dinner . . ."

One Week Later

E L E N A

There. My eyes flit to the clock in the Vicomte Café. It's five-thirty and I've finished my proof-reading. Business has been good recently and it's satisfying, sending it off five minutes before my deadline.

I get up and pay, giving Antonia a tip. In the High Street I head into the delicatessen, checking the list that he gave me, picking up organic vegetables and fancy cheese. He wants to cook tonight, though he's suggested I choose a dessert. My eyes rest on a chocolate cake—I suffer a faint shiver of horror. Once a favorite, not something I can eat since the trauma of the attic.

I sometimes still suffer nightmares about my confinement. I'm trapped back in there, and the walls are shrinking in on me and Sophia is down below, laughing, and I'm screaming, banging the floor. I remember the night I escaped. Finn came climbing up the ladder, his arm bandaged: Sophia had actually injured him. He whispered that she had lost it. That I had to trust him. That it was too dangerous for her to know I was alive. He told me to eat some cake—I forced it down, desperately hungry, the sugar and chocolate queasy in my stomach. He was going to pretend he had given me a drug and then carry me down. I must play dead. He would put me in the boot and drive me to safety. He knew it was a lot to ask, but it was the only way he could get me out alive. He showed me the wound beneath his bandage. *If she did this to me, imagine what she might do to you . . .*

My heart was beating so hard when he carried me down. I was terrified she'd see the trembling in my fingertips. But she was preoccupied with her role, opening up the boot; she'd been fed a story and she believed it. The car journey left me covered with bruises as I tumbled about. Desperate to get me away, Finn drove too fast. Nausea swirled in my stomach. I fought back the urge to throw up.

A few miles on, he stopped the car by a verge. As he opened the boot, fear overwhelmed me. *Was he lying? Going to kill me after all?* I tumbled out, tried to run but didn't get very far. I collapsed on the road in exhaustion. He came running over to me, curled his arms around me, held me tight.

He found a coat in the back of the car to cover me so that he could check us into a hotel in Padstow, the nearest town. My feet were bare and filthy; the hotel staff frowned but didn't comment. Up in our room, he ran a bath for me, bathed me and washed my hair. Room service was delivered. He told me to mind my stomach, eat slowly. As I ate, energy and strength flooded back into me. Finn talked and talked, nervous, halting. He told me the same story that I had pieced together, only there was more about the death of his mother, who had fallen from a window— pushed, he believed, by his father. The pain of growing up without her, the agony of seeing his father bully his half-sister. On and on, he talked, skirting away from their illicit love affair until I pinned him down with a direct question and he just spread his palms, gazed at them in shame.

"I'm so sorry," he kept saying, over and over.

"You can call the police right now," he said, giving me his mobile.

"I think I should," I replied tersely.

He looked to be on the verge of tears. "I had no idea Sophia was even following us to Crugmeer. I should have seen the signs, how upset she was getting, but I had tunnel vision—all I could think about was seeing you and how much it meant to me that you had even come. When she drugged you—I still can't believe she did that!—I put you in the attic to protect you. You were never meant to be locked in. And then it was stalemate. You were safer there than out, but God, I thought Sophia would come to her senses . . ."

"She lost the plot," I said.

"Yes. You have to remember too—from her point of view, she had so much to lose. I inherited this house when our father died, and it's in my name only. We never thought about putting it in both our names because we were devoted to each other—the idea of either of us ever deserting the other was unthinkable. But . . ." He coughed and took a sip of water, swallowing. "As the years went by, I began to crave a normal life. We invaded the lives of other couples with our switches and they were supposed to envy us—but I found myself envying *them*. Their marriages, even if they were cracked, their routines, their authenticity. For Sophia, it was different. A part of her always remained detached, saw other people's lives as theater.

"I don't think she can survive without me. That's what I've realized. And it breaks my heart, because I love you, and I want to be with you, and in trying to . . . to have that normal life I want, I've put you through hell and nearly destroyed you." He pushed the phone toward me, looking haggard with defeat. "Call them. I can't keep this up any longer. We deserve to lose everything."

I pushed the phone away. His confession had made tears prick in my eyes despite everything, but I was too exhausted to cope with any more. I got into bed and curled into a ball. He sat beside me, stroked my hair as he watched me sleep. When I woke up, I reached out for him, and he laced his fingers through mine . . .

———————

Now, having done my food shop, I walk back to Wimbledon Common. Spring is here, in the birdsong and in the trees, and we might even spot a Womble in the long grass, as we like to joke.

I turn off at Murray Road. Opening the door, I find Séverine in the hall, pulling on her coat. She grins at me as I fish money from my purse. I've upped her pay in recent months and we enjoy a chat from time to time about her family.

In the kitchen, I put the veg in the fridge and open the back door. Lyra comes bolting in, tail a-bristle, no doubt in some feud with a neighbor's cat. I put down some prawns for her, her favorite.

Upstairs, I apply makeup. There's still that excitement I feel before his arrival; each homecoming has the thrill of a first date. I wait breathlessly for the sound of his Jaguar pulling into the driveway. I know he'll be exhausted from that long drive from Cornwall. I always fear that he won't come, that she'll persuade him to stay, but as the months have passed, my confidence has grown that he will.

I run downstairs, fling open the front door. We embrace in the hallway; he covers my mouth with kisses. In the living-room, he gives me a gift, telling me he picked it up in Crugmeer. I open it up: handmade chocolates.

"Go on, I know you want to," he teases me, and watches me eat a rose cream, sighing with delight.

We go into the kitchen and he starts to prep the meal for me.

"Is the little one okay?" I ask, not quite able to say his name.

"All's fine," Finn says briskly, putting peelings into the bin: *subject over.*

But it hangs between us, the fear, wondering how long we can get away with this.

And then it fades, as Finn laughs and jokes and makes his delicious sauce for our creamy Tuscan salmon. I am touched by the pleasure he's taking in it. For him, this is all still a novelty: the closest he's come to the conventional relationship he's always craved.

It's not conventional for me. It's completely fucked up. I'm dating a guy who's still in a relationship, albeit non-sexual, with his half-sister, who gave birth to my ex's baby. Anil, one of the few people who knows the situation, has teased me that she's his *madwoman in the attic*. But, as much as I loathe Sophia, I can't classify her as a psychopath anymore. I understand why she needs Finn; I understand why she can't cope with my existence. Sometimes I fear there's an unkind streak in me that relishes the fact that we're dictating the game now, she's the delusional one. Even so, the lies constrain my life: Adam still thinks I've gone traveling and my concerned family have, reluctantly, agreed to keep quiet about where I am . . .

But . . . as Finn looks around and gives me a kiss, my heart turns over. My life is a hundred times richer here than it ever was with Adam, when I followed all the norms.

Finn sits down and we raise our glasses, smiling softly at each other.

It's a fragile situation. A sandglass has been tipped: we can't get away with this forever.

But for now, we're happy.

ACKNOWLEDGMENTS

The Switch might have languished on my computer unpublished, had it not been for Cathryn Summerhayes being so enthusiastic when I first showed her the idea. Thank you for believing in my book, for reading the final draft speedily despite a hugely challenging family situation, and then selling it with such passion.

A huge thank you to Emily Griffin at Penguin Random House UK and Jeramie Orton at Pamela Dorman Books: such passionate and brilliant editors who supported me and steered me through various drafts. It's been a joy to work with you, and thank you for making *The Switch* a much better book. Thank you to my publicist, Laura O'Donnell, my managing editor, Rose Waddilove, Lynn Curtis for copy-editing and Sarah-Jane Forder for some sharp proof-reading. To Issie Levine for marketing and creating such exciting proofs, Henry Petrides for a striking cover, Jane Glaser, and everyone at Penguin Random House UK and Pamela Dorman Books US.

I have been lucky to work with excellent film agents Addison Duffy and Jason Richman at United Talent, and Nick Marston at Curtis Brown. Thank you to Matt Tolmach, Camilla Grove, and Paige Tolmach at Matt Tolmach Productions for your passion for *The Switch* and seeing its TV potential!

ACKNOWLEDGMENTS

Thanks for love, support, and friendship: Zakia Uddin, Anna Wilson, Victoria Connelly, David and Leesha, Anna Maconochie, Alex Spears, Venetia Welby, Susanna Crossman, Ben Pester, Sam Byers, Lola Jaye, Dylan Evans, Simon Lewis, Tom Tomaszewski, Harold and the Shark, and Matthew Turner.

A very special thank you to my dear Andrew Gallix.